BA
FOR
ME

Heidi Perks worked as a marketing director before leaving to become a full-time mother and writer. Her first novel, *Now You See Her*, was a *Sunday Times* bestseller and a Richard and Judy Book Club pick. Heidi is a voracious reader of crime fiction and thrillers and endlessly interested in what makes people tick. She lives in Bournemouth with her family, where she is writing her next thriller.

Praise for Heidi Perks

'A highly addictive and thrilling read.' *Heat*

'Subtly, elegantly told… it is razor sharp and impossible to put down.' *Daily Mail*

'Seriously page turning.' Lisa Jewell

'Gripping.' *Good Housekeeping*

'I was totally hooked from the first page.' Amy Lloyd

'I couldn't go to bed until I knew how it ended.' Jenny

on

What readers are saying:

'This is a read **not to be missed**!!!'

'Family secrets, mystery and intrigue. This is
the perfect book that **won't disappoint**.'

'A surprising plot and **lots of twists** with interesting
characters. **I loved the writing style** and the setting
of the story.'

'*Come Back For Me* is easily **the best thriller I've read in
a long time**.'

'Lots of twists and turns, **guaranteed page-turner** that
keeps you guessing until the end.'

'*Come Back For Me* was a really **engaging and
addictive** read, about family secrets, a tight-knit
community and family ties.'

'**Fascinating** family drama with more than a hint of
psychological thriller.'

'A fantastic thriller that **grabbed me from the start**.'

'Full of twists and turns, this book **will have you
riveted** to every surprise event.'

'I literally finished this book in a few hours - **I couldn't
tell myself to put it down**.'

'A definite must read.' Hollie Overt

'Perks has a real knack for throwing red herrings at the readers - I had a long list of suspects and theories, but **she still managed to pull it out of the bag and surprise me**.'

'If you're looking for a thriller with plenty of **mystery and intrigue**, you've got the **perfect** book here.'

'The **twists and turns** held me rapt throughout, and when it was all revealed it left me a bit **gobsmacked**. And very shocked!'

'This book had me **gripped from the start**, will be looking at more from this author.'

'What really sets Heidi Perks' stories apart is that they are thought-provoking. **The characters and situations will stay with you long after you have finished the last page**.'

'The combination of a **strong story, realistic characters and brilliant writing** gives you **one of the best books I've read in the last year**.'

'An **absolute cracker** of a read.'

'This is a **must have** for your holiday reading pile.'

'**Another gem** from Heidi Perks!'

'Keeps you reading **late into the night**!'

Also available by Heidi Perks

Now You See Her

COME BACK FOR ME

HEIDI PERKS

Typeset in 10.58/15.9 pt Palatino
by Integra Software Services Pvt. Ltd, Pondicherry

Printed and bound in Great Britain by Clays Ltd, Elcograf S.p.A.

Penguin Random House is committed to a
sustainable future for our business, our readers
and our planet. This book is made from
Forest Stewardship Council® certified paper.

arrow books

1 3 5 7 9 10 8 6 4 2

Arrow Books
20 Vauxhall Bridge Road
London SW1V 2SA

Arrow Books is part of the Penguin Random House group
of companies whose addresses can be found at global.
penguinrandomhouse.com.

Penguin
Random House
UK

First published in Great Britain by Century in 2019
First published by Arrow Books in paperback in 2020

www.penguin.co.uk

A CIP catalogue record for this book is available from the
British Library

ISBN 9781787460782

Typeset in 10.58/15 pt Palatino

by I................................ ....Publisher

Printed and............in Great Britain........by CPI......S.p.A.

For my husband, John.
For believing in me.

And for Bethany and Joseph.
I believe in you.

EVERGREEN ISLAND

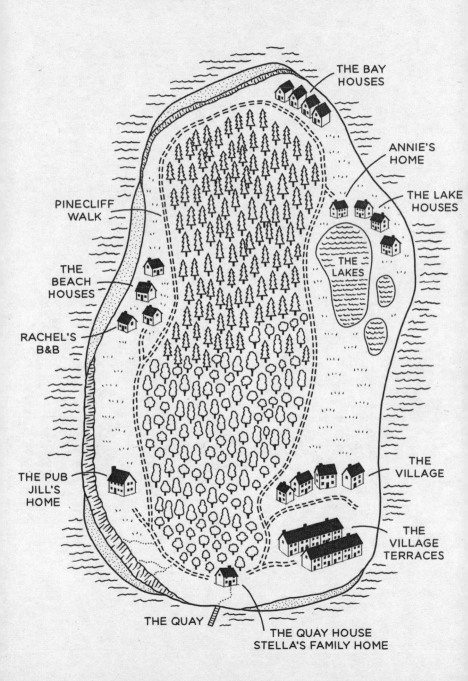

THE BAY HOUSES

ANNIE'S HOME

THE LAKE HOUSES

PINECLIFF WALK

THE LAKES

THE BEACH HOUSES

RACHEL'S B&B

THE PUB JILL'S HOME

THE VILLAGE

THE VILLAGE TERRACES

THE QUAY

THE QUAY HOUSE STELLA'S FAMILY HOME

Evergreen Island

9 September 1993

We left in a storm. The sea was rising in sharp clumps of angry waves, rain hitting my feet like bullets. Dad must have known we shouldn't be making the crossing to the mainland, yet he stood on the boat, one hand frantically flapping for one of us to reach out and take it. The hood of his red mac had whipped off his head, the rain plastering his hair to his scalp. He yelled over the wind for us to get in, but we wouldn't move from the end of the jetty.

The boat rocked violently as it tugged at the rope that kept it tethered to the dock, and I noticed Dad's other hand gripping tighter to the steel railing of the steps. 'Get in, Stella,' he shouted.

Thunder cracked overhead and the sky lit up with magnificent streaks of light. Behind me our house flashed bright between the silhouettes of our tall pines, making it look like something from a horror film. I pushed my hands deeper inside my raincoat, clutching Grey Bear harder to my chest. I didn't want to leave the only home I had ever known, but I had never seen my dad so determined. His jaw was set, his teeth bared. It wasn't like him to be so persistent, so unrelenting, and I found myself shrinking further back.

'I'm not going anywhere,' Bonnie screamed from beside me. 'We'll all die if we do.' My sister held her hood tightly against her head but I could just make out the paleness of her face in the moonlight. Bonnie had yearned to leave the island for years, but this wasn't the way she wanted to go.

'We will not die and we need to go,' Dad yelled back. He turned to me and added more softly, 'I promise you. It's fine. We'll be safe.' Dad owned the small ferry that he was demanding we board, and he'd run the thirty-minute crossing between Evergreen and Poole Harbour every day for the last sixteen years. If anyone could take us to the mainland safely, it was him, but we'd never dared attempting a crossing in weather like this before. Mum wouldn't usually let us out of the house when it was this bad.

'Why can't we wait till morning?' Bonnie was begging.

I stared at the water, its white foam bubbling and spitting in rage. 'Because—' Dad shouted. 'God, will you both just *get in*?' He flapped his hand again, his gaze drifting over my shoulder to where Mum was coming down the jetty. Her head was low, arms tucked inside a plastic poncho as she trailed a suitcase behind her.

'Where's Danny?' Dad yelled as another flash of lightning lit up the sky, making both Bonnie and me jump. I counted, too quickly, only reaching two before thunder roared overhead. The storm was creeping closer.

My brother trailed behind Mum, shrouded in a shapeless black coat that hung over his bulky body, reaching the ground.

Bonnie started shouting again, gesturing at the sea as it rose and dipped, higher and lower than I'd ever seen it go. Another loud crack filled the air and I yelped as a branch from one of the pines fell to the ground beside me. I jumped out of its way as the wind carelessly tossed it along the jetty.

For a brief moment, Dad stopped yelling and stared at the branch. My tears were already bleeding into the rainwater that soaked my face, but my heart twisted every time I thought of leaving my beloved island. All I wished was for Dad to realise that whatever we were doing, it wasn't worth it.

'I do think we should wait, David.' Mum's voice was high-pitched, her eyes wide as she looked from him to the water. 'It wouldn't hurt to stay another night. We could leave first thing ...'

We held a collective breath as Dad took his eyes off the broken tree and glared back at her. 'No, Maria. We go *now*.'

'I don't understand,' I said. Dad was the easy-going parent. The one who allowed another half-hour of play or a chocolate digestive even if we'd just brushed our teeth.

'Mum?' I cried, turning to face her. Why wasn't she doing more to stop him? Mum understood more than anyone how much this island was a part of me, that I wouldn't be able to survive without it. She loved Evergreen as much as I did.

She stared back at me, the fear I'd seen only moments ago replaced by a blankness. 'Mum—' My voice trembled as I waited for her to demand we go back to the house, but instead she placed a hand on my back and started moving me towards the steps of the boat. I hesitated but she pushed harder until I had no choice but to get on, ignoring Dad's outstretched hand as I scurried to one of the few benches that sat undercover.

Danny silently followed, sitting behind me, turning to stare out of the window. He wouldn't look at any of us, though there was nothing unusual in that.

'I don't want to go.' I searched each of their faces in turn. Only Bonnie looked at me as she settled beside me. Her leg shook against mine and I couldn't remember a time when we had been so close.

Removing my hood, I looked back at the island through the scratched glass of the boat where the rain still lashed against it. I could have drawn a line right through my heart where it was splitting in two.

Tears continued to trickle down my cheeks as the wind rocked the boat heavily to one side, making Bonnie yelp. I reached out my hands to steady myself, letting go of Grey Bear. Maybe Bonnie was right and we wouldn't make it to the mainland, but for some reason Dad was determined to try. Maybe I no longer particularly cared if the sea swallowed me up.

At eleven, I wasn't prepared to accept our parents' hurried reasons for leaving the island. I couldn't believe that this was for good and I couldn't understand one bit why they were dragging us away in the middle of a storm. 'Will we come back?' I whispered to my sister.

Bonnie's hand shook as it reached for mine under my mac. 'No,' she said, 'I don't think we ever will.'

PRESENT

Chapter One

My clients sit on the sofa opposite me. Her arms are crossed tightly in front of her chest; he is leaning forward, his hands clasped between his widely stretched legs. I could easily fit in the gap between this couple, and in each of their sessions they are moving further apart.

Her jaw is so tense I can almost see it pulsing as she stares at me. I'm surprised she hasn't cried today – she has in every other session. Her husband keeps glancing over at her, but she won't look at him. Each time he does, his eyebrows twitch as if he's either wondering where it all went so wrong or what he should do about it.

'I don't know what more to say,' he mumbles, and she laughs and shakes her head, mouthing something so quietly I can't work out what it is. 'I'm sorry,' he continues.

'God!' she cries and looks up to the ceiling. Her determination is so resolute I can see her willing the tears not to fall.

I hate this time of the session, but already the minute hand has ticked past six. Tanya will be waiting for me to leave so she can close up behind me. Looking after reception means she is always the last one out of the door.

'I'm afraid—' I start, but my client interrupts me as she pulls herself off the couch and grabs the cardigan that hangs limply on the arm.

'I know,' she says. 'Our time is up.'

'I'm sorry,' I say. I would take them both to the pub and let them carry on talking if it wasn't so unprofessional. 'Before you go, is there anything else you want to mention?'

'I think he's said enough today, don't you?'

Her husband chews on the corner of his lip but doesn't look up as he stands and reaches for his jacket.

'Do you ever wish you'd never asked a question in the first place?' she says quietly as she follows me to the door.

'Do *you*?' I ask her.

She moves her head, but it is so slight I can't tell if it is a nod. 'I can't not know it now, can I?'

I shake my head. No, she has to face the fact her husband once slept with someone else. I consider telling her to come and see me on her own but already she is talking to Tanya, fixing a date for them both the following week.

When they've left, I lock up my room and wander over to the desk where Tanya is pushing her thick glasses higher up her nose and tapping furiously on her keyboard. She doesn't look up until I'm almost on top of her. 'I'm off then,' I say. 'Sorry I was a little late.'

The phone rings and she checks the line before answering, 'Stella Harvey's office.' I still feel a tingle of pleasure every time I hear her say those words. As she explains the pricing structure of my family counselling sessions I consider, not for the first time, how much money I could save if I didn't have to pay a share of Tanya's salary. I'd had little choice, though, when I'd rented the room with the others in the building. Next to me is a physiotherapist and further down the corridor a chiropodist and a reiki healer, but none of us work full-time and I don't believe we really need a receptionist.

Tanya hangs up and turns back to her keyboard to close down the computer. 'Prospective clients,' she tells me. 'A young couple having problems with their daughter. They're going to call back next week.'

'Thanks,' I say. 'Are you up to anything nice this weekend?'

'Mike and I are visiting his parents. What about you?'

'I'm having lunch at my sister's tomorrow,' I tell her.

'And how is Bonnie?' Tanya raises her eyebrows.

I laugh. 'She's fine. Her husband's away this weekend,' I say, though I'm not sure why I mentioned it. I don't even know whether this means Bonnie will be happier or more pissed off.

Tanya nods, her lips pursed, and I imagine her thinking back to the one and only time she met my sister. I know she wasn't impressed, but I stopped bothering to defend Bonnie long ago. At some point I got past caring what anyone else thought or feeling the need to explain that, with so little family left, I can't be blamed for wanting to cling to her.

Besides, no one has ever been able to understand our relationship. Not even I could explain all the intricacies that tie us together. In most ways we are polar opposites. But I'd made an unspoken promise eighteen years ago, soon after Danny left, that I would always be there for my sister. That was when I began to wonder if it wasn't all Bonnie's fault she was the way she was.

Mum used to whisper to me at night sometimes. When she thought I was sleeping she'd creep into my room, pulling the duvet back over me where I'd kicked it off. I'd liked her kneeling on the floor beside me, her warm breath on my face, the smell of Chanel washing over me, lingering long after she'd left the room.

'My everything, Stella,' she would whisper as she gently stroked my hair. 'You're all the babies I ever need.'

Maybe that left no room for Bonnie.

Tanya and I leave the office together. She turns left as I cross over towards the park, a cut-through on my twenty-minute walk home, past the cathedral and to my flat that sits just on the outskirts of Winchester.

I like the walk, even in January when the only light is from the street lamps and the cold air bites at my skin. It gives me a chance to mull over my client list for the following week and, as I always do on a Friday, vow to invest more time in building up my business.

Making a decision to set up on my own as a family counsellor hadn't been done on a whim. I was never one of those children who'd decided early on what job they would do. Even after A levels, I still had no idea and it took twelve unhappy years in recruitment and a satisfying redundancy package for me to make the break.

Four years ago I'd signed up for the training and obligatory counselling I had to undertake myself before I could counsel others. My supervisor had underlined the importance of the latter early on. Carrying childhood scars or unresolved issues from previous relationships could make my advice biased.

I'd tried declining the opportunity but it was clear this wasn't something I could get out of, and I knew if I pushed much harder I would raise suspicion about my own family dynamics. But I had filed away most parts of my life into neat little boxes and hidden them deep. We were very good at that as a family. I had learned from the best, even if it did go against everything I expected from my clients.

'*So why are you interested in family counselling?*' was the first question I'd been asked in my introductory session.

I told the counsellor how lucky I'd been growing up. That I'd had very loving parents and my upbringing on the island of Evergreen had been idyllic. I said I was interested in familial relationships and always thought I'd had an ability to listen and help. I told her the truth up to a point. The point where we left the island. Or maybe just before that.

My counsellor had been eager to know more about Evergreen, as most people are. 'And only one hundred people lived there?' she'd asked me, stunned.

I nodded. 'Just over. I knew all of them and they all knew me.'

I told her how wonderful it was as she gaped back at me. 'I honestly loved it,' I laughed. I knew some people thought it was claustrophobic, but there was nowhere else on earth I had wanted to be.

'And you didn't find it too remote?' Another popular question, because even though the ferry only took thirty minutes, you couldn't see Evergreen from the Dorset coast.

'I didn't,' I told her. My sister, however, had hated the fact that in the winter months my dad's ferry only ran once a day. But then my sister had hated all the things that had made me love it.

'You say you were eleven when you left,' she went on. 'How old were your siblings?'

'I was the baby of the family. Danny was fifteen,' I told her, 'and Bonnie was seventeen.'

She nodded, though I didn't know what she had gleaned from that, and all the time I carried on smiling, careful not to let cracks show. I knew she would soon be prying deeper into the end of our last summer on the island and the years after we'd left. She would want to know what triggered my family to break down, and I wouldn't be able to tell her. Every one of us had secrets we'd held too close and because we'd never spoken about them, they'd torn us apart in the end.

I wanted to help other families talk because that's where we went wrong, only I wasn't going to tell her that. Instead I breezed through what happened after we left, highlighting only the bare facts.

Now I try to banish the memories of the sessions I'd endured, as a drop of rain splats on my head. Soon I need to dive under cover of the nearest shop before I'm drenched. I must have left my umbrella at work, I realise, as I meander towards the wine shelves of a convenience store, choosing a seven-pound bottle of Sauvignon Blanc while waiting for the worst of the rain to pass.

Back at my flat I pour a glass and sit by the window in the kitchen watching the rain that is now steadily drumming against the pane. Despite having little to do this weekend and regardless of the fact I don't work a usual five-day week, I still get that Friday feeling and have fallen into a comfortable routine: once I have finished this glass I'll make a curry, then have another drink with Marco in his flat above mine while ignoring his pleas to join him clubbing.

As it is, I don't get back to my own flat until just before ten, but I'm not ready to go to bed just yet. Instead I snuggle down on the sofa with a blanket, flick on the TV, then grab a magazine from the coffee table and idly thumb through it.

The news comes on and I glance up. A reporter is standing outside a house, holding a large umbrella while the wind whips her ponytail from side to side. My eyes drift to the ticker tape along the bottom of the TV screen and then back again to her. I don't recognise any of the details behind her at first and am about to turn back to the magazine when something catches my eye.

They've caught it at a funny angle, but there's a distinctive window in the top corner of the picture, circular with obscured glass. I inch forward on the sofa and grab the remote again, turning up the volume so I can hear what the reporter is saying over the hammering that's beginning to beat in my ears.

It's funny I didn't recognise it immediately when every detail is etched on the inside of my eyelids. When all I need to do is call up my memory and I can paint a picture of a thousand pixels in intricate detail. But then it doesn't look the same. Not entirely.

The windowsills have been painted a deep teal and now the camera is panning out so I can see more of the house. There are colonial-style white fascia boards and a conservatory at the front. It doesn't look like my home any longer. Yet unmistakably it is. The white picket fence that runs along the left-hand side is still there. Dad had put that up one summer to separate our garden from the path that runs alongside it. On the right, tall pines still drape the length of the garden.

I feel my pulse racing quicker and I try to ignore it to focus on the reporter's words. 'Clearly the whole island is in shock,' she says.

I look back at the ticker tape reeling its breaking news; the words '... *Island last night'* roll out of sight to the left and a new headline about Syria follows.

'And the police aren't able to release any more details as yet?' This comes from a woman in the studio, but the screen is still filled with the view of my house and garden, panning out further still and exposing a white police tent that is flanked by officers. It has been erected on the right at the rear of the property, tucked neatly in between the house and the trees that separate the garden from the woods beyond.

'Not yet, but the forensics teams have been working here all day,' the reporter says.

I look back at the tape. *'Body found on Evergreen Island last night,'* it now reads in full. I scrunch my hands up tightly, willing the blood to rush through them and stop the numbness from spreading up my arms.

A body has been found on the island. And even though no one has said it outright, it's clear it's been buried in the garden of my old house.

Chapter Two

I watch with morbid curiosity as the news filters through in sharp pieces: the current owners were building an extension to the side of the house; excavations ran deeper and wider than expected; last night one of the builders noticed a bone that turned out to be a hand and in turn there was the rest of a body.

The reporter tells us it was a shocking discovery for both the builder and the owners. Around the back of the white tent, she points to the exact spot the body was found. My eyes are wide as I take in every detail, my hands clawing the fabric of my jumper. To anyone who doesn't know the island it looks like it's right in our old back garden, but to me, an islander, I can now see it's actually just outside, at the point where the garden merges into the woods.

But the thing with Evergreen is that most of the houses don't have fences separating private land from that around it. Where we lived, in the Quay House that sits just back from the jetty, we only did on one side – the white picket fence – because it was the only one completely exposed to the public paths. Every other side was lined with trees, but it means the boundaries were blurred. And it means you'd be forgiven for thinking the body was dug up from the garden and it's already clear this is the way they're spinning it.

I cannot tear my gaze away from the TV because this, I realise, is the first time I've seen my house since that night. The night we left.

With my eyes glued to the screen, I reach for my mobile. My fingers tremble as I press Bonnie's number and lift the phone to my ear. She answers just as it's about to go to voicemail. 'Yes?'

'Have you seen the news?'

'No. I'm getting ready to go to bed. Luke's not well and—'

'Turn it on,' I interrupt. 'BBC.'

'Okay, okay, give me a minute,' Bonnie huffs. I imagine her strolling into the kitchen and flicking on the small flat-screen that sits on the wall above the counter. 'Christ,' she says suddenly. 'Is that our old house?'

'They found a body,' I tell her. 'Right outside our garden.'

Bonnie is silent for a moment. 'It might as well be in it,' she says eventually.

'I know. But you can tell it's not. Look at it, it's just on the edge of the woods.'

'Bloody hell. Who is it?'

'They haven't said. There's barely any details.'

I hear Bonnie suck in air through the gap between her front teeth.

'They haven't even confirmed if it's male or female. Surely they can tell. They say forensics are all over it.'

'Well, someone on that island knows who it is,' she says. 'Oh my God,' she adds with a short laugh. 'Can you imagine them all? They'll be like vultures.'

'It must be awful for them, Bonnie.'

'I know, but seriously. You couldn't do a thing on that place without everyone else knowing. I got my period and the boys found out within twenty-four hours.'

She was right. I hadn't been able to dangle a foot over the cliff edge without Mum finding out before I got home. Danny couldn't fall out of the tree he'd been hiding in without it being whispered around the island within hours, but then there'd always been an interest where Danny was concerned.

'One of them must have done it,' she says suddenly. The thought sounds like it interests her, like this isn't real but simply a drama we're watching.

'We don't know that.'

'Oh, come on. Who else would bury a body on that island?'

Again she's right, but I don't want to think about it. 'Do you think we know who it is?' I say. 'The body, I mean.'

'Probably not. It's been so many years since we left.'

I nod but don't answer.

'*Or,*' she goes on, making the word sound dramatic, 'it could have been there all the time we were living in the house. We could have been walking right on top of it and we'd never have known. No one believed me there was something off about that place.'

'There was nothing *off* about it.'

'They're probably digging up a whole load of bodies right now.'

'Bonnie!'

'Oh, lighten up, Stella. We haven't lived there for twenty-five years.'

'I know, but . . .' I murmur without finishing my sentence and sit in silence until Bonnie finally speaks.

'I like what they've done with the house.'

I stiffen at her words. 'What do you mean?'

'They painted it, it looks good.'

'Have they?' I reply. 'I hadn't noticed.' She must know I'm lying. How could I miss the deep teal paint that makes it look so modern, so unlike ours?

Bonnie lets out a snort before asking, 'Are you going to call Dad?'

'I guess.' I know I should but I don't relish the thought, not least because I don't speak about the island with Dad any more.

'Have you spoken to him lately?' she says.

'No.' The familiar surge of guilt washes over me. 'I need to go and see him. Maybe I'll do that instead.'

'When the witch isn't there.'

'Olivia seems to be working a lot at the moment. There's a good chance she won't be there if I go during the week. Would you come with me?' I ask, hoping, but already knowing what the answer will be.

'No,' Bonnie replies bluntly.

I sigh. 'I'll call him in the morning,' I say. A familiar tightness has already wrapped itself around me. It always feels like it's compressing my lungs, forcing me to breathe harder. I want to speak to him but it's not the same any more. It feels like he's altogether a different dad than the one I had on Evergreen, but there are times when I temporarily get him back again and I never know which is harder.

'It makes you think, doesn't it?' Bonnie says, bringing me back to the moment.

'What?'

'Whether we know whoever did it.'

After I hang up I carry on watching the news, flicking between channels, chasing the story, but there are no new reports and at some point I fall asleep on the sofa. I dream of the island again, as I have been doing lately. I am chasing my friends through the woods. They are laughing and I am too, but then they disappear and now someone is chasing me. When I wake my heart is fluttering and my neck is caught in a crooked position on the cushions.

I'd stopped dreaming about Evergreen a few years after we'd left but had started again straight after those sessions I'd endured during my training as a counsellor. Now I don't know how to make them go away. Each time I wake from a dream, I hear my counsellor's voice. *See, this is why it's important to flush out the demons.*

But there were never any demons on Evergreen. In my eleven years there I could stack my happy memories on top of each other and they would reach the sky. In one session, I'd skimmed over my parents' divorce by stating categorically that none of their problems started until much later. Until after we had left the island and moved to Winchester. When my dad had lost his soul to an air-conditioned office with blacked-out windows in the city – that was when they were no longer happy. I told her that a few times, though I wasn't sure I believed it myself, but I wasn't prepared to open the lid on that box.

It is not even three a.m., and I should be going back to sleep, but I glance at my iPad. There have been times in recent years when I've wanted to look up my house online. After my first counselling session, when we had dissected Evergreen in more detail than I'd been prepared for, I'd returned to my flat and opened up Rightmove, tapping the Quay House address into the search bar but deleting it before I hit Enter. I hadn't been ready to see how it might have changed.

I had previously managed to look up some of the islanders, though. Many times I'd searched for my once best friend, Jill, but I'd never been able to find her. Even some other names I'd tried like Tess Carlton and Annie Webb – the woman we called Aunt, though she was no relation. I hadn't been so surprised to find she wasn't on Facebook – by now Annie must be in her eighties.

But my dreams have left a bitter taste in my mouth and instead of scouring the web I find myself reaching for my childhood scrapbook that hides in the magazine basket beside the sofa. Always this is a comfort, a reminder of blissful times, and I can already feel my pulse slowing.

It falls open at the place I last looked, where a feather is stuck with brown, now-faded Sellotape which is curling at the ends. I press it down, but as soon as I release my finger it springs back up. One day I must go through the book and carefully mend pages and stick pieces in again before the whole thing falls apart irretrievably.

I know every page by heart, so much so that I don't know if it brings back actual memories of the island or if the photos and memorabilia have taken over because I've looked at them so many times. I turn over a page and catch a photo before it flutters out.

It's one Mum had taken of my friend Jill and me that last summer. We were sitting on the sand, our heads so close that tendrils of our hair wound together – mine, tinged golden from the sun, and Jill's amber curls floating in the wind. We had such different hair, yet blended together it created something beautiful.

I run my fingers over Jill's face. If I close my eyes I can hear her laugh, but in this photo she isn't smiling. Mum had caught us unawares and I can still hear Jill's urgent whisper in my ear, *'Don't tell anyone,'* before Mum shouted out at us to *'Say cheese for the camera!'* I wonder if Mum had noticed then that something wasn't right.

I snap the book shut and inhale a deep breath that catches in my throat. I had kept my promise that I wouldn't tell for the whole summer, but in the end I hadn't been able to keep it. Maybe that had been a mistake, but it's too late to consider that now.

Chapter Three

The following day I contemplate how lunch with Bonnie will play out since our conversations about Evergreen have always been strained. I put it down to the fact we saw our upbringing in starkly different lights. Sometimes I wonder how we could have come from the same family when our perceptions of growing up are so different.

Bonnie opens the door and stands aside, ushering me into the long hallway and out of the rain that hasn't stopped since last night. 'Luke's still sick. He ended up not going away,' she says as she brushes past and leads me to the kitchen at the back of the house.

'Oh? What's wrong with him?'

'A cold.' She sighs loudly. 'He's in bed. Complaining. I told him not to come out in case he's contagious.'

'You could have come to my house instead of keeping your husband upstairs,' I say.

She looks taken aback at the suggestion. 'I'd already got lunch.'

I raise my eyes at her lack of compassion as I slip my coat off and hang it on a hook by the back door.

'What do you want to drink, tea or coffee?'

'Tea. Thanks.'

'I was looking forward to him getting out of my hair this weekend. He's doing my head in.'

'He's always doing your head in,' I say, thinking of my poor brother-in-law upstairs and imagining at some point he'll appear to say hello anyway.

'Well, he's been more irritating than usual. He's signed the boys up for boxing classes, can you believe it? Why the hell does he think I want them boxing?' She stops when her oldest, Ben, comes into the room.

'I want to do boxing, Mum,' he says. 'You said I could.'

'I know I did.' She watches her twelve-year-old for a moment and then turns away.

Ben shrugs and I open my arms to pull him in for a hug. 'Your mum worries about you, that's all,' I murmur in his ear. 'She doesn't want you getting hurt.'

'And it's expensive,' Bonnie says, 'on top of everything else.'

I roll my eyes at Ben who grins. 'I swear you've grown again,' I tell him. 'You're nearly as tall as me.'

'Yes, but you're short, Aunt Stella.'

'Hey,' I laugh. 'Five five is not short.' He has always joked about my height, though compared to Bonnie, who's at least four inches taller than me, I often feel tiny.

'Mum,' he says, 'can you take me to Charlie's? It's raining.'

'No way. That's why we bought your bike. He's only around the corner, and besides, I have your aunt here.'

'I don't mind—' I start.

'Uh-uh. He has transportation. And legs.'

'Fine. See you later, Aunt Stella.' Ben gives a wave and he's gone.

'He's such a handsome boy,' I say when the front door closes behind him. 'They both are.'

'I know.' Bonnie pauses, watching the space he has left before turning to fumble in cupboards for tea bags and mugs. 'I dread the day they bring home girlfriends.'

I pull out a chair at the table as Bonnie finishes making tea. 'There's no more news about the body,' I say.

For a moment she doesn't answer, and I wait for her to change the subject as she often does. 'Did you call Dad?' she says.

I shake my head. 'Not yet. Don't you *ever* want to see him, Bon?' I ask. 'Don't you miss him?'

Bonnie screws up her mouth and looks away. 'I wasn't as close to him as you were.'

'That's not what I'm asking, and you were still close.'

'Neither of them had much time for me.' She brushes her hands flat across the work surface.

'That's a ridiculous thing to say. You used to tell me the opposite was true,' I remind her, thinking back to the rare times she'd opened up.

'That was in the early years when they were always trying to fix me,' she says. 'At some point they gave up. Probably when you came along,' she adds. 'I'm joking.' She peers at me over the rim of her mug. 'Anyway, they loved you the most, anyone could see that.'

'Bonnie, that's just not true.'

'It is.' She scrapes her chair back sharply. 'And I'm long past caring. I'll get lunch ready. It's only soup.'

'That sounds great,' I say, wondering why she couldn't have rescheduled if she hadn't gone to much effort. 'Where's Harry?' I ask.

'He's at a friend's too. I swear they spend more time at other people's houses than they do at their own these days. I never see them.' Bonnie dips her head. It's easy to see how much she misses her boys even if she won't say it. 'I guess it's what comes from going to a normal school and living in a normal city – the opposite of what we had. I can't imagine what they'd be like if they had to live in the kind of confinement we did.'

'Was there really not anything you liked about Evergreen?' I ask her.

She turns to face me. 'Nothing. I had no life, no friends—'

'You did,' I say, 'there was Iona—'

'One.' She turns back to the stove muttering, 'And that was only for one summer.

'I thought of Danny the other day,' Bonnie goes on. A leap of conversation for her. A missed heartbeat for me. 'I don't know what made me start thinking of him, but it was about a week ago.'

I don't know what to say so I wait for her to continue.

'No, actually I'm lying,' she says. 'I know very well what made me think of him. I saw this weird older kid at the boys' rugby game. He was standing on the sidelines, just staring at the others. It reminded me of the way Danny used to do that.'

I pull at the paper napkin in front of me, tearing a little corner off and rolling it between my fingers.

'Our brother freaked everyone out. I hated him for that ...' Her words trail off as if she's no longer talking to anyone but herself. Bonnie pours soup into two bowls and brings them over to the table, going back for a loaf of bread and a knife.

'You didn't hate him,' I say quietly as she sits down.

She widens her eyes at me. 'I did. Since the moment he was born. I swear that was when everything changed – at least, that was when Mum started taking me to those stupid Stay and Play sessions on the mainland with the woman who used to try and make me talk.'

I open my mouth to ask about the sessions but Bonnie is already going on. 'I could never believe you *didn't* hate him. I never knew what you found to talk about when you both used to sit in that treehouse. You spent hours in that thing together.'

We did, but we'd never really talked. Instead we did our own things alongside each other, like little kids do before they learn how to play. Danny would draw while I read or played with my Barbie dolls.

'Do you remember that time he fell out the tree and I thought he was dead?' Bonnie says. 'He didn't move, he just laid there.' She hangs her arms out to the side, her tongue lolling out of her mouth. She looks comical and it's hard not to smile. 'He'd been secretly watching Iona and me and the branch had snapped beneath that heaving body of his and he just plopped on the ground at our feet.'

'Vaguely.' Was that the time she'd been screaming at Mum in the kitchen about him?

'I wished for him not to move for a moment, and then he did, and I wanted to kill him. He was always watching us. He embarrassed me so much,' she says. 'No one understood that boy.'

'No one tried,' I murmur.

'As far back as I can remember he was always playing on his own, wheeling those cars of his round and round in the sand. I used to ask myself why they spent so much effort trying to work me out when anyone could see it was Danny who needed help.'

'When did those sessions stop?' I ask her. 'The ones Mum took you to.'

'Stay and Play?' Bonnie shrugs and scoops up a spoonful of soup. 'When I was about seven. I don't know. Whenever it was that Mum suddenly whisked me out of there one day and said she didn't need to know any more.'

'Any more about what?' I ask but I know Bonnie won't go further. She tells me she doesn't have any more answers, but I'm not sure if it's the truth or if she simply doesn't want to face them.

'He only got worse as he got older,' she says, turning the attention back on Danny. 'That last summer he was a nightmare. You must remember the sleep-out at the beach?'

'Of course I do.' I had been there too when Danny was accused of grabbing one of the girls.

'And the way he was with Iona,' she murmurs. 'He made it awkward for me. I was surprised she hung around as much as she did when Danny was there.'

'He liked her,' I say, 'because she was so nice to him.'

Bonnie looks away, but not before I notice the tiniest flicker of a cloud passing over her face. 'I went to Mum's grave the other day,' she says. 'Did you put those flowers there?'

I sit back in the chair. I shouldn't be surprised by Bonnie's change of topic but she still manages to catch me off guard. I don't bother answering when she knows I go every week and leave flowers.

'She would have hated what's happened, wouldn't she?'

I nod, and in a way I'm glad she's not here to see it.

'Do you want coffee?' Bonnie asks after we've finished lunch.

'Please,' I say as I help her tidy the plates.

'You know it's times like this when I could murder a glass of wine,' she says, looking at me as she waits for a reaction.

'Bonnie, I don't know what you want me to say to that.'

'Oh, come on, you're the counsellor. If you can't come up with something no one can.'

'I counsel families whose relationships are in trouble. Not recovering alcoholics.'

'Isn't it all linked?' she asks as she watches me carefully. When I don't answer she says, 'It's not like I want to get drunk. I just get bored with coffee and tea.' She turns and glares at the kettle. 'How's work going, anyway?'

'It's good,' I say. 'I'm really enjoying it.'

'Any interesting clients?'

I laugh. 'You know I can't tell you.'

'Oh, come on. Don't I get any perks for being your sister? Just a little something, you don't need to tell me names.'

'No!'

'You're boring. *I'd* tell *you.*'

'I don't doubt it,' I smile.

'So, no men you like the look of?'

'Bonnie!'

'Seriously, how else do you think you're going to meet someone? And some of them are in the perfect position – unhappy in their marriages. All you need to do is give them a nudge in the right direction.'

'Well, there aren't any I like anyway.'

'Maybe you're better off single.' She pours hot coffee into mugs and we fall into a silence before she says, 'Do you ever think about finding Danny?'

'Of course I do, but I wouldn't know where to start.'

'Do you think Mum knew where he was?'

'I can't imagine she didn't,' I say, taking a mug. I'd always blamed Mum for letting him go. Even at twenty-two, Danny hadn't been old enough to really fend for himself and I couldn't understand how she'd allowed it.

That had been eighteen years ago and I'd wanted to scour the country looking for him. I'd imagined us finding him curled up, shivering on a dark street corner, and we'd pile him in the car and take him home where he belonged. But all Mum had said was, 'I lost him a long time ago.'

She was right about that. Anyone could see how Danny had withdrawn even more since we'd left the island, only no one commented on the fact he hadn't once picked up his pencils and drawing pad. 'Maybe she kept in touch with him but never told us for some reason,' I go on.

'Why would she do that?'

'I don't know. Maybe he asked her not to.'

'Why would he—'

'I don't know,' I snap. 'That's the problem, isn't it? We'll never know.'

Bonnie nods and I wait for her to say something about Mum, but instead she says, 'Do you think he's still alive?'

She offers me a biscuit, grabbing one for herself and pushing it into her mouth as she looks at me expectantly.

'God, Bonnie. What a thing to say.'

She shrugs and continues to watch me as she chews intently. 'I think Mum probably did know where he was,' she says finally, her voice much quieter. 'I can't imagine her never looking for him.'

That evening, while the news is still spilling out the same brief headlines, I finally pick up my iPad and scour the pictures that various websites are showing, poring over them in search of familiar faces.

I have always wondered what happened to the people I grew up around and who might still be on the island. Those who were once such a part of my life that I could never have imagined one without them. I zoom in close on a picture of a crowd near the police tent, studying their faces for a hint of recognition, but the more I enlarge the photo the more granulated it becomes. Despite this I trace my finger across the people until I stop. Standing a little further back, away from the huddle, is a woman I'm sure I recognise.

I click off the picture and open another and now I can clearly see it is Jill's mother, Ruth Taylor. She is standing alone by the café in a photo the press have captioned 'The local village'. I study her face, its roundness, her mouth skewed as she stares at something out of the shot. She looks older, of course, her hair now completely grey.

So, they never left the island. For many reasons I'd always hoped Jill had.

I sigh as I return to the first photo and lean back. Every one of these people will have to answer questions in the next few days, and I'm sure that if the police don't already know who the body belongs to, they soon will.

No one is able to set foot on or off the island without everyone else knowing about it. No one could have been buried under its earth without at least one of its residents knowing who it is.

Chapter Four

I used to beg Mum to take me back to Evergreen. I'd done so ever since the night we left right up to just before Danny had packed his bags and a year after Dad had gone.

'We could still go back,' I suggested over breakfast. 'Dad was the one who made us leave and he's not here now.' Whatever level of truth there was in the reasons they gave us, it was clear it had been *his* decision for us to get on that ferry.

'I don't think so, Stella,' Mum said.

'I don't understand why not. We were happy, we—'

'The time isn't right,' she cut me off, eyes jerking towards Danny who was spooning Cornflakes into his mouth.

'Danny was happy there,' I persisted, annoyed she still wouldn't consider it. 'Weren't you, Dan?'

My brother looked up but didn't answer as he pushed his chair away, carried his bowl to the sink, and hurriedly left the kitchen. Mum had to see how miserable living in the city was making him.

'You know he'd be happier,' I told her. 'At least say you'll think about it.'

She muttered she would, but less than two weeks later, Danny left. One day he heaved a heavy rucksack on to his back and told me he was going. Mum stood by the gate as we watched him, her face pale and haunted. She wore the exact same expression she'd had when she'd picked up the phone to the hospital the first time Bonnie had been admitted: like her world had fallen apart.

Her arm stretched up as if she was trying to reach for him, but as far as I knew she never made any effort to stop him. After that I began to question how Mum could have let the others leave too. Throughout my childhood she'd been the one holding us together, but each time one of them walked out the door I felt the snap of my family breaking further.

After Danny, I gave up asking about Evergreen. My heart was no longer in it and, once Mum died, the thought of the island without her seemed impossible. But the news has dredged up memories and stirred emotions I'd all but forgotten and, for once, I envy Bonnie's ability to paper over it with her usual detachment.

Sunday morning I call my sister early. More than twenty-four hours after the news and I'm still procrastinating over speaking to Dad. 'They say the body is female,' I tell her. 'But I don't understand how she's never been reported missing. Surely someone noticed she'd disappeared.' I pause. 'We knew everyone on that island. I still can't help thinking we know her.'

'Like who? Tess Carlton?' Bonnie says, plucking a name from nowhere. 'One of the Smyth twins? You think one killed the other?'

'Bonnie, that's a dreadful thing to say.'

'We'll find out soon enough,' she murmurs, already losing interest in what I want to dissect. My attention drifts to the TV. They are in the garden again, the cameras panning around it and the dark woods that lie beyond, thick with trees where the sun only catches the very top of them. They look ghostly from this angle. Most visitors steered clear of them, but as children we'd run through the woods to the parts the light didn't reach without a moment's pause and no one thought anything of it.

Somehow the cameras have managed to catch a menacing side to the woods and for a moment I see them how everyone else will too: like they are haunted.

When I hang up the phone to Bonnie I think of the girls I knew back then. We ranged in ages, many of which fell between mine and Bonnie's: Tess Carlton, the daughter of my mother's best friend; Emma Grey; Bonnie's friend Iona;

and of course Jill. Yet my memories of most of them are sketchy apart from Jill.

The last time I saw my friend was after Mum's hurried attempts to tell me about the plan for us to leave the island. I wasn't interested in the rental house in Winchester or the extra income from Dad's new job and had raced to Jill's house where she'd told me to meet her in our secret place in the clearing.

I hadn't accounted for her dad following. It meant she had to whisper in my ear when she told me she couldn't bear the thought of me leaving.

Tears flowed down our cheeks as her dad stepped nearer, telling her she needed to come back to the house. Now he was too close for me to ask her what was so important he couldn't give me and my best friend some time together. But by then nothing Bob Taylor did surprised me.

I'd clutched on to Jill's arms, searching her face as she trembled in my grip. 'Don't be scared,' I said, hoping he wouldn't hear. I chanced a look in his direction, but she was shaking her head at me. How I wished he would leave us so I could talk to her properly. 'We'll write to each other,' I went on. 'I'll write first and send you my new address. Promise me you'll write back?'

Jill nodded, her eyes glazed with tears she tried to blink away. 'Promise. We'll always be best friends.'

'Blood sisters' promise,' I replied and we pressed our fingers together until her dad yelled at her and she finally pulled away. 'I'll miss you,' I called out, my voice cracking with the weight of my pain.

'I'll miss you too,' she cried back.

I kept my promise and wrote to Jill a week after we'd settled into the first house in Winchester. I rushed to the door every time the letterbox rattled. A week later I wrote again, begging her to write back, adding my address to the envelope, just in case she'd lost it the first time. I never once heard from her.

That afternoon the doorbell rings, rapidly followed by a loud knock.

'Give me a chance,' I mutter, putting my cup down, tea slopping over the rim and on to the coffee table. When I open the door two men are standing the other side, one tall with closely shaven hair, the other at least a head shorter.

'Miss Stella Harvey?' the taller one asks. 'I'm PC Walton and this is my colleague, PC Killner. Nothing to worry about, we'd just like to talk to you about an incident you may have heard of on the news. We're hoping we can come in and ask a few questions.'

'I don't understand,' I say, shaking my head, but at the same time stepping aside so they can enter my narrow hallway. 'Why do you want to ask me questions?'

'We're talking to everyone who's lived on Evergreen, but like I said, it's nothing to worry about,' he assures me as they both walk forward and stop at the point where you can either go left into my small kitchen or right into the living room.

I gesture to the latter where there's more room for us to sit but don't think to offer them a drink as I perch awkwardly on the edge of Mum's old rocking chair. 'I lived there a long time ago,' I say. 'We left in 1993.'

PC Killner nods as he pulls out a notebook and clicks a pen. He traces his finger along his notes and then looks up at me. 'And could you confirm when you moved there, Miss Harvey?'

'I was born there,' I tell him. 'In 1982. My parents arrived in ...' I pause and think back. 'It was '76 or '77. My sister was a baby.'

He nods again and glances down.

'Why?' I ask, shuffling forward until I'm nearly falling off the edge of the chair. 'I mean, it was so long ago, I don't understand how this could help you.'

Walton smiles. 'Routine procedure.'

'But it was ages ago,' I repeat, trying to work out what it means. Do they think the body has been there years? Do they want to talk to me because I was living there at the time it was buried?

'I know.' He smiles again. 'And we realise you were young when you left, Miss Harvey, but we'd like to gather some information and then we'll be on our way. I don't intend taking up much of your time.'

I purse my lips, pushing myself back until I can feel a small cushion pressing into the base of my spine. My heart flutters, threatening to race, but Walton's smile seems genuinely warm and I remind myself there's nothing I know about the body.

He asks me to confirm who I lived with and where, and I tell him that along with Mum, Dad, Bonnie and Danny, I lived in the Quay House. My heart skips a beat at the thought he might have already spoken to Bonnie, but again I tell myself there's nothing she can add. We'll only be giving them the same information.

Regardless, having two policemen in my living room is making me on edge and I try relaxing my shoulders and loosening my jaw. Will the policemen be watching my mannerisms the same way I do my new clients, or are they purely interested in gathering facts and moving on?

'Who were your closest neighbours?' Walton asks.

'We didn't really have neighbours,' I tell him, explaining how the Quay House sat at the end of the jetty away from any other houses. Killner turns over his sheet and looks at what appears to be a map of the island. I can't help but strain to get a better look at it.

'To the left you have the Pines pub?' He peers up at me.

I nod. 'That was where my friend Jill Taylor lived with her mum and dad. Ruth and Bob,' I add when they look as if they are both waiting. 'I don't know if they're still in the same house.'

Killner gives me a thin smile and I realise it doesn't matter what I know because they already know more. 'And on the other side is the village,' he is saying. 'Perhaps you could confirm who lived in the closest terraces to you?'

I think back to the rows of small houses that backed on to a cluster of shops. Calling it a village is an overstatement, but it was a central hub, a place where the adults caught up and bought essentials. 'The doctor always lived in the end terrace nearest us,' I say, 'but there were a few different doctors in the years I lived there.'

He asks me to work backwards as best I can and I name the doctors I remember, though my time frames are vague. As Killner makes notes, I catch Walton looking at a photo on the shelf in the corner of the room. 'That's my mum. She died ten years ago in a car accident.'

'I'm sorry to hear that, Miss Harvey.'

I watch his eyes take in the many other photos that line the mantelpiece. All but one are pictures from years back. When we were young. When we lived on the island. Walton's eyebrows furrow into the glimmer of a frown. What must he make of so many pictures taken so close to his crime scene adorning my shelves? I'm comforted he can't see the rest of them hanging in my bedroom.

'Will you be speaking to the rest of my family?' I ask, bringing his gaze back to me as he reaches for a frame and holds it up.

'We will.'

'My dad's—' I start, but he interrupts me as he peers closer at the photo.

'This is your sister?'

'It is.' I shuffle to the edge of the chair again.

He taps his finger against the glass of the frame and turns to Killner who gets up to join him. 'This bracelet she's wearing,' he goes on as I stand too and take the photo from him. 'Do you remember it?'

'Yes. I made it,' I say.

His head snaps towards me.

'It's a friendship bracelet. I made a few of them the summer we left. I sold them.'

'Can you remember who to?'

'God, no, I mean, just some of the girls.'

'Could you write me a list of who you recall having one?' he asks.

'Well, yes, I suppose,' I say.

He smiles again but it no longer feels genuine and this time, when he tells me once more these really are just routine questions and there's nothing for me to worry about, I no longer believe him. 'Thank you for your time,' Walton says, handing me a card and asking me to get in touch when I've written my list.

Once they've left, I watch them through my living-room window as they chat to each other by their car, PC Walton laughing at something his colleague says. My hands tremble as I call Bonnie and I consider the thought that, deep down, there might be a tiny part of me that relishes being drawn into what has happened because it links me to the island again.

But as Walton looks up at my window, it vanishes as quickly as it came, and I'm left with an unnerving dread that one of my bracelets could be in any way involved.

'Can you hear me?' I ask as Bonnie picks up, static fuzzing in my ear. 'Where are you?'

'Tesco. And I've got hardly any reception. Hold on.' I wait for a moment until she comes back on the line. 'Is that better?'

'A little. I've just had the police round.'

'Luke said they've called at ours. What do they want?'

I relay their questions as she drops things into her trolley.

'So they're making sure no one's lying,' she says. 'Why do you sound so worried?'

'Lying about what?' I ask, ignoring her question.

'Who was or wasn't on the island, I suppose.'

I finally hear them drive off and I retreat from the window. 'I don't like this,' I admit. 'Bon, I think – I don't know, I get the feeling we might have been there when it happened.'

'They're just asking questions,' she says, sighing. 'They're probably speaking to everyone who's ever been there. Why are you panicking?'

'They were interested in the friendship bracelet I made. You were wearing it in a photo. They asked me to write them a list of everyone who had one.' Come to think of it, I don't recall Bonnie ever wearing it, but I pick up the photo again to see it for myself, tied around her wrist.

Bonnie doesn't speak.

'Did you hear me?' I say.

'Yes. I heard you. Why do they want that?'

'I don't know, but it means—' What does it mean? We know who the body is? We know the person who killed her?

'It means nothing. They're probably looking into loads of things right now,' she snaps, but there is no conviction in her words.

'I don't like not knowing what's going on. I feel so …' I pause, searching for the right words – like I should be there instead.

'Stop obsessing over it,' Bonnie says. 'Every conversation we've had this weekend is about the bloody island. I don't want to talk about it. I don't even want to think about it.'

Her reaction doesn't surprise me, but the news has tipped me off kilter and, while Bonnie might want to shut out her thoughts, I haven't been able to. I can't stop my mind from going to places I've always avoided and now all the boxes I'd once locked away are rising to the surface. There have always been many questions I've wanted answers to but have never been brave enough to pursue.

'Bon,' I start, cautiously, 'the way we left, those last few days—' I break off, not knowing how to finish the sentence. Still not knowing if I'm sure I want to.

'What?'

'It's just – is there anything you remember about it that I don't?'

'Of course there isn't. What the hell would I know?'

A lot more than me, I think. She was six years older, more aware. 'We never really spoke about anything …'

'Because there's nothing to speak of,' she says. 'And don't go bringing up why we left again. They told us they needed the money that Dad's new job would bring in. Clearly the ferry was making a pittance. I don't know why you can't accept that.'

I don't believe you can, either, I think as Bonnie reels off the facts like she's learnt them by heart. I know this means she is holding back on me. But then, aren't I holding back on her too?

When I hang up, I pick up the photo that had caught the policeman's attention. It's one of the five of us, taken that last summer. I look at it closely, at Mum and Dad's smiling faces, his arm slung over her shoulder, her hand clasping his.

What happened to us all?

As much as I need to have that conversation with Bonnie, there's a greater part of me that doesn't want to. Because then I would have to admit I've lied about what happened before we left. And the reason I lied was because I'd thought, if I did, it would keep us all together.

Chapter Five

That night, while Evergreen is no longer a headline, my own personal interest has heightened. I pore over the internet searching photos, names, anything that relates to it. The more I find out, the more I have to know. It has become a drug. How I managed to keep myself away for all these years, I'm no longer sure.

A couple of weeks into my own counselling sessions, I was asked, 'How often do you think of your old island?' I thought the way the counsellor said 'your old island' made it sound like a fictional land rather than the only place I've ever called home.

'Not often.' I cocked my head, mirroring hers. We were both as inquisitive as the other to know what was really going on inside each other's heads. For my part I wanted to know what she was getting at and why she kept coming back to Evergreen. Something in our first meeting had fuelled her therapist's interests.

When the ensuing silence got to her, she went on, 'You clearly wish your parents had never taken you away from it. Do you think you've given yourself the chance to settle anywhere else?'

It was an interesting question, and not one I'd really considered. 'I don't know. I guess.'

'You're thirty-two. You're having a change of career. You live in a rented flat. You want to devote your time to helping others and you also spend a lot of effort on your sister. Who you still live less than ten minutes from,' she stated, as if this wasn't a good thing.

The heat spread up my neck and across my face. 'You make it sound like I'm a failure,' I blurted.

'No.' She shook her head. 'Not at all. Or rather I'm sorry if I do – I applaud your decision to train in a new vocation. I just get the impression you spend an inordinate amount of time worrying about Bonnie and ...' she paused and I caught a flash of pink colouring her own cheeks '... living in the past. Seeing it as all rosy is common, but maybe not too healthy for someone at your life stage. Planning for the future is—'

'I thought that's what I was doing,' I snapped, blinking as my eyes watered. 'Retraining. And I can't help worrying about Bonnie when she's the only family I have.'

'Yes,' she said, looking like she wanted to add more. Maybe about why I always brushed over my feelings around losing every other family member.

'And in answer to your question,' I went on before she could continue, 'I very rarely think about the island.'

This was, of course, a lie, and she knew it. I had become like Bonnie in the way she used to hide evidence of her drinking. My scrapbook was squeezed in between magazines; I had shoeboxes at the bottom of my wardrobe stuffed full of Mum's old photos.

I had been fighting a yearning to return for years and I'd thought I'd overcome it. But ever since Friday night, I feel like I'm losing the fight. And since the visit from the police I no longer think I can stay away. I should be back there, helping to find out why someone buried a body on the edge of my old garden and what my bracelets have to do with it. I should be back among the people I used to love because I actually can't bear the thought of not being with them. And I should be back because I want to know why we left when it was clear we would never be happier anywhere else.

My pulse flutters as I carefully compile a list of the girls who had one of my bracelets. When I'm done I look over the names before emailing them to the police. My eyes rest on the name at the top, and I know I'm not going to get any answers sitting in my flat.

Monday morning I try to focus my thoughts on a new family – a couple and their fourteen-year-old son who, in the mother's words, has trouble committing to school.

She talks quickly, outlining her worries as if she's ticking off a shopping list, and it's clear how nervous she is. Every time she relays a situation she reminds me she doesn't agree with her son's behaviours. However, I don't get the impression she wants to belittle him; rather, I think she needs me to know that she's just a good mother, trying hard.

I feel for her. She comes across as guilty for letting it get to the point that her son's hardly in school and they are all in therapy. I can imagine she feels the same way I did yesterday with the policemen in my living room.

I nod as I listen, every so often turning my attention to her husband and child. The boy fiddles with the balled-up coat in his lap and looks as if he wants to be anywhere but here. His face is blotchy with patches of red, and as his gestures become more frantic I can sense he's had enough. As soon as his mum pauses for a breath, I ask him to tell me what a good day looks like to him.

He grunts and shrugs, but for the first time since he sat in my office he looks up and catches my eye.

By the end of the session I've garnered his parents' misaligned priorities but I still feel there's much more to glean and I suggest I spend half an hour alone with him at the start of our next session.

As I watch them leave, my mind drifts to Bonnie and the woman our parents took her to see on the mainland. Not for the first time I wish I had Mum here to ask what her intentions were. There have been many times when clients have left and I've thought about how I'd do anything to have both of my parents in front of me, talking.

I'd ask Mum how she could have let Danny go and Dad what he was looking for when he met Olivia and if he ever found it. Whether he realised she was Mum's polar opposite, or if that was his intention.

Now he is living in a house that's as stark as his relationship, where there is no drama, no cross words, no raised voices. No laughter, no holding of hands or secret kisses when they think I'm not watching. That was what he'd always had with Mum.

Secretly I thought he deserved Olivia when he first moved in, but then once Danny left I began to wonder whether any part of it was Mum's fault. Certainly that was the way Bonnie saw it.

Outside in reception, I casually run the idea past Tanya that I've been considering visiting the crime scene. She pushes her glasses up her nose by habit and, as I wait for her to answer, I realise I'm hoping she'll tell me it's a good idea.

'FOMO, they call it,' she says. 'Fear of missing out.'

'You make me sound like a voyeur,' I reply. 'Just say if you think it's an awful idea.'

'I think it's an awful idea. Personally, I wouldn't want to go anywhere near it, but then I have no interest in returning to the town where I grew up.' She shudders. 'What does Bonnie think?'

I shake my head. My sister would only deter me.

'She doesn't know?'

'No. And anyway, it's just a thought,' I say, brushing off the idea like it is only that. I look up as my couple from last week arrives, and direct them through to my room.

'Look,' Tanya goes on when they are out of earshot. 'I just think if you want to play detective you need to be careful. The police won't thank you for sticking your nose in.'

'That's not what I want to do. I just want to see some of my old friends again.'

I do also want to find Jill and ask why she never once wrote to me. I've never revealed to anyone how much I tore myself apart searching for clues for what seemed utterly inexplicable. I'd been desperate to cling to our friendship. The pain of being forgotten and so easily discarded had ripped through me, though I'd never let on how much when my family was already taping over cracks and trying to form some semblance of a normal life in a new city.

But it's only one of the many boxes whose lids are starting to flip open. Now there are voices in my head I haven't listened to in years and I can't get them to shut up.

'Have you spoken to your dad about it?' Tanya is asking.

I snap my head up, pull myself out of my thoughts. 'Not yet,' I say, turning towards my office. The fact is, I don't want to open up a conversation about the island with him, because while he's the only one who could tell me why he made us leave, I'm not entirely sure I trust him any longer.

I have barely asked my clients how they are when she blurts out, 'I don't think I'll ever forgive him. All I can see every night is him with her.' The words catch in her throat and she looks into the corner of the room to hide her face from her husband. As it is, he is studying his hands, folded in his lap.

'I don't think he should have told me,' she says. 'I think he only did it to ease his own conscience. He thought he'd feel better for it.'

'That's not true,' he murmurs and I ask him if he can explain what he means. Really I just want him to talk.

'I don't know what you're asking,' he says.

'She means why did you tell me,' his wife spits.

He glances over at her. 'Because you kept asking. You begged me to tell you. I thought it's what you wanted.'

'What I wanted?' she cries. 'What I wanted was for you not to sleep with another woman.'

The colour drains from his face and he hangs his head again. There's little he can say to make amends, but at the same time I must coax him to try. Meanwhile she is continuing to talk but keeps coming back to the same thing – that she wishes she didn't know.

'Would you do it differently if you had the chance?' I ask her.

'What?' She screws her eyes up at me.

'I mean, if you went back to the point when you begged your husband to tell you the truth. Would you ignore what you thought you wanted to know?'

She continues to regard me and I realise it's an odd question, but I'm interested in her answer. I lean forward in my chair, ignoring the voice telling me I shouldn't use my clients for my own purposes.

'I don't ...' She shakes her head and in that moment looks so confused that I lay my palm flat on the table between us and tell her it doesn't matter. I didn't mean to catch her out.

'There's no right or wrong answer,' I say, though my minor slip means I need to backtrack and make her feel comfortable again.

I move the conversation on, but at the end of our session, once her husband has left the room, she pauses and says, 'I think I always would have asked him.'

She looks so sad and I touch her arm lightly. 'I think any of us would do the same,' I assure her. 'Despite the outcome, we'd always beg for honesty.'

Because isn't the torment of wondering worse than the truth? I have gone back and forth in my head playing out too many scenarios, trying to bury my own questions that would have burnt through my skull if I'd let them, and now I fear they will. In my own training, I learnt that we are better equipped when we know what we're up against.

I follow them out, and once they've disappeared at the end of the road I hold my face up to the grey sky, my hand circling my wrist where my own friendship bracelet once was.

There were secrets that summer. We all had them, though I don't understand how we got to that point where it all went so terribly wrong. And the more I try to separate everything, the more it blends together until it becomes one large tangled mess, leaving me thinking if I can pick apart one piece the rest might unravel.

The body; our departure; Jill's silence – what if it's all linked somehow? The thought tears through me as the sky closes in and I can't bear the foreboding sense that it could be. All I know is that I have to find out and I can't do that here.

I go back into reception and wait for Tanya to finish a call. When she hangs up I tell her I'm rearranging my clients for the next few days. 'I don't have many and I can fit them in next week,' I say.

She eyes me over the rim of her glasses.

'I can't *not* go,' I tell her, almost breathless at my decision.

Chapter Six

By eleven thirty the following morning I am standing at the edge of the harbour, waiting in line with a number of other passengers who would have once been waiting for my dad's small ferry. Now double-decked bright boats line up like ducks in a row and a kiosk sells tickets for around-the-island cruises. One thing hasn't changed, though – there is still only one run a day in winter to Evergreen and it's leaving in fifteen minutes.

My parents would have hated that a large company took over, but I'm pleased for its generic unfamiliarity. I don't know how I would have handled seeing someone else in Dad's place.

In my left hand I clutch a ticket, rubbing its edge with my fingers to the point it is starting to disintegrate.

Someone once told me that the difference between fear and excitement is two inches, and what I once thought of as a flippant remark now feels closer to the truth than ever. Everything I fear about setting foot on Evergreen also excites me, and the two mould together until I can no longer separate them.

From the mainland I can't see Evergreen. Blocking it are other islands, mostly uninhabited, and Evergreen hides behind them, out of sight. Most of the other passengers will disembark at Brownsea, an island set up for tourists. Hardly any of them venture as far as Evergreen.

Last night I rang the number of a woman named Rachel who was renting out rooms in her house on the island. She didn't call it a B&B, but I took from her posting she intended as much. I doubted she was busy. Regardless of recent events, January wouldn't drive many visitors, but still she was reluctant to let me stay.

'It's just for three nights,' I begged.

She pulled in a tight breath. 'I don't know what you want to come over here for at the moment anyway. And you're not police?'

'No,' I said. 'But my family lived on the island a long time ago. There are old friends I want to see.'

'Like who?' she tested me.

'Annie Webb,' I said, thinking of the one person most likely to still be there, if she were still alive. I held my breath as I waited for an answer.

'I don't know ...'

'Please,' I begged. 'You'll hardly know I'm there.'

'Three nights?'

'Just three.'

'Fine,' she huffed, 'I'll see you tomorrow,' and promptly hung up.

I wondered how many paying guests she'd actually ever had. Most of the visitors to Evergreen went because they were looking for an adventure, but there was little to do on the island that couldn't be done in a day.

Dad often came back after work and relayed the comments he'd overheard, like 'What a quaint existence', and 'Why would anyone want to hide away from the rest of the world?'

I didn't like the way visitors spoke of the island as though there was something secretive about it. 'Why would they say that?' I asked Mum, but she used to laugh it off.

'They're jealous,' she told me. 'Who wouldn't want to live here?'

'But why do they think we are hiding?' I persisted. I imagined Evergreen tucking itself in tighter behind Brownsea so no one would know we were there. And then I pictured all of us islanders crouching down behind the trees as soon as someone stepped off Dad's ferry so we couldn't be seen.

Mum tried her best to explain it wasn't meant that way. 'Some people just don't see the beauty in it,' she'd said. 'Not like we can.' In time, I realised there was something magical and mysterious about the idea of us hiding. But now, I am standing on the other side. I am the one searching, and I don't know who's hiding from me.

'Are you coming on?'

I look up sharply at the man on the ferry, before glancing down at the steel walkway.

'We need to get going if you are, love. Are you waiting for someone?'

'No, I'm ...'

'You need a hand?'

I shake my head and inhale a deep lungful of sea air that feels like a brick as it jars in my throat. 'I'm coming,' I say, and he stands aside to let me pass. Despite the cold, I climb to the top deck and find a seat on the right-hand side because it is from here I will see Evergreen most clearly.

As we pull away from the jetty, my stomach lurches and I close my eyes to quell the sensation I'm about to burst. I have thought about this moment forever and now that I am here it is surreal. Questions flood my mind: will it still look the same? What if I don't see anyone I know? How will Jill defend her reason for not staying in touch? What's it going to be like to stand in front of my old house again? My eyes snap open and I grip on to the side with the hand that still clutches my ticket. It is that, I realise, which scares me the most.

We reach Brownsea where most of the passengers climb off. I am the only one on the top deck now. Dark clouds threaten rain, but I am here because I know it's only a matter of moments until I catch a first glimpse of my island, and I want to see it clearly and not through the steamed-up glass below.

Once more I lean towards the edge, my breath sticking in my throat, tears pricking my eyes as we begin to round Brownsea, until piece by piece I see it. A thin line of sand. The skyline of the trees. The points where those trees dip and you can see where the reservoir lies beyond. The opening of the quay, bare of boats, waiting for our arrival.

I cry out and hold my hand over my mouth. My heart races as my gaze sweeps across the horizon one way and then back the other, trying to take it all in. For this is what I've dreamt about since the day we left. Seeing this sight again. Coming home.

Evergreen Island

1 July 1993

When Maria looked back to the start of the summer she often asked herself if she'd had any sense of foreboding of what lay ahead. Did anything feel amiss or had there been a change in the wind as it blew over the island? She always came back to the same conclusion – there was no possible way to know how much everything was about to change, and therefore there was nothing she could have done differently. But the thoughts would continue to taunt her, that possibly she just hadn't been watching closely enough.

It started one very hot day at the beginning of July. She could remember it so clearly, and if there were such a thing as a switch that could divert your life on to a completely different track then that was the moment she'd have chosen to use it.

From Danny's bedroom Maria had a good view of the jetty. Especially on clear days, like that morning, when the sky was a perfect pale blue and the sun dappled the surface of the water, making it look like it was covered in tiny crystals.

She'd soon see David's boat when it pulled into the quay and right then she was watching her daughter, Stella, standing on the dock, waving wildly. She could probably see her dad coming back. It was only the first return run of the day and David would be turning around more or less straight away. With the summer forecasted to be a hot one, they expected good business to set them up nicely for winter.

It was past ten, which meant David was running a few minutes late. She pulled away as she contemplated whether to join Stella or stay out of the way. There were newcomers scheduled to arrive on this run and unusually there were eight of them in total – a family of five, the new doctor and his girlfriend, and the young girl who was studying on the island as part of her geography course. Maria was torn between wanting to see first-hand what they were like and ignoring the fact they were arriving at all.

Soon her husband's ferry came into view. Five minutes and the passengers would be disembarking. She could be there in two.

Taking a deep breath, Maria walked slowly down the stairs. Usually the start of the summer holidays was her favourite time of year. The promise of long, lazy days ahead with the children, eating outdoors when David finished working.

It had crossed her mind there wouldn't be many more summers like this, her concerns centred on the fact that the last of her children were growing up. She could already sense Stella tugging away from her a little more than in previous years. She'd have thought that with two older children she'd be used to it, but it was her youngest she yearned to keep closest.

In the garden Maria wandered to the trees that lined the boundary between the house and the jetty. As she drew near, Bonnie appeared on one side of them, her head hung low, her shoulders tense. 'Do you want to come and see the newcomers with me?' Maria asked. 'I'd like to have you with me.'

Bonnie looked up at her, her face blank. 'Why would I want to do that?'

'There's a girl coming, only a couple of years older than you,' Maria said. 'Iona. She's nineteen, I think. Anyway, she'd probably be grateful to know someone her own age and—'

'I'm not five,' Bonnie snorted. 'I can make my own friends.'

'I know you're not,' Maria said patiently as she watched her daughter storm off.

Bonnie shook her head and carried on walking towards the house. She hated the way her mother did this. Always trying to tell her how to live her life. Both her parents had been doing it as long as she could remember, though her mum was undoubtedly worse. It had started with the Stay and Play sessions they used to drag her to, with the woman who'd watch her play with the stupid toys they laid out while she talked at Bonnie.

Afterwards Bonnie would have to leave the room and sit with someone else while they discussed her. They always let Danny stay, perched on her mum's lap, sucking on that dummy that was always in his mouth.

Bonnie knew they must have been looking for something in her, but she didn't know what. She only knew that the toys were a distraction to get her to open up.

One time the woman was particularly interested in the way Bonnie never looked at her when they were talking, so the next time Bonnie stared straight at her. She learnt that if she paid close enough attention to their questions, she could tell them whatever it was they seemed to want to hear. Something must have worked, because one day her mother stormed out, grabbed her hand, and they never went back. Bonnie remembered listening to her parents talking that night when she was supposed to be in bed, and hearing her mum utter the words, 'Sometimes nothing good comes from being honest.'

At first it was exciting to hear her mum say something so unexpected, but the moment passed quickly and then it just left her uneasy. God knew she had enough things she was already worrying about.

Now her mum was back to her old tricks, trying to get her to make friends, and it was for that exact reason she was going to refuse to have absolutely anything to do with this Iona.

Maria stopped at the thin line of trees and hesitated, hidden from view. Everyone came to the island for something, which was why she was always so wary of newcomers. It would only be a matter of days before she and the islanders started talking about them, drawing conclusions as to what the new people expected from Evergreen, what they might be running from. Everyone had a reason for coming here.

At the other end of the jetty Stella had her arms around her dad's stomach. He'd pulled her in tight and was kissing her head. Maria loved watching David's affection for his children, though she wasn't entirely sure it was always fairly distributed. Yet another thing she'd glossed over, when maybe she should have paid more attention.

He looked up over his daughter's head, glancing around, and Maria knew he was looking for her so she stepped out.

A woman was climbing down the steps of the boat, looking harried. She had dark hair pulled into a tight ponytail and was calling behind her. 'Come on, Freddie. Freya, take his hand, get him down the steps.'

Clearly this was the Little family. Maria smiled at the mother as she hurried up the jetty, suitcases tightly clutched in both hands. 'I'm Maria, welcome to Evergreen,' she said as they passed, just as Annie Webb had when they'd stepped off the boat all those years ago.

The woman paused, looking around. 'Feels like I'm on some TV show, you know, surviving on a desert island.'

'I'm sure you'll love it,' Maria replied, though she wasn't sure in the slightest. Already she had the sense the Littles weren't cut out for Evergreen. 'If there's anything you need, I live in the Quay House,' Maria went on, indicating behind her.

When the Littles passed, Maria greeted the new doctor. His girlfriend barely looked up. Her cheeks flushed pink and she looked like a deer trapped in headlights. It made the contrast with Iona, who was stepping off the boat behind her, even starker.

'Mrs Harvey?' the student asked, holding out her hand. She had long eyelashes and a short shock of brown hair that had been shaped into a pixie cut. It suited her small face perfectly, though the hair looked a shade too dark for her pale skin. She pushed her sunglasses on top of her head and Maria was taken aback by the brightness and intensity of the girl's green eyes. 'I'm Iona. I'm here for my sandwich year.'

'A sandwich year?' Maria asked, shaking her hand and smiling at the young girl's warmth.

'It's a year out of my degree,' Iona said. 'I'm studying geography, hence ...' She waved her arm about her. 'Your island looks beautiful.'

'Thank you.' Maria beamed. 'It is.'

Maria watched her stride off towards the village, only spotting Annie Webb when the girl was out of sight.

'So that's the lot then?' Annie asked.

Maria nodded and let out a breath. 'Seems like it.'

'And how are you, Stella?' Annie said, turning to Stella who was now leaping up into David's struggling arms. 'You're too big for your father to lift any more. You shouldn't be doing that at eleven. Eleven,' she repeated, shaking her head. 'I remember the moment you were born.'

'You were the first person to see my face,' Stella grinned.

'I was,' Annie said, 'and your mother was lucky I was here. There was no chance of *you* making it to the mainland. Not like your brother, of course, who didn't want to come out.'

'Danny made something cool for the treehouse,' Stella said at the mention of her brother. 'It's a wooden chest. I can put my notebooks and pens in it so I don't have to keep taking them up there.'

'Danny made that?' Maria asked. 'That's lovely.'

'That boy's always been good with his hands,' Annie murmured as David called out that he'd see them all later.

Maria turned from Annie to wave. Her husband looked guarded as he pulled in the rope for a quick turn-around, but she knew why. He wouldn't like the fact she and Annie were watching the newcomers with such interest, but

David was wrong to think it was Annie who disliked change. Annie was the one who made *her* feel better about it.

Maria had always been surprised that David didn't understand her closeness to Annie. Surely anyone who knew their whole story would have realised why she'd become so dependent on her. After all, Annie was the only one who knew the truth about why they'd come to Evergreen. Well, not the *only* one, but Maria tried not to contemplate the others.

Yet over the years David had become almost irritated by their friendship, as if he were jealous of the way she often turned to the older woman rather than him.

'You know he's up there, don't you?' Annie said and Maria turned back.

'Who?'

'Danny.' Annie gestured to a tree and Maria eventually spotted her son's sandalled feet dangling between its branches. His feet were bigger than hers now, the size of a man's, which didn't seem right. He'd had another growth spurt that spring and was only two inches shorter than David. He looked like a man but he was still a child, and Maria couldn't think of a time when he'd be ready to leave home.

She shook her head and sighed. She knew what Annie would be thinking, but what did she expect her to do? She couldn't ask Danny to stop hanging around in trees when it was the only place he seemed happy.

Maria hadn't known then how much that summer would change them. By the end of it the island that she had once loved, her safe place, would become one that none of her family could ever return to.

Danny knew they had spotted him, but it wasn't as if he was hiding. He just wanted to see what all the fuss was about. His parents had been talking about the newcomers for the last few nights and he knew his mum was nervous about their arrival though he really didn't get it. She was so friendly to everyone, it didn't make sense that she wasn't happy to meet new people.

Contrary to what they suspected, Danny didn't mind strangers arriving because it gave him others to watch. It got boring when the same old people did the same old things. Hardly any of the islanders did much out of character. He hoped this lot would be interesting and would make the summer pass quicker. He liked it when Stella sat in the treehouse with him, but already he worried that she would be off with Jill all the time.

Everyone else thought he didn't like talking to anyone and sometimes it meant mealtimes could pass and they'd completely ignore him. Stella was the only one in the family who didn't either hate him, like Bonnie, or talk for him as his mum did. Actually his dad was pretty good, but he was always working.

Danny pulled out his drawing pad and turned to the back page where he started a list. There were three new girls on the island but he didn't know their names so instead he drew pictures of them. Then he tucked the book under his arm and climbed out of the tree.

PRESENT

Chapter Seven

For a moment I am unable to move as I stand on the end of the jetty. My hands are numb and clenched tightly inside my pockets, my fingers curled too tight. Little things have changed that remind me how many years have passed since I've last been home, like the whitewashed planks of wood under my feet and the steel posts lining the jetty with rope knotted around them to act as a railing. It might look attractive, but it's not the same, and I wish I could rip them away to find what I remember.

Mum's voice fills my head. *It's too commercial. Look at it all set up for the tourist trade, I'm surprised Annie allowed it.*

If she's still here, Mum. Maybe she's not. Rachel from the B&B didn't confirm it.

No. She'll still be here, Mum says as a cold gust of wind blows, catching me off balance as it hits me face on. Any stronger and it could have taken me into the sea, and I look over my shoulder uneasily as I step away from the edge.

My legs feel like liquid. The other few passengers have disappeared and already the ferry is preparing to leave. I pull a hand out of my pocket and clutch the bag that weighs down on my shoulder, forcing myself to walk forward, my eyes wandering to the trees just off to the right in front of me. Any minute I'll be able to see through them to my house the other side.

I keep moving to where the jetty ends and the path sweeps past it. In either direction I would pass my garden. To the left the path opens up on to Pinecliff Walk, the main route to the cove at the other end of the island. This way leads past the length of my garden with the white picket fence. To the right, the path winds inland to the village, and then further on to the lakes.

I take neither. Instead I step over the well-trodden ground and creep forward towards the trees until my house starts to come to me in fragments. Jigsaw pieces of brick and glass and roof tile until I'm suddenly at the bottom of our garden.

My chest aches from the scent of a familiar blend of heather and pine that is so overpowering I find myself reaching for a tree to stop from swaying too far. I make no move to wipe away the tears running in rivers down my cheeks until I'm soon sobbing, choking down great lungfuls of air. I collapse against the tree, unable to take my eyes off my house. My precious home. *We should never have left you.*

Memories flood back as I search its windows, all of them closed and curtained. No one can see in. No one, most likely, wants to look out. I seek out my old bedroom window that sits on the far right side, next to Danny's, imagining my old heart-dotted curtains hanging on the other side of it.

I don't have to close my eyes to smell Mum's casseroles and roast dinners wafting through the house or hear her voice calling us in for tea, and I grip tighter to the tree to keep from running up to the front door.

It takes me a while to notice the police tent, even though you cannot miss it. Its presence is overwhelming as it perches in the corner at the very edge of the woods.

My eyes flick back and forth between the house and the activity unfurling. A man wearing a black overcoat is bent over, raking a patch of ground. He lifts his head to call someone, pointing at whatever he's found.

I tear my gaze away and look back at the house. For all the years that have passed, I could be hiding in these trees right now, waiting to jump out on Mum. How time can slip into the ether as if it never existed. I can't even imagine I've had a life anywhere other than Evergreen and yet there have been twenty-five years of it.

I used to weave through the pines I'm standing amongst until I got to the only tree that ever mattered, but even from here I can see it's not the same. At some point my treehouse was ripped out, leaving it naked.

I let out a groan as pain tears through me, shrinking back when someone near the tent looks in my direction, reminding me I'm effectively spying on a murder scene.

I turn my attention on the bare tree again. Dad built us the treehouse. I'd begged him for a year before he finally found enough wood and spent a month hammering in nails, fixing it like a nest into the branches.

He built it the year I turned ten. I'd had two summers in it before I never saw it again, but I had climbed its wooden ladder every day. Often I would take a blanket and, if it was dark, a torch and a Tupperware box of sandwiches, and would sit in it for hours, reading books, colouring, writing in my diary.

'It's an accident waiting to happen,' Bonnie had muttered more than once.

'It's beautiful,' I'd cried. 'Daddy's made this for us.'

'Us?' she laughed. 'You wouldn't get me in that if you paid me.'

'Danny?' I'd turned to my brother. 'You like it, don't you? You'd come up there with me.'

Danny had shrugged as his eyes trailed up its makeshift ladder. He'd spent as much time in it as I had. Never with anyone but me, but often he'd go up there alone, sit on its platform, and look out. What he was looking at, I had no idea.

But now the treehouse is gone and the windowsills have been painted teal and a shiny new conservatory stands at one side. Now there is a white tent in the garden and blue-and-white police tape tied around the trees, and if I'm not careful, a detective will come over and ask me what I'm doing.

'You okay?' A voice behind me makes me jump and I turn, still slumped against the tree, and wipe a hand furiously across my tear-streaked cheeks. A woman about my age is staring at me oddly, an amused smirk on the edge of her lips. She pulls her dark navy parka tighter to her, one hand gripping a camera that hangs around her neck.

'I'm fine, thanks,' I mumble.

She gestures over to the tent. 'Horrible business, isn't it?'

I nod, unsure how to answer, deciding that saying as little as possible is best.

'Do you live here?' she asks, and there's something in the way she says it that suggests she already knows I don't.

When I shake my head she slowly holds out a hand. 'I'm from the *Bournemouth Echo.*'

'Oh, hi.' I shake her hand. 'Do they know anything more about the body, then?' I ask as casually I can.

'Not as far as I'm aware.' She continues to watch me carefully, her lips threatening to break into a grin. 'You don't look the type to have come for a nose,' she says.

'I'm not.' My fingers automatically reach for the hard skin on my thumb and begin picking at it.

'Do you mind if I get your name?'

'Why do you want that?'

'I'm just writing something up on general public concerns, that kind of thing. To be honest, if I go back with nothing, my boss will have me and I'm running out of things to report on.'

I hesitate, toying with the idea of making one up, but in the end I tell her the truth. 'Stella. Stella Harvey.'

'Stella Harvey,' she repeats slowly, nodding as she bites her bottom lip. She glances back at the quay. 'How long are you here for then, Stella? You know the passenger ferry doesn't come back until tomorrow?'

'I know. I'm staying at one of the beach houses,' I tell her. 'Just for a couple of nights.'

'Well, it would be good to catch up with you, Stella Harvey,' she says, but before she goes to leave, she pauses and adds, 'I'll probably see you around.' And with a swing of her camera, she smiles and wanders off towards the white tent and the huddle of officers.

I decide to stop by Rachel's house so I can drop off my bag, taking Pinecliff Walk to avoid the police tent.

It's clear up close that the picket fence isn't the one my dad put up. From a distance it looked the same but this one has clearly been installed by a professional, with its neat, straight lines and perfect points, and I have an overwhelming urge to kick it.

Up ahead, the new conservatory flashes brightly, its glass sparkling against the backdrop of blinds that have been pulled closed. I wish the new owners would let me see some part of the life they have inside, but it's blocked from view and I have to make do with the outside.

Still I contemplate whether they've made the small kitchen any bigger, or if they've knocked down the partition Dad had put up to give Danny and me a bedroom each. It wouldn't have taken them long to notice you could hear everything through the thin wall. I sigh deeply as I take one last glance before carrying along the path as it bends away.

Pinecliff Walk snakes along the coastline for a mile and a half until it reaches the furthest point of the island – Pirate's Cove. Sometimes it meanders so close to the edge that there's a clear view of the sea, but at others you're too far away and have to imagine the water beyond the trees or at the bottom of cliffs. At these points other little tracks spider off it, some well-trodden routes and others more makeshift cut-throughs to the cliff and beaches below.

There was one path in particular we'd made ourselves that led to my secret place by the small clearing, and it's at the tip of this that I pause. It's funny that even after twenty-five years a wave of nausea washes over me as I glance to my left.

I'd loved that place once, but when I'd turned up on Jill's doorstep on my last day and she'd suggested going there, I'd frozen. I hadn't told her why I no longer wanted to return to that spot. I hadn't told anyone what had happened there only two days earlier. Instead I'd reluctantly agreed to meet her there and had buried my secret. It was the first box I'd shut the lid on.

Further up the path I pause again, this time when I'm at the top of the driveway that leads to Jill's house. Even if I knew my old friend still lived there I'm not sure I yet have the courage to knock on the door.

My question tingles on the edge of my tongue: *Why did you never write, not even once?* I'd lost count of the number of letters I sent before I eventually gave up. But now that I am in grasping distance of finding the answer, I find my feet picking up again. I tell myself it is the thought of seeing Bob Taylor that deters me, but I know it is more than that. I know I am still unsure if I'm ready for what I might discover.

In contrast, Rachel's house, set among a scattering of beach houses a little further along, is less familiar and imposes no vivid memories. I knock loudly on her door as spots of rain begin to fall, and by the time she opens it my hair is wet.

Rachel is at least a head shorter than me and somewhere in her early fifties. Her brown hair streaked with grey is pushed back from her face with a thick navy Alice band. She is wearing a wool cardigan that falls to midway down her calves and, as she peers at me from the other side of large round glasses, she effortlessly gives the impression she isn't pleased to see me. I offer my name though I'm sure she knows who I am.

'Come in,' she says as she lets me into a large but dimly lit hallway. Too much dark mahogany furniture lines the walls and there is little space for us to stand but right in the middle of a red woven rug. 'I didn't want any guests,' she reminds me. 'I don't want you staying any more than three nights.'

I shake my head. 'I won't,' I assure her, the unfriendly welcome making me think even three is too many.

'I double-lock the door at nine in the winter but it's too dark to be out past then anyway. There are no streetlights on the island,' she goes on, 'but I assume you already know that, don't you? You said you used to live here.'

'I did. A long time ago.'

She nods as she moves to a bureau and pulls out a book from its top drawer, flicking through the pages until she finds the last one to be written on. 'I need your name, address and telephone number in here.' She taps a pen against the pad and hands it to me. 'Then I'll show you up to your room. You can pay me in cash now or when you leave, it's up to you.'

'I can do it now,' I say as I begin writing.

'I make breakfast at eight but you'll need to sort yourself out for anything else.'

'That's fine.'

'There's a shop and a café in the village but they shut early in winter.'

I nod. 'Thank you.'

She waits for me to finish writing and takes the book from me, reading my address. 'So how long since you were last here?'

'About twenty-five years,' I say.

'And where did you live?'

'The Quay House,' I tell her, and wait for the inevitable widening of her eyes and parting of her mouth. She reaches out to hold on to the bureau beside her, and as her gaze roams my face, I can tell she is searching for clues as to what this means.

'I was only eleven when we left,' I say, shrugging, hoping she might think I therefore have little memory of the island. I'm relieved when she tells me to follow her upstairs to a pleasantly large and clean, but dark bedroom. The trees outside the window sap what little light there is, made worse by more mahogany furniture and a deep purple bedspread.

Rachel fumbles in her pocket and produces two keys. 'These are for your room and the front door, but as I say, I'll be double-locking at nine.' She begins to back out but pauses before heading down the stairs. 'I only agreed to you staying because you said you had friends here, but if people don't take kindly to you coming back, then—' She breaks off, leaving me no wiser as to what she'd do. No doubt tell me I'd need to go.

'We don't need any more upset. We've been through enough the last few days and can do without more people poking their noses in,' she says, looking at me pointedly. I go to protest but Rachel carries on, quieter now. 'This was a good place to live until last Friday and now ...' she shakes her head '... now you're better off just keeping your business to yourself.'

'I promise I'm not here to cause any trouble,' I tell her and eventually she nods and leaves.

I dump my bag on the bed, pulling out my purse and phone and stuffing them into my coat pockets. Her accusation that I'm only here to be nosy riles me, and I hate that she thinks she has more right to be here than I do.

Outside I wind back round the path to the village. Despite the overcast day, it is eerily quiet. My gaze flicks around the shops, taking in the changes. The bakery has been replaced by a convenience store. Bistro tables sit empty outside the refurbished café. My stomach growls and I'm about to stride over to get something to eat when the journalist suddenly emerges.

She grins again when she spots me and wanders over, her camera still swinging carelessly from side to side. 'So what are you actually doing back on the island, Stella Harvey?'

Evergreen Island

10 July 1993

There was a particular day, during the first week of summer, when two occurrences began brewing that would lead to fatal consequences by the end. It's possible the tracks had already been laid too firmly, but Maria would later consider how her own actions had not helped to divert her family to safety.

She had seen little of Stella, though she didn't begrudge her spending time with Jill. In fact, she'd insisted her daughter not feel bad about it (even though she would have liked to see more of her) because friendships were important.

Jill had been waiting by the gate for Stella right after breakfast, a rucksack weighing down on her bony shoulders. Maria had given them fruit and cake to pack into their bags and, as she stood in the doorway and watched them running up Pinecliff Walk, she found herself peering a little more closely.

'What's up?' David appeared beside her, making her jump. He kissed her head, slinging an arm over her shoulder. 'You missing your girl?'

'A little,' she admitted, though it wasn't just that. She'd noticed Jill looked thinner that year. It was easy to spot under the girl's spaghetti-strap top and the denim shorts she'd also been wearing last summer. Maria shook her head and nestled into her husband. She didn't want to mention her concerns just yet, but she'd keep an eye on Jill.

What she'd also considered was that she'd have no clue what to do about it even if there were a problem. Ruth Taylor had her head in the sand about almost everything, and the idea of addressing anything so personal to Bob was – well, out of the question.

'Are you staying for lunch?' she asked David.

'I wish. It's so busy today I shouldn't even be taking a break, but I couldn't resist popping back to see my gorgeous family.'

Maria laughed. 'Well, you'll have to settle with just me. I've no idea where Danny is, but look, Bonnie's down the end of the garden with Iona.' She made him stop to watch their oldest child. 'She looks so carefree,' she went on, a warm glow spreading through her body.

'Yes, that's good,' David said as he trundled into the house, and the moment was gone.

'Don't you think?' she persisted, following him into the kitchen. 'Maybe all she needed was to find a good friend and now she has one.'

'Maria,' he said, stopping her. She heard him sigh even though he tried his best to hide it. 'You mustn't keep worrying over Bonnie. She's fine.'

But things had never truly been fine, and this was one thing – the only major thing – they'd never agreed on.

'Well, I've invited Iona to dinner tonight,' she went on, refusing to get niggled, 'so please don't be late.' As she spoke Maria glanced out of the kitchen window at her daughter with her new friend. They were laughing, engrossed in conversation, and it was such an unusual sight that Maria almost wished she could take a photograph.

'You see, I'd never get a view like this back at home,' Iona said, stretching out on the lounger.

Bonnie watched her friend's movements. Her long legs made her look like she could be a dancer. She uncrossed her own and slid them down the sunbed until they were almost touching Iona's. 'I guess it's pretty good,' she said.

'You're joking, right? It's amazing.'

Bonnie looked to the sea and the hustle of the people on the jetty. There were so many of them, as there always were on summer days, stepping off her dad's boat, excited to see what twee little place they lived in. Sometimes she felt like she was in a bloody zoo.

'I can't believe you don't realise how wonderful it is. If I lived here ...' Iona trailed off but it felt like an intended pause to Bonnie when she added, 'Well, I wouldn't want to go anywhere else.'

Bonnie snorted. 'You really wouldn't miss everything out there?' She gestured in the direction of the mainland.

Iona shrugged. 'I don't think so.'

Bonnie glanced away and saw her dad between the trees, walking down the jetty towards his boat. Maybe she should try and see Evergreen how Iona did, but she didn't think she could. There was just something about it she really didn't like.

'It's so kind of your mum to invite me to dinner tonight,' Iona said. 'It's not easy when you don't know anyone.' Bonnie didn't get the impression there was anything Iona wouldn't find easy. Her friend leant her head closer still, dropping her voice even though there was no one near. 'I don't like spending too much time in the house in the village,' she said. 'I think the couple is a bit weird.' She grimaced before breaking into a grin.

Bonnie laughed as warmth spread over her. She wanted Iona to share more, things she wouldn't tell anyone but her. To think she hadn't been going to bother making an effort. Bonnie was so grateful Iona had sought her out instead.

But then her mind drifted to the other bit Iona had just said and the warmth started to dissipate. She wished Iona wasn't coming to dinner tonight, sitting around the table with the rest of the family. Why did her mum always have to ruin everything? She was doing it again, watching over her. Waiting for her daughter to do something that would suddenly click – a light-bulb moment when she'd know what was supposedly wrong with Bonnie.

She sank back against the lounger and mulled over ways she could convince Iona not to come. The thought of keeping her new friendship to herself was much more appealing.

Danny's face dropped when he walked into the garden at dinner time and saw Iona sitting at the table. It was bad enough when Jill came, but he was kind of used to her. Even though they'd all known Jill for years, she still didn't say much to any of them but Stella.

The chairs were squeezed in a little tighter and there was practically no gap between Bonnie and Iona. Danny slunk around the other side of the table, pushing his own chair closer to Stella's.

Iona was chattering away like a bird. Her voice was all high-pitched and excited and Bonnie was giggling like a child. He supposed it was better than hearing his sister moaning, but already it struck him that if he closed his eyes he wouldn't be able to tell their voices apart.

His mum's arms stretched over his shoulder as she placed a bowl in the centre of the table and told Iona she hoped she liked chilli. He thought it was a funny thing to say when the poor girl could hardly say she didn't. Sometimes people weren't very perceptive.

When his mum pulled her arm back, she rested it on his shoulder and Danny knew she was trying to tell him she hoped he was okay.

He only hoped Iona would carry on rattling away to Bonnie and wouldn't talk to him. He didn't even want her to look at him. He hadn't seen any other girl like Iona before and suddenly she was glancing up and smiling straight at him and Danny thought that the burning through his chest was going to make him puke all over the table.

From now on he was just going to have to avoid her, though he didn't like the idea of that either.

Maria should have realised sooner how uncomfortable her son would be. The moment she'd seen him dragging his chair alongside the table she knew she'd done the wrong thing, but it was too late to change it. What was right for one child was clearly not for the other, and her eyes brimmed suddenly at the sight of her three children who could not be more different. How she wished they could all be more like Stella.

Not for the first time, she questioned whether they'd made the right choices and whether Evergreen was still the right place for them. Their haven sometimes felt like it was suffocating them instead, and every so often Maria worried that they'd trapped themselves here.

By the end of the summer she would know that they'd made a mistake in coming in the first place and that, sooner or later, the truth would find them wherever they were.

PRESENT

Chapter Eight

The journalist smiles as I gape back at her. 'You don't recognise me but I wouldn't expect you to. I only knew you for one summer before you all disappeared.'

I cock my head to one side. There is something vaguely familiar about her thin face with the splattering of freckles on her nose and her sleek dark hair that's pulled back into a ponytail.

'Freya Little,' she says. 'My family arrived at the start of the summer and you were gone by the end of it.'

'I remember,' I say. 'You had two brothers. Didn't all your names begin with F?'

She grins. 'Freddie and Frankie. Ridiculous, really. Were you going in for something to eat?'

I nod, glancing at the café.

'Let's go for a walk first,' she says and starts ambling in the direction I just came from.

'I can't believe you recognised me after so long,' I say, walking alongside her.

'As soon as you told me your name I could see how little you've changed,' she says. 'Your hair's still the same.'

I reach up to touch the ends that fall just below my shoulders. 'It's shorter,' I say. 'It was always so long when I was young.'

'Did you know how much I used to look up to you?' Freya asks.

'Why would you have done that?'

'You always seemed so sure of yourself, so certain about everything on this island. Not in a horrible way, more like you knew you were meant to be here. I, on the other hand, knew we definitely weren't.' Freya raises her eyebrows as she cuts off the path and heads towards the coastline to the side of the jetty.

'How do you mean?' I ask, following her to sit on a bench that overlooks Brownsea Island.

'Mum wasn't happy the day she arrived here and we all suffered because of it. I know my mum can be a bit loud for most people, but they didn't give any of us the time of day. We were ostracised. Everyone else huddled together and made a decision we weren't wanted. They were one big clique and we weren't going to break into it.'

I raise my eyes as I carry on looking at the water. That wasn't particularly the way I remembered it.

'It's breaking now, though,' she says and I turn to find her watching me. 'There are fractures,' she goes on. 'Though some of them are sticking closely together. But that was my story,' she says, pausing to take a deep breath, 'and I'm sure it's not as interesting as yours. What made you up and leave that summer, Stella?'

I look down to where my hands are balled in my lap, wrenching them apart and pulling my coat tighter against me. I wonder if Freya really believes this is a simple question for me to answer or if her journalistic radar can tell it's anything but. 'My dad got another job, we needed the money.' I regurgitate the excuse like I believe it myself.

I wait as she nods, musing over my answer. She doesn't ask more, though I'm certain this hasn't satisfied her but rather she's just biding her time. 'So, you saw your old house on the news,' she states. 'That must have been a shock.'

'It was,' I agree.

'And that was why you came back? You thought that by being here you might get more answers?'

'Maybe,' I admit.

'You won't get any more here than you will watching the news. Nothing will be released until they're ready.'

'You think the police already know more?' I ask.

She dodges the question as she says, 'In fact, you won't get any answers that easily on Evergreen. Sometimes you only leave with more questions. Do you want to know what I think?' she asks and I nod because it's easier than answering her questions. 'I think more than one person living on this island knows *exactly* who the body is, only none of them are saying.'

'Who are you talking about?' I ask, staring back at her, wishing I could flatten down the corners of her mouth which look like they're constantly amused by me.

'I don't know for certain but I'm going to make sure I find out. Too many of them are like closed books, but, with pressure, one of them will snap open.'

I shift uncomfortably on the bench and turn back to the sea. Despite the fact I know someone must have buried the body, it's still unsettling that it could be someone I know.

'You had an older brother and sister,' she recalls. 'They didn't want to come back with you?'

'No,' I say. 'Bonnie has a family to look after.' I don't add that I still haven't told her I'm here. I know I should call her to explain.

'And Danny,' she says, as if suddenly remembering his name. 'I felt sorry for him. He was a loner and kids can be cruel.' She stops and I have an unexpected flashback of Freya on the beach the night of the sleep-out while all the other girls were causing a commotion. 'How's he doing now?' she asks.

I don't want to tell Freya I haven't seen my brother in eighteen years. That I wish I could have stopped him from going or that I know how cruel those kids were and I never did enough.

'Danny moved away a while ago,' I say. 'We don't really keep in touch.'

She nods again. 'So the police been to see you yet?'

'Why are you asking me all these questions?' I say. 'Am I some news story for you?'

'No. Not at all. Well, not yet anyway,' she adds and then smiles. 'Relax, Stella. I'm not grilling you for an article. It's blatantly obvious you have no more knowledge than I do about the body. Clearly that's why you've come back and it's what I'm here for too.'

'So why the interest in me?'

'I think you could be helpful,' she says, shifting so that she can get a better look at me. Since the start of our exchange, Freya's had control, and every piece of her body language tells me she knows that. 'I guess it depends how much you want to involve yourself with this.' She waves a hand behind us in the direction of the police tent.

'I don't understand what I can do.'

'You can talk to the people who won't talk to me. You'd have a better chance than I do.'

'What makes you think that?' I ask.

She laughs. 'Because you know most of them and your family was once liked round here. Many of the islanders are closing their doors in my face. I think they'd be more likely to speak to you. And in return,' she goes on before I can answer, 'I can help you with some of the things you want to know.'

'Like what?' I ask. 'You told me yourself you don't know anything.'

'I can tell you who the police are most interested in. The ones they've been back to see more than once.'

I nod slowly.

'There's already a question, isn't there?'

'What do you think the police already know? You said they'll release the details when they're ready. Do you think they know how long the body's been there?'

'A pathologist could have established that very quickly,' she says. 'I imagine they already know who the body is.'

'Oh,' I gasp. 'So why aren't they saying? Why hasn't it been on the news?'

Freya shrugs. 'They must have decided it isn't in the public interest to let it out. Maybe they're letting this lot stew.'

I shudder, pulling my coat even tighter, reaching inside my pockets, to feel for my phone. All of a sudden I have an urge to call Bonnie and my mind is drifting back to the interest the police showed in my friendship bracelets.

There were five girls on my list including me. They were, at least, the ones I remember – Jill, Bonnie, Tess Carlton, Emma Grey. What could any of us have possibly had to do with the body?

Suddenly I feel like I should never have come back. I don't want to get involved in Freya's games – I can't trust her – and yet I find myself asking, 'You say the police have been back to see some of them more than once?'

Freya nods.

'Who?'

'Susan Carlton; Annie Webb; Bob Taylor. You remember the names?' she asks.

'Yes,' I say with a tight breath. They were my mother's best friend; our adopted aunt; Jill's dad. 'Do you know why they're focused on them?'

'No,' Freya says, with a short laugh. 'But maybe they're the ones you could start talking to?'

'I'm not sure I want to get involved,' I say. 'And I don't see what you think I'm going to find out that's going to help. If the detectives couldn't get anything out of them, they're hardly going to tell me. Besides, they could have been questioned for any old reason.'

'Sure. But let's face it, Stella, we're both here with questions and I think yours are probably lying deeper than you'd care to admit.'

I glance back at her, screwing up my eyes.

'The body was found in your garden,' she says. 'I'm sure that's a big part of the reason you're back.'

'Outside it,' I growl, angry at her suggestion. I stand up.

'Only just,' she says, looking behind us. 'Oh, wait up,' she adds, grabbing my arm over the back of the bench as I begin to walk away. 'I'm sorry! That was careless and uncalled for. I'm like that. It comes with the job. Please. I'm sorry,' she says again, releasing me. 'I didn't mean anything. Look, maybe we can talk some more tomorrow.'

I shrug as I pull my mobile out of my pocket. 'I need to go,' I mumble. 'I have to call my sister.'

Freya shakes her head. 'Not around here, no reception anywhere on this island.'

I look down at the phone and sure enough there are no bars. I stare at it a moment longer before tucking it back into my pocket. I had never before thought of Evergreen as isolated, but now I've never felt more so.

Chapter Nine

Back in the village I go into the café where a blast of warm air hits me as soon as I open the door. A young girl at the counter smiles at me. She looks no more than fifteen, with her dark blonde hair tied into a ponytail, and a bright pink apron that she wipes her hands across. 'How can I help you?' she asks.

'Hot chocolate, please, and something to eat.' I glance at the blackboard behind her, settling for a chicken mayonnaise sandwich.

'Find yourself a seat and I'll bring it over,' she says, gesturing to all the empty tables. The only other customers are two young girls on bar stools by the window, their backs to the room as they giggle over something.

I pick a table at the edge of the room. 'It's quiet,' I say, looking over my shoulder as the girl piles a large spoonful of filling on to a slice of bread.

She nods. 'It is. Are you here because of the body too?'

Her directness shocks me and I glance at the girls who have stopped laughing but are still deep in conversation.

'I'm guessing you must be either police or press because that's all we've had since Saturday.'

'I'm neither,' I tell her.

'Oh?' She comes around the counter with my sandwich, setting it on the table and lingering. 'What are you doing here, then?'

'Actually I used to live here. A very long time ago.'

'Oh, cool. Maybe you knew my mum?'

I cock my head to one side questioningly.

'Emma Fisher? She's lived here all her life. She was Emma Grey then.'

'Yes, I knew Emma.' She was three years older than me, the same age as Danny.

'We live over in the terraces,' she says. 'Number two, you should go and see her.'

'Oh, well ...' I stammer, trying to recall what more I can of Emma other than the fact her name was on my list.

She was quiet. Her parents kept to themselves. I never really knew what to say to her. 'She lived in the village when we were young, too,' I say, details coming back to me – Emma had long blonde hair sliced neatly across her back in a sharp cut.

'My grandparents are still there. Number eight. The same house they've always been in.'

'So your mum never left the island?'

'No. She met my dad and he moved here for a few years, but they split up when I was five and he went back to the mainland. It's just been me and Mum ever since.' The girl smiles and goes back around the counter to finish making my hot chocolate.

'And what about you?' I ask, when she comes back. 'Do you like living here?'

'You sound like the journalists.'

'I'm sorry.'

She shakes her head. 'It's fine. It doesn't bother me like it does many of the islanders.' She places a mug in front of me.

'Thank you. How do you mean?'

'They hate the fact people are prying into their lives. I don't know, it's like they suddenly all feel guilty. That's what my mum says, anyway. She says it's enough having a policeman on your doorstep to make you feel like you've done something wrong.'

I nod, knowing what she means.

'I kind of get it,' the girl goes on, 'but she hasn't been hounded that much. Anyway, that's why no one's coming out of their houses.' She rolls her eyes. 'We've all been told to stay away from the press so I think they find it easier to hide away altogether. Did you like living here?'

'I did,' I smile. 'I liked it a lot.'

'I think I get the best of both worlds because I stay with my dad as well. He always said it was too claustrophobic. Some of my friends hate it.'

'My sister did too,' I tell her. 'She couldn't wait to leave.'

'Is that why you did?'

I shake my head. 'No, not really. My dad got a job in Winchester. I'm Stella, by the way.'

'I'm Meg.' She gives me a smile that lights up her face. 'And I like it, in answer to your earlier question. Well, at least I think I do.

'No one knows who it is,' Meg goes on, sliding into a seat opposite me. 'Straight after they found the body it was horrible, you know? Everyone was talking about it and you could tell they were all looking at each other differently. Mum told me I wasn't to trust anyone, but I think she's over-reacting. I mean, I've known these people all my life.'

I nod as I take a bite of my sandwich. Whatever warning Emma gave her daughter clearly hasn't been heeded. The journalists would have pounced on a young girl like her, naive, ready to tell them what they wanted.

Meg leans in closer again as she says, 'I don't like it, if I'm being honest. People are starting to gossip about who might've done it. I hope it's not someone who still lives here.'

I give her a small smile. 'I guess the best thing you can do is just stay out of it.'

Meg looks up as a man enters the café. Pushing her chair away, she stands and says, 'You should definitely visit my mum, I think she'd like to see a friendly face.' For the first time in our short conversation I see her eyes cloud. 'She's more on edge than ever,' she adds more quietly.

'She might not even remember me,' I say quickly.

Meg nods but carries on looking at me intently. 'Maybe not, but could you just drop by, perhaps?'

She looks so hopeful that I find myself agreeing. Besides, I figure, it can't do any harm.

A straight path, wider than any other on the island, backs on to the village, lined with small terraces on either side. There are sixteen in total, eight on each side in perfect symmetry, and they all look exactly the same. It is the only part of Evergreen that looks man-made.

As I knock on the door of number 2, it's starkly obvious how close Emma still lives to where she grew up, and I try to imagine what kind of life she's had.

A shadow flickers on the other side of the door and I step back in anticipation, but no one answers. I'm about to knock again when the curtains to my left twitch and a woman's face appears.

I hold up my hand in a semi-wave. Emma's face is instantly recognisable, pale and framed with a light blonde bob and a sweeping fringe that hangs slightly too low, covering her left eye. She looks thinner than I remember. Emma doesn't wave back but eventually drops the curtain and opens the door, looking at me quizzically, her eyes flicking over my face.

'Emma?' I ask and hold out my hand. 'You may not remember me. I lived here a long time ago. I'm Stella Harvey.'

Emma continues to study me then hangs her head ever so slightly to one side. 'Stella Harvey,' she repeats quietly. 'You left when we were kids.'

I nod and look over her shoulder, wondering if she's going to invite me in. 'I just met your daughter, Meg, in the café and she suggested I visit you. I know this is a surprise but I promised her I would. Though maybe it isn't a good time?'

Emma cautiously steps to one side. 'I was just waiting for someone, but you can come in.'

I step in but already wish I'd said I wouldn't bother her. It's clear she isn't comfortable with my turning up on her doorstep, and neither am I. Yet I follow her through to the living room where she ushers me into an armchair in the window as she perches on the sofa opposite, her fingers curling around each other in her lap. Every so often her eyes drift to the window behind me. She doesn't ask what I'm doing here.

'Meg's a lovely girl.' I search for safe ground.

'She is.' Emma relaxes into the sofa. 'She's only just sixteen but she's got a good head on her.'

'It's wonderful that you've stayed here all these years,' I say.

'Is it?' She looks at me under her long eyelashes.

'It's what I always hoped I'd do.'

Emma stares at me blankly, chewing the inside of her mouth. 'It's not too great any more,' she says finally.

'No.'

'Oh, of course,' she says suddenly, throwing a hand to her mouth. 'It's where you lived. The body – I mean, it was in your old garden.' Her face has gone a shade paler; it looks as if it's been washed white.

I don't bother protesting it was just outside it, fearing this is the reaction I'll get from everyone. In contrast to Emma's, my cheeks are burning.

'No one knows who it is,' she blurts.

I lean forward in my chair. All of a sudden she looks very ill. 'Emma? Are you okay?'

'No, of course I'm not okay.' She laughs nervously, her eyes widening as if I just asked her the most ludicrous question. 'A body's been found on our island.' Her fingers continue to play in her lap, catching my attention, and I realise it looks like she's counting on them.

'It's a dreadful shock,' I say. 'I couldn't believe it when I saw it on the news.'

'Is it why you're back?' she asks, eyeing me carefully. She leans closer as she says, 'If I were you I wouldn't have come anywhere near.'

I bow my head, inclined to agree with her the more hours that pass. 'My sister and I were saying we can't believe none of us know of anyone who went missing,' I say. I ache to show her we're on the same side, that I'm not someone to fear. I want her to realise I have a right to be back, even though it's becoming apparent no one else agrees. Maybe I should tell her the police have asked for my help. That possibly we could work out between us what link they have found between my bracelets and the body. But for now I say, 'I'm sure the police will find out who the body belongs to soon. Then people might feel a bit better about it . . .' I drift off when I notice her gawping.

'This isn't a TV drama,' she says. 'How the hell do you think we'll all feel better when we know who it is? There aren't going to be less questions then, they'll just be different ones.'

'I'm sorry, I only thought—'

'You don't live here,' she snaps. 'So don't pretend to understand.' Her eyes drift over me again and out to the window.

My body is burning. I want to scream at her that of course I understand, but I bite my lip as I turn to see what's caught her attention. There's no one there and when I look back she focuses her gaze on me again.

I take a deep breath, shifting in the armchair. Maybe it's time to leave, but while I'm here I might as well ask: 'Who still lives here that I might remember?'

'Probably most of them.' She is so quiet I can barely hear her. 'Not many leave.'

I shuffle uncomfortably, thinking it's no surprise Meg's worried about her mother; the woman is clearly a nervous wreck. 'Annie Webb?'

Emma arches her eyebrows, her mouth twisting into a faint smirk. 'Of course Annie's still here.'

'And the Smyth twins?' I ask, trying to keep the conversation light, grappling for names while I pluck up the courage to ask after the only one I really want.

Emma shakes her head. 'No. They were some of the few who went. Years back. Their cousin, Freya Little, is here again, though. She's a journalist. Snooping around, asking too many questions like this is all far too exciting.'

I nod. 'I've already met her.'

'Yes, well, don't tell her anything,' Emma mutters. 'You can't trust her.'

'I've got nothing to tell her,' I say as she suddenly leaps off the sofa and brushes past me to get to the window. She raps her knuckles against it and I turn to see whose attention she's trying to get, but whoever it is has already gone.

'I have to go.' Already she's edging towards the door.

'But—'

'There's someone I need to speak to.' With Emma opening the door, I have no choice but to get up and leave.

'I wanted to ask about Jill,' I say, as she steps out after me. She hurries down the path to the gate and it doesn't look like she's heard me. 'Is Jill still here?' I say, more loudly.

Emma stops and looks over her shoulder. Her mouth opens as her eyes dance over me. She seems to be looking right through me and it's such an eerie stare that I find myself shrinking back, the hairs on my arms pricking cold.

With a vague shake of her head she eventually turns and begins scurrying up the lane. 'Emma?' I call, though she doesn't answer as she rushes to the man waiting for her at the end of the lane.

I watch them talking and, when Emma gestures behind her, the man looks at me. There is something familiar about him but I can't place him. Emma continues to talk, gesturing nervously in the air, and I watch as the man's face pales. He doesn't take his eyes off me but at the same time he looks like he's seen a ghost.

Evergreen Island

13 July 1993

Something else changed that summer. It was the very first year Danny had shown any interest in going to the sleep-out on the beach where all the kids would take their sleeping bags and stay the night. Maria couldn't fathom why this year he wanted to go. It broke her heart as she watched him carefully packing an overnight bag: a toothbrush; a bar of soap, both tucked into a washbag. She closed her eyes and contemplated telling him he wouldn't need either of those things, but then, imagining his reaction, she crept away.

She knew it would be better if he didn't go. Maria could protect her son by keeping him away, even though David would disapprove. But at the same time she'd always longed for Danny to want to join in, and that was why she was fighting her desire to stop him.

How could she know what was the right thing to do? Remove your child from what might hurt them, or let them face it and hope they'll be stronger for it in the end?

David often told her she mollycoddled Danny. 'He needs to learn how to toughen up,' her husband would say, though there was always a glint of something else in his eyes. Fear that maybe he didn't believe his own words?

The thought of Danny sleeping on the beach with the other kids tore at Maria. She could imagine exactly what it'd be like – a group of kids tightly packed around a campfire, the older boys showing off with their guitars. Meanwhile her son would be tucked into his sleeping bag on the outer edge of the circle, not knowing how to join in even if he wanted to.

Maria tried brushing the thoughts away as she retreated downstairs and into the garden. She jumped when she caught sight of a figure suddenly appearing to the right of the house. The trees were so thick there anyone could wander in from the woods. She'd often considered asking David to build a fence around that side too. There was no way of knowing what was their garden and what was the woods, but usually the only people who used it as a walkway were her friends. As it was, her visitor today wasn't. And he knew perfectly well where he was walking.

Danny zipped up his bag and stood back to look at it. It was the first time he'd packed his own things for a night away and he was pretty sure he'd remembered everything. His mum had been asking questions and he knew she couldn't understand why he was suddenly going this year when every other he'd outright refused, but there was no way he could tell her his reasons.

He'd heard stories from Bonnie and Stella over the years so he knew what to expect and that he might end up hating it. He'd have to make an effort talking to people if he wanted to fit in, and he also knew he'd probably find it all too much and would end up sitting on his own.

But yet his skin was tingling at the prospect and now there was no way he was backing out. He patted his bag, with the drawing pad tucked in at the back, as he gave one last glance around his room. How bad could it be?

Bonnie lingered by the back door, half listening to her mum's conversation with Bob Taylor, half keeping an ear out for Iona. She was annoyed because she didn't want to go to the bloody sleep-out on the beach. Nothing exciting ever happened there. And to top it off, this year her brother was going, which meant he was bound to do something embarrassing. She eyed him cautiously as he scuttled past her, calling out to their mum that he was off.

For some reason Iona thought it sounded fun and had promised they would keep an eye on Danny, which had made Bonnie's mum practically leap up and hug them.

When Iona came out of the toilet Bonnie asked again, 'Are you totally sure you want to go? We could do something on our own instead?'

'You don't have to come,' Iona said, smiling, her eyes raised as she waited for an answer.

Bonnie fiddled with the strap of her bag, suddenly feeling even more annoyed. 'No, I'll come,' she snapped and then, worrying it might have sounded bad, she rearranged her face into a smile to hopefully show she wasn't that bothered. Iona looked at her curiously but she had no idea how much Bonnie was wrestling inside.

'Bonnie, seriously, don't come if you don't want to.' Iona's eyes were screwed up, her head cocked to one side.

'Why *can't* we do something on our own?' she blurted. There, she'd said it now, but she immediately wished she hadn't. She didn't want Iona to think she was being clingy. 'I just find these nights so babyish,' she added and gave a laugh that even to her sounded strained.

'Are you sure you're okay?'

'I'm fine,' Bonnie said. 'Totally fine.' But she wasn't. Inside she was screaming, wanting to kick out with her foot and throw down her bag, slamming her fists on the counter.

Iona linked her arm through Bonnie's. 'Come on, we're in this together,' she said and already the bubbles that were fizzing in Bonnie's stomach began to subside.

*

Maria thought Bob Taylor did it on purpose. There was no need for him to come around the back of the house. She listened patiently to him blathering on about cutting back trees, but he always managed to put her on edge. He'd done so ever since he'd arrived on the island twelve years ago with Ruth and Jill. Annie had told her about their arrival a week before they came, and the thought had even swept through Maria's mind that they could be friends with the new family.

But then she'd met him and knew it could never be. He had held out a hand to David, barely acknowledging Maria as he talked far too loudly about how pleased they were to be coming to the island. While Ruth slunk behind him, not once did he ask them any questions, for that would have stolen his one-man show. On the surface his words were effusive, but she knew they were hiding something darker. She knew Bob and Ruth had a secret. And just like Maria and David, they had come to Evergreen to hide from it. They had been tiptoeing around this fact for so many years that by now Maria thought that, as much as she disliked Bob, she could probably trust him.

But during the summer weeks that stretched ahead, that trust would be tested to its limits. And by the end of it Maria knew that putting distance between her family and Bob Taylor had become not just a necessity – but a matter of life and death.

PRESENT

Chapter Ten

The last time I saw Annie was the day before we left when I watched her and Mum talking in the garden. I remember her clutching on to Mum's arms, her mouth forming a perfect circle, shaking her head as if she either couldn't believe we were going or didn't agree with it.

When they came into the kitchen Annie's arms had twitched at her side before she'd reached to hug me. 'Look after yourself, Stella,' she said. 'Look after yourself.' I'd expected to see tears in her eyes when I pulled back, but they were completely dry.

Like everywhere else on the island, there's no sign of movement by the lakes, which feel deathly still. Even the water looks like a sheet of ice. Slowly I walk around them towards Annie's home, the first one in the staggered line of houses.

Annie had always watched over me like I was one of her own. She might as well have been family – she'd become a surrogate aunt to us all – and it seems silly that I feel so apprehensive. But then nothing on the island is the same as it once was.

I approach the house, knocking loudly on the front door, my rap echoing on the other side. There's a faint sound of footsteps that gradually get closer until the door slowly opens and I'm face-to-face with her.

I hold my breath as I take her in. Her skin droops on her cheeks, sunken into the bones, which in turn makes her eyes look wider. A curve in her back bends her over so she hunches forward. I release my breath and smile through the shock of how much she has aged. 'Hi, Annie,' I say.

'Stella?' She leans her head to one side. 'Stella Harvey?' Her hand shakes against the door frame. 'Rachel told me you were coming and I wondered when you were going to visit me.' She pauses and smiles. 'Well, my dear, there's no point us standing in the doorway getting cold. You'd better come in.'

I step into her large hallway, memories flooding back. The grandfather clock still in one corner; the tapestry of a forest hanging on the wall. 'Let me look at you,' she says, taking hold of my arms and turning me to face her. She shakes her head, a smile cracking her lips. 'All these years,' she says. 'I don't know if I'd have recognised you if I wasn't expecting you.'

'It's good to see you, Annie,' I say as she ushers me through her living room and into the kitchen.

'And what can I get you to drink? You always used to ask for hot chocolate.'

'Whatever you're having,' I smile.

'We'll have tea,' she says as she sets about looking for cups. 'Sit yourself down,' she commands, and I pull out a chair by the small round table that still stands in the centre of the room. I sat here so many times, allowing Annie to ply me with hot chocolate and biscuits. I used to take handfuls of Jammie Dodgers and custard creams, stashing them in my pockets to eat in the treehouse. She seemed proud when I'd leave with a stomach full of sugar.

'So many years,' she says wistfully.

'Twenty-five,' I say, and she nods.

'I know, I remember it clearly.' She turns to me with watery eyes and comes over and sits opposite, two mugs placed carefully on coasters. 'I was so sorry to hear about your mum. It was very sad when she passed. Terrible accident,' she murmurs. I don't know how she'd have heard about it since she hadn't come to the funeral. Possibly my dad had thought to call her. 'She was a special woman ...' Annie goes on, her voice drifting away.

'But it's lovely to see *you* again.' She pushes herself as straight as she can, holding out a hand across the table. 'I missed you and your family a lot, you know.'

'I'm sure not as much as I missed everyone, and the island.'

'Only you choose now to come back.' Annie shakes her head as if this is a grave mistake on my part. 'I wish you hadn't. This isn't a good time for you to be here, Stella.'

'I was so shocked when I saw the news,' I say. 'I couldn't believe it.'

'And that's why you've come?'

'I don't know,' I admit. 'It's part of it.' I look out towards her garden. In the summer it used to be filled with heather and roses and bushes of lavender. Now it looks bleak and stark. 'There are things I need to find out,' I say. 'Things that have been playing on my mind for too long.'

Her eyes are wide and she pulls her hand away and wraps it around her mug, dipping her eyes to her tea as she slowly takes a sip. I expect her to ask what I mean but she doesn't. 'Have you seen anyone else since you arrived?'

'Only Emma Grey,' I tell her, frowning at the oddness of our encounter. 'Oh, and Freya Little – the journalist.' My mind drifts back to what she'd told me about Annie being one of the few the police had been keen to talk to. I hate the idea that she expected me to interrogate Annie, yet the fact Freya clearly knows more than I do means I'm loath to tell her I want nothing to do with her. 'It's very quiet everywhere,' I add.

'People are frightened. First the body and then all the questioning. Journalists like that Freya try to turn us against each other, I swear.'

'It must be horrible.'

'It is.' Annie's gaze drifts out of the window. 'You'd hope something like this would bring a small community together, but ...' She shakes her head.

'Why do you think it hasn't?' I ask.

'Because of people like her, as I said.' Annie turns back to me. 'The police have to ask their questions, but those journalists want even more from us. It's better to keep to yourself. Then you can't be drawn into farcical conclusions.'

'Are *you* alright, Annie?' I ask. 'No one's hounding you, are they?' Annie was always the matriarch of our island. The thought of her being pestered by someone like Freya bothers me.

Annie shrugs. 'Oh, I can look after myself,' she says, though her tired eyes say different. 'For some reason everyone thinks I have all the answers, though.' She gives me a thin smile and I shrink back. She must know that's why I'm also here, though it's different answers I'm looking for.

'Tell me what you're up to now.' Annie plumps out her words as if this is much more important than anything else.

'I'm a counsellor,' I say as I relax my shoulders, picking up my mug. 'I counsel families.'

'How wonderful. I can imagine you doing exactly that,' she smiles. 'You were always so caring about everyone. And how is your sister?'

I tell her that Bonnie is married with two boys she idolises, but not that every time I see my sister I nervously watch her for signs she might be teetering on the edge of having a drink. Thinking of my sister reminds me that I still haven't spoken to her or told her where I am.

I glance over at Annie's telephone perched on the windowsill, wondering whether I should ask to borrow it, when she carries on, 'The day your parents arrived on the island, Bonnie screamed her head off like she was determined she wasn't going to like it here.' She pauses. 'I'm glad she's finally happy. And how about your father?'

'Well, Dad moved away,' I start. My eyes flit from her gaze as I fumble with the handle of my mug.

'I realise he left, love,' Annie says. 'Your mum wrote to me at the time. But do you see him much? Is he still with the other woman?'

'Olivia. Yes. Somehow they're still together, and no, I don't see him as much as I'd like.' I let out a deep breath. Her eyes crease as she regards me, waiting for me to tell her more, but instead I say, 'I didn't know you were still in touch with Mum?'

'We weren't really. Only if there was something important. She sent me a long letter telling me your father had gone. I think she was more upset about his choice of woman than the act.'

'Seriously?'

'I'm being flippant.' Annie waves a hand dismissively. 'And what about your brother?' she asks, and I wonder why Mum didn't consider Danny's leaving important enough to mention.

'Danny went too. We lost touch with him, but I think it's the way Danny wanted it.'

'He never came back?' Annie leans away and turns her attention to the garden again. So, Mum *had* told her.

'Things didn't turn out well,' I say as we fall into a burdened silence.

Eventually Annie murmurs, 'But now you're here again. And like I say, this isn't a good time. As lovely as it is to see you, Stella.' She stops and shakes her head as she turns back to face me. 'You should return when all this has died down. When everyone ...' she pauses, searching for the right words '... when everything's back to normal.'

I drain my tea and place my mug on the table, carefully pushing it aside. 'Annie, Mum really loved it here, didn't she?'

Annie cocks her head to one side.

'I know she never wanted to be anywhere else.'

She fidgets in her chair but doesn't answer.

'What I don't get is that she suddenly let him take us away.'

'I don't know what you expect from me, Stella,' she says, her voice soft but firm.

'If anyone knows what happened, you do,' I persist. 'You and Mum were so close. She looked to you like her own mother. Especially when Gran died.'

Annie shakes her head, hanging it low.

I take hold of her bony arm, squeezing it gently though I'm scared to press too tight. She feels so fragile between my hands and it saddens me how much the last few days must have taken their toll. 'Mum trusted you. I know she would have told you whatever was on her mind.'

Annie looks up at me. 'What do you mean?'

'Did she find something out?' I say.

Her lips are parted, her head giving only the glimmer of a shake, and I see something behind her eyes that she's holding back from me. I wait for her answer. In my work I have become hardened to silences.

Straightening herself, she asks, 'Whatever are you getting at, Stella?' Her voice wobbles with uncertainty and I can almost see her held breath. Her question has been asked to detract attention. Annie knows why Mum agreed to leave, I am certain of it.

I have never before spoken to anyone about what I saw before we left. To do so now would mean unleashing everything I've buried in one of my boxes.

'Did she find out Dad was having an affair?' I say, the words tumbling out.

'An affair?' Annie's rigid body softens as she sinks against the back of her chair. 'Why would you think that? Oh, Stella. I don't think for one minute your father would have had an affair.'

Annie seems so amused by the idea, and strangely so relieved, that I find myself smiling back, ignoring the voice inside my head saying, *But I saw him.*

She pushes away from the table, taking the mugs to the sink and rinsing them. When she wanders over she doesn't sit down but instead hovers by the table. 'It's the past, Stella,' she says softly. 'The best place for many things to stay.'

'It's *my* past, though. I have a right to know what made us leave.'

'You have no right at all if your mum didn't want you knowing.'

'So, there is something. I'm begging you, please tell me.'

'There's nothing I can tell you,' Annie says, though I know she means there's nothing she is *prepared* to tell me. All these years and she still remains loyal to Mum.

I sit back, deflated. For a moment we are both silent, but I don't want to lose the track of our conversation and I'm not ready to leave, even though I get the impression she'd like me to.

Eventually I nod as if I've accepted what she's telling me, and for now I change the subject to the body. 'It must be frightening,' I say, 'when no one knows anyone who went missing. You must all be wondering who it is.'

'Of course we are.' Her face falls into a frown.

'But no one has any idea?'

'You still assume I have all the answers, Stella,' she says. 'You're beginning to sound like Freya Little.'

'I don't mean to,' I say. 'I just can't help wondering if we knew her.'

Annie nods slowly but doesn't answer.

'I hoped I'd get the chance to see some of my old friends while I'm here, too.'

Annie smiles and reaches out a hand to the table, leaning on it and stretching out her leg. She looks as if she's in pain and I wish she'd sit down again, because it makes me feel uncomfortable too. 'Like who?' she asks.

'Jill.'

A shadow crosses Annie's face and for a moment she looks at me with a blank expression. She shakes her head. 'Oh, my dear.' She pulls her hand away and clasps both hands together tightly before letting go and reaching out for me. 'I thought your mother had told you. Honey, Jill's dead.'

Chapter Eleven

'Jill died? When? How? I mean, what happened?' My hands shake as Annie reaches for them, wrapping her own around mine in an effort to still them.

'Many years ago,' she says softly. 'She was nineteen.'

'But that was – that was *ages* ago. How come I never knew?'

She continues to look at me, shaking her head.

'Mum can't have known, she would have told me something like this.'

For a moment Annie doesn't reply, then says, 'She knew. I told her the news myself.'

'But – but – why didn't she tell *me*?' I stammer, pulling a hand away to wipe the tears.

'I can't answer that.' Annie leans awkwardly again and I want to force her into a chair. 'Most likely she didn't want to hurt you.'

'That's crazy. Even if she didn't, she still shouldn't have kept it from me. God!' I cry out. 'I don't believe it. I came back here hoping to see Jill.' The tears are flowing down my cheeks now. No amount of wiping will stop them from dampening my skin but my hand brushes them away regardless. 'What happened?'

'She got ill quickly.' Annie lets go of me and picks up a box of tissues from the sideboard, passing it to me. I take one and hold it beneath my eyes. 'It was too late to do anything.'

'How was she ill?' I ask, desperate for more details.

'She had chest pains and was struggling to breathe. She suffered heart failure in the end. It was all very sudden.'

'Heart failure?' I repeat. 'At that age? And no one knew there was a problem?'

'No,' Annie says, shaking her head vigorously. 'She had a rare condition. But you mustn't go asking her parents for any more details. Bob and Ruth never got over her death,' she murmurs, a shudder rippling through her body, making her shiver.

I look at Annie for a moment longer but she won't return my gaze. 'We were so close,' I say.

'I remember. You were inseparable.'

'Maybe Ruth would like to talk to me?' An image of the woman I'd seen in the online photos hovering on the outskirts of the groups flashes into my head. I can't imagine how devastated she must have been by her daughter's death. 'I'm sure she would,' I go on. 'My mum would have given all the time in the world to Jill if it were the other way round.'

'No,' Annie says adamantly. 'Ruth has never got over it. Even seeing you back here will cause her too much pain. Please stay away from both of them. All this business,' she mutters, 'I keep telling you, it's *not* a good time for anyone, Stella.'

I shake my head, unable to process it all. I have always respected Annie, the whole island does, yet I don't see how she can expect me to leave without speaking to Ruth. Not now. 'If only Mum had told me ...' I trail off, not knowing how to finish the sentence.

'There's a bench,' Annie says finally. 'Up on the cliff above the cove. Her father put it there for her. Maybe you could visit that.'

'On the cliff?' I say. 'But—' My heart stops as memories of us fill my head. All the times I used to run along as close to the edge as I dared while Jill lingered behind, calling me back nervously.

'That's where he wanted it,' she interrupts. Annie knows as well as I do how scared Jill was of the clifftop, and the fact Bob chose that spot to place a bench in her memory knots in my stomach. 'And after that, my dear,' Annie goes on, 'I really do think it's best you go home.'

Grief and anger merge in waves as I leave Annie's house. A cold wind whips through the air and I decide to veer into the shelter of the woods instead of taking the path to the cliffs. Here the air is cooler but stiller, and I wind through the thick trunks, creating my own path, though skirting the edges, too uncertain to delve deeper into them as I'd once have done without a second thought.

Pushing my hands further into my pockets, I carry on until I'm back on the path by the clifftop, where I make my way over to the bench that perches proudly on its edge.

A bronze plaque on the back reads, 'For our daughter, Jill. You will always be in our hearts.' I run my finger over the engraving, fresh tears already flowing as I imagine Ruth writing the words, searching for the right ones that say everything she wanted to in such a small space. I remember how hard it was when we did it for Mum. Bonnie and I had argued over them and eventually settled on something that didn't do justice to how I felt.

But to write them for their own daughter must have been unbearable. Torn apart with grief at the loss of their only child – I can't imagine what Bob and Ruth went through, losing Jill at such a young age.

I sit on Jill's bench and look out to sea, saying a silent prayer for my old friend. A lump lodges in my throat, making it ache, as the memories of us playing together run through my head like an old black-and-white movie. I can see us standing on the clifftop, a few feet further back from where I am now. She clutches tightly on to my hand and I count down from ten. 'Six steps forward,' I tell her, 'that's all we have to do today.' I feel her hand tighten but she is giggling. And I am too until we both laugh so much we fall on to our bottoms and lie on the ground instead, looking up at the sky.

We didn't know then what the future had in store for us. I'd had no idea that by the end of that summer I would leave the island. Jill had had no idea that she only had another seven years to live.

But what I do know is that, despite Annie's warning, I cannot leave Evergreen without seeing Bob and Ruth.

Evergreen Island

13 July 1993

It was only a matter of hours until Danny stormed back from the sleep-out, his eyes wet and red, Maria's fears confirmed. He brushed past her as he ran up the stairs. She called after him but already his bedroom door was shut.

Minutes later Stella arrived, panting, and when she came into the kitchen she dropped her bag and bent over, clutching her knees as she took deep breaths.

'What happened?' Maria filled a glass of water for Stella and pulled out a stool. Perching on the edge of it, she took hold of her daughter's arms. 'Did someone say something? And why are you so out of breath?' Her questions kept coming as she waited for Stella to straighten up and take a sip of water.

'I ran all the way back,' she said. 'I couldn't catch up with him. He wouldn't stop.'

Maria might be cross with Danny later for letting his little sister run all the way without looking after her, but for now she just needed to hear what had happened.

'He didn't join in from the start. I tried getting him to, but he just sat in his sleeping bag by the cave.'

Maria nodded. How she wished she'd listened to her heart and not her husband.

'Next time I looked around I couldn't see him,' Stella said. 'I told Jill I should look for him but someone was toasting marshmallows and ...' She paused and glanced away.

'Stella, you've done nothing wrong.'

'We carried on talking and I kind of forgot all about Danny and then there was this shriek. Everyone jumped up and we couldn't work out who it was, but someone started running out of the cave screaming that he grabbed her.'

'That Danny grabbed her?'

Stella nodded.

'Who?' Maria asked. She raced through the girls in her mind. Jill – God, what would Bob say if it were Jill? Iona – what would she say if it were her?

And then there were the ones who were most likely to make something up for attention. Emma Grey?

'Tess,' Stella said solemnly, and Maria's heart sank because they both knew Tess Carlton had never been the type for dramatics and also because she would have to face her best friend, Susan.

*

Danny pounded his fists into his pillow. 'Stupid, stupid, stupid,' he repeated.

His heart beat rapidly and tears stung his eyes. He'd heard Stella calling out behind him but he hadn't stopped.

Why had he sat in the cave in the first place? If he hadn't he would never have seen Tess, and then he would never have had to run away.

He knew the answer to that, but he also knew it wouldn't sound right to anyone else.

He'd been watching them. Drawing them in his pad. It was the reason he'd wanted to go to the sleep-out. He was right about people; most of the time they acted the same way, but when you watched certain ones closely, they'd occasionally do something you least expected. He wasn't sure if this made him more excited or more on edge, but either way he was definitely more interested.

Automatically Danny reached out a hand and grabbed for the pad, then leant over and slipped it under his bed. He was sure no one else saw things the way he did because they never looked hard enough.

They wouldn't see tonight the way he did, either. They would take Tess's side, and who could blame them? They weren't likely to take the side of the weird kid.

He knew what they said about him but he didn't care. He didn't like engaging in conversation but it didn't mean he was weird. They didn't get how your body could feel like it was on fire every time someone stared down at you and asked you a question. And that if you opened your mouth to answer all the words would dry up.

But he'd seen the way Tess had looked at him in the cave. He'd counted the seconds of silence before she'd let out a piercing scream.

It wasn't how she'd made it seem.

Bonnie was fuming. With gritted teeth, she climbed the steps to the top of the cliff, her legs shaking. The entire evening had been a write-off.

Behind her Iona was chatting away to Tess, who by all accounts seemed to have got over the whole incident in the cave pretty quickly. Bonnie stopped suddenly on the step, which forced Iona to crash into her.

'Hey!' Iona cried. 'Everything alright, Bon?'

'Fine,' she muttered. 'I thought I saw something in front of me.'

'Like what?' Tess called out.

Bonnie closed her eyes and bit her lip. *Like what?* she mimicked in her head. Iona had told Tess she would take her home, which meant their evening together was over. Tess could walk home on her own; she only lived in the bloody house at the end of the cliff path. Why did Iona have to be so damned nice?

Bonnie started climbing again.

'Bon!' Iona said, laughing. 'Didn't you hear Tess? She asked what you'd seen.'

'Sorry, I didn't,' she called back breezily. 'I don't know, Tess, maybe a slow-worm.'

'Eughh,' the girl said and Bonnie rolled her eyes. She knew she was being unreasonable but she couldn't help herself. Iona was *her* best friend, and because of Tess's dramatics she was being taken away from her.

'I'll come back with you and we can drop Tess home then go and do something else, shall we?' Bonnie called back.

'Don't you think you should check on your brother and sister?' Iona said. She'd already commented that Stella shouldn't have been running home on her own. 'Anyway, there's no need, I'll go in with Tess and probably stay for a bit.'

They reached the top of the steps and Bonnie was glad for the lack of light, which meant they couldn't see how cross she was. 'Fine, I'll see you in the morning,' she snapped and barely turned back. She had no idea why Iona was so keen to drop into the Carltons', but she wouldn't give them the satisfaction of knowing she was upset.

Maria glanced up as David walked into the kitchen. She ushered Stella away and told him what had happened. She could see the pain on her husband's face; it matched that in her heart.

'Talk to him before making any judgements,' he said.

Of course she was going to, but she was also scared about what he might tell her. 'I knew he shouldn't have gone.'

David frowned. 'We can't keep him locked up.'

'Where did we go wrong?' she whispered, tears pricking at her eyes. 'Was it my fault? Did I spend too much time focusing on Bonnie?' She had loved Danny the moment he'd come into the world but had felt guilty her oldest child was draining her attention. And Danny had been so placid.

'Of course it isn't your fault,' David said, but his voice was flat. She felt him pull away and she looked up at him. Did he think it was?

'What is it?' she said. 'You do think I spend too much time on her.' Her heart hammered a rapid beat and she already knew she didn't want to hear his answer. She'd always feared he might one day open up, and if he did they might never come back from it. In the end she would be right, but that day Maria was relieved when David shook his head and told her there was nothing. Rubbing her arm, he motioned for her to talk to their son.

Maria climbed the stairs and stopped outside Danny's door. She tapped on it quietly, easing it open. His body was a mound in the bed, his duvet pulled over him. She couldn't see his head but she could hear his breaths coming short and fast.

Easing herself on to the end of his bed, Maria reached out and touched his leg. He flinched but the rest of him didn't move. 'Danny,' she whispered. There was no reply. 'You can tell me anything.'

She waited a moment and then rubbed his shin before getting up to leave, when from under the cover she could just make out his voice. 'It wasn't how it seems.'

Maria knew in that moment whatever her son had done, she would do what was needed to put it right. She would do the same for any of her children.

PRESENT

Chapter Twelve

When I wake the next morning my brow is dripping wet, my pyjama top clinging to my skin in patches of damp. My sleep has been laced with dreams that entwined and made no sense and it takes me a moment to remember where I am and only a fraction longer for the news of Jill to hit me again.

Jill's name was the first on the list I'd sent to PC Walton. I wonder if he already knew she'd died and had crossed her off as soon as he read my email. Then scanned the remaining four names, prodding his finger against the one of most interest.

I throw back the thick purple bedspread, checking the time on a phone still empty of bars. I tap on it regardless, knowing there won't be messages or emails, but still I hope there might have been a crack of signal at some point during the night.

There is nothing. And it is already eight thirty, which means I have missed breakfast. By the time I've showered, dressed, and made my way to the dining room there's no sign of Rachel, but she has left out a few boxes of cereal, some milk in a jug, and a kettle on a sideboard so I can make a cup of tea.

This morning I will pay Bob and Ruth a visit. Even though the idea of rapping on their door paralyses me, I cannot spend the next two days on the island avoiding them.

Thoughts of them circled my mind before I fell asleep last night. They were a couple of contrast. On the few occasions Jill and I were in her kitchen, Ruth had melted into the background, always busying herself cooking or cleaning, occasionally tittering at something we'd said, but never integrating herself into our conversation like Mum had. She'd give the impression she felt like a spare part whenever I was there. Her timidity only amplified when her husband was around. Bob threw himself into rooms, larger than life, full of misplaced character and usually too much beer.

Jill had tried to explain this was because they lived in a pub and that he had to accept drinks when he was offered one. I thought their family could all do with Bob getting a different job, but then I also couldn't imagine him doing anything else.

Jill didn't always defend her dad. I knew she didn't like him and it was only guilt that stopped her from uttering the sentiment aloud. There were two occasions where she had bruises on her arms and once I'd touched the purple flesh without thinking, making her wince. 'I'm sorry, does it hurt?' I'd asked. 'Where's it from?'

She quickly pulled her sleeve down and changed the subject but I wouldn't let it go. 'Tell me what happened,' I persisted. 'We're best friends, remember?' I turned over my hand to display my middle finger where I'd cut myself a year before. She'd done the same and we'd pressed them together, swearing ourselves 'blood sisters'. We'd got the idea from a film but had both been too scared to cut our wrists like the girls in the film had.

'Best friends,' she nodded and pressed her finger against mine. 'He didn't mean to do it. He just grabbed me too hard when he was cross. He said sorry and promised it won't happen again. Then – then he started crying. I ended up telling him it didn't matter.'

I shuddered at the thought of a man like Bob crying. 'Are you going to tell your mum?' I asked.

'Dad told me not to because she'd be upset. You mustn't tell anyone. You need to keep it a secret. Blood sister's promise.'

'Promise,' I said and we pulled our fingers away.

I hated the thought of keeping a secret from Mum only slightly less than I hated what Jill's dad had done to her. But a blood sister's promise meant keeping my word.

Bob didn't keep his. And by the end of the summer I'd caved in too and told my mum what was happening.

I don't know what she did about it but shortly after that we were gone.

My stomach churns as I turn on to the gravel lane that leads to the pub. Overgrown plants trail and wither on either side of the track and as I get closer to the building I can see how unloved it looks. Paint is peeling off the windowsill into curled strips that only need a light tug before the whole lot could be ripped off.

I knock on the side door, my heart thumping in time with the beat. It takes a moment for a figure to pass the obscured glass but eventually three bolts clank and the door slowly opens. On the other side of it is a shadow of Jill's mum. Ruth Taylor's eyes are hollow and rimmed dark underneath. Her hair is almost entirely grey, with a thin fringe, and falls just above her shoulders. 'I don't want to talk to any more press.' She stares at me with a frown that creases her sad eyes, though she doesn't make a move to close the door, and I wonder if actually she would quite like to talk to someone. She looks at me more intently and I can see there is recognition.

'I'm Stella,' I say, smiling.

'Oh my!' She holds a hand over her mouth as the frown disappears. 'I haven't seen you in years.'

'No. And I'm sorry to turn up unannounced. I hope you don't mind me coming by, only—' I break off, watching her expression carefully. 'Only I've just heard about Jill.'

Ruth's face falls again but she opens the door wider and stands aside for me to enter. She gestures me into their open-plan back room that sits behind the pub. Not much has changed. A large TV hangs on a wall over the fireplace but the kitchen has the same eighties look with its red leather bar stools and red and white splashback. Like Annie's, I find it surprising how, inside their walls, they are almost frozen in time.

Ruth drops into a chair and, not knowing what else to do, I sit too. 'Bob's not here,' she says.

'That's good,' I reply without thinking, 'I mean, I—'

She breaks me off with a wave of her hand.

'I'm so sorry about Jill. It's a huge shock.'

Ruth's eyes mist over like a film has been draped across them. Her fingers fiddle with the edge of a cream doily that sits under a fruit bowl. When she stops they continue to shake. 'It was when it happened. She got ill very quickly,' Ruth says, in a repetition of what Annie told me yesterday. 'She couldn't get her breath, she said her chest was hurting her.' Ruth's hands clench into fists and I can't help but glance at them. 'We took her to the hospital on the mainland when the doctor here couldn't do more. They admitted her to run some tests. I wanted to go private,' she murmurs, almost looking through me as if caught in a distant memory. 'She had *sudden cardiac failure*,' she says as if she's uttered the same words countless times before. Her entire speech feels like it's been learnt by rote.

'I'm so sorry. I can't believe it could have happened to her at that age.'

'She had something very rare,' Ruth says.

'What was it?'

'Nothing I'd heard of. Hypertrophic cardio—' Ruth breaks off suddenly and turns away, tears pooling in the corners of her eyes as she clamps her mouth shut. I wait for her to go on but she doesn't finish the sentence. 'They told me there was nothing I could do,' she says quietly. 'Oh, dear me.' She pulls her hands back to fumble in her pockets for a tissue, which she uses to dab at her eyes. 'No one's asked about Jill in such a long time.'

'I'm sorry. I didn't want to upset you. Maybe I shouldn't have come.'

'No, no,' she says. 'It's nice talking about her. It feels like she's been forgotten. Bob doesn't speak of her and anyone who knew her won't – they just don't—' She stops again and adds in a whisper, 'No one talks about her to me.' She scrunches the tissue, clenching it tight in her hand.

'That must be hard,' I say, willing her to open up further. It's clear the woman needs to talk.

'It is,' she cries.

When it seems she isn't going to go on I say, 'Why don't you think they do?' I hear my counsellor's voice but Ruth doesn't notice as she shakes her head.

'I don't know,' she says quietly. 'I used to think they were told not to.' Her eyes are glazed over and I can see she's back all those years ago. 'It hit Bob hard.' Suddenly she snaps her focus back to me and her hands stop scrunching. 'She missed you a lot when you left.' Ruth smiles sadly before her face drops. 'Anyway, that was all such a long time ago.' She reaches out for the doily and stares at it intently as she begins fiddling again.

'I missed her too,' I say. 'I wrote to her a few times but she never wrote back.'

'Oh.' Ruth grabs a handful of the cotton, releases it, and then flattens it down. 'Oh right,' she goes on. 'I don't know why she didn't do that.' She gives a small shake of her head but won't meet my eyes and I can immediately tell she knows exactly what stopped her daughter from keeping her promise, but I also know this isn't the time to press her. 'I saw you put up a bench for her,' I say instead. 'On the clifftop.'

'That was Bob's idea. He said it was her favourite place. You know, I never knew it was,' she adds, her eyes shadowing again. 'I sit on the bench every day. People keep walking if they see me. I guess they think they'd have to talk to me about her.'

'People often don't know what to say regarding death so they find it easier not to mention it. Maybe they also think you want that time alone.'

Ruth nods.

'I had many friends who didn't know how to handle me when my mum died,' I say.

'Annie told me about your mum.' I wait for Ruth to express some kind of condolence but she adds nothing.

Mum and she were never close, but as far as I knew they were friendly. It surprises me that she offers nothing.

Ruth frowns and pushes her chair back. 'I have things I should be getting on with,' she says, when there's a sudden noise outside and we both turn towards the window. When I look back she's already standing, flattening her skirt, her eyes flicking from me to the glass.

I'm conscious it's probably Bob and that he'll walk through the door any moment, but there's more I want to ask Ruth. I never intended to follow Freya's request to question my old friends, but at the same time I want to know what they do. 'It's nice to be back but I wish it was in better circumstances,' I say. My words spill out quickly.

Ruth nods. 'Yes. It's a horrible affair.'

'Does anyone have any idea what happened?' I ask, expecting Bob to crash into the house any minute.

Ruth glances across at me. 'Why would we?' Her hands hang at her sides, but her face looks frozen as she glares at me.

'I hoped someone would know something, that's all.'

She doesn't move until the side door suddenly flings open, making her head snap towards it.

'That damn woman,' Bob is shouting as he enters, 'never looking where she's going. She came straight into me—' He stops abruptly when he notices me at his table. 'Who are you?' he demands before turning to Ruth. 'I told you not to keep letting these lot in. We've got nothing more to say—'

'She's not from the papers,' Ruth interrupts shrilly, shaking her head a little more than necessary. 'This is Stella Harvey. She was Jill's friend when they were children.'

He turns to me. 'Maria and David's kid,' he says slowly, his cold eyes roaming over me.

'I just came by to pass on my condolences,' I say, pushing myself out of my chair.

Bob's face pales, his eyes growing wide. 'What the hell are you on about?'

'Jill,' Ruth says quickly, in that high-pitched voice again. 'She's come to talk about Jill.'

His face relaxes slightly. 'Oh, Jill,' he says. 'Right.'

For a moment I don't speak as I wonder what it might be that Ruth is afraid her husband will say. 'I've only just heard. I'm so sorry,' I tell him.

Bob breathes in, his lungs sucking the air from the room. 'Only just? Our daughter died sixteen years ago. And that's why you came back, is it?' he asks with a hint of sarcasm.

'Well, no, I didn't find out until I was here.'

He drops his bag on the floor and folds his arms across his chest as his eyes bore into me. 'So what the hell did you come back for?'

Ruth's hand grabs for the doily again, twisting it into a tight ball. I have no need to explain myself to Bob, but at the same time I have no idea how I'm going to get out of their house without giving him something. And right now that is all I want to do.

He leans forward, his face almost pressing against mine as he says, 'Your family left a long time ago. There's no need for any of you to return. So whatever you think you're doing back, you aren't wanted.'

He pulls away and stands aside, motioning to the open door. 'I don't want to see you around here again,' he says, and I know he doesn't just mean his house. He means the island.

As soon as I reach the top of their lane, out of sight of the pub, I pause, trying to regain control of my breath. I never expected a warm welcome from Bob but I hadn't been prepared for that.

Clenching my fists, I stand rooted for a moment, undecided what I can possibly do next. Freya was right. I've been here twenty-four hours with no answers, only more questions.

'Stella!'

I turn at the sound of Ruth calling me, quietly but urgently. She scurries up the lane, glancing back at the pub, which means Bob likely has no idea she's taken the risk of coming after me. 'Thank you.'

'For what?'

'For talking about Jill. It's been years since I've heard her name spoken aloud.'

'Oh Ruth, I'm so sorry.' I reach for her hand but she pulls back. 'We can talk about her again if you like? I've got so many stories from our childhood I can share with you.' The chance to meet her somewhere else would be good. Where Bob won't walk in.

Ruth bites her lip as she glances back again. 'Bob can't mind you talking about her,' I say, though I doubt this is the issue. 'Why doesn't he want me here? I don't understand.'

'I shouldn't have come out,' Ruth says as she turns to the pub, but before she walks off she pauses, looking over her shoulder. 'It wasn't my fault,' she says, shaking her head. 'I didn't – I didn't know.' Her eyes are filled with tears.

'Of course you couldn't have known,' I say, but as I watch the way she searches my eyes, I can see she believes she should have. 'You can't blame yourself for her illness,' I go on, gently. 'It wasn't in your control.'

Ruth shakes her head again, her mouth parting, and I can tell there is something she needs to get off her chest, something she needs to rid herself of. But in the end all she says is, 'You can't understand.'

Chapter Thirteen

It's a relief when I throw open the door to the café and see Meg's friendly face smiling at me. I order another hot chocolate, this time with whipped cream and a comforting amount of marshmallows on top.

'You look frozen. I didn't think it was as cold today,' she says, eyeing my thick coat.

'I am a bit cold,' I smile, though it's not the weather that's causing goose bumps to sweep across my skin. My encounter with the Taylors has left me shivering.

'There are a few more people in, at least,' she says, and I look around at the customers, murmuring quietly in small huddles. A sense of apprehension still lingers in the air.

When she places my hot chocolate on the counter Meg adds a plate with a large slice of Victoria sponge. 'On the house. You look like you could do with it.'

'It looks amazing. And thank you,' I say, immediately warmed by her thoughtfulness. 'So how do you cope with no mobile signal round here?'

'WiFi,' she says. 'You can use the café's if you want?'

'Oh, God, yes, that would be great,' I say as she passes me a card. I pull out my phone and tap in the code.

'Mum said you went to see her yesterday. How did you find her?' Meg asks.

'She was fine,' I lie, smiling. 'It was lovely to see her.'

Meg shakes her head and sighs. 'No, she's not. She's anything but fine. That's a shame, I was hoping you might see it for yourself.' She shrugs as she turns her back and continues to slice a carrot she was midway through chopping.

I want to tell her I did see it, but at the same time I don't know what good it would do Meg. When the door pings and a customer walks in, I instead find a seat in the corner of the café and call Bonnie's number.

'Where the hell are you?' she shouts as she answers the phone.

'It's good to hear your voice,' I say. She thinks I'm being sarcastic, but she doesn't realise how much I've missed it in the past day and a half.

'I tried calling you and even went to the flat. Where are you?'

'I just came away for a few days.'

There is a moment's pause and then she snaps, 'Oh God, no. You haven't gone back there. *Tell me you haven't.*'

'I am on Evergreen,' I say, glancing around at the customers. 'But only for three nights. I'm coming back Friday.'

'Why, Stella?' she cries.

'I had to.'

'You just couldn't stay away.'

'No, I couldn't.'

'And what do you think you're going to find exactly?'

'I just want to know what happened.'

'And you can't watch the news like any normal person?'

'I don't just mean that,' I say, dropping my voice as I hold the phone closer. 'The reasons we left—'

'You're not going to tell me you think our parents put the bloody body there, are you? Is that what this is about? You think we left because they *murdered* someone and buried her in the garden?'

'No! That's not what I'm saying. It just – us leaving changed everything, Bonnie. It wrecked *everything*,' I say.

'And you think you want to know why?'

'Don't you?'

The truth is I have no idea if I do or not. I've spent twenty-five years convincing myself I don't. That I know who my parents are, that my life on Evergreen was exactly what I always believed it was. But I know my parents had secrets too.

'No. I don't,' she says into the phone and I can hear her teeth are gritted. 'I can't see what it matters any more. That's the trouble with you counsellors, you think you have to dig up the past to help you find the future. You don't. You just get on with it.'

I sigh, ignoring her rant. 'I found out Jill died.'

'What?' she gasps. 'What happened?'

I tell Bonnie the brief details I know.

'That's awful.'

'I know. Mum knew, though,' I say. 'Annie told her when it happened. Why didn't she tell me?'

'It doesn't surprise me. Mum didn't tell us everything,' Bonnie says. 'Do you remember that rabbit you found when you were eight? You wanted to keep it as a pet. You begged them to let you. Danny said he'd make it a hutch.'

'I remember. It ran off.'

'No, it didn't. Dad pointed out it had myxomatosis and Mum told him they had to get rid of it. We never saw that rabbit again.'

I remember Mum crouching in front of me, looking into my eyes and telling me wild rabbits loved to run free. I shake my head. 'That's hardly the same thing,' I say. 'People tell kids things like that so they don't get upset.'

'The point is Mum omitted telling us things if she wanted to.'

'You're talking about a wild rabbit. She should have told me about my best friend dying.'

'I agree with you,' Bonnie says. 'She should've.'

'It feels so wrong.' I take a deep breath, releasing it slowly. 'I haven't even seen her in twenty-five years but I feel like I've lost a good friend.'

'She was a good friend.'

'She was the best,' I say, tears springing to my eyes. I wipe them away quickly. 'Apparently she had heart failure. But it all seems weird.'

'How do you mean?'

'Do people that age suddenly get heart failure?' I ask.

'Of course they do. It can happen at any age.'

'I don't know, Ruth acted like there was more to it. And she was odd about Mum dying, too. They always got on, didn't they?' I ask.

'As far as I know. Why?'

She just totally dismissed her death. And Bob Taylor said none of us should have come back.'

'Well,' she pauses, 'he's right.'

I roll my eyes. I won't be able to get Bonnie to agree with me. We are both silent, but when she starts talking again my attention drifts to the man who's just entered the café. A black woollen hat is pulled low over his forehead, and his chin is covered in roughly shaven stubble. When he pulls off the hat I recognise him as the man who'd been talking to Emma yesterday. He glances around the café and starts to walk to the counter when he catches my eye and suddenly stops.

'Stella?' Bonnie is shouting in my ear. 'Are you listening to a word I'm saying?'

'I'm listening,' I say. His dark eyes seem to penetrate right through me before he abruptly swivels on his feet and walks straight out the door. 'Actually, I have to go,' I tell Bonnie. 'I'll call you again later.' I hang up amid her protests.

'Meg, who was that man?'

'What man?' She looks up but of course he's no longer in sight.

'He just came in the café. Messy stubble, grey hair, really dark eyes. He looks so familiar.' And he clearly knows me, or at least he did when Emma told him who I was.

She wrinkles her nose. 'Could be Graham?' she tries flatly. 'Sounds like Graham Carlton. Lives up in one of the bay houses. Married to—'

'Susan Carlton,' I finish. 'She was my mum's best friend. Of course,' I say, a glimmer of recognition coming back to me.

'Why do you want to know about *him*?' she asks, her top lip curling at the last word.

'No reason,' I tell her as I watch the window to see if he's still around. 'They were leaving that summer,' I murmur, remembering how upset Mum was when Susan told her they were going. How she'd cried when an estate agent brought people over to view her best friend's house.

'Guess they must have changed their minds.'

I'm leaving the café when Freya suddenly appears on the path in front of me, as if she's sprung out of thin air.

'Hey.' She lifts her hand in a wave, her face drawn. She's lost the sparkle she had yesterday. 'Where are you heading?' she asks.

I shrug. 'I'm not sure. I might just head back to my room for a bit.' In truth I haven't a clue what to do and if there were another ferry today there is part of me that could go home. An eerily deserted island where no one is happy to see me isn't the return I envisioned.

'I'll walk with you,' she says and nods in the direction of my old house. 'Let's avoid that, though. I've had enough of it for now.'

'I haven't been talking to people like you asked,' I say. 'I don't have anything to tell you.'

Freya shrugs. 'That's fine,' she says, surprising me, and as we walk she makes small talk about everything but the body. By the time we reach Rachel's I know more about Freya than I could have imagined, and when she stops by the front door and turns to look at me, I suddenly wonder if she's been lulling me into a false sense of security.

'What is it?' I say, cautiously.

Freya drops her gaze to the ground and kicks at a stone. When she looks up she says, 'I thought you'd want to know the police are about to release a statement. About who the body is.'

'Oh.' A shudder ripples through my body. 'Oh God,' I say. 'You're telling me this because I know her.'

Freya nods slowly. Her eyes flick between mine.

'Go on,' I urge.

'It's Iona,' she says. 'Iona Byrnes.'

Evergreen Island

18 July 1993

Maria had toyed with the idea that it might be better if Iona *didn't* come for dinner for a while. Especially after everything that had happened at the sleep-out. That it should be the five of them, drawing back in together, the way they always had when something had happened.

Sitting around the dinner table had always been a family event, but that summer she had opened the door to Iona and now there was a sixth person merging into her family and Maria knew it was time to stop it.

But five days later and she didn't act upon her feelings because she'd watched Bonnie's face as her daughter's friend appeared in the morning. It had lit up when Iona pulled her out to the garden to talk.

Instead of listening to her gut, Maria had allowed herself to be swallowed up by her eldest child's joy and later that day, when Bonnie came crashing into the

153

house, telling her Iona would be coming for dinner, Maria relented.

She hadn't been able to spot the earlier signs that disaster lay ahead, and there would soon be another coming. Yet still Maria continued to brush them aside. Could she really have been expected to predict the level of fall-out?

Of course she could.

After what they'd done she should have always been on guard, whatever guise the threat came in.

Bonnie loved that Iona said she had something really important to tell her. Her friend had pulled her to one side when the rest of the family were milling about in the kitchen, making breakfast, discussing what they planned to do for the day.

Stella had announced she was going to the beach again with Jill and it was almost comical the way their mum seemed so upset by it. Clearly she wanted to spend every day with Stella, but her little sister was completely wrapped up in her friend and their stupid secrets.

Whatever they were, Bonnie doubted they were anything as important as Iona's. When her friend whispered that she had something to say, Bonnie's tummy did a funny little dance.

Since the God-awful night at the sleep-out when her brother's antics meant Iona went off with Tess, Bonnie hadn't felt right. Every time anyone spoke to her she'd wanted to scream at them to shut up. Her insides had felt like they were knotted into lumps of burning iron. It was the exact same way she used to feel as a child, right after Danny was born. Like she'd do anything to get the imposter out of the way.

But it was her that Iona wanted to tell her secret to, not Tess. And that was probably because Tess was only fifteen and she'd always been so sickly sweet. Iona must have found that out for herself by now.

'Let's go to the woods,' Bonnie suggested. It was already a scorchingly hot morning and her shoulders were burnt from the day before. She had to wear a T-shirt to cover them up, which meant she wouldn't be able to put her bikini on. She was by far the palest member of the family and she hated that her skin didn't turn the nice bronze colour Stella's did.

She and Iona linked arms as they walked around the back of the house. Their conversation skimmed over Take That and how much they loved Robbie, and who they liked most in *Beverly Hills, 90210*. When they were deep in the woods, Iona pulled Bonnie down so they were sitting by a tree. For a moment they were silent and Bonnie knew they were building up to something big. She could feel the anticipation fizzing inside her that at last she was being told a secret she would forever keep to herself.

'So,' Iona said, chewing the corner of her lip as she grinned. 'This is a little bit naughty.'

'Go on,' Bonnie said. She laughed out loud, stopping quickly when she feared it sounded childish.

'I'm kind of seeing someone.'

'Oh?' Bonnie felt her heart dip. She hadn't been expecting this.

'And you mustn't tell a soul.'

'No. Of course I won't.' She wouldn't, but already the secret felt tainted. Did this mean Iona would be spending less time with her? She would have to ensure that didn't happen. 'Who is it?'

'Oh.' Iona looked away. 'I can't tell you that.'

'Why not?' Bonnie snapped.

Iona looked at her out of the corner of her eye. 'I just can't,' she said. There was the glimmer of a smile on her lips and Bonnie couldn't help but stare at it.

'So why tell me anything if you can't tell me who it is?'

'Don't be like that,' Iona said, hanging her head to one side. 'We're friends, you just have to trust me.'

But Bonnie couldn't bring herself to accept that. In fact, the way Iona was looking at her, threatening to break into a grin, made the knots in her stomach tighten again. 'I don't get why you can't tell me who you're seeing.'

'It has to be a secret, that's why. No one can know.'

Bonnie's head started to whirl. It had to be someone she knew. Maybe he already had a girlfriend. Or maybe he was much older. She slumped back against the tree as Iona started talking about something different and soon Bonnie knew she would have to wait before she found out.

'Don't be cross with me,' Iona said as she reached for Bonnie's wrist.

Bonnie felt a tug and looked down to where Iona was pulling on the threaded bracelet Stella had given her the day before. Her cheeks flushed when she realised she hadn't taken the thing off. Her sister had made such a fuss of it being the first one she'd made but Bonnie was going to remove it before anyone else saw.

'What's this?' Iona said. 'Is it a friendship bracelet?'

'Yes.'

'Oh no, who's your other friend?' Iona was laughing. 'Should I be jealous?'

Bonnie wished she would be and toyed with the idea of making up a friend just to see how Iona would react. Only deep down she knew Iona wouldn't be bothered at all. And on top of that Stella had already made a dozen more bracelets and had started selling them, and if Iona found out the truth Bonnie would look stupid. 'My sister made it,' she said eventually.

'Well, it's cute.'

Bonnie peered down. 'I want you to have it,' she said, untying it.

'Oh, okay, thank you,' Iona was saying though Bonnie didn't even look up as she focused on wrapping it around her friend's wrist.

And that way, she thought, *everyone will know you're my friend.*

*

Danny was grateful his mum had stopped asking him about the incident at the beach. Hopefully she'd accepted it hadn't meant anything.

It really hadn't. He'd been just as shocked as Tess had when she came into the cave and acted like she was going to have a wee. Danny had leapt up. There was no way he could keep hiding if she was going to pull her pants down. It would be awful if he watched and then someone found out.

Instead he ran past as quick as he could but the cave was narrow and he ended up slamming into her on his way through. He almost hit the rocks when she started screaming, a little too dramatically, in his opinion.

He definitely wished he hadn't gone to the beach in the first place. He hadn't needed to watch *her* that night, there were plenty of other opportunities. Especially when she was around their house almost every evening for dinner.

Maria was just popping the chicken in the oven when there was a loud rap on her kitchen window. She looked up to see Susan Carlton. Her friend was clearly here to discuss Danny and Tess, and Maria felt dreadful that she hadn't made the effort to call on her. She didn't like to admit it, but she had been avoiding her.

'Come in,' Maria called, her eyebrows furrowed as she dropped her oven gloves on the side. 'Can I get you a tea?'

Susan glanced at her watch as she appeared in the open doorway. 'I'd say it was time for wine, wouldn't you?'

Maria felt her shoulders melt. 'Definitely,' she smiled. 'I'm so sorry—'

Susan waved a hand in the air. 'Don't be. I just thought I'd better come before it got more awkward.'

Maria filled two glasses with a nice Chablis David had brought back from the mainland and they went outside. She took a deep breath. 'Danny hasn't said much,' she started, 'but he tells me it wasn't what it seemed. I don't think he intended to grab Tess or hurt her in any way. What does Tess say?'

Susan sighed. 'Her exact words were that she'd gone into the cave to go to the toilet and was pulling her trousers down when Danny suddenly rushed out from the shadows and grabbed.'

Maria winced as she watched her friend. There was something distant about Susan as she gazed ahead of her, and she didn't think it was just what had happened between their children. 'I'm so sorry,' she said again. 'I know Tess wouldn't lie but I can't believe Danny meant anything by it.'

Susan shook her head and reached for Maria's hand. If anyone else understood Danny, it was her two friends. Both Susan and Annie knew first-hand how little Danny gave, but they also knew he wasn't the type to hurt anyone.

Maria was pleased they'd spoken and she felt she could put the incident behind her. Move on. In fact, she'd let her guard down completely by the time she served dinner outdoors, and was already thinking about other things when Iona said, 'It was a terrible thing that happened the other night.'

Maria watched Bonnie's mouth drop open, her fork caught midway as she prodded a potato.

'I hope you're feeling okay about it, Danny?' Iona went on.

Maria glanced at her son, his cheeks burning, his bottom lip twitching. 'I don't think—' she started as Danny pushed back his chair, one of its legs catching in the ground, sending it flying as he ran off to the treehouse and up its ladder. Every one of them turned and watched him.

Stella, she could see, was desperate to go after him but Maria held a hand over her daughter's to keep her from doing so. David tapped his fingers on the table, unsure what to do about the sudden explosion. Bonnie's face had flared an angry red, her jaw set hard, and Maria wished, just for once, that she could see through her wrath and love her brother for who he was, like the rest of them did.

'Oh dear, I think I might have said the wrong thing,' Iona said at last.

If the girl expected the others to assure her she'd done nothing wrong, she was in luck, for David spoke up. 'It's really not your fault, Iona,' he was saying and soon he'd managed to move the conversation, stilted and edgy, while Maria continued to stare at the ladder.

She couldn't bring herself to reassure Iona. Not when the girl's words felt hard and empty, almost planned.

As she looked at her daughters and their guest, and the empty seat where her son should be, unease settled over her. This wasn't what her family dinner should look like. One of them missing. Someone different in his place.

Nerves skittered through her body like a thousand bugs, but still she didn't realise the true extent of how this stranger could tear her family apart.

PRESENT

Chapter Fourteen

Freya watches my reaction closely. I can feel the intensity of her stare as my life feels like it's chipping apart again, tiny fragments falling away.

'Why have you told me it's Iona?' I say. 'Surely you're not supposed to.'

Freya leans her head back, looks at a spot in the distance. 'I didn't know whether to or not, I still hadn't made my mind up until we got here. To be honest, I wanted to give you some kind of warning.'

'Why would I need a warning?'

Freya looks at me like I'm stupid. 'Because as soon as the news comes out this lot are all going to react and—' She sighs and breaks off. 'Oh, come on, Stella. She was always at your house, with your family. The islanders are all so keen to point fingers, and as soon as the ones who didn't know you find that out, they'll all be turning to you for the answers you don't have.'

I tear my gaze away from her.

'You know I'm right,' she says more gently.

'Why are you looking out for me?'

She shrugs. 'I feel like you might need a friend. Listen, I need to go, but here, take my number.' She passes me a card. 'And just be careful. Like I say, they'll draw links even where there aren't any.'

An hour has passed and I haven't left my room. My mind whirs with images of the Iona I remember, full of life, laughing and joking around our dinner table. As much as it breaks my heart to think she was killed, there is someone else who it will affect even more. I need to tell Bonnie before she hears it elsewhere.

As I walk back to the café and past the white picket fence, I see a crowd gathered beside the police tent on the other side of our old garden. The news must have already spread, bringing out the islanders to swap their theories and chase gossip. It doesn't surprise me, it's what they've always done, only today it is more overt.

Chastened by Freya's words, I linger for a moment, watching them, careful to keep my distance. But I have nothing to hide and I refuse to feel guilty over something I have no more idea about than any of them. Eventually I walk around the garden until I'm on the outskirts of the group of mostly unfamiliar faces. Women and men younger than me, some with small children of their own; teenagers; an old couple shuffling their way to the front. A detective is answering their questions calmly, satisfying their need to be fed first-hand details. They look excitable as they chatter among themselves, in contrast to the smaller group who are huddled together by the line of trees that mark the edge of the woods.

These are the people I recognise. Annie is speaking to Ruth Taylor. Both of them look on, still and solemn. To their right is Graham Carlton, his black hat pulled low over his head again, and next to him is another woman who when she turns in my direction I see is his wife, Susan, though she has aged almost beyond recognition. Her thin frame is stooped, her once blonde hair a shock of white. From where I stand her skin looks grey.

My eyes flick between the two groups. The islanders I know and this new, younger group who continue to be animated, their voices rising. And somewhere hovering between them is me.

I glance to my left to where a reporter is being filmed, and when I look more closely I see she's the one who reported on the body last Friday night. Already it appears the news is being broadcast to the rest of the world, which means Bonnie might already know, and will assume I hadn't bothered telling her. By instinct I pull out my phone but of course there's no signal.

I know I should go back to the café and call Bonnie straight away, but Annie has noticed me and splinters from her group as she beckons me over. The closer I get, the more the others line up like a mini row of soldiers, waiting for me to reach them.

'Stella.' Annie holds out her arms. 'I take it you've heard,' she says gravely.

'I can't believe it's Iona.' I let her take my hands.

She nods. 'You remember the rest of us?' she says, waving her arm behind her.

'I do.' I turn to Susan. 'It's good to see you again.'

'Only wish it were in better circumstances,' she says, then she holds out her arms too and pulls me in for a hug, murmuring in my ear, 'I am so sorry about your mum. She was a dear friend. I missed her a lot when you all left.'

'Thank you,' I say as she releases me, and when I look up I notice Graham has walked away.

'My dear,' Annie says, taking hold of me again. 'Let's have a walk.' She steers me on to the path that leads to the village. She is walking slowly and it looks like the weight of her heavy coat is drowning her small body. 'I was rather hoping you wouldn't still be here,' she says once we are safely out of earshot. 'Especially now we know who the body belongs to,' she adds, her voice dropping even though there's no one else around.

'What do you mean by that?' I ask.

Annie pauses, her arm still linked through mine. Worried eyes search my face and I can see how much this is putting a strain on her. 'I know what some of them will be saying, I've seen how it works. They draw their own conclusions. Of course Iona was only here that one summer and—' She breaks off and looks back at my old house. 'And then as far as everyone understood it you all had to leave, only days apart. It's better you go home, Stella. Back to Winchester and your sister.'

'I don't understand.'

'I think you do.'

'No, I mean she was called away, I remember that. But she must have come back.'

Annie shakes her head. 'The day she got on that ferry was the last time anyone saw her.'

I turn away because I can't bring myself to look at Annie.

I know this isn't true. I know that Iona came back again before we left because I saw her. Only I never told anyone else.

And I know that one other person saw her too, and it's time we spoke.

Chapter Fifteen

There are so many people milling about the village that I'm reluctant to use the café's internet to phone Bonnie, but I have no choice.

I am glad Meg's not there and I don't have to swap pleasantries with the stranger behind the counter as I focus on what I need to do. As soon as my mobile picks up the WiFi, I see there are sixteen missed calls from my sister. My heart beats rapidly as I dial her number.

'Finally!' she screams when she answers. 'Do you have any idea—?'

'I'm sorry,' I say quietly. 'There's no reception here at all and—'

'You could have called me as soon as you knew. Not let me see it on the news,' she shouts.

'Bon, I've only just found out. I came straight back to the café so I could speak to you. They must have aired it immediately.' Silence. 'Bonnie?' I say.

'It's Iona,' she says finally. 'I mean, shit, Stella.'

'I know,' I murmur. 'I'm so sorry.'

'She was the only friend I had on that God-awful island. Who would kill her?' she says angrily. 'And how the hell did no one know she was missing?' Bonnie sucks in a tight breath. 'I only knew her one summer. Why does it hurt so much?'

'If she meant something to you it doesn't matter how long you knew her.'

'It's the fact she was murdered,' Bonnie says. 'That's what makes it so awful.'

My mind strays to Jill. Would her death have been even harder if she'd been killed? I don't have the answer.

'She was the only friend I had,' Bonnie says again. 'The first person who wanted to spend time with me. I never had that before her.'

'Of course you did,' I say, though I know this isn't true.

'No one wanted to be friends with me. But she did.'

I shift on my chair, keeping an eye on the customers, making sure no one is listening. 'Bonnie, you remember she was called away?' I say. 'What exactly happened? Wasn't she called back to see a sick relative, was it an aunt?'

For a moment Bonnie doesn't speak, then she snaps, 'What are you still doing there?'

'I'm coming back,' I sigh, thinking of all the people who don't want me here either. 'I'll have to wait until morning now, though,' I go on. 'Please tell me what happened when Iona left.'

'What are you getting at?'

'Just – I don't know – how did she seem to you? She must have been upset when she got the call, especially if it meant she had to suddenly go home.'

Bonnie is silent again.

'Bon, you were the closest one to her,' I urge. The more my sister clams up, the more my stomach ties itself into knots. What is she hiding?

'I realise that,' Bonnie snaps. 'It means the police will be back again and they'll want to know why you're there, digging around for something completely irrelevant.'

Is it irrelevant? Something supposedly made Iona leave – or at least made the islanders think she did – but the fact remains she was here again only two days later. And after what I saw and who I saw her with, my mind is going into overdrive, spilling out conclusions I can only pray aren't right.

'I mean, your timing couldn't be more perfect,' she goes on. 'It's going to look suspicious.'

'Alright, Bonnie, I told you I'm coming back. Will you just tell me what I'm asking for? Was there anything you remember about what happened when she was called away?'

'No,' she says after a beat. 'Nothing at all.'

I clutch the phone hard against my ear until my knuckles turn white, glancing around, but the customers are fewer now and those left are chattering among themselves. 'You're sure about that?' I hiss.

'Totally sure,' she replies sharply.

I grit my teeth, shaking my head. *What are you holding out on me, Bonnie?* 'And she definitely left the island? You didn't see her again?'

'No, I never saw her again.' Bonnie's voice is smoother now, which lets me know at least this is the truth.

'Did she have any other family?' I ask.

'No,' Bonnie says. 'She hadn't seen her mum in three years and had no idea who her dad was. She told me she used to pretend he was a rock star when she was a kid, that he made loads of money and one day he'd come back for her.'

'That's kind of sad,' I say, despite the other thoughts racing through my head.

'I don't know. She laughed about it when she told me. God, I can't believe she was killed.'

'But she had this sick relative,' I go on blindly. 'I mean, whoever that was must have realised she was missing.'

'Why are you interrogating me? Do you think *I* killed her?' Bonnie snaps.

'No,' I say. 'Of course I don't.' I squeeze my eyes tight, pressing my fingers against them. 'But you tell me you saw her leave the island and—'

'I never told you I saw her leave,' Bonnie interjects. 'I didn't. I was supposed to, but—' She pauses. 'I never turned up. We'd had an argument. The last time I was supposed to see her I never went and now she's dead.'

I hear a cry escape her and wish I could be with Bonnie right now so I could wrap my arms around her. But I also need to get some answers. 'How do you know she left, then?' I ask, fearing I already know.

'Because Dad told me she did,' she retorts. 'Are you more interested in playing detective than my feelings? And you're the counsellor ...'

But I'm no longer listening. Dad would have been the last one to see Iona because he'd have taken her back on his ferry.

Yet I'm pretty sure my dad was lying.

On Wednesdays Olivia is always at work, which means she won't be at home, looking after Dad. This is a good thing, I tell myself as I dial their home number and wait for the connection. It's him I need to speak to. I listen to the rapid beats of my heart and when he answers I draw in a tight breath. 'Hi, Dad, it's me, Stella.'

'Stella ...' His voice is warm and soft, and as my heartbeats slow I toy with the idea that I could have an entire conversation with him that doesn't need to even nudge the edges of what's happened. I could avoid it altogether.

'How are you, my darling?' he asks and the familiar cloak of guilt wraps itself around me. I know he probably doesn't remember how long it's been since I last saw him but it feels like he is brushing over it because he'll always forgive me.

My fingers play with the seam of my coat, rubbing it roughly as my breath lodges in my throat. 'I'm good. How are you, Dad?'

'Not so bad, love,' he says. 'Not so bad. I've been in the garden. It's starting to rain. Have you got rain?'

I glance outside the café window. The sky has darkened and it looks like it might start. 'Not yet,' I tell him.

'And how's Andrew?'

I close my eyes at the name. How he manages to pluck it out so easily every time I have no idea, but Andrew and I split up two years ago. 'Fine, Dad,' I say. 'Andrew's fine.'

'That's good,' he murmurs, his voice drifting away, and I wonder if there's a chance Olivia is there. Often I'd have to haul Dad back into my conversation when she was; we'd always be pulling him like a tug of war.

In the early days I asked Dad if I could see him on his own and to my surprise he once agreed. But when I turned up at the café I saw Olivia hovering over the table, flapping the menu in front of him as she impatiently waited for him to choose.

'I thought she wasn't coming,' I said, as I slipped on to a chair opposite him and she went to order.

'Oh, you don't mind, do you, love?' he smiled, asking so casually as if he had no idea there was a problem, or if he did he was too scared to confront it.

She won in the end. She got the prize. Maybe I let her or maybe eventually I didn't see the point of the fight. If he wanted to leave Mum for someone like her I wasn't going to change anything.

'Dad, listen, I'm back on Evergreen,' I tell him and wait for his reaction. One of Olivia's unspoken conditions was that we forget Dad had a life before her, and as such any talk of the island between us faded many years ago.

'Oh? What are you doing there?'

'Well, did you see the news at the weekend?' I ask. 'Do you know what happened?'

'The news ...' his voice fades.

'About Evergreen,' I prompt. 'It was on TV. They found a body on the island.'

'I don't really remember watching the TV,' he says.

'But do you know what's happened?' I go on. 'Where they found the body?'

There is silence for a moment as I wait for him to answer. 'I think I do,' he says at last. 'I think someone came to talk to me about it.'

'Dad,' I say patiently, dipping my voice so the remaining two customers don't hear me. 'They found a body buried just outside our garden. Dad ...' I press, a little louder. 'Did you hear what I said?'

'Yes, my love, I heard, but it's really raining now. I think I need to bring the clothes in.'

'You have clothes out there?' I mutter. 'Dad, did you know that they've identified the body?'

'No,' he says slowly, more definitely this time. 'No, my darling, I didn't know that.'

I wait but he doesn't ask. 'It's Iona,' I tell him. 'Do you remember her?'

'Oh yes,' he says gravely. 'Yes. I do remember her ...' he trails off. 'Is our treehouse still there?' he asks suddenly. 'I built that for you. You and Danny loved it in there.'

'We did,' I say.

'I built it well.' I can hear his smile seep through his words. 'Your mum was worried it would collapse, but I bet you anything it's still there.'

'Yes, Dad, it's still here,' I lie, pain pressing at my heart.

'You wanted to sleep in it,' he is saying.

'I did once,' I admit, smiling sadly at the memory. 'It was too cold, though. I didn't last the night.'

See, we were happy. I do remember it right.

'We had good times on the island,' I murmur.

'We did, my love.'

So what happened? Why did you make us leave?

'Dad,' I start, 'you told Bonnie you took Iona back to the mainland at the end of the summer.'

A pause. 'Did I?'

'Do you remember her leaving? She was called away for a sick relative.'

There is the sound of clanking in the background and I imagine him rooting through drawers, his mind somewhere else entirely. The noise stops. 'Yes. I took her back,' he says, 'when she had to go.'

'Did she ever come back?'

I wait.

'No, love,' he says eventually. 'I don't think she did. Love, I can't find my ...' he stops again, 'oh, you know that thing. The thing that goes round ...' I blank out his words as his frustration rises and I know I have lost him again.

I fight back the tears when I hang up. They are tears of exasperation, anger, and a desperate need to get to the truth. But at the same time there's a fear that if I do I won't like it.

You are *lying, Dad.*

Before the end of that summer I never would have believed it was possible. Not my dad. He was the most straight-up person I knew. In conversations like we've just had, I see snatches of that dad again. Since his dementia diagnosis, there have been plenty of pieces of him that have been taken away from me but many have been given back. When he takes me to happier times on the island it makes it hard to believe he could lie.

Outside I take a deep breath of the cold fresh air, a few spots of rain drop on to my face, and for a moment I stand awkwardly in the middle of the small cluster of shops, not knowing which way to turn.

As the rain starts falling more heavily, flashes of bright umbrellas begin to pop up, but through them I catch sight of Meg, her arms flailing wildly in the air, her face as hard as stone as she shouts at her mum.

Emma's face is passive, willingly taking whatever her daughter is throwing at her. I fall in step behind a couple of young girls sheltering in a shop doorway under a large pink brolly and move closer to Meg and her mum.

'Why won't you just leave it?' Meg shouts, fear dripping from her words. 'Keep away from him.'

Emma doesn't answer, but as the young girls dip into the shop I am left exposed and staring straight at Meg and her mother. Emma turns and gapes at me while Meg throws her hands in the air. 'I give up,' she screams, before running off.

'Emma, is everything alright?' I venture.

Her face is wet with rain but I can make out tears glistening in her eyes.

'Emma, are you okay?'

She shakes her head, almost imperceptibly, before she too walks away, in the opposite direction of her daughter, leaving me alone again, hair plastered to my scalp as water drips down the back of my neck.

The sooner I get off this island the better.

When I let myself into the B&B Rachel stops rifling through the drawers of her bureau and looks up. 'Take off your shoes, you're leaving a puddle on the floor,' she says, eyeing me cautiously.

I do as she says, pairing them up neatly by the door.

'You'd best get a towel,' she murmurs, going back to whatever she was looking for. 'And I suspect you've heard the news.' She pauses again and glances over her shoulder. 'The body. A young girl who lived here a long time back.'

'Yes, I heard,' I say.

'Did you know her?'

I nod.

'I'm sorry.' She turns back to her desk. It won't be long before she hears just how well we did know Iona. 'There's a note for you on the sideboard,' she adds. 'It was on the mat earlier.'

I pick up the envelope, turning it over in my hands. My name has been written on the front in block capitals. 'Thank you,' I say and when she doesn't respond I go up the stairs to my room.

I close the door behind me, ripping off my wet coat and throwing it on the bed, then slide a finger under the seal of the envelope and peel it open, pulling out a small sheet of notepaper. The writing mimics that from the envelope – all in block capitals.

My eyes skim over the words but I have to reread them before I can take in their warning.

STOP DIGGING. YOU WON'T LIKE WHAT YOU FIND.

I glance back at the door, half expecting Rachel might have followed me up. My breaths are shallow as I turn back to the note, reading the two lines over and over until they blur in front of me.

I sink on to the bed and tears sting my eyes as a sense of desperation overwhelms me. I am out of my league. My fingers tremble as they continue to clutch on to the piece of paper, its warning staring back.

I want to get off the island now. Maybe, I think, there is some way I can get back without having to wait until morning.

Dropping the note, I close my eyes and allow images of Dad to plague my mind. He knows more than he's telling, but surely, I cry silently, he had nothing to do with Iona's death.

Yet there's a fragile strand that links my dad to her and it's one I've spent the last twenty-five years trying to erase from my mind.

It's the reason I couldn't go back to my and Jill's secret place. The reason my family began to break down.

And now what if someone else knows about it too? Someone on this island, and for whatever reason they don't want me digging any more?

Because I'm certain I saw my dad and Iona together before we had to leave. Together in the clearing. Only I don't understand how that fragile strand means Iona ended up deep in the ground.

Evergreen Island

5 August 1993

David was always aware when Maria was watching him. He could sense her eyes penetrating his back and when he looked in the mirror, after spitting out a mouthful of toothpaste, he caught her hovering behind him. He rinsed off his brush, slotted it back into the pot, and turned to face her.

'There's something about Iona,' she said.

David had to agree. There *was* something about the girl, the way she brightened up Bonnie, how she was always so keen to please everyone around the table. But he knew Maria didn't mean those kinds of things. Her face was pinched, which meant she was worrying herself over something.

'I can't put my finger on it,' she went on.

'I thought you liked her.'

'I did. I do – I …'

David didn't like that Maria got so wrapped up with everything, twisting things around, making problems where there weren't any. They were always the little things too. In his mind it was the one big thing she should be anxious about, but his wife seemed to have miraculously glossed over that as if it didn't play on her mind.

In this way, David thought, they could not be more different. He lived with it hanging over him every day. They just never spoke of it.

He refused to agree with his wife about her recent concern. 'Iona's a lovely girl. Don't go there, Maria.'

Maria sighed. 'I don't see her doing much university work,' she went on.

'Oh, for heaven's sake.'

'I'm just saying,' she murmured, gnawing at a patch of skin on her thumb. He gently prised it out of her mouth, knowing she was nervous. What did she really think there was to be afraid of with Iona?

He kissed her on the head and moved past her. He wouldn't be drawn into this. Not when he was beginning to really like the girl.

The following morning Maria was still agitated by her conversation with David. She shouldn't have to prove to him that she was beginning to realise there was something odd about Iona's behaviour, but it seemed she was going to have to.

By the end of the summer she would wish she'd tried even harder to get David to see that side of Iona, and maybe he would never have done what he did. But the fact was, at this point, Maria didn't really understand the depth of it herself.

That morning she had just got a chance to sit down with a coffee when she heard Bonnie screaming outside. She sprang out of her chair and shot to the door as Bonnie approached. 'What the hell's happened?' she cried.

'I hate him!' Bonnie yelled.

'Who do you—'

'Danny. Jesus, who else? He's been sitting up a bloody tree in the woods again. Watching us, listening to us.'

Maria's stomach clenched. She'd spoken to Danny, choosing her words carefully, reminding him he shouldn't be watching people.

Bonnie stared at her. 'We were sitting under the tree, talking, and then he fell out of it and landed by our feet. It's obvious he's obsessed with her.'

'He fell? Is he okay?'

'God, Mum!' Bonnie shouted. 'Clearly he's not okay, he's tapped. In the head.' She prodded the side of her own with her forefinger.

'Is he hurt, Bonnie?' Maria found herself yelling back.

'I don't know. I don't care.'

'Oh, what's wrong with you?' Maria muttered as she ran out of the house, calling behind her, 'Where is he?'

Bonnie followed, snapping back that he was in the woods. Already Maria was running towards her son.

'This way.' Her daughter pointed left and Maria raced forward when she saw a figure slumped on the ground.

'Danny!' she called. Her son was curled in a ball, wrapped up into himself. If it weren't for his size, he'd be mistaken for a child. 'Danny,' she said as she crouched next to him, touching his leg and shaking him gently.

He opened his eyes but then shut them again quickly. 'I wasn't doing anything wrong,' he murmured.

'Are you hurt?' Maria asked and he shook his head.

'I wasn't spying. Bonnie says I was listening to their conversation. I wasn't.'

'You were,' Bonnie cried out from behind Maria. 'You bloody well were.'

'Bonnie, will you just shut up,' Maria said. Her daughter's feet were planted defiantly apart, her hands on her hips, her face white as a sheet.

Danny had opened his eyes again at the sound of her raised voice.

'What did you hear?' Bonnie was asking him, but Maria was looking around.

'Where's Iona?' she asked before Danny got the chance to answer. Where could that girl have gone so quickly if she was only here a moment ago? With all this fuss going on, why suddenly run away?

'You have to do something,' Bonnie snapped and Maria turned back. It seemed none of them were listening to each other. 'Every time Iona looks around, he's there, watching her.' Eventually Bonnie stormed off, towards the house.

Maria pulled her son up until he was sitting. 'Were you listening to them?' she asked.

Danny shrugged.

'Because you know we talked about that.' She gave a small sigh. 'You can't eavesdrop on other people, Danny.'

He didn't answer for what felt like an eternity and she was about to give up and haul him to his feet when he said, 'I don't even know why they're still friends.'

'Who? Bonnie and Iona?'

Danny nodded. 'It's not like Bonnie's ever happy when she's with her any more.'

Really? Could she have actually missed that? Maria found herself shaking her head as she regarded her son. She couldn't imagine it to be true, but if it were, she would have to watch that girl even more closely.

Danny feared he might have gone too far when he told his mum what he did. But he also wanted to get the heat off him. The fact was he had been watching Iona and he couldn't stop. He was drawn to her like the moth that had kept him awake the night before, buzzing about the landing light. She was so intriguing, made up of so many different things. She wasn't like anyone else on this island. Watching her excited him, and every time, he saw something new.

PRESENT

Chapter Sixteen

In winter on Evergreen the evenings are long. Longer still when there is nowhere to go. Since returning to my room I have made myself a prisoner, much like the islanders have done over the last few days. Soon everyone else on the island will know Iona was practically a part of my family.

I'd convinced myself I was desperate for answers but now all I want to do is bury my head like Bonnie.

It's eight p.m., and I am lying on the bed, my thoughts circling, and each time they complete a loop I am back where I started – my hope that I am jumping to conclusions that Iona's death had anything to do with Dad.

A loud knock on the front door below startles me and I push myself up against the headboard, listening to Rachel's footsteps on the hard floor. I pray it is her they've come to see and not me. I don't relish the thought of any of the islanders asking me questions or reminding me I'm not wanted.

There is a murmur of voices, then footsteps on the stairs, and I swing my legs off the bed, moving to open the door a crack, releasing my breath when I see Freya on the landing. 'Hello again,' I say.

'She didn't want me coming up.' Freya rolls her eyes.

I smile, amused that Freya got past Rachel, and invite her in, watching her gaze swoop around the room before she plonks herself down on the end of the bed.

'I didn't expect to see you again so soon,' I say. 'What's it been like out there? Are they still all around, talking about Iona?'

'No. They all cleared off back to their homes when it got dark,' she says and I sit next to her, studying her expression. Her eyebrows are arched into a small frown. There is more she wants to tell me, but I'm afraid to ask.

'I still can't get my head around it,' I say, not taking my gaze off her.

'Of course.'

'My sister's upset and I feel like I need to be there for her. I think I should probably leave in the morning,' I rattle on, realising I need her to understand I'm not running away.

'Yes, I guess,' she says. It's not the answer I expected.

'Bonnie relies on me quite a lot, you see,' I go on. 'She has Luke and the boys, but whenever anything goes wrong it's me she turns to. To be honest, it gets a bit too much at times, you know, the pressure of always having to put her first.' I give a short laugh. 'Do you know, in some ways I think I was rebelling against her when I came back to the island? I knew she would hate it and that made me more determined. But now—' I break off. 'Actually, Freya, I thought you'd tell me to stay,' I admit. 'I thought you'd want me to carry on talking to people, especially now we know it's Iona.'

She turns away and stares at my closed door. 'I feel like I'm the bearer of bad news every time I see you.'

A familiar sensation of numbness spreads through me again, starting at my fingertips, making me squeeze them tight. 'What's happened?'

Freya dips her head, looking at her hands clasped in her lap.

'Will you just tell me what's happened,' I snap.

'I'm sorry,' she starts, 'and I shouldn't even know this, but a couple of hours ago someone confessed to Iona's murder.' Already her words are ringing in my ears.

'No. No,' I say. 'Oh God, *no.*' I cradle my head in my splayed hands, rocking it back and forth as my stomach sinks. *Dad, what have you done?* I should have been with him. I should never have broken the news on the phone. He doesn't understand what he's just done. He can't realise what this will do to his life.

Freya's words are muffled but they come through anyway. 'I could get into trouble for telling you.'

'It's my fault,' I cry. 'I spoke to him earlier. I told him everything. I should have done it face-to-face.'

'Really? I thought you hadn't seen him in years.'

'What?' I look up at her. 'What do you mean?'

'Your brother,' she says. 'Danny's just confessed to killing Iona.'

Chapter Seventeen

The following morning I cannot get off the island quickly enough. All night my thoughts have tumbled over each other, reaching crescendos of fear, trying to make sense of what Danny has done.

In the morning I wait until the last moment to slip out of my room, leaving a note for Rachel on my bed to tell her I'm going a day early. I don't want to see her. I don't want to face any of them. It won't be long before they learn of my brother's confession, and when that happens I won't be here.

As soon as I'm on the ferry and the mainland is within sight, my phone springs into life. I call Bonnie, and when she doesn't answer I leave her a message to call me back urgently, that I'm on my way home but I need to speak to her.

Once I'm at Poole Quay I call her again but there's still no answer, and when, half an hour later, the same thing happens it crosses my mind she's doing this on purpose – letting me know she has control back after I left her. I'm nearly in Winchester by the time she calls, and by then she's already heard the news from a police officer.

'When did you find out?' she shouts.

'This morning,' I lie. There's no point reiterating my lack of phone reception. 'I got on a ferry as soon as I heard. I've been calling you ever since.'

'I didn't have my mobile on me.' A lame excuse but I don't bother arguing.

Instead I tell her I'm going straight to her place and within twenty minutes I'm ringing her doorbell.

'Aunt Stella.' Harry breaks into a grin as he answers the door. 'Mum said you'd gone away.'

'Hi, Harry.' I kiss him on the cheek as he lets me pass. 'Why aren't you in school?'

'I'm sick,' he says and coughs loudly. 'Mum's in a weird mood,' he adds quietly. He raises his eyebrows at the sound of a pan crashing to the kitchen floor, followed by Bonnie swearing. 'Are you sure you want to stay?'

'I'd better,' I say, confident he's unaware of what's happened.

Harry follows me through to the kitchen, announcing my arrival like I am the Queen. It's something he's done since he was little but today his mum barely looks up. 'See,' he whispers, loud enough so he knows Bonnie will hear. 'Weird mood.'

'Harry, give us some space,' she says, straightening her back and rubbing the base of her spine. 'Please,' she adds softly, and I wonder why Bonnie only ever reveals her fragility with her children.

As soon as he's left, she turns to me. 'Our brother.' She shakes her head, her face pale. She's taking deep breaths and I can tell she's trying to control herself.

'I feel as sick as you do,' I tell her, taking her hand and leading her to the sofa by the back door. My stomach has been churning for the last seventeen hours. 'Tell me what the police said to you. I don't really know any details.'

As we sit she tells me what little she knows. That this morning Danny was taken to Dorset to be questioned regarding Iona's death.

'From where?' I ask but she shrugs, shaking her head.

'I don't know, and I'm not sure what evidence they have. It must be pretty substantial.'

'Bonnie,' I say, realising she doesn't know everything, 'he walked into a police station and *admitted* it. I'm sorry, I thought you knew.'

She pulls her hand away and swivels on the sofa until she is glaring at me. 'No. God. I didn't.'

'But I don't get why he would have done it,' I say. 'It doesn't make any sense.' Every time I think of the possibility that my brother could have killed Iona, waves of nausea surge through me.

'The bastard. The bloody bastard. Why would he kill her?'

'I thought he liked her.' I slip off my shoes, pulling my feet on to the sofa and hugging my knees against me. This is what I can't stop playing out in my head. That every time they were together, I believed Danny liked her.

'He was obsessed with her. And that's a big difference to liking someone as a normal person would. We should have known,' Bonnie says. 'Urrgh. You remember that bird, don't you?'

I nod, feeling sick as I had then.

'Mum was picking feathers out of Danny's jumper for days. Even she didn't know what to say for once.'

'He said he'd found it like that,' I murmur, though his story had conflicted with the one Iona told Bonnie, and I'd seen his drawing for myself. The bird didn't look right. It was so unlike his other pictures.

'We should have guessed he'd do something like this one day,' Bonnie says. 'I just never thought he already had.'

'Bonnie, don't talk like that.'

'You're not seriously defending him?' she spits out. 'You've just told me he's admitted it. He's kept this a secret for twenty-five years and, shit, our parents must have, too.' She hangs her head in her hands, her fingers digging into her skull. 'I thought it was my fault. All this time and I thought it was my fault we left.'

'What do you mean?' I bend my head to look at her. 'Why would you think it was your fault?'

'It doesn't matter.'

'Yes, it does—'

'No,' she snaps. 'It doesn't.'

After a moment I say, 'Because you and Iona had that argument?'

'Just forget I said anything,' she says angrily, and I turn my head to look out the window. I'm about to speak when she says, 'Danny followed her once. When she left our house he followed her to the clearing by the cliff. She had to shake him off and lose him.'

'That doesn't sound like Danny.'

A picture of my brother springs into my head. His big hulking frame, his head always hung low as if he wasn't looking where he was going. I never saw him like they did. To me he was just my brother: lost, but above all gentle. My heart sinks with pain that my brother could have done this, because it doesn't make sense that he was capable of it. 'It must have been an accident. Danny's never hurt anyone.'

'You're defending him again,' she cries. 'Just like Mum and Dad always did. I don't know what's wrong with you all. Can't you accept he's not right and that he's done something horrendous? He needs to be punished.' Her voice rises and we hear a thump on the floor above us. Bonnie raises her eyes to the ceiling and her words are quieter when she says, 'I haven't told Harry. I'm not going to tell either of the boys, and Luke's not here so he doesn't know yet. Of course you'll have to speak to Dad about it, that is if he hasn't already been locked up too.'

'Bonnie, we don't know any of the details, you can't start assuming—'

She storms over to the patio windows, her fists clenched tightly by her sides as she stands with her back to me. 'I'm not speaking to Dad,' she says. She is taut with tension, like a coiled spring about to burst. 'I don't want anything to do with any of it. I'm not going to let my family suffer.'

This is *your family*, I want to say, but she doesn't see it like I do. While Bonnie can and will distance herself from them, I'll be the one picking up the pieces and trying to put them together. Because this is the only family I have.

I rest my head on the back of the sofa, trying to make sense of those pieces. 'If they did know, do you think that's why Mum let Danny leave?' I say.

'I don't know. Our family is screwed up.'

I can't argue with that. 'They must have thought they were protecting him, doing the right thing. Wouldn't you do it for your boys?' I ask.

'Don't even go there,' Bonnie cries. 'Don't you dare compare my boys to Danny.'

'I'm not,' I say softly. 'I'm just asking what you would do if they'd done something awful. If there was nothing you could do about it. What would you do, Bon? I'm asking you to help me understand,' I plead, when she doesn't answer.

'If they killed someone I would not cover it up,' she says, but how can she say this for certain unless she's been in that position? Surely a parent would do anything to protect their child?

'Do you remember that drawing pad?' I say after we've fallen into a silence. 'The one Danny used to sketch people in?'

'Vaguely.'

'I wonder what happened to it.'

'Why?'

'I don't know. He seemed to get people. He wasn't interested in the trees or the beach or the sea, but he was interested in people.'

No one was allowed to look in his book. It was always tucked under his arm when he went up to the treehouse but he never once showed anyone. Then one day, Jill and I went up to the treehouse ten minutes after he'd come down. He can't have realised he'd left it behind, but I saw it poking out from beneath one of the cushions.

Only when Jill left did I pull it out, flicking through its pages, expecting to see reams of words that I told myself I wouldn't read. But there weren't words. It was filled with cartoon drawings, caricatures of people, speech bubbles coming out of their mouths, and they were good. Really good. And even though I knew I shouldn't be looking, I couldn't help it because it was clear his characters were based on people we knew.

'Do you think they'll let me see him?' I say.

Bonnie swings around, her face aghast. 'Why would you even want to?'

'I want to talk to him.'

'No! No way. I don't want to be one of those families you watch on the news, standing by a killer. I don't want people thinking we condone him. I just want – I want this to go away,' she exclaims. 'I don't want to deal with everyone knowing my brother's a murderer. I can't deal with it,' she says, covering her face with her hands. 'I can't deal with *any* of it.'

I stand up and pull her in to me; her body shakes against mine. 'It isn't going to go away,' I say. 'We have to face it.'

'No, we really don't,' she says, pulling back and looking up at me. Her face is streaked with tears. 'We've had nothing to do with Danny for eighteen years. So, there's no need to start now.'

'It's not as simple as that, Bonnie.'

'Why isn't it?' she says in a childish demand.

'Because you're not considering what I want.'

'You've done what you wanted. You went back to that place when you shouldn't have. Now we just need to leave this alone. Please, Stella, I'm begging you. Stay out of it.'

But all I can see is my brother, his long legs dangling out of the treehouse, clutching his book to his chest like nothing else mattered. Whatever he did, I don't believe he intended to.

'I don't want you digging any more,' she says, and my mind drifts to the threat which I'd tucked into my coat pocket before I left.

Bonnie looks fearful, as if there's more she doesn't want me finding out. She pulls out of my grip and wanders away. With her back to me, she braces herself before opening up the dishwasher and unloading it.

No, I'm sure she's just worried about what will happen to her and the boys following Danny's confession.

'Bon, why did you say you thought it was your fault we left?' I ask her.

She pauses; a mug in her hand stops midway between the dishwasher and the counter before she slams it down. 'I was once told something,' she says. 'But it was a lie.'

'What—'

'It doesn't matter,' Bonnie snaps. 'And you still haven't reassured me you're going to drop all this raking over the past.' She straightens and turns to me. 'Stella?' she prompts when I don't answer.

'I will,' I say, though I already know that is impossible. My brother is sitting in a police cell and I need to know if he should be there, because I can't deny there's a part of me that doesn't believe he should.

Chapter Eighteen

I have barely stepped off Bonnie's front steps when I get a call from a Detective Harwood who says he would like to speak to me. I agree to meet him in two hours and he gives me the address of a house near Bournemouth, so close to where I have just come from this morning that I wish I had known before making the forty-minute drive back to Winchester.

As soon as I get home I peel off my clothes and stand under a shower, piping-hot water raining down on my skin until it almost scalds me. I need this sting of pain to focus on as my head is a mess. In many ways thinking about my brother and what I can do is easiest, because as soon as I stop my head is filled with thoughts too difficult to accept: that everything I once believed was a lie.

When I'm out of the shower I grab my scrapbook and take it to my bedroom. Relieved to be lying on my own bed again, I let the book fall open at the first page. Mum and I started it when I was ten. Its first entry is a newspaper clipping of the islanders protesting against the proposed development of a boutique hotel. There's a picture of us all gathered together in solidarity – Mum and Annie at the front of the group. *Annie Webb and Maria Harvey lead protest to keep island a sanctuary*, the headline reads. I had proudly cut out the article and pasted it into the book.

I flick to the last page, an entry made on 3 August 1993. I remember the day clearly. It was burning hot, I had stripped down to my swimming costume and was standing under a sprinkler in the garden when Mum came out and turned off the tap.

'We need to save water. Let's play something,' she'd suggested. 'How about the alphabet game?'

This meant taking turns to find something on the island that started with a particular letter. I had stuck in various things we'd found and had written up others like the caterpillar I'd spotted crawling up a tree.

Now I rub my fingers gently over a daisy and a feather stuck side by side in my book, both long ago turned brown and limp. The list stops at M. I don't recall if we finished it or not. I can't even remember how the day ended.

I flick through the pages one at a time, poring over them, searching for clues I know don't exist, and eventually toss the book across the bed, letting out a scream. Rolling on to my side I thump my clenched fists against the pillow, burying my head in it, grabbing handfuls of white cotton until I can't squeeze any tighter. Pain and frustration rip through me.

This is my family. These are the people I'm supposed to trust most.

But I no longer trust any of them.

The interview suite in Dorset is in a room at the back of a house. High ceilings and intricate coving are the only interesting features in what is otherwise a blank canvas. The walls are magnolia, bare apart from a digital clock that flashes bright red, and two cameras pointing towards each of the sofas.

'You're here as a witness,' Harwood tells me once he has pointed out that the interview is being videoed. 'You're free to leave whenever you want. But as we explained to you earlier, your brother is under arrest for murder.' I nod as he goes on, 'There will be times when this may be frustrating for you, but this is a one-way interview. If you have questions we'll never lie to you but there may be times when we won't be able to give you information.'

'Okay.' I smile weakly as I pick up the glass of water that sits on the small table in front of me. My blood burns as it speeds around my veins like cars on a race track and I can't sit still on the sofa as I lean forward, then back, before shuffling to the edge again, folding my hands in my lap.

But I am grateful for his kindness when he asks me if I'm okay to proceed. And I'm also grateful for the fact that at least someone is telling me they won't lie to me even if they can't give me everything I need.

The detective asks what I know about the incident and I tell him there's absolutely nothing. He seems to accept this as he moves on to wider questions about Iona and my family. Did we see her often? How well did I get on with her? How about my sister? My mother? My father?

To start I tell him that during that summer I had always thought Iona was friendly and good fun, but that it was Bonnie who had formed a very close friendship with her. Though I don't add it was closer than anyone else before and possibly even after.

I say that Mum was the one who instigated the dinner invites so I'd assumed she liked her, but what I don't say is that at some point those invites must have dried up because in the last couple of weeks Iona stopped coming over. I realise I'd never given this any thought before now.

And Dad? My chest is tight as I tell Harwood that Iona and he got on well, that he made her laugh with his stories. I push my clammy hands beneath me, willing the fabric of the sofa to dry them out.

My omissions sit in hard lumps in my throat and it crosses my mind that one day I may have to tell a courtroom why I never said more.

But Harwood isn't pressing me; instead he wants to know what other friendships Iona formed on the island. His question surprises me and I can't work out where he is going with it when surely he must only be interested in my brother.

'It was so long ago,' I say, 'and I was only eleven.' It feels as if all my answers have been vague and I have a strange desire not to disappoint him.

'I appreciate that, Ms Harvey,' he says. 'But can you think of anyone else she used to hang out with or talk about?'

'Well, there was one girl,' I say, the only person I ever saw her laughing with. 'Tess Carlton.'

Harwood searches through the pages of his pad. 'Susan and Graham Carlton's daughter?' His eyebrows are raised when he looks up. I nod and he continues to look at me for a moment too long. 'And you say they were friends?'

'I saw them going to the mainland together, so yes, I suppose they must have been.' Now I think about it, it was an odd friendship, with Tess only fifteen.

I suddenly wonder whether Tess was the cause of Bonnie's argument with Iona, but I can't consider it for long as Harwood is talking again. 'Tell me about your brother's relationship with Iona Byrnes.'

Even though this is what I've been anticipating, the air sticks in my throat like sickly treacle. I swallow loudly. 'Well, to be honest I saw no relationship between them. I mean, my brother, he ...' I pause and take a sip of water.

'Danny barely ever spoke to her even though she was at our house a lot.'

'How did he behave when she was around?' he asks.

As I remember it, Danny was no different with Iona than he was with anyone else, but I do recall the way *she* was with *him*. 'She tried to talk to him a lot,' I say. 'I mean, she was always asking him questions, trying to bring him into the conversation. We all knew better than to push Danny, but I guess Iona showed him a lot of interest.'

'More than other islanders did?'

'Yes. None of the other girls gave him the time of day.'

'Why do you think Iona did, then?'

I shrug. 'At the time I thought she was being friendly.'

'And how did Danny respond to the attention?'

'I think it made him feel awkward. He wouldn't have liked it. And he didn't really engage with her.'

'What about the things that weren't being said?' Harwood asks. 'The mannerisms, behaviours.'

The things that people don't say are, of course, what I've learnt to look out for in my job. But back then? I shake my head as I realise I didn't really notice.

Harwood doesn't speak. Instead he regards me as if he's waiting for more. I recall Bonnie's words about Danny always watching Iona that summer, but I never saw it for myself.

As far as I knew Danny was up in his trees drawing. My mind flits to his book and the pictures inside.

'What is it, Ms Harvey?' the detective asks and I realise my lips have parted.

'He used to draw her a lot,' I admit. 'But then he drew everyone,' I quickly add. 'He had a skill for it, his drawings were so detailed and accurate.'

'But he drew Iona more than anyone else?'

On the pages I had seen, he had. They started on the night of the sleep-out. Iona and Bonnie were depicted in the centre of the page; the small circle of kids gathered around the fire behind were only a blur. He must have spent ages watching her, copying her. 'I suppose,' I say weakly. 'I can't be sure.'

Harwood nods as if this is good enough and my earlier desire to be useful has been replaced by a heavy guilt. He flips over a page in his pad and asks if my family knew Iona before she moved to the island.

'No, of course not.'

He looks up, waits a moment.

'We met her the day she arrived,' I say. 'I remember it.'

Again there is an uncomfortable pause and I mirror his questioning expression. 'Why do you ask?'

The detective shakes his head as if his question isn't relevant, but I can tell it is. For some reason he thinks we might have met her before. 'Tell me about the last few days of your time on the island,' he says. 'Can you recall anything at all that's in any way unusual?'

Apart from the fact we were hauled away in the middle of a storm?

Apart from the fact I saw Iona again when everyone else thought she was gone?

I shake my head, knowing my lie will eat away at me, but I don't know what good can come of the truth. There is nothing useful in telling the detective I believe my father was having an affair with her. Not when Danny has already told them he killed her.

I sink back, drained, as Harwood checks the time on his watch. Hopefully we are done because I have nothing left to give.

But he has another question for me and asks it with his head cocked, his eyebrows furrowed. 'Was Danny ever violent?'

'No,' I say emphatically. I feel the prick of threatening tears. 'Never. He was the gentlest person I know.' My mind skims past the image of the bird, the way he said he'd wrapped it tightly so he didn't drop her. I so wanted to believe him. 'That's why none of this makes sense,' I say.

Harwood nods and sits back in his own sofa. He chews on his bottom lip as he considers whatever it is he wants to tell me. Eventually he says, 'Your brother says he and Miss Byrnes argued the night of September the eighth.'

I try not to react at the date. It was our last whole night, the one before we left.

'He says he pushed her backwards and she fell over a cliff. Is there anything about his story you recall?'

I stare at him in utter shock, shaking my head.

'And Danny tells us this was the last he saw of her,' Harwood says.

I frown. 'But – she was buried in the woods,' I say.

'She was.' He doesn't add any more as this information hangs in the air.

'How is my brother?' I ask. 'Is he doing okay?'

'He seems to be holding up alright.'

'I don't know anything about—' I break off. 'I don't know where he's been living or anything really,' I add, a little more quietly, ashamed for my part in our distance.

'He's been living in Scotland,' the detective tells me as I raise my eyes. 'Quite a solitary lifestyle. He walked into a police station in Girvan yesterday afternoon.'

I nod though I've never heard of the place.

'He paints and makes sculptures, sells them on his website. He's a talented man.'

'He always was,' I say. 'Detective, one of the other policemen asked me about my friendship bracelets ...?'

'Yes. We found one near the body.'

'Oh. I see,' I say, shuddering.

Iona wasn't on my list. She had never bought one and I wonder if this means it was Bonnie's. But Harwood isn't interested and instead he's saying, 'Ms Harvey, your brother has asked to see you.'

'Really?'

'If you would be willing—'

'Yes, God, yes, of course.'

'Good. Good.' He nods as he watches me carefully and I wonder if he is truly happy about this scenario or whether he's still making his mind up about it. 'We can arrange for you to be taken to the station from here if you like.'

Evergreen Island

18 August 1993

After the incident of Danny falling out of the tree, Maria had been torn between putting some distance between her family and Iona, and having the girl sit around her table just so she could watch her more closely. In the end she had settled on the latter. As it would turn out, Maria soon realised the girl's motives were not as they'd first seemed. But, as would also be evident by then, it was far too late to do anything about it. Iona's claws were already firmly hooked into Maria's family.

Bonnie kept her eye on the garden ten minutes before dinner time. Her stomach bubbled with what was no longer a pleasant sensation. She hoped Iona wouldn't turn up. She had prayed her mum wouldn't invite her again and all the muscles in her body felt like they had turned to stone when the invite had been tossed at Iona that morning. Why couldn't her mum see she didn't want her any more? Weren't mums supposed to know when something wasn't right?

Bonnie had had to go along with it, smiling, pretending that Iona's words the day before hadn't knifed into her. If she admitted to anyone, including herself, that they had, she feared her world would blow up.

Shit, she thought, as she saw Iona waltzing in through the side gate. She thought she might throw up. The only thing she could do was forget what Iona said. Push it out of her head. And besides, if she didn't, she might end up losing the only friend she had.

By the time Bonnie got downstairs Iona was already engrossed in another of her dad's stories. Later, during their meal, she would continue to laugh along with something else he was telling them. Bonnie hadn't heard a word of it. She didn't think her mum had either; her attention was elsewhere. It seemed to be on Iona because her eyes kept drifting to her, watching behind her sunglasses.

Suddenly her mum interrupted the story and said, 'We know so little about you, Iona, tell us more about yourself.'

Bonnie could feel her friend stiffen. Iona had told her many things about her life before Evergreen but there was no way she'd bring them up at the dinner table. If she ever did she would deal them out slowly, one card at a time, like she had with Bonnie.

That was how it felt. Iona had a whole stack of gems and she kept them close to her chest, but then every so often, when Bonnie least expected it, she would drop one on her and sit back, waiting for her reaction, like she'd just lit a firework.

Bonnie didn't like that. It wasn't like the beginning of summer any more when she'd felt excited to be part of Iona's world. Now it somehow felt wrong. Like for every card Iona played, Bonnie was supposed to play one too. And every time Iona would point out the differences, how lucky Bonnie was, how grateful she should be.

The day before Iona had been in Bonnie's bedroom, her eyes sweeping around it until she found a snow globe Bonnie had been given a few years ago. Iona cradled it in her hands, releasing her fingers so the globe slid to the edge of her palm. Bonnie's heart fluttered nervously and she wanted to reach out and take it back. Her mum had bought it for her but she knew how stupid she'd sound if she told Iona to be careful, so she did nothing as she watched it roll from side to side.

Iona grinned. 'You know, you really do have too many things,' she said as she stopped rolling it.

Bonnie glanced around her room. She wanted to protest but didn't know what to say when it was probably true. She had always got most things she'd asked for. When she was young, birthdays and Christmases had been stacked with presents. After one of the Stay and Play sessions when she'd shown an interest in one of the toys, her mum had bought her one the very next day.

'Our lives couldn't be more different, could they?' Iona was saying sweetly. 'How did we ever become friends?' she joked before pulling Bonnie into a tight embrace. 'You know, there's something I've been meaning to tell you.'

Bonnie could never have predicted what was about to spill out. If she had, she'd have held a hand over her friend's mouth to stop her from uttering the lies.

Maria was sure Iona looked uncomfortable. All she'd asked was for the girl to tell them about herself, but she was brushing it off with, 'Oh, there's really very little to tell.'

Bonnie had stopped eating, she noticed. Her fork hovered midway to her mouth and now she had put it down on her plate, a piece of pork still speared on the end of it.

All she wanted was to learn more about the girl. Maria felt at a disadvantage not even knowing Iona's background story.

But David had moved the conversation on. Maybe he'd noticed their guest didn't want to talk or maybe he was oblivious. Whatever it was, she finished dinner frustrated.

Helping David stack the plates, she followed him to the kitchen when he started telling her he'd seen Graham that morning. She was biting her lip, ready to interrupt and say that wasn't important when he announced, 'Did you know their house is on the market?'

'What?'

'Susan's idea,' David said as they stopped by the sink. 'You don't know anything about it?'

'No.' Maria shook her head, shocked. 'She hasn't said a word.'

'That's strange.'

It was. She couldn't imagine why her friend hadn't confided in her, but then she'd also noticed Susan wasn't herself of late. 'I'll have to speak to her,' she said as David pulled her in for a hug.

'You're happy here, aren't you?' he asked. 'You wouldn't want to leave?'

'The island?' she gasped. 'No! Never. Why would I?'

'Just checking.' He smiled as he kissed her on the head. 'You seem a little – anxious at the moment.'

Maria shrugged and let her shoulders relax. Suddenly the idea of telling him she needed to know more about her daughter's friend seemed trivial. She watched him go outside and heard him call goodbye to Iona who was strolling out the side gate, then turned to the sink and started scrubbing a pan.

When she caught sight of Bonnie hovering in the doorway Maria laughed. 'You made me jump,' she said, her face falling as Bonnie glared back at her. 'Everything okay?'

'Why did we move here?' Bonnie said suddenly.

'Sorry? What?'

'I said, why did we move here? Why did we come to this island in the first place?'

Maria smiled despite herself. 'I've told you the story before,' she said. 'We wanted to move away from Birmingham and have a different life. Your dad saw the ferry for sale and it was a perfect opportunity—'

'Yeah, yeah, I know that story, but what's the real one?'

'That is the real one,' Maria replied slowly. She glanced quickly at David, who'd appeared behind their daughter, a stack of plates laden in his hands.

'You can both save the rehearsed speech. I'd hoped one of you might be honest with me,' Bonnie snapped before storming out the room.

'What was that about?' David whispered to her. 'You're shaking.'

'I just ...' She looked behind her to the door that Bonnie had just disappeared through. 'I just have this feeling, David, that it's going to come out.'

She had been right. It wouldn't be long before it did come out. What she hadn't been prepared for was the extent to which she would be betrayed.

PRESENT

Chapter Nineteen

I am in the police station waiting room by five to four. My stomach churns as I unsuccessfully try to focus on an old black-and-white film playing on a TV, my insides twisting themselves into knots which pull tighter with every breath.

By the time I am called through to see my brother, I feel like I will throw up, but I grab my bag and coat and follow Harwood down a corridor to a closed door at the far end. I wish I had someone else by my side, but the only person who should be here would never show even if I asked her. Besides, I couldn't bring myself to even tell Bonnie I had willingly agreed to see our brother.

After eighteen years, I only have the pictures in my head of what Danny might look like and most of those, I realise, are simply a version of the twenty-two-year-old I last saw.

'Ms Harvey? Are you okay?' Harwood's voice snaps me back to the present.

'I don't know what to expect,' I admit. 'I haven't seen him in so long. Is he already in there?' I gesture to the room that sits behind the door.

'He is.'

'Will you be with me?'

'No, it'll just be you and Danny. Are you still happy to do this?'

I nod faintly. For all the denials that plague me, the fact is my brother has told the police he pushed Iona over a cliff and potentially I have to accept this.

Harwood pushes the door open and I step inside. There is a man seated at the table, though he isn't anything like the one I imagined. This one is thirty-nine, forty next month. He has short dark hair that is trimmed neatly around his ears and the front sticks up in a small quiff, with only a faint appearance of grey. His wide eyes, a deep chestnut brown, hide behind thin silver frames and I mouth his name like I expect him to shake his head and tell me I have the wrong room.

Danny stands as the door closes behind me. Tears spring to my eyes as I slowly walk over and, by the time I reach the table, he has sat down again. All the time he doesn't take his eyes off me.

I sit silently. My mouth opens but no words come out. I want to tell Danny he looks good. That despite what he says he has done, he looks handsome and smart. His mouth twitches as if he too is searching for the right words and it seems like an eternity before I speak.

'I've missed you,' I say. The words splinter into the air and he raises his eyes above my head as if he's trying to catch them. Really I know he's struggling to hold his emotions, because it's what Danny always did: looked over our heads when he didn't want to cry.

Immediately we are kids again. I am back with my brother in our treehouse, curled up on the cushions, silently doing our own things. Tears roll down my cheeks and I fumble in my bag for a tissue I know I don't have, resorting to wiping them away with my sleeve.

'Thank you for agreeing to see me,' he says finally, in a deep, gravelly voice that doesn't sound right. It isn't the one I've had in my head, but then maybe the years have replaced my memories with false ones.

'Of course. I've wanted to see you for years.'

'I mean for coming now. Now you know what I've done.'

'Oh Danny,' I say, letting out a deep breath. 'You're my brother.'

He looks further away, staring at a point in the corner of the room. I want to reach for his hands but they are out of sight and we fall into another silence that weighs down on me.

I search his face until the boy behind it peeks through. I see him now behind the lines under his eyes, the light stubble on his cheeks.

'I hear you've been living in Scotland?' I ask.

He nods.

'The police mentioned a place called Girvan. I've no idea where that is.'

'It's on the west coast,' Danny tells me. 'I live outside of it.'

I nod, though still none the wiser. 'He said you sell your art online?'

'A little. I make things; paint. I have a website.' He pulls his hands out and lays them on the table. They give him something else to look at as he dips his eyes and studies them.

I must have looked my brother up on the internet hundreds of times, yet never once did I find him.

'I don't use my name,' he says as if reading my thoughts. 'I go by D. Smith.'

'I'll have a look,' I say, unsurprised he's chosen something unrelated. 'It's good to see you, Danny,' I add, 'even with what's happening.' I bow my head, cheeks flushing. 'I always hoped you'd come back, you know.'

Danny breathes in deeply through his nostrils as he sits back and I watch him for a moment, waiting for him to say whatever is clearly on his mind.

'You never wanted to?' I ask.

He shakes his head. 'I couldn't.'

'I hated not knowing where you'd gone. I couldn't bear imagining what had happened to you.' Tears start trickling down my cheeks again and as Danny looks up I notice his hand flinch. His eyes drift to my cheeks, wide with pain, and it looks as if my tears may break him. I quickly wipe them away again. 'Did Mum know where you were?'

'Yes,' he says quietly.

'How come she never said anything to me?' I ask, shocked.

'Don't blame her. She knew I wanted to be on my own. You know I was never very good at living among people.' He gives a small smile. 'She was trying to do right by all of us,' he says. 'Bonnie hated the island, I hated the city ...' he drifts off. 'How is Bonnie?'

'She's fine.' I smile. 'You have two gorgeous nephews. Ben and Harry, they're twelve and ten.'

'I don't expect she's handling any of this ...' He floats a hand off the table and waves it slightly.

'Bonnie's fine,' I say again.

He breathes in deeply and when he releases his breath says, 'They don't believe me.'

'The police?'

'I know they don't.' His eyes search mine imploringly as he drops his voice and adds, 'But I'm telling the truth.'

I edge forward, staring at him intently. His eyes don't flick away; they look at nothing but mine. His gestures imply that he's telling the truth.

'So why do you think they don't believe you?' I ask.

'They're asking me things.' He screws his eyes up now, his forehead creasing. 'Saying she was buried in our garden.'

'It wasn't *in* it,' I say. 'It was in the woods.' I shuffle on the hard chair. 'It was pretty near our garden. Are you saying you didn't know that?'

He gives such a small shake of his head I can't be sure I saw it.

'Danny, what are you saying exactly?'

'Stella, I killed her.' He lowers his voice even further and leans across the table towards me. 'And I should be punished for it.'

'But if you didn't bury—'

'I know what I did,' he interrupts me. 'I know I must have killed her and I need you to make sure they know it too.'

'Danny, what do you mean, you *must have*?' I say.

'Will you just do that for me?' Danny cries. He curls his hand into a fist and thumps it against the table. 'I want to go back to my cell now,' he calls out, looking about, making me think we are being watched. There are no cameras, no flashing lights, yet it is only a matter of seconds before the door opens and Harwood appears.

'Danny—' I start as my brother buries his face in his hands.

'Please. I just want to go now,' he mumbles and refuses to look at me as I'm led out of the room.

Chapter Twenty

'He says he thinks he must have done it,' I say on the phone to Bonnie after Harwood drops me back at the interview suite. I leap out of the way as a car swerves close to the kerb, sending a puddle splashing towards me.

'I can't believe you went to see him. You said you wouldn't.'

'No,' I say, 'I don't think I ever did. But that's not the point. The point is he doesn't know, Bon. He says he *thinks* he must have. Not that he *did*. And not only that, he says he didn't bury her.' I don't bother admitting he didn't tell me this outright.

'So why the hell would he confess? Of course he did it, he's going to say anything to get out of it now. He's scared.'

'He's not trying to get out of it, he wants me to get the police to believe him.'

'So, what's the problem?' she cries out. 'Tell them that and we can all move on with our lives.'

I sigh as I open my car door and climb in. 'Bonnie, isn't there any part of you that wants to believe he might be innocent?'

She laughs. 'Do you really think I want to live with the fact my brother killed my best friend? Only the odds aren't exactly stacked in his favour right now, are they? Think back,' she goes on. 'Remember all the times he's done something that wasn't right—' Her voice suddenly cuts out and when I look down at my phone I see my battery is dead.

I drive straight to Bonnie's. She leads me down the hall, but on the way I pass Luke lying on a sofa in the living room. 'Are you feeling better?' I ask as I pause in the doorway.

Luke pushes himself up and turns around to look at me. 'Oh, hey Stella.' His eyes flick to Bonnie who has stopped beside me, irritation bubbling off her.

'Come on,' she snaps as she pulls my arm and drags me through to the back. 'He's watching TV, we can sit in here instead.'

'What does Luke think?' I ask as she unscrews a bottle of lemonade and pours us both a glass.

Bonnie shrugs. 'I don't know,' she says, handing me a drink. Her hand is shaking, I notice, only slightly but it is there.

'What's happened?'

'We had an argument. Fantastic timing, isn't it?' She rolls her eyes and walks over to the sofa, expecting me to follow. 'My whole life is cracking apart and to top it off my husband and I fall out.'

I sigh as I sit down next to her.

'I can't stop thinking of the last time I saw Iona,' Bonnie says. 'It plays on a loop in my head.'

I open my mouth to ask her about it but already she's going on, 'We used to talk about everything.' Tears glisten in her eyes, but when she catches me looking she turns away.

'You saw how close we were,' she says. 'I never had a better friend than Iona. I loved her.'

'I know you were close, Bonnie,' I say softly, thinking back to how Bonnie always wanted her for herself. I'd once watched, mesmerised by the way their arms moved in sync as they cut their food. The time I'd sat in the seat next to Iona, Bonnie had roughly dragged me out of it. I was never allowed near her Sindy dolls when we were younger, and when she found me trying on her roller boots she'd screamed so loudly Mum had raced in from the bottom of the garden, no doubt expecting to see one of us dead on the floor.

I need to remember that, however callous my sister is being over Danny, Iona was once a good friend so this must be hitting Bonnie doubly hard.

'I hated the way the police were asking about our friendship, trying to pick it apart. I mean, I know it was only a few months ...' Bonnie trails off.

'What did they ask you?' I say and she outlines their questions which were similar to the ones Harwood asked me.

Bonnie downs the dregs of her lemonade and shakes her glass as if she's contemplating a top-up. Her actions are more frantic than usual, though I put it down to the questioning.

'I didn't tell them about our argument,' she says, setting the glass firmly on the side table. 'It wasn't important.' She doesn't look to me for confirmation so I don't give any. After all, there were things I kept to myself too. Neither of us, it seems, has been completely honest.

'It was so stupid,' she mutters, opening the bottle again and topping up her glass.

I get the impression she wants me to ask her what it was about but when I do, she snaps, 'I just told you it wasn't important.' She glares at me as if goading a reaction, but I just shrug. 'What did they ask you anyway?' she says, and almost scornfully adds, 'You didn't even know her that well.'

'That's what I told them. All I could say was what little I did know.'

'Which was?'

'The basics. That she was over as part of her university degree—'

Bonnie laughs suddenly and then says, more quietly, 'That wasn't even true.'

'What do you mean?'

'She didn't go to university.' She studies me carefully, looking pleased that she's caught me out, but as I stare back at her, incredulous, her expression changes. 'She just said she did,' she adds.

'But ...' My eyes follow Bonnie as she pulls herself off the sofa. 'I don't understand. What did she come to the island for, then?'

She shrugs and says, 'She liked to tell stories. That was just one of them. Anyway, I need the toilet.'

'Bon,' I call as she disappears. I wait for her to come back and when she does she asks me if I've spoken to Dad. I shake my head, refusing to let her determine the conversation. 'You didn't answer my question. Why did she come to the island if it wasn't for part of a course?'

Bonnie drops on to the sofa, hunching her body stiffly as she stares out of the patio doors. 'I don't have a clue why she came.'

Sometimes when people are lying they change positions quickly. Nerves make people fidget. I have learnt to spot the ones whose heads suddenly turn in a different direction. But I also notice the ones who don't move at all. It means they are preparing themselves for confrontation. And as Bonnie is immobile, my guess is she knows exactly why Iona came to Evergreen.

But maybe it's not relevant, I think, knowing better than anyone that pushing her will get me nowhere. It's been a long day, and as I haven't been home for the last two nights, I tell her I need to go after half an hour. I'm passing the living room when Luke shoots off the sofa and follows me to the door. 'I'm going to the shop,' he tells Bonnie, jangling his car keys in one hand. I kiss my sister on the cheek and say I'll call in the morning, then follow Luke out of the house.

'What's happening with you both?' I ask as we walk to the end of their drive.

Luke glances behind him. 'She won't talk to me. She didn't even tell me about your brother until she'd already been questioned by the police.'

'You're kidding?'

He shakes his head. 'She's told me I can't mention it to the boys, which is madness, because at some point they'll find out and then they'll be furious we've kept it from them.'

'I agree. They should know what's happening, and preferably before one of their friends says something.'

'She doesn't want to talk about Danny, at least not to me.' He gives me a sideways glance but I shake my head.

'You're not the only one.'

'Yeah, well. She keeps shutting me out and ignoring everything, and to be honest, Stella—' He breaks off and looks back at the house again. 'To be honest, I'm sick of trying.'

'Oh Luke, don't say that.'

'It's true. She's never wanted me to be there for her. It's always you.'

I can't argue with this. Bonnie has often reminded me, 'Blood is thicker than water.' The last time she said it was when I sat with her in rehab on the day she'd been released. 'I'm glad you're here, Stella,' she'd said. Her small suitcase was packed and ready by her feet. Her eyes were wide as they gazed up at me like I was the older sister. She looked like a child, I remember, as we both sat there with renewed optimism that this time would be the last we'd see of the place.

'Where else would I be?' I said. I wasn't surprised when it was me she'd called to pick her up and take her home. It was always me. Never Luke.

'Who else would I ask?' she'd said in return.

I wish I could remind her that blood is thicker than water when it comes to Danny, too.

Luke's keys jangle loudly in his hand. 'You know, it was never the case I didn't want to be there,' he tells me.

'I know that,' I assure him, though I hate the way he talks in the past tense.

He looks down at his feet, kicking a stone away. 'I think she's been drinking,' he says. 'Of course, I don't know for sure because she won't admit it to me and she does a bloody good job of hiding it.'

'Shit. Shit.' I look up at the sky. I could see there was something in her actions tonight but I hadn't wanted to go there.

'I'm sorry, Stella, but I can't—' He shakes his head and I catch a tear glistening in the corner of his eye. 'I know you don't need this right now.'

Over the years there have been many occasions when I've walked away from my sister with an unsettling sense that things weren't right. In the early weeks of Bonnie being sober, I was constantly on edge. I knew when she'd snuck in a drink because I could read the signs clearly. Guilt was etched on her face, her fingers jittering with fear that she'd be caught out. As the years passed, and she subsequently stopped drinking, it's become harder to read, though I've never stopped looking.

Any other time I would have been paying more attention.

I slam my front door behind me, furious with myself and even more so with Bonnie. The last thing I need is for all my concentration to be focused on her and I hate that it even crosses my mind that this is why she's doing it. Danny is the one who needs me right now.

I throw myself on to my bed, lying on my back, and in each direction I look, photos of the past peer back at me.

Me and Mum on the beach, our hair whipped up above our heads in the wind. We are laughing as we look at each other.

Dad and I on the jetty, him crouching down to my height, his checked cap on, our cheeks pressed together, our smiles wide. We both hold an ice-cream and I have a splodge of his on the end of my nose from where he tapped me with it.

In nearly all the pictures Dad is wearing his cap – the one Mum had bought him one birthday and he proclaimed he would never take off. He wore that cap every day as far as I remember. He was wearing it the time I saw him with Iona and somehow this makes his deceit much worse.

I turn away, training my eyes on a different photo that sits on a shelf the other side of the room. This one's of me and Jill, our arms linked tightly through each other's to protect a bond we would never break.

I move on quickly, my eyes flicking along the shelf.

Bonnie, Danny and me all lined up stiffly beside each other like we had nothing in common apart from the fact we were siblings.

Next to it, Danny and me hanging out of the treehouse. My face full of laughter at something Mum must have said. Danny's is a blank as it always was, his eyes staring far into the distance.

I curl on to my side, pulling up my knees and wrapping my arms around them, closing my eyes so I don't have to look at the pictures any more. Not when they make the walls close in on me until I can't breathe.

And not for the first time, I envy my sister for having a drug to clutch on to.

The following morning I call Dad because we need to have a conversation about Danny. 'It's Stella,' I say as Olivia picks up.

'Oh, Stella ...' My name comes out long and painful, like she's doubled over in shock. 'The police were here. They want to question your father. Your brother's been arrested for murder.'

'I know. That's why I'm calling.'

'I told them absolutely no way is he speaking to them, he isn't well. He's got dementia,' she screams like this is something I don't know. 'They're saying they can get a doctor in there and another adult. But not me. They say it should be someone else.'

'Have you spoken to Dad about it?' I ask.

'He's unclear and so vague. I think he frustrated them.'

'But what's he said to you?'

'Nothing. He's not talking about it. Every time I try he shuts down, and I don't know—' She breaks off, then adds more quietly, 'I don't know if he's doing it on purpose.'

'Can I speak to him?'

'No,' she says, a little too sharply, but then she goes on. 'As I said, he's not well. He hasn't got up yet. He's drained.' We fall into a silence before Olivia says, 'If your brother – if he did what he says he has, then David must have known. He'd have known, wouldn't he?'

'I don't know,' I say, though I'm also sure he must have. 'But I think there's a chance Danny didn't do it.'

'I don't know what else to do,' Olivia goes on like she hasn't heard me, and I realise it's the first time I've heard a side of her that needs reassurance from me, that's willing to show a weakness.

Were it over anything else I would have revelled in the moment, but I find myself telling her everything will be okay, asking her to get Dad to call me as soon as he's up to it.

I hang up but I can't settle. It's Friday and I'm due in the office late morning for my rearranged clients that I'd pushed to the end of the week.

But there are too many things I can't seem to straighten in my head. I pace back and forth in my kitchen, making breakfast, forgetting what I'm doing midway through a task. I worry what good I'll be to my clients, since my mind keeps lingering on what Bonnie told me. *Iona liked to make up stories.*

I have begun to consider that if Iona didn't come to Evergreen to study, she must have come for something else important.

Eventually I make the decision to drive to Dad's when I finish work. We need to have a conversation face-to-face, because he's the only one who can give me the missing jigsaw pieces.

Evergreen Island

23 August 1993

Maria would not give up. Despite Iona's deflection, she would make it her business to know more about the girl. Even then she knew that finding out what Iona was doing on their island would be paramount to keeping her family safe.

But towards the end of August she was still seeking a glimmer of insight. Her day had started by wandering along the harbour on the mainland, people-watching, looking at the expensive yachts and perusing the shops. She had gone to the mainland alone and been lost in her thoughts when she spotted Iona dipping into a clothes shop on one of the backstreets. She had another girl in tow, but from where she stood Maria couldn't see who it was. It was funny that her first thought strayed to Bonnie as she wondered what her daughter was doing without her friend.

Despite Danny's suggestion that Bonnie wasn't happy in her company, her daughter had slunk into the girl's shadow again, though the friendship did seem more lopsided than when it had started.

Maria found herself strolling to the shop, creeping into the corner of it, where she hovered, surprised to see Iona having an intense discussion with Tess Carlton. Her hiding, eavesdropping, was a ridiculous charade and if the girls spotted her she'd have to pretend she'd been there all along, but she couldn't help listening to snatches of their conversation over the music.

'I'm so glad we're good friends,' Iona said, linking her arm through the young girl's as she yanked clothes on their hangers along the rail. 'Isn't it nice to have someone to talk to about everything?'

Maria felt herself bristle as Tess simpered with joy. She'd watched the same gestures sprinkle like confetti over Bonnie.

'You can tell they haven't a clue what to do with him,' Iona went on.

Maria's hands started to tingle and her cheeks burned. 'He completely creeps me out, to be honest. I can't bear the way he looks at me over the table. I feel sorry for Bonnie, I really do, but—' Iona broke off. 'I suppose you can't always choose your family, can you?' she said boldly.

Maria felt the blood draining from her.

'It was so funny what happened in the cave, wasn't it?' Iona went on.

'I don't know, he looked really upset,' Tess replied.

'Yes, well,' Iona brushed her off. 'I think he deserved to be taught a lesson, though I'm not sure it's worked. Every time I look around, he's there, and it always makes me so nervous when I suddenly catch him, like he's creeping up on me.'

Tess didn't answer.

'Anyway, much more important than that. When were you going to tell me you were leaving the island?'

Maria froze, as it appeared had Tess. 'What do you mean?' she asked.

'Your house is for sale. Didn't you know?'

Maria imagined Tess shaking her head. Susan had only recently confirmed it to her best friend – how the hell had Iona heard? It was clear Susan hadn't wanted to talk about it, which was why they'd not put a board outside the house.

'It would be a shame if you left, don't you think? Especially now we're such good friends.'

'Well, I suppose ...' Tess was clearly as confused as Maria. What was Iona up to? Maria was certain this bizarre friendship had absolutely nothing to do with Iona wanting Tess to stay.

'Maybe you could have a word ...' Iona was saying when Maria stumbled forward, colliding with a rail as she did so. She stopped quickly, grabbing on to it to steady herself. The girls hadn't noticed, but when the door pinged open and a woman entered, she took the chance to flee before they saw her. Her heart was in her mouth as she ran to the ferry, so betrayed by the girl she'd invited to sit around her dining table every night.

Danny had taken his drawing pad and pencils and headed towards the slip of beach that ran alongside Pinecliff Walk. He knew the small clearing was where Stella and Jill liked to meet. They called it their secret place, even though anyone could find it. Mostly no one wandered past because it wasn't on a man-made path, and today Stella was at home so he knew he wouldn't be disturbing her.

He liked the spot, too. Right by the edge of the cliff, there was a great view of the sea and the other islands. It was a good place to go when he needed to get away completely.

Only today, just as he was getting his pencils out of their case, he heard a sound behind him. By instinct he scrambled into the gorse. He knew it was probably a stupid thing to do, but often he did these things without thinking.

His heart somersaulted when he spotted Iona. She must have come back on the last ferry. He'd watched her go that morning, and now she was strolling along, eyes hidden behind dark glasses, humming an unrecognisable tune.

He pulled back deeper, praying she wouldn't see him. He'd tried to be more careful since he'd fallen out of the tree. She carried on walking towards him and then, as she drew near, she crouched down and stopped humming.

Danny held his breath, but she must be able to hear it coming out short and sharp. He waited for her to pull back the branches and demand he tell her why he was watching her again.

But then she stood, sliding her glasses on to the top of her head, smiling that beautifully weird smile of hers that at first he'd found so difficult to draw.

He'd got it now, though. He'd learnt just to make the eyes much darker so you couldn't see into her. How to twist the lips at a slight angle and then the resemblance was uncanny. Danny wondered whether anyone else saw as many faces as he did, but he had captured every one of hers in his book.

'I hope you're not following me,' she said, which was clearly absurd when he'd been there first.

David pulled out the chair beside him for Iona. She was such a pleasantly warm girl. He enjoyed her company and had been about to ask after her day on the mainland when Maria leant over the table and said, 'David, can you light the candles?'

He smiled at his wife as he looked up, but she was glaring back at him. She'd been in a funny mood for the last couple of weeks and he was tired of it. It was summer, their favourite time of year, and they should be happy. If she didn't want Iona to join the family every night, which he suspected was her issue, then why didn't she just say so?

He lit the wicks as Maria ladled chilli into Stella's bowl, passing the spoon to Bonnie. Iona must be able to sense the frostiness, but she was covering it up nicely with a level of maturity his wife wasn't showing.

Picking up the bottle of wine, he popped out the cork and sniffed it though he had no idea what it should smell of. As soon as he placed the bottle on the table, Iona took it and poured herself a large glass.

Out of the corner of his eye he caught Maria's intense stare. And now Bonnie, who was glowering at her friend's glass. David opened his mouth to tell Bonnie she could try a little drop if she liked, but something stopped him. Maybe it would only bring attention to the age difference, and he didn't want to encourage it.

Instead he settled in to enjoy his meal when Maria suddenly demanded across the table, 'Tell us where you were living before you moved here, Iona?'

For heaven's sake. She was on that again.

To eliminate any atmosphere, he played along. 'Maria's right. We know nothing about your family.' He smiled warmly as the pinkness on Iona's neck turned a hue darker.

'My mother moved around a lot since I was five,' Iona said.

'Like a traveller?' Stella piped up.

'Yeah, something like that.'

'Do you live in homes?'

'Of course they live in homes,' Maria snapped. She was still staring at Iona, and David felt incredibly uncomfortable with the turn the conversation had taken.

'Lots of travellers live in caravans,' Stella went on regardless.

'Well, I lived in a house, but it was nothing like this.' Iona had leant in towards Stella now. 'Nothing at all as grand as the one you and your brother and sister have all been brought up in.'

David cocked his head. It sounded like there was a hint of jealousy, but then it wasn't hard to see why.

'No, we lived in places *much* worse than this,' Iona was stating.

'Did your mum miss you when you came here?' Stella asked, and Iona laughed loudly while Bonnie jolted upright, sitting so tensely that only her hands moved as they scooped up a forkful of peas that all tumbled back on to the plate.

'No, I don't think Mum missed me one bit,' Iona said, smiling, which he found an odd thing to do given what she'd said. 'My mother is not a nice woman. She's done things you would never believe.'

'Oh?' Stella's eyes widened and David decided to cut in before Iona said something inappropriate for a family dinner.

'So where do you come from originally?' he asked.

There was a pause and he waited, slightly apprehensively now if he were being honest.

When she turned to him she flashed another smile and said, 'Birmingham, David. I come from Birmingham.'

'Oh, how lovely.' He smiled back, trying to avoid looking at Maria. He knew what would be racing through his wife's mind and he'd have to defuse it later when she came to him, panicked.

They had left Birmingham and Maria's mother, Joy, behind them seventeen years ago and if he never saw that place again it would still be too soon. He felt a slither of unease but he shook it off. This was Iona, after all. He couldn't possibly have anything to worry about.

PRESENT

Chapter Twenty-One

I have managed to squeeze in four sets of clients back-to-back, but it means that by the time I get in the car to drive to Dad's, I could do with climbing into bed instead. On the way I mull over whether *I* need to talk to someone, as Tanya suggested after she'd taken one look at my pale and strained face.

I'd agreed that it would ease my burden, but when she told me she'd found the number of my one-time counsellor I brushed off the suggestion. I don't have the energy or the inclination to open up an entire can of worms. If I talk to anyone it has to be someone who at least knows part of the recent story. And there is only one person who springs to mind.

Before I can give it too much consideration, I press the number for the only other person who knows as much as I do right now.

'Hey Stella, it's good to hear from you,' Freya answers. 'I'm in the middle of something, but how are you doing?'

'Fine,' I say automatically, before admitting, 'Actually I'm not.' My fingers tug at a loose thread on the bottom of my cardigan as the other hand taps against the steering wheel.

'Do you want to tell me?' she says after a beat. 'Maybe we could meet later?'

No. Because you're a journalist and I shouldn't trust you.

Yes. Because I don't know who else to turn to.

I ignore her suggestion to meet and say, 'I went to see Danny yesterday.'

'Oh?' Her interest is piqued.

'He looks different to how I imagined he would. So much better.'

'Well, that's good,' she says evenly. 'Did he tell you what happened?'

'No. Well ...' I hesitate. 'He says the police don't believe him.'

I hear her suck in a breath. 'Interesting.'

'I haven't a clue what to think.'

'But Danny still says he killed her?'

I don't answer her question, but say instead, 'They asked me lots of questions about Iona. It got me thinking that there's more to her than we knew.'

'Right ...' Freya answers cautiously.

'Forget I said anything. I've just got too many things going on in my head.'

I hear her tapping on a keyboard. 'Are you writing down what I'm saying?'

'What? No. Of course not. I'm sorry, I'm trying to get something done for my boss. Sorry. Where were we? So did Danny say he killed her?'

I sigh. 'What he actually said was that he had to have.'

'What does he mean by that?'

'I don't know,' I say. 'I wish I did.'

'I'm sorry, Stella. I'm going to have to call you back. Is that okay?'

'Sure,' I say, but she's already hung up, leaving me feeling I was wrong to think I could confide in her.

I feel even more frustrated and despondent by the time I reach Dad's. He opens the door, wearing a thin cotton blue dressing gown that comes to his knees, revealing his striped pyjamas beneath. He looks at me blankly and shakes his head, and for a moment we stand awkwardly in the doorway.

'Dad, it's five p.m. You're still not dressed,' I say gently.

'You must be here too early. I didn't think you were coming until later.'

'I didn't say I was coming. Can I come in?' I nod behind him and he opens the door wider and lets me through while he lingers by the bottom of the stairs. 'Maybe that's why you're surprised to see me?' I say hopefully, as he continues to watch me cautiously.

He shakes his head again as I wander past. My heart thumps as I take a breath, considering whether I need to tell him who I am, when he suddenly cries out, 'Stella!'

'Yes, Dad?' When I turn he is smiling at me and still I feel my skin tingle each time this happens. 'Shall I make us a cup of tea?' I ask, smiling back. 'I take it you've had your lunch?'

'I, erm . . .' He frowns.

'Don't worry.' My heart splinters. 'Shall I make a sandwich anyway?'

'No. Don't bother, love, I'm not hungry.' He holds a hand against his flat stomach.

'So what time were you supposed to be here, then?' he asks as he follows me into the kitchen and watches me boil the kettle.

'I didn't say, Dad. This is just an extra visit.'

'Oh. Okay.'

'How are you feeling? Olivia says you haven't been well. Is it a stomach bug?'

'Yes, love, probably. I can't stop sleeping and my head's all fuzzy.' His hands shake as they rest on the table. When the tea is made I pass him a mug and sit down next to him, taking his hands in my own, and for a moment all I can think is that there are so many years we will never claw back, and is it now far too late?

'It's a lovely day,' I say, nodding outdoors. 'Cold, but at least it's stopped raining.'

He gazes out of his back door at the neat little garden beyond. 'I had the, erm ...' he waggles a finger as he searches for the word '... you know, the man here yesterday.'

'Man?'

'Yes.' He looks agitated. 'He wasn't wearing a uniform. You know what I mean.'

'A policeman?'

'Yes.' He slaps his hand back down on the table. 'A policeman was here yesterday wanting to talk to me.'

'Did he ask you any questions?' I say.

'No, love.' Dad screws his eyes up as if I must have known this. 'I wasn't well.'

'Do you know what they want to talk to you about?'

He raises his shoulders, splaying his hands out in front of him.

'I think it's about Danny,' I tell him. 'And the body they found on the island.'

'Do you remember that treehouse I built for you?' Dad breaks into a smile. 'I started thinking about that for some reason.'

'I remember it.' I smile sadly.

'It took me a week and you and Danny were so impatient for it to be ready. I put it in the oak tree,' he says. 'I expect it's still there.'

'I expect so,' I say, my heart sinking again.

'You spent hours in it. Danny too. He was always up a tree,' he says, but the light has faded from his eyes. 'He spent more time up there than on the ground. Your mum always thought it best to leave him but I wasn't so sure.'

'Really?' I ask, intrigued by this difference of opinion that I never remember seeing.

'She over-compensated for both of them,' he murmurs, adding in an even softer voice, 'especially Bonnie.'

'How do you mean, Dad?' I say and he looks up at me sharply, like he didn't realise he was speaking aloud.

'She was always a good mother,' he tells me. 'She adored all three of you. Above anything you mustn't ever forget that.'

I smile and lower my eyes. 'I think the police wanted to talk to you about Danny.'

Dad studies his thin fingers which are covered in papery skin and dotted with too many sunspots.

'Do you know anything?' I ask, reaching out for one of his hands when they start to shake again, his fingers making tiny taps on the table. 'About what happened to Iona?'

His eyes begin to water and I squeeze his hand gently. 'She was found. On the island,' he says.

'I know, but do you know any more?' I persist. 'Do you think Danny had anything to do with it?'

He looks up at me, his lips parted, as he groans, 'Ohhh. Oh dear, Stella. I don't know. I think maybe. I think maybe he did.'

'Oh.' I pull my hand away, my pulse racing wildly. Now that he's said it I realise it is so far from what I expected.

Dad frowns, his brows furrowed deeply, and he circles his fingers on the table like he wants to add something but he doesn't have the words. When he does, it's a non sequitur. 'I used to love my ferry. I was very happy on that boat.'

'You were, Dad.' My words are no more than a whisper. 'I used to come and meet you when you came back. I'd wait at the end of the jetty for you.'

'You were always there. Waiting for me. We were very happy there once,' he says. 'You more than anyone. You were born on that island.'

'I know. Annie Webb delivered me.' I smile at the memory of the story I always begged my parents to keep telling me. 'You said we would never have made it to the mainland.'

My dad's shoulders rise ever so slightly.

'Thank goodness she was there,' I go on. 'Her being a midwife.'

'Annie was always there,' my dad says, but he is no longer wistful as he stares at the table, and for a moment I think I've lost him until he adds, 'We would never have gone in the first place if it wasn't for her.'

'You knew Annie before you went to Evergreen?' I ask, completely surprised.

'No, maybe it wasn't her doing,' he continues, circling a finger anxiously on the table as he ignores me, clearly irritated by whatever thought has come into his head. 'It was Joy's doing.'

'Gran?' I ask.

Dad shrugs. 'Yes, but that's something you'd have to ask your mum about.'

'But I can't, Dad,' I say, leaning towards him. 'I can't ask Mum any more, can I?'

He purses his lips. 'I don't suppose you should, anyway.' He sits back and looks at me. 'How is she doing? Is she well?'

'She's ...' I shake my head. 'Dad, she's ...'

'I am sorry about what happened between her and me,' he says quietly. 'I never wanted to see her hurt. I never wanted any of it to turn out like it did.'

'Oh, Dad. What happened to us?' I say, tears pooling in my eyes now.

'I loved her very much, you know.' He frowns, asking, 'Are you staying for tea? I imagine Olivia will be back soon.'

I glance at my watch as Dad gets up and walks to the sink, looking out at the back garden. 'Dad, you remember Iona, don't you?' I say.

'Yes,' he answers quietly.

'Do you know why Iona really came to Evergreen? I know she wasn't at university.' I watch him closely, certain I can see his shoulders tighten.

'She came looking for someone,' he says. 'But I don't believe she ever found them.'

'Who was she looking for?'

Dad shakes his head. When he turns he looks agitated, pressing the heel of his hand into the edge of the sink.

'None of that matters any longer,' he says. 'It was all such a long time ago.'

'Some things do matter,' I say and he looks at me quizzically. 'I saw you, Dad,' I blurt as my client's words come back to me. *I can't not know it now, can I?* 'I saw you with her,' I go on, less sure. 'Were you and Iona – were you having an affair?'

Dad stares at me, incredulous. 'What? No!' he cries. 'How could you even ...' He shakes his head, almost manically, his eyes wide as he pushes himself up, scanning the room like a frightened child. 'Where's Olivia?'

'I'm sorry,' I say, as I stand up too and approach him. 'I didn't mean to upset you.'

He stalks out of the kitchen and I quickly follow, finding him standing by the front door, his fingers curling and uncurling around the bottom of the banister. 'I don't ...' He looks up the stairs and then back at me, his eyes searching for something, but I don't know what to give him. 'I don't know what I'm doing,' he says eventually, and he looks so scared.

I take both his hands and squeeze them between my own. 'It'll be okay,' I tell him, and as he keeps watching me I feel the weight of what he's expecting – that somehow I can make this better.

Suddenly a key turns in the lock and the front door swings open. Her perfume wafts in before she does. The familiar scent of Poison that always catches in my throat.

Olivia steps inside and slams the door shut, her eyes flicking between me and Dad and then trailing down to our clasped hands. 'What's happened?' she says, dropping her handbag and grasping my dad's elbow. She twists him to face her in a practised manoeuvre that leaves us automatically letting go of each other. She's got him again.

'What's going on, David?' she demands.

Olivia and I both watch in horror as a tear escapes the corner of his eye and rolls down his cheek.

'Will one of you tell me what the hell's going on?' she demands, turning to me.

'I just came to speak to my dad.'

'David, why don't you go and get yourself dressed.' He nods and obligingly makes his way up the stairs. Olivia continues to glare.

'I needed to talk to him.'

'You're worse than the police,' she hisses. 'Hounding him.'

'His son's in prison,' I cry. 'Having confessed to murder. I need to know what Dad knows.'

'I have doctors and solicitors working for your father,' she says flatly. 'Clearly he isn't in a state to get hauled into their stations and sit there for hours being asked about something that happened twenty-five bloody years ago. He can't remember my *name* some days,' she adds, slapping a hand against her chest.

'But he does remember the past,' I say. 'And you know that.'

*

Back in the car I slam my palms hard against the steering wheel, accidentally hitting the horn, which makes an old lady stop and look at me. I ignore her as I fling my head against the headrest and close my eyes. My teeth are gritted so tightly my jaw aches.

As I reach into my pockets for my phone, my hand brushes against the piece of paper that is still inside. I pull it out, unfolding it.

STOP DIGGING. YOU WON'T LIKE WHAT YOU FIND.

The warning doesn't make sense. If someone knew my brother had killed Iona, then why would they want to keep it a secret? Why warn me off and not go straight to the police?

I glance up, looking out of the front windscreen. Unless there's something else they don't want me finding out.

Chapter Twenty-Two

Early Saturday morning I am called back into the interview suite to see Detective Harwood and this time he seems more agitated. 'Your brother is adamant he killed Ms Byrnes,' he tells me. Like me, he is grappling for the truth but can't quite get to it, and he's feeling the pressure.

Danny has now been held for nearly forty-eight hours and my limited online research tells me they only have ninety-six in which to question him. This means by Monday morning they need to either charge my brother or let him go.

'He says he arranged to meet her at a point on the island by the edge of a cliff.' Harwood passes a map of Evergreen to me, prodding his pen at a spot. I pull it closer and peer at the mark his pen has left, taking a deep breath and then passing it back to him.

'I know exactly where that cliff is.'

'Why do you think he might have arranged to meet her there?'

'I can't think why,' I say, refusing to acknowledge it's the exact spot I used to meet Jill. Our secret place. The only reason I can think of is that Danny didn't want to be seen.

But it is also, of course, the spot where I saw my dad and Iona, and an unwanted image of them flashes in my head. Even when I blink it doesn't disappear. Dad was so adamant yesterday that he didn't have an affair. And yet I saw him – I'm sure I did. I see his cap vividly and it is this I keep coming back to.

'Daniel says this is where he and Ms Byrnes fought and then he shoved her. He saw Iona fall back over the edge.' He prods again at the map; this time his pen marks a spot on the thin stretch of beach below.

'But what your brother describes is inconsistent with what we know. And where she was found. This area, here.' He points to the spot just outside my house where Iona's body was dug up. This time he uses his finger to circle around it. 'Who had access to it?'

'Well – everyone,' I say. 'It's on the edge of the woods. Anyone could go there if they wanted: islanders, visitors ...' I trail off.

'So day visitors would pass by the end of your back garden?'

'No, I said they *could*. There was access to it. But they rarely did, and usually it would have been because they'd got lost. The people that came to the house that way were friends, though most of the islanders used the gate. I think it seemed like a more polite entrance. Mum preferred it.'

Harwood nods, though I sense his impatience. 'So, who in particular do you recall coming to the house via the woods?'

'Annie Webb and Susan Carlton usually, but they lived in that direction.'

'Anyone else?' he asks.

'Not that I recall.'

'Did anyone used to spend a lot of time there?'

I shake my head.

'Or avoid it?'

'No.' I look at him quizzically.

'Did either of your parents have a strong affinity with the place?'

'It was on the edge of our garden,' I say. 'But neither of them went there more than anywhere else.'

Harwood nods but I can see he isn't getting what he wants. 'What about over these last few days? You've just been back to the island, did you see anyone hanging around there more than you'd think usual?'

'There were loads of people there the day we all found out it was Iona, a huge crowd,' I say.

'Who did you recognise?'

I list the group lingering by the trees: 'Annie Webb, Ruth Taylor, Susan and Graham Carlton, only Graham . . .' I falter as I recall it '. . . he didn't stay. I was going to talk to him but he'd already walked off.'

'Okay.' Harwood nods, watching me carefully, as if this is at least a nugget of interest. 'Was anyone in particular missing from the crowd?'

'Bob Taylor wasn't there. Neither was Emma Fisher, though I saw her right after in the village with her daughter. They were having an argument,' I add. 'I don't know what about.'

'Great. This is all very helpful, Stella,' he tells me, though his face is deadpan and I'm not entirely sure it's getting him anywhere.

'Also ...' I pause, still unsure if I want to pass on this information. 'Someone sent me a note. With everything that happened with Danny, I forgot to tell you about it on Thursday. It told me to stop digging.'

'Do you still have it?' He looks up as I dip into my coat pocket and pull it out.

An hour and a half later I have finally finished answering the detective's questions. I tell him I need the toilet, so we say goodbye and I turn right, passing the hushed voices spilling out from other rooms. My mind is so focused on what he has asked, and what he may do with the note, that it's not until I'm heading for the exit I suddenly stop.

'... not just even the fact the body was found somewhere else entirely,' a man is saying. I duck back against the wall, making sure I'm out of sight. They must be talking about

Iona but their words are low and I strain to hear only snatches of the conversation.

'... injuries from falling could have killed her ...'

'... not sure?'

'No. Doesn't seem like it ...' someone says before their voices fade. I press closer.

'... to make it look like she hit a rock?'

'Yes. More like a blunt instrument.'

A door at the far end bangs and a woman comes out, eyeing me suspiciously. I peel myself away and follow her to the main door.

Is this why Harwood thinks Danny isn't guilty? Do they know more that means his story doesn't stack up?

My heart is hammering as I step outside and on to the street. The sun is trying to break through the clouds, but the wind has picked up. I wrap my coat more tightly around me. The forecast for the next few days isn't good. Storms are coming, they say, though right now the white clouds don't seem to threaten rain.

From inside my bag my phone is ringing and Freya's number flashes. 'I've just had an interesting conversation,' she tells me before I've had the chance to speak.

'Really?' I rub a hand over my sleep-deprived eyes, dodging a cyclist who swerves on to the pavement and then back on to the road without any awareness.

'With Iona's mother.'

'Oh?' I stop short. There was only one time I remember Iona mentioning her mum and her words had been so cold they'd made me shudder. The same mother who hadn't noticed her daughter was missing for twenty-five years.

'I'm going to meet her,' Freya says excitedly. 'I'm catching the train up now. I get the sense there's something she's holding back on. I'm hoping she might tell me, but—' Freya breaks off. 'Well, to be honest, I don't know how much I can trust what she's saying, and I thought you might like to come.'

My stomach flutters with the thought of meeting the woman who could tell me more than most about Iona. She's become something of an enigma, and if there's anything that can help me piece together what happened between her and Danny it's worth pursuing. Especially if my brother's version of the night she died isn't accurate. 'Okay. I'll come,' I say quickly.

'Great. I'll meet you at New Street station at three.'

'New Street? Where's that?'

'It's where Iona's mother lives,' she says. 'Birmingham.'

Chapter Twenty-Three

Freya told me she'd arranged to meet Iona's mother, Ange, in a pub in Balsall Heath. When she added that she didn't fancy walking into a bar like that on her own, I looked it up on my phone, silently agreeing with her while wondering why the area, Balsall Heath, rang a bell.

Though my parents were originally from Birmingham, they never said much about their lives before moving to the island. What little I knew was that they'd bought their first house in Shirley, not far from Gran's house where Mum had grown up. With their having no interest in returning, it meant I'd never visited myself.

I drive to New Street where I meet Freya, whose excitement is bubbling off her. She strides across the station, looking for the taxi rank, leaving me trailing in her wake.

'The police must have already spoken to her,' I call as I hurry to keep up.

'Of course they have.' She briefly pauses by the exit before spotting a queue of cabs. 'Her mother was the one who confirmed the body was Iona's, so the police will have been all over her.'

'Then what's she going to tell us that she hasn't told them?'

Freya shrugs. 'Maybe nothing.'

'So, this could be a wasted trip.'

She turns to look at me. 'You can't think of it like that. There's always a possibility she'll add something new.'

'I'm surprised she agreed to meet you,' I mutter as she leans forward to speak to a driver, reeling off the address.

'What's the matter with you today?' Freya asks as we climb in the back.

I shrug. I don't feel like telling her that I'm anxious about meeting Ange. 'I don't know what to expect,' I say. 'I'm not used to this like you are. I'm not sure why you asked me along anyway, especially when I was no help to you on the island.'

Freya looks at me quizzically.

'You asked me to speak to people. So far you've pre-warned me about things you probably shouldn't have, but I don't know what I've given you. Except that perhaps I'm the centre of a story?'

Freya sighs and rolls her eyes. 'Is that really what you think? That I'm using you?'

'I don't know what I'm thinking about any of it,' I murmur. 'I'm so tired I could burst into tears right now.'

She reaches over and squeezes my hand. 'The night of the sleep-out I didn't think Danny did anything wrong.'

The image of Freya there flashes into my head again. She'd hung back from the small group of girls clustering around Tess. 'What do you mean?'

Freya pauses. 'He looked scared stiff. I thought he was innocent. I don't know, something doesn't feel right about him confessing, either ... Anyway,' she adds, 'I'm not surprised Ange is happy to meet. As soon as I mentioned a free lunch she jumped at the chance. Money talks, and for some a lot louder than others.' Freya smiles, and I may be wrong but I think she is genuine.

'Ange sounds revolting,' I grumble. 'Happy to discuss her dead daughter for a free lunch.' I shudder at the thought. 'The fact she didn't know Iona was missing makes me feel sick.'

'Well, we don't know what went on.'

'No, but still—'

'And that's what we'll hopefully find out today. They could have been estranged for good reason. We can't judge her before we've even met her. I thought you'd know that more than most.'

Freya is right to a degree. People always have the ability to shock. I see it with my clients all the time and have learnt not to take preconceptions in with me. Plus I only have to look at my own family. Yet Ange is one person I don't think I'll be wrong about.

'Anyway, she might be able to give us something that can at least in part explain what happened on that freaky island or why Iona was there in the first place.'

'Why do *you* think she was?' I ask. I don't mention what Dad told me about her looking for someone because I'm still not entirely sure I trust what he says.

Freya shrugs. 'No idea. We moved there because our cousins were there and Mum thought she wanted that kind of life, but why do other people decide to move somewhere so remote?' She spreads out her fingers and starts to count on them. 'Work; or because they're running from something. Or someone,' she adds. 'A nineteen-year-old girl on her own coming over to live on that island ...' she pauses '... there's got to be a reason.'

I mull over the thought that Iona could have been running from someone.

'Ange was insistent we meet in this pub,' Freya says, peering out the cab window as the driver pulls up outside. 'Apparently it does good food, though I don't know what bar it'll be set at.'

'Don't worry, I'm not expecting much,' I say quietly. 'Balsall Heath sounds so familiar,' I tell her as I climb out, looking around and then up at the red-brick pub that sits on the street corner. 'But I don't know why.'

*

I follow Freya closely as she swings open the heavy doors and marches in, totally unfazed by the look of the pub and its clientele. A row of men perch on stools along the bar. One of them glances over his shoulder but his body barely moves enough for him to see who's come in. In the far corner a woman raises her head and looks at us questioningly, and when Freya lifts a hand she nods in return.

'Who have you said I am?' I whisper, grabbing Freya's arm as she strides over. 'Am I supposed to be working with you?'

'She doesn't know you're coming. Tell her you were a friend of Iona's if you like.'

I don't have time to answer as we reach the table and Freya shakes the woman's hand. I quickly offer to get the round, which consists of a large white wine for Ange and two Cokes for Freya and me. When I return to the table they're already deep in conversation, Freya saying how grateful she is for the woman's time, even though it's quickly apparent Ange has little else to do. I slide in silently beside Freya and as they talk I study the woman, trying to find any resemblance to the young girl I remember.

Ange's fingers are yellowed from nicotine, the same shade as her teeth. Her greying hair has flecks of auburn and is scraped back into a ponytail. There is something familiar about her green eyes that flick nervously between the two of us, but it's not Iona's I see in them.

They settle on me as she warily watches me sipping my Coke.

'My name's Stella,' I say, smiling. Ange's hands shake as they grip on to the stem of her wine glass. 'I'm a friend of Freya's and I knew Iona too. I'm so sorry about what happened.'

'Your fault, was it?' she says.

I open my mouth but I have no words. She laughs at me in a deep cackle. 'Joking with you, love.'

I smile again but her inappropriateness makes me feel nothing more than revulsion. Freya glances at me but I can't look at her.

'Already had the police asking a load of questions,' Ange says. 'So don't know what you want.'

'Well, I'm just interested in Iona's back story, what happened before she went to Evergreen. Have you always lived here, Ange?' Freya asks.

The woman nods. 'I was born here. Same as Iona,' she says. 'She got away but I never did.'

'So, when did you stop seeing her?'

'A while before she went over there. Can't remember how long.' Ange takes a quick slug of wine. Her eyes peer over the rim of the glass, focusing on the table, and I'd bet she knows exactly how long it was.

'And did you know she planned to go to Evergreen?' Freya asks.

Ange gives a slight nod, slowly looking up.

'It's a funny place to go,' Freya says, leaning her body forward as if whatever Ange tells her is in complete confidence. 'I'm surprised she'd even heard of it, living in Birmingham, so far away. Many people don't know it exists. It's not a big island.'

'No,' Ange says. 'One hundred and two people.'

I lean forward myself. So, Ange knows about it.

Suddenly the door swings open and Ange looks up at whoever's just walked in. I go to turn as she says through gritted teeth, 'Don't look over.'

'Who is it?' Freya asks.

'Someone I owe money to. I can't pay it yet. Haven't got it but I will.'

I flick Freya a look but she's watching Ange. 'How do you know about Evergreen?' she says and Ange turns back and shrugs.

'Ange, what was Iona doing there?' Freya asks again. 'This could be really important. Maybe I could help out with whatever issue you have with that man who's just walked in.'

Ange laughs. 'It'd take a lot more than you could pay me.' She chews the corner of her lip and I sense she's deliberating.

'However things ended between you and your daughter, you must want to know what happened to her,' I say. 'There must be a part of you that needs answers.'

'I have answers.' Ange stares at me. 'Some boy killed her. He admitted it.'

'The police don't believe that's the truth,' I blurt and she cocks her head slightly. 'So if there was a reason she went …' I pause, hoping to encourage her to fill the silence. I can see she is weighing it up as she tips her glass back, draining the last dregs of wine.

'She was looking for someone,' she says at last. So Dad was right. 'I told her not to go anywhere near that island, but she was a stubborn bugger.'

'Why didn't you want her going?' Freya asks.

'Because I knew it wouldn't end well. We had a row about it. Huge one. Knew for sure I wouldn't see her again after that. She called me things you don't call your own mother.'

And I'm sure you said worse, I think as Ange stares down at her empty glass. I'm not sure if there's any guilt or regret behind her glazed expression, or if the sadness of losing her daughter is nothing compared to what her life has become.

'Who was she looking for?' I ask.

Ange pushes her glass across the table towards me.

'I'll get you another one,' Freya says, but she needs me to move before she can get out of the booth and I'm not budging until Ange answers.

'Her sister,' she says, looking up as the man she owes money to starts walking over to our table.

'Her sister?' I ask sceptically, as Ange speaks to the man. 'I haven't got your money today, Frank, but I'll get it.'

Frank's muscled arms hang at the sides of his body. Tattoos creep out the top of his sweatshirt, climbing his neck. His eyes roll over both me and Freya as he sums us up, obviously unable to reach a conclusion as to what we're doing here.

'A word?' he says, gesturing to the door then marching towards it.

Ange shuffles across the seat, but Freya reaches out and takes hold of her arm as she stands. 'Who was her sister?'

Ange pauses. 'Her name was Scarlet.'

'I don't know of any Scarlet,' Freya says, but Ange has already pulled her arm away to follow Frank to the door. 'I'll get you another wine,' Freya calls after her. 'Come back in, Ange, and I'll get you something to eat, too.' Freya nudges impatiently for me to move so she can get to the bar.

'There was no one called Scarlet,' I say when she returns. 'I knew everyone on the island and there was no one with that name.'

Freya stands by the table, her fingers tapping it impatiently as she watches the door, waiting for Ange to come back in.

I look over my shoulder. 'She's been a while. Do you think she's okay?'

Freya doesn't acknowledge me as she strides across the pub and disappears outside. When she comes back her eyes are wide with anger. 'She's gone.' Picking up her phone, she scrolls through for what I assume is Ange's number. 'No answer. Shit.'

'Do you think Iona got the wrong place?' I ask.

'No,' Freya says, grabbing her bag, infuriated by Ange's disappearance. 'I think Scarlet changed her name.'

Evergreen Island

25 August 1993

Bonnie stood at Stella's window, watching her mother in the garden below. She was chattering away to Susan, pouring them both glasses of wine like they had no cares in the world. Bonnie's fingers trembled as she touched the pane of glass, lightly at first because she didn't want to bring attention to herself.

All she wanted was for Susan to leave. For her mum to tell her friend to go and then to come and find her. Bonnie hadn't been downstairs in over two hours, yet her mum hadn't once thought to see if she was okay.

She wasn't. Not one bit.

Pressing the heel of her hand more firmly against the glass, she watched Susan lean in, sharing some piece of gossip, no doubt.

Gossip made her sick. She didn't want to hear any more, ever again.

If she pushed harder she could shove her hand right through the window.

The thought intrigued Bonnie. Maybe she should. Maybe then she could jump out with the shattering glass and finally her mum would notice that something was up.

She didn't miss the fact that the one time her mother wasn't cooing over her shoulder, Bonnie needed it more than ever.

But then did she really want to talk to her? Maybe it was better to stay hiding upstairs. To keep her hands over her ears and tune out the rest of the world, like she had as soon as Iona had left the house earlier.

She didn't want to see her best friend again. She didn't.

But then on the other hand she couldn't bear the thought of never seeing her again.

She wondered where Iona was right now. Who she was talking to, laughing with. Sharing things that she should be sharing with her. Her body ached at the thought that Iona might be off with Tess again.

How could you hate someone and yet want them so much at the same time?

Maybe she could forget what Iona told her. Blank it out.

Yes. That was what she needed to do. Pretend it had never happened. They would go back to being best friends.

She glanced down at her mum. Fury and rage filled her body and she slammed her fist against the window as hard as she possibly could.

The glass didn't shatter. No one even looked up.

*

Danny was happy that day. Some days he just woke up that way. He loaded his rucksack with two packets of cheese and onion crisps and half a pork pie, and in the back compartment he slipped in his drawing pad and pencils.

He was heading into the woods, so he'd tied a fleece around his waist, stretching it into a tight knot at his stomach. In the woods he found a tree and climbed up with ease, skimming up its trunk with the agility of a gymnast. Despite his weight he was an impressive climber. Tucked between the branches, Danny pulled out a packet of crisps and tore into them greedily. Crunching loudly, he didn't stop until he'd finished, eyeing the other bag before deciding to keep it for when he was hungry.

He took out his pad and scanned the woods, finally settling on a pretty sandpiper fluttering around a nearby trunk. He buried his head in his pad, feeling the wetness of his tongue as it poked out the corner of his mouth in concentration. Every so often he would glance up, searching for the bird, scrutinising its feathers before copying it on to the page.

When he finished, he leant back and stared at the picture. He wasn't happy with it. Something wasn't right with his drawing, but he couldn't work out what. Maybe he wasn't close enough. He needed to get a better look at the bird. Danny grabbed his stuff and slid down the tree, making his way to the trunk she was still flapping around.

She didn't look happy, he thought as he strained up to look. She was frantic, her wings beating rapidly. He dropped his things on the ground and continued to stare as she suddenly flew hard into the tree and then landed with a thump beside his boots. Danny crouched down, gazing at the creature, reaching out to touch its broken wing. He pressed a finger gently on her stomach. She wasn't breathing.

He stood and unknotted his fleece, carefully laying it on the ground, and then gently picked up the bird and wrapped it inside.

'What are you doing, Dan?'

Her words melted in the air like thick syrup, and he looked over his shoulder to where Iona stood behind him. She knelt beside him, her eyes drifting to the tears he knew were leaking from his eyes. Then she turned to the pad, to the picture of the bird. He quickly shut it before she looked at the drawing on the other page. Before she recognised herself.

'The bird – it flew into the tree.'

'I know,' she smiled. 'I saw it happen.'

'I was going to take it to the beach and bury it in the sand. It's a sandpiper.'

'I didn't know that.' Iona tilted her head to one side and continued to smile at him. She was talking to him as though he was a child and he didn't like it, but he stood and walked out of the woods towards the beach.

The bird still cradled in his arms, he turned around to see her still watching him, grinning. He didn't feel happy now. He never did when she was around any more.

*

Maria passed Susan the bottle of wine and watched her friend slowly fill her glass. They were both focused on the bottom of the garden where David was fiddling with the broken leg of one of the loungers.

'I still can't believe you're actually going,' Maria said.

'I don't think I have any other choice.' Susan's words were definite but tinged with sadness. 'Graham's made it that way.'

If there was anything Maria could say to make her stay, she would, but she also knew it was probably best for Susan. It would take something pretty seismic to change her mind now.

Maria watched Stella appear between the trees, kneeling down beside her dad.

'I used to envy you having three children,' Susan said. 'I always wanted more.'

'I know you did.'

'Tess—' Susan started before breaking off.

Maria looked across at her friend who tipped her glass to her mouth, her lips parting as she took a gulp of wine.

'What about Tess?' Maria asked.

'Something's got into her. She's coming out with all these weird notions lately, and it isn't like her. I think – I think getting off the island is the right thing for her, too.'

Maria bristled. She didn't like change. But she had felt it coming anyway.

'Do you think you can trust anyone completely?' Susan asked, and Maria cocked her head as she watched David tossing the chair leg to one side, hands on his hips as he looked at the wreck before him.

She considered the question carefully and eventually said, 'Yes. I do.'

What a fool she had been. Only two weeks later she would realise she couldn't even trust the one person closest to her. And if she couldn't trust him, then she couldn't trust anyone.

PRESENT

Chapter Twenty-Four

I stand aimlessly outside the pub on the corner of the road while Freya paces back and forth, making calls. 'Still can't get hold of her?' I ask when she finally hangs up.

'She's not answering. Probably thinks she's said too much already.'

'Maybe someone knows where she might have gone?' I suggest.

'Like who?'

'I don't know. The barman?'

Freya looks at the closed doors. 'Wait here,' she mutters. I can see how irritated she is, and I am too. The fact that Iona had gone to Evergreen looking for a sister has thrown her story wide open.

When she returns, Freya's shaking her head. 'He says he doesn't know where she lives but she comes here most days.' She glances at her phone again. 'But that doesn't help. I have to get home. It's my grandad's ninetieth tomorrow.'

'I could stay,' I suggest.

Freya looks at me quizzically.

'I mean, I could find somewhere for the night and try again tomorrow. I've got nothing I need to rush back for.'

'You want to do that?'

I shrug. If I want to find out who Iona was looking for, I have no choice. 'It can't be far from where my parents used to live. I could look around the place, see where they grew up.'

'Okay. Well,' Freya hesitates. 'Call me as soon as you talk to her.'

'I will.'

She nods at the pub. 'And don't speak to any strange men.'

It's nearly six p.m. by the time I've collected my car and checked into a Premier Inn near Shirley. I've bought essential toiletries and figure that once I've eaten I'll have an early night before looking around the area in the morning, to try and find Gran's old house. Once alone in my room, I try calling Bonnie. It doesn't surprise me that I haven't had one call from her in the last forty-eight hours. She is holding back on me so that I'll go running to her, and if I leave it much longer, it will only be worse. I'm apprehensive as I tap on her contact, dreading the thought I'll hear in her voice that she's had a drink. When her mobile rings out I hang up and try the landline, but still there's no answer.

Exhausted, I run a bath. Sliding into the hot water, I breathe out a sigh as it begins to release the ache in my muscles. With everything that's been going on lately, I knew I'd risk Bonnie slipping away from me, and I hate that I've allowed her to.

I sit up when my phone begins to ring, then stretch to grab it from beside the basin. 'Bonnie,' I answer, clambering out the bath, reaching for a towel and struggling to wrap it around myself with one hand. 'I was trying to call you.'

'So I see,' she says bluntly. 'Where are you? I saw your car wasn't outside your flat.' Her tone sounds measured, which brings me some hope she's sober.

'I've been out with Freya.'

'Seriously? So what have Cagney and Lacey discovered this time?'

'Actually, we came to Birmingham.'

Bonnie is silent. 'Birmingham?' she says after a moment, her pitch rising.

'Freya was in touch with Iona's mum and she agreed to meet us.'

'Her mother?' She is yelling now. Another pause. 'What the hell are you playing at?'

'Bonnie,' I say calmly, trying to defuse her over-reaction. 'I know that for whatever reason you don't want to hear this, but I think there's a chance Danny didn't—'

'This isn't about Danny,' she says, an odd tone to her words now, and I try to figure out what could possibly be unnerving her. 'Why did you visit Iona's mother?'

'Please, calm down, Bon. Because I want to know more about what Iona was doing on the island. And this *is* about Danny—'

'And?' she interrupts. 'Did you see her mother?'

'Yes.'

'Oh …' Bonnie is laughing, but it isn't a happy sound that fills the line. 'You have to be kidding me. When are you ever going to stop, Stella?'

'Bonnie, I don't know what—'

'What did she say?'

I slide down on to the edge of the bed, scooping up the towel which keeps slipping off me. 'That Iona was on the island looking for a sister.'

Bonnie doesn't answer.

'Someone called Scarlet.'

Still she doesn't answer, and it takes me a moment to realise she's hung up.

I check my signal to find four healthy bars and soon my phone flashes with a call again.

'Why are you doing this?' Bonnie cries.

'I'm just trying to find out—'

'Are you coming home now?'

'No, actually I'm staying in a Premier Inn in Shirley for the night because I want to—'

'You're still there?' she shouts.

'I am, and Bonnie, will you stop interrupting me.'

The line goes dead again, and I stare at my phone before throwing it on to the bed.

Five minutes later Bonnie is calling again.

'I don't want you seeing her,' she pleads.

'Bon, are you crying? What are you scared of?'

'I'm not scared of anything. I just want you to come home.'

I sigh in response.

'Will you?'

'Bonnie, I know you don't like what's going on but you have to let me do this. Bonnie?' I say as I check my phone and see she's hung up on me a third time.

When she doesn't call back, I go to the restaurant and order a burger. There's no point in us having the same conversation over and over, but by ten p.m., when I'm ready for bed, I feel the need to try. Her phone goes straight to voicemail and I don't leave a message.

Half an hour later I'm drifting asleep when a loud knock on my door makes me sit up rapidly, blood rushing to my head. 'Who is it?' I call out as I pull back the covers.

'Me.'

'Bonnie?' I make my way across the room, opening the door as she pushes past me. 'What are you doing here?' As I switch on a lamp that fills the room with light, I see she's unsteady as she plops down on to the bed.

'Tell me you haven't been drinking.'

'I had one.'

'Bonnie,' I sigh. 'Don't lie.'

'It isn't a lie. I have only had one.' She at least has the presence to look guilty as she avoids my gaze and fiddles with the corner of the duvet.

'But even one . . .' I shake my head. 'And you've driven all the way here. Why did you do it?'

'You weren't there,' she snaps. 'I needed it.'

'You didn't even talk to me first,' I say, sinking on to the bed next to her. 'You always promised you'd do that if ever you got to this point.'

'You don't have to look quite so disappointed in me,' she says. 'I can carry that weight for the two of us.'

I shake my head. 'I'm so angry with you. After everything—'

'Don't you want to know *why* I had a drink?' she asks, her eyes filling with tears. 'Why I had to have one glass of wine?'

'Of course I do.'

A tear trickles down her cheeks and she dips her head but doesn't bother wiping it away. 'I'd been trying so hard,' she says in a whisper. 'I didn't want to. But you haven't been there, Stella.'

'I'm always at the end of the phone.'

'That's not what I mean. You're not there in the sense that I want one thing and you want something completely different, and I can't – I can't handle it.' Her hands continue to fiddle with the duvet.

'What is it you can't handle?'

'All of it. The past.' She holds her head up and stares at the ceiling. She doesn't seem to care that tears keep sliding down her cheeks and roll off the end of her chin. 'I was seventeen when I had my first drink. It was three months after we'd left the island. By the end of the night I'd had more than I could count, but it was the first time I'd stopped thinking.

'The voices in here had been quieted,' she says with a sad laugh, tapping the side of her head. 'And it was a good feeling, you know? Not having to think.'

I reach for her hand and hold it in mine.

'Mum and Dad didn't notice because they were both wrapped up in their own problems. I pretended I didn't care, but it hurt,' she says, her voice melting.

'Oh, Bonnie,' I say.

'I think they expected me to disappoint them. I swear there was never anything wrong with me as a child, yet they insisted on taking me to those bloody Stay and Play sessions. Can you tell me why they thought *I* needed some shrink watching over me, and not Danny?'

'I don't know,' I say softly. 'I was too young.'

'I was condemned from an early age.'

'Bon, that's not true. Mum and Dad loved you, you know they did.'

She laughs. 'It was like they didn't know what to do with me. They must have known something was wrong, but I honestly haven't a clue what it was.' She pulls herself straight and wipes a hand across her face. 'Anyway, that's why I had a drink today. Because I can't deal with all the crap that's being dragged up again. I made a choice long ago to blank it all out and now it's resurfacing.' She shuffles away until I have no choice but to pull my hand back. Taking a deep breath, she asks, 'What did her mother tell you about Scarlet?'

'Nothing,' I admit. 'Just her name. I met her in an area called Balsall Heath, though. How do I know that place?'

'It's where Gran worked,' she says.

'Was it?' My grandmother was a social worker in the seventies, working with families who lived in slums. 'Dad said something about Gran being the reason they went to the island. Do you know anything about that?'

Bonnie looks up, shaking her head.

'He might have it wrong,' I sigh.

'You know, I read about a survey the other day,' Bonnie says suddenly. 'About mothers who admit to having favourites. Most commonly it's their youngest.' She looks at me expectantly. 'And that if grandparents do, it's typically the oldest. Do you think if Gran had still been around I'd have been hers?' she says. 'I doubt it.'

Choosing to ignore her, I say, 'Did Iona ever mention anyone named Scarlet to you?'

Her eyes drop to my mouth and I can see there are thoughts racing through my sister's head as she works out which ones to say aloud. Her fingers tap against her leg. 'Please tell me,' I plead. 'Is that what you argued about? Because I don't believe you can't remember. Did she ever tell you who Scarlet was?'

'She was lying,' Bonnie sighs. Her hands have stopped tapping but I still see them shaking as she grasps them tightly in her lap. 'That's why we fell out.'

'She can't have been. Not when her mum told me there was a sister.'

'She was lying, because she said it was me.'

If it's possible for my heart to temporarily stop beating, it has done so. The air around me stills, catching our breaths, and even then I know it's a fraction of time I will never get out of my head.

Chapter Twenty-Five

'Iona told me I was her sister and that I'd been taken when I was a baby,' Bonnie tells me.

'What the hell does she mean by that? That Mum and Dad kidnapped you?' My heart has raced back to life again and now it beats furiously as I push away from the bed, pacing the short space between it and the wall.

'She said the reason I was taken ...' Bonnie swallows, and I can hear her words catching '... was so they could give me a better life. Only they left her behind.'

'That's ridiculous.' I shake my head. 'Bon, you must know it is, it sounds like a fairy tale.' I crouch in front of her, reaching for her hands, prising them apart. They feel so cold against mine. 'You don't believe any of this, do you?'

'I was never even going to ask Mum, but I couldn't help myself. I broke one day. She told me it wasn't true.'

'Well, there you go.'

'She's hardly going to say, "Oh yeah, that's exactly what happened," is she?' Her eyes flare defiantly but her body has slumped.

I shake my head. 'But you know it doesn't make any sense.'

'Mum made me think Iona was jealous and made it all up. I was beginning to think she might have, you know, the way she was always cooing over the house and that damned island as if we lived in a palace.'

I realise I am frowning at Bonnie as she speaks, looking like I don't agree, for she snaps, 'She was. You just didn't see it.'

'I'm not saying she wasn't,' I reply, though if anything it always appeared the other way round. 'What about Dad?' I ask.

'He was ...' Bonnie gazes past me, thinking back. 'Dad was distant. He didn't really talk about it. While Mum was going crazy that Iona had even said such a thing, he seemed more concerned about Iona.'

I push myself up angrily and pace towards the wall again.

'What's wrong with you?' she snaps. 'Will you stop doing that?'

'Bon, I think Dad might have been having an affair with her.'

'What?' she laughs. 'That has to be the most absurd thing I've heard.'

'I saw them together. After she was supposed to have left the island.' I turn to my sister. 'I know Dad lied about taking her back, or at least about not seeing her again.'

'What were they doing?' she asks hesitantly.

'Kissing.'

'No! No. That's totally not true.' Bonnie snorts though she's staring at me as if she isn't sure any more. As if something else is dawning on her. 'That's totally sick. I mean, God ...'

'She never said anything to you?'

'That she was seeing *my father*?' Bonnie laughs but her face has paled. 'Of course not,' she mutters. 'But I knew she was seeing someone. She'd just never tell me who.'

'Dad says he wasn't. When I saw him yesterday he seemed totally convincing. Only ...' I pause, shuddering. 'Bonnie, the place I saw them was the spot Danny says he killed her.'

'Oh my God!' Bonnie cries. 'This is getting even more horrendous. You have to stop.' She falls into her hands as they clutch her head, her fingers digging into her scalp. 'Just stop talking about it now. I wish I'd never come.'

I sit on the bed beside her again and for a while neither of us speak.

'I never stopped wondering if what Iona said was true,' Bonnie eventually says in a whisper. 'But I decided I never wanted to know. And I don't. I just can't – I can't even go there.' She looks at me imploringly. She needs me to drop what I'm searching for. I can't keep unearthing our past, because for Bonnie that's where it needs to stay.

She isn't like me. Or my client who admitted she would have begged for the truth regardless of its outcome. I was wrong to think everyone would. For my sister, it's easier to accept that what she doesn't know won't hurt her.

I wave a hand in the air. 'Iona must have got the wrong person. There's no way Mum and Dad were capable of kidnapping a child,' I say, though my thumping pulse reminds me I don't know what to believe any longer.

'I don't want to know, Stella,' Bonnie says again.

She glances at the bed. 'I'll sleep here. We'll both go home in the morning.'

'Yes.'

'Promise me, Stella.'

'We will,' I say.

'I want you to promise.'

'I promise,' I tell her.

'It's sad, isn't it?' I say when we are lying together in bed. It's the first time we've done this since right after Danny left when I'd turned up on her doorstep. Only this time it's my arms that are wrapped around Bonnie. 'That we never felt we could tell each other the secrets that have been eating away at us for so long.'

Bonnie nods but doesn't answer.

'Maybe if we'd all been more honest, things could have been different,' I say.

'Maybe if they'd been more honest I might not be here,' Bonnie murmurs. 'I meant nothing to Iona, did I?' she says.

I pull her closer. 'How come you were still friends with her after what she said?' I ask, and feel her stiffen in my arms.

I don't think she's going to answer, but at last she says, 'I didn't have any others.'

I close my eyes, burying my head in her hair, holding her tighter still. 'Did you give her your friendship bracelet?'

She nods.

'She was still wearing it when she died, Bon. I think maybe you did mean something to her.'

I know that in the morning Bonnie will continue to persuade me to leave without looking for Ange. I now understand why the thought of digging into the truth is unbearable for her.

I'll have to cross that bridge then, but as we lie together I ask myself whether I can stop searching and put my sister first.

It's only a fleeting question.

There's no way I can walk away now.

Chapter Twenty-Six

I dream of the island again. My sleep is plagued with distorted images: the people; my secret place; Mum. She is always at the forefront, and when I wake I am cold but laced with sweat.

In my dream Mum had stripped off mask after mask, each time revealing another layer that was never her. I can't shake it from my head, because if there was one person I could rely on it was her. She was my safety blanket.

Would you tell me the truth now, Mum?

Not that long ago I'd have said with certainty that she would. I lie next to Bonnie, trying to untangle Mum's decisions, and it comes to me that maybe all she was doing was hoping to protect us. Maybe she thought the truth was too hard for us to hear.

Bonnie is snoring gently. I push off the covers and swing my legs from the bed. It also occurs to me that I'll never know. Death has a way of making that a certainty.

It's just after ten when Bonnie leaves, reminding me again that I'm to drive home too. I tell her I want to look around Shirley and she begrudgingly accepts this. The truth is, I'm dithering over my decision.

There are possibly answers that are a ten-minute drive away. But then I came looking for ones that could help Danny, not throw more shade on my family. Plus I made a promise to my sister, and I already know how much damage I would cause by breaking it.

I am pacing the car park when I get a text from Freya, making sure I let her know as soon as I find anything.

I sigh, kicking my foot against the wheel of my car.

I am torn in two, yet I can't deny there is a greater tug on one side. And I know, deep down I know, that at some point in the future my need for the truth will outweigh everything else.

This is why, an hour later, I'm back at the pub in Balsall Heath. I hold my hand over my bag as I push open the heavy door, and the smell of stale beer hits me immediately. The barman from yesterday is rubbing a cloth around a pint glass. He looks up, surprised, as I walk over. 'What can I get you?'

'Just a Coke, please.' I glance around. 'I was hoping to find the woman I met yesterday. Ange?'

He gives one nod but doesn't respond.

'I was with another woman and we sat in that corner.' I point to the booth at the far end of the bar. 'The guy who came in looking for her, he looked like he knew where to find her, and you said she comes in most days.'

He stops cleaning his glass and lays the tea towel on the bar. 'I don't know why you're here again, love, and I have to say I don't think you look like a copper, but take my advice and keep well away from both of them.' He arches his eyebrows, straightening his back as he begins to wipe around the glass again. He has pitted skin and a few missing teeth, and still I have no idea if I can trust him to help, but he's the only hope I have.

'Please,' I beg. 'This is really important.'

'She left you suddenly, yeah? Didn't seem like she wanted to talk to you. I don't want to know what kind of trouble she's in now.'

'She's not in any trouble,' I say.

'Doesn't sound like it.'

'I just need to ask her about her daughter. That's all it is, I promise.'

He opens his mouth to speak when the double doors bang open. Closing it again, he turns his back on me, but not before I've seen his face pale. I look around as the man with the tattoos walks in.

'Should I ask him?' I hiss across the bar.

'I wouldn't,' he says quietly over his shoulder. 'Stay out of it. You don't want him thinking you have anything to do with her. You've got to hope he doesn't recognise you. The usual?' he asks, turning as the man approaches the bar. When he has his pint and has sunk into a booth in the corner, I ask the barman again.

'Can you tell me where she lives?'

'One of the bedsits off London Road, as far as I know, but I can't tell you where exactly.'

'Thank you so much.' I take another sip of my Coke and lay out a five-pound note on the counter, telling him to keep the change. As I turn to leave he leans forward.

'Seriously, you don't want to get involved with her,' he says.

It's a five-minute drive to the end of London Road where terraces of Victorian three-storey buildings, once beautiful homes, have long since fallen apart into run-down B&Bs and bedsits. I pull up by the corner of the road and, with no idea where to start, find one that's slightly more well-kept than the others and ring its bell. An elderly man comes to the door in a brown dressing gown that flaps open at the knees, and after apologising for disturbing him I tell him who I'm looking for and give a description of Iona's mother.

He doesn't have a clue who I'm talking about, so I try the next door and then the next, until there are only a few more left. I'm giving up hope when I finally find someone who thinks she knows her, directing me to the end of the terrace.

I don't believe Ange will actually be here but when I ring the bell, she answers, her face dropping as she takes me in. She glances awkwardly over her shoulder as she asks me what I'm doing here.

'I just need to speak to you,' I say. 'Can we go somewhere and talk?' I indicate the green over the road where there are empty benches opposite a small, deserted bandstand.

Ange nods, rummaging in her pocket for her keys before closing the door behind her. 'What is it you want?' she asks as we sit on a bench. A wind whips through the trees and I notice Ange shiver as she pulls her thick woollen cardigan tighter. She looks up at the sky. 'Storm coming, I reckon.'

'I need to know if the girl Iona went looking for is my sister,' I say.

She looks at me, seemingly interested in what I'm asking, but doesn't respond.

'I found out she told my sister, Bonnie, that they were, but I don't know if it's true. I have a photo,' I say, pulling out my phone and scrolling through until I find one of Bonnie and me. I enlarge Bonnie's face but for a moment hold the phone in my lap where Ange can't see it. 'I know it's a long shot. I don't really expect you to recognise her.' Regardless, I pass the phone to Ange.

She stares at the photo for a long while and I wait, my breath tight in my throat. 'I don't know,' she says, 'it could be, I suppose.' She hands the phone back.

'There's nothing about her you remember?' I say. 'No birthmarks or features?'

Ange shakes her head.

I sigh as I let the phone drop on to my lap. Ange watches a squirrel intently as it runs across the path in front of us and darts up a tree.

'What actually happened to Iona's sister?' I ask.

The squirrel disappears but she carries on gazing into the distance.

'Why are you so desperate to know?'

'Because I need to know if it's Bonnie. I need to know if my parents did something that—' I break off. 'Please. My mum died. I can't ask her.'

Ange gives a small flick of her head, watching me carefully. 'Someone once asked me how desperately I needed extra money,' she mutters, after a pause. 'Get myself on the right track, you know, sort myself out. I laughed in her face, told her she hardly needed to ask. All she had to do was look at the clothes me and the kids were wearing, look at the shithole we were living in.

'She wasn't laughing, though. She had a dead-straight face, and so I asked what she meant. What I had to do for it.'

'What did she say?'

'She looked at the baby and said there was this really nice couple who desperately wanted one but they couldn't have one of their own. Said they could give her a real nice life, lovely clothes and all that.'

'She asked you to sell your baby?' I gasp.

'You got no idea, so don't try making out you have,' Ange snaps. 'I didn't have enough money for food for myself, let alone to feed them. And I wasn't well,' she goes on. 'Got taken into the hospital a couple of times and I couldn't look after the girls. She'd told me enough times she wouldn't let them get taken from me, but I didn't believe her. I knew one day I'd be in hospital and they'd be gone.'

'You knew this woman?' I ask.

'She was my social worker. One of the good ones.'

I pull back, my heart racing, trying not to put together the facts that link my family to this woman.

'She told me the amount they were willing to pay.' Ange lets out a chuckle. 'Didn't know anyone who had that kind of money to throw about. So I said, "What about the other one?"' Ange pauses. 'But Iona was older and they didn't want her. Told me it would be too risky, that at her age she could remember or talk too much. Anyway, in the end I said yes. They could have the baby. It actually wasn't the hardest decision I had to make.'

'Didn't you ever regret it?' I ask, feeling sick as I listen to her. How could someone be so desperate as to sell their own child? How could anyone even suggest it?

'Should say I did, shouldn't I? That would be the right thing. Only I didn't. I had money and was told I could sort myself out, and me and Iona could have a better life too. Everyone was happy.'

'Only you weren't?'

'Not really cut out for motherhood.' She grins sadly, lowering her eyes. 'Thought it was best for us both when Iona left me. She found out what I'd done and couldn't bear to look at me, so I thought she was better off without me.

'I thought she'd moved on with her life,' Ange goes on. 'I never expected her to return after what she knew.'

'That's why you never reported her missing?'

'Never knew she was,' Ange says bluntly, though tears are glistening in her eyes. 'Just never even realised till the police came knocking on my door a few days ago.' She reaches down and pulls out some little white pills from her pocket, wrapped in tissue, which she counts out with shaky fingers.

'I really don't think you should be doing that here,' I say.

Ange laughs at me. 'These ones are prescription. I have to take them or else something else might kill me off.'

'What's wrong with you?' I ask, eyeing the tablets.

'You wouldn't have heard of it. Hypertrophic cardio-myopathy. Sounds proper posh, doesn't it? It means . . .' She starts to tell me but my mind blanks out. Suddenly I know exactly who Iona had been looking for.

Chapter Twenty-Seven

'Iona got the wrong person.'

I gaze at the outline of Ange's face, the sharp chin, the short nose, and reel back. There's something so familiar about her. I was right that it wasn't Iona's eyes I saw in hers; it was Jill's.

She twists round to look at me. 'What you talking about?'

'She got the wrong person,' I repeat. 'She thought it was my sister, but it wasn't; it was my friend Jill.'

Ange looks at me out of the corner of one bleary eye. 'And how do you know that?'

'Because Jill had the same condition as you. Only I don't think her parents knew. She died when she was nineteen. The same age Iona did,' I say, holding my hand to my mouth as the realisation sinks in.

Ange's deep breaths sound hollow and raspy, as if she can't quite catch them.

'Are you okay?' Part of me wants to take hold of her hand which is shaking in her lap. Another part recognises she's done this to herself.

'Fine,' she says. 'I'm fine. I should be getting back anyway.'

'Wait. I know who it is, this changes everything. We can go to the police. If we tell them what happened, that we know who bought your baby, then—' I break off, my heart thumping.

Then what? Does it mean Bob and Ruth knew who Iona was? Does it mean *he* killed her?

'Then they can find out what happened to Iona,' I finish.

Ange shakes her head as she moves to stand.

'You have to want that.' I grab her arm. 'We have to go to the police.'

'No. We don't,' she says firmly.

'Why not?' I cry.

'What I did was illegal.'

'This is *murder*. What could be more important?' I'm incredulous that she's lost two children but is still refusing to talk. 'What's more important than putting your daughter's killer behind bars? The right person,' I add.

'I owe people,' she cries. 'Okay? I owe too many people.'

'So?'

'So ...' She pauses. 'If I confess, I have no chance of paying them off.'

'I don't understand.'

'I just can't talk to the police,' she hisses.

'Are you being blackmailed? Is it the people who took your baby? You think they can help you?'

'This has got nothing to do with you,' Ange snaps.

'Of course it has! My brother could be locked up for something he didn't do.'

Ange turns away from me.

'Are they still paying you? You want their money more than knowing what actually happened to your daughter?' I say, though I already know the answer to that. This is a woman who didn't even notice Iona was missing for twenty-five years; she's hardly going to care now.

'You know *I'll* go to the police now, though, don't you?' I say as she pushes herself off the bench. But she doesn't appear to be listening any longer as she walks off across the green. 'Wait!' I run after her.

'You don't know what you're dealing with.' Ange pulls her arm away as I try to reach for it.

'You're scared,' I say as she steps on to the road without looking. 'I get that, but you don't need to be.' I check for cars, hurrying to keep up with her. At her house she slips past the open gate and on to the short path.

'You know nothing about my life at all.' Ange glares back at me, her eyes wide with fear, her hand reaching for the low brick wall that separates one terraced house from the next.

'I'm sorry, but I do have to talk to the police, Ange. Helping my brother is too important, and now I know my family had nothing to do with it—'

'You know, my Iona wasn't a stupid girl,' she interrupts. 'You say she thought my Scarlet was your sister?'

'Yes, but I know she wasn't—'

'But why did Iona think she was?' Ange asks.

'I've got no idea, she was obviously wrong.'

Her hand grips more tightly on to the wall, flakes of red brick crumbling beneath the pressure. 'She was mistaken, but not for no good reason. You see, my baby wasn't the only one taken to that island.'

I step back, my right foot tipping off the edge of the kerb.

'There was another before mine. That's how I knew it was safe.'

I shake my head, refusing to take in what she's saying. My heart is like lead as it bangs heavily inside me.

'Maybe your family isn't innocent after all,' she says, turning towards her front door. 'Maybe you shouldn't go running to the police either.'

'Do you know?' My voice breaks as the words catch in the air. 'Do you know that for a fact?'

Ange pauses, one hand pressing a key into the lock.

My head is ringing, but finally Ange gives a small shake of her head and I have a momentary flutter of relief. She pushes the door open.

'Ange, please,' I cry, following her as she steps inside the house. 'Who was your social worker?'

Her face is blank as she turns to close the door.

'Was her name Joy? Please,' I sob desperately, as she shuts it.

I sink back against the wall, burying my face in my hands, eyes focused through my fingertips on a man rummaging in a bin, pulling something out, tossing it back in again. Ange's words make my thoughts scuttle around my head as aimlessly as his actions.

Iona got the wrong person.

Yes, my gran was a social worker, but she might not have been the same one.

They're coincidences. Nothing more.

I close my eyes, breathing deeply, slowly, pulling my hands away as I tip my head to the sun which is shooting like an arrow through a slit in the clouds.

I will call Harwood. Tell him what I know.

Only *what if I'm wrong?* I close my eyes again, trying to shake away the thought.

If I talk to the detective I'll be setting a whole new wheel in motion, and who knows what their investigations might turn up.

There is less than twenty-four hours until they could charge Danny with murder and maybe, just maybe, the only thing I can do to help my brother is to go back and dredge up the truth.

Evergreen Island

5 September 1993

Maria needed to seek Iona out. She wouldn't let it fester any longer. The previous day Bonnie had come to her and uttered the words: 'Is Iona my sister?'

She hadn't confirmed where it had come from, but to Maria it seemed obvious Iona had put the thought in her head. And as Maria had seen her daughter in front of her, trembling, she knew it was time to confront the girl and find out once and for all what she thought she was doing.

Iona was driving herself slowly through the family like a knife, but Maria approached her with the certainty she could stop her going deeper.

She'd found her in the village, carefully holding a cake in her hands, picking the cherry off the top and popping it into her mouth. There was something so innocent about the way she looked, so fragile, and for a moment Maria paused. At nineteen she was barely an adult.

She began to walk over as Iona spotted her, looking amused at what she must know was going to be an awkward conversation. It didn't take much for Maria to be on guard again, all thoughts of feeling sorry for the girl immediately disappearing. 'Iona. I think we need to talk.'

'Oh?'

Maria hated confrontation at the best of times, and right now this was one of the worst. 'Let's walk,' she said, gesturing to the path. Iona fell into step beside her and for a moment they were silent. 'Bonnie's getting some strange ideas,' she said at last.

'How do you mean?' Iona inclined her head to one side and looked at Maria.

'Yesterday she asked me if you were sisters.'

'Sisters?' Iona laughed. 'Where did that come from?'

'You,' Maria said, but she was already doubting herself. She'd been so certain Iona had put the idea in Bonnie's head, she hadn't stopped to ask if it could have been concocted by Bonnie.

'Why would I tell her that?' Iona screwed her eyes up as if the idea was completely ludicrous.

Maria fumbled in her pockets, searching for something to hold on to. 'I don't know why you would,' she said. 'That's why I'm asking you.'

Iona smiled in such a way that already Maria was feeling like a fool. 'Is this why you came to see me? Are you worried about Bonnie?'

'No, of course I'm not, why would I be?'

'I don't know, Maria, you seem concerned about a few things recently.' Iona brushed a hand casually against the bushes on the side of the path as they walked and Maria wondered how she'd never seen this side of the girl. Had every one of them missed it?

All of a sudden she felt a rush of panic for all her family, but especially Bonnie, who'd been dragged into the girl's web. 'I'm not worried about my daughter,' she said as she continued striding ahead with what seemed like less purpose than she'd set out with.

'And did she tell you I'd told her we were sisters?' Iona asked, with that smile again that looked more like a smirk.

'Well, no, not exactly.'

'Then it's in her head,' Iona said bluntly.

Maria faltered. She realised she'd been naively expecting Iona to admit what she'd said and to tell her why.

'You must notice the way Bonnie follows me around,' Iona went on, her tongue flicking out as it licked the icing on her cake, her expression suddenly serious. 'She's clinging to me. I'm the only friend she has. I think she'd like it if we were sisters, don't you?'

'Iona, stop.' Maria turned abruptly and halted her in her tracks. 'Why are you here?'

'You asked me to walk with you.'

'Just tell me the truth,' Maria snapped. 'What are you doing on our island?'

'*Your* island?'

'Please be honest. Why did you come to Evergreen?'

'The funny thing about honesty,' Iona started, 'is that often the people who ask for it aren't being so themselves. Do you really want the truth, Maria?' she asked. 'Are you sure that's what you want?'

Maria's heart thumped furiously. Of course she did. Of course. 'Yes,' she said quietly.

'Then why don't you go first. Tell me what *you're* doing here. What made *you* come to this island in the first place? And be honest, Maria.'

Maria stared at the girl. She looked so much older than nineteen now, so much wiser and more knowing. But what could Maria say to her? Because she knew that maybe Iona already knew the truth.

'Stay away from my family,' Maria said, her words shaking. She shoved her hands deeper into her pockets and turned from Iona, picking up her steps again, walking as fast as she could. She wanted to get away. The girl frightened her but she also knew there was nowhere she could go. Not on this island. This place was supposed to make her feel safe, but there was nowhere she could hide.

'Wrong answer,' Iona called out shrilly from behind her.

It would only be another four days before hiding wasn't an option anyway. Before running became the only solution. What Maria hadn't known in that moment, as she'd stumbled into her kitchen, hands catching the sink, was that she was about to make everything worse for them.

Her pulse raced as she grabbed an upturned glass from the drainer and filled it with cold water, her eyes only then darting to the corner of the room where Stella was watching her.

'Hey, darling.' Maria put the glass down and spun round. She was breathless but Stella didn't seem to notice, absent-mindedly chewing on a chunk of her hair. Maria reached out and prised it away.

'I need to talk to you, Mum.' Stella was wavering on the edge of tears.

'What is it?' Maria gasped. God, what was it? She really didn't think she could take any more.

'It's about Jill.'

Maria's heart did a merry dance, but she kept her composure as she nodded and asked Stella what was bothering her.

'She made me promise.' A single tear escaped, rolling down Stella's cheek. Maria could see how much this was troubling her.

'Tell me,' Maria urged soothingly. 'You know that's what I'm here for. To take any worries away from you.'

Stella nodded. 'He's done it again,' she said quietly, and Maria feared she knew what was coming.

'Who's done what?' she asked.

'Her dad – he's hurt her.' Stella sobbed as she crashed against her mum's chest and Maria wrapped her arms around her daughter, nestling her head against Stella's.

'You've done the right thing,' she said.

'You have to promise you won't say anything,' Stella pleaded and Maria said she promised because oh, how much easier it would be to keep quiet than to face Bob. But a child's safety was involved. And despite everything, that was paramount.

When Maria looked back at that afternoon many years later, she could still vividly recall Bob's face when he opened the door to her as he wiped his grubby hands on a tea towel, tucking it into the waistband of his trousers. How his face had dropped when she'd started speaking. She'd told him she was worried about Jill, that she was only looking out for her, and had expected him to shout, at least say something, but the quieter he remained the more she dug herself into a hole.

Eventually Maria stopped talking. The look on his face was pure fury. Fire burnt from his eyes, his hands clenched into tight fists by his sides. She had overstepped the mark. She stood there, frozen with fear, preparing herself for whatever punch he would, quite literally, throw at her.

Instead he leant forward, his face contorted in anger. 'Don't you dare think I owe you anything after this,' he said, his voice measured and unnaturally calm. All the years of mutual trust and silence had fizzled away in one short moment. 'I don't ever want your daughter near mine again. Now get the hell off my property.'

She had run and not looked back. The next time she had seen Bob they hadn't discussed the encounter, because by then there were other, more pressing matters.

But when Stella would beg her to go back to the island, pleading with her that now David and Bonnie had left the family home, and it could be just the three of them, the idea would run down Maria's spine like a shard of ice.

Four days after that encounter at his door, she would be tethered to Bob again in ways she could never have imagined.

And because of that, her family would never be able to return to Evergreen ever again.

PRESENT

Chapter Twenty-Eight

It is four p.m. and I'm running along the harbour to the last of the bright yellow boats. On weekends there are two ferries a day, and the final one is about to leave.

By the time we reach Evergreen the sky is thick with black clouds. Lights begin to flicker on along the jetty, but there should be enough daylight to find my way to Rachel's.

I haven't called ahead to check she is happy for me to stay another night. I haven't particularly planned what I am going to do. I'd driven straight from Birmingham to Poole, ignoring the voices in my head, because if I'd listened to them I feared I would stop the car. There were already too many good reasons for me to do just that, including my promise to Bonnie, but I knew if I did I might not get to the truth. And for as long as Danny is sitting in a cell, believing he killed Iona, I will not give up looking for it.

The air is cold but fresh as it slaps against my face, rainwater dripping into my open mouth as I stand on the end of the jetty. Behind me the ferry chugs away and I'm suddenly alone on an island where night is crawling towards me fast and I can be certain the islanders don't want me. It is hard to believe I once belonged. Holding my hood against my head, I finally hurry forward while I can still see the way.

It takes Rachel a while to come to the door and when she opens it her face falls.

'I'm just here for the night,' I tell her. 'I'm going again in the morning.'

She shakes her head, eyes narrowing. 'You aren't staying here.'

'But …' I look past her to the empty hallway. 'You must still have the room available. And like I said, it's just for one night.'

'I don't care if it is, you aren't staying here,' she says firmly, leaning towards me as she adds, 'I know why you suddenly ran off. I know what your brother has done. Evil.' Rachel screws her face up in disgust. 'And people aren't surprised. He used to frighten all the girls.'

'You didn't even know him,' I protest. 'And that's not true at all.'

'None of us want you back on this island. You realise that, I hope.' She stops and shakes her head. 'I only wish I'd never given you a bed in the first place.'

I grit my teeth, hesitant. I don't know where else to go, but I won't plead for a room now. 'My brother's innocent,' I say. 'And I'm going to prove it, then you and the whole bloody island will really have something to talk about.'

I turn away, expecting to hear the slam of Rachel's front door, but as I walk to the path in the quiet I realise she must be watching me go. Only when I'm at the corner do I finally hear it close.

'Shit,' I mutter, kicking at the gravel beneath my feet. The few beach houses clustered around me are shrouded in darkness. There is only one place I can think of going – Annie's.

The light is fading fast and I stick to the path, but as soon as I approach the clifftop above Pirate's Cove a warm yellow beam shines out from the back of the nearest bay house belonging to Susan and Graham Carlton.

It is getting darker and I should get to Annie's, but then I never did speak to Susan when I was last here. And apart from Annie, she was the closest one to my mum.

In the latter years I didn't visit the Carltons' house much, but often when I'd pass I'd see Mum and Susan sitting on a swinging seat beside the front porch, laughing over a glass of wine. The seat is still here. Tonight the wind catches it, rocking it back and forth, and, empty of people, it's a disquieting sight.

The light shining from the back illuminates their garden which is exposed to the clifftop, bordered only by a low hedgerow. A figure, doused in black from the shoulders down, is standing at the far end, looking out to sea, the wind picking up her hair and whipping it about wildly.

I walk to the side of the house, and while there's a break in the rain I pull my hood back and call out, 'Susan?'

She doesn't respond.

I clear my throat to call out more loudly, when she moves her head ever so slightly, as if she wants to look over her shoulder but can't quite make it.

As I pass along the side of the house, she inches around further and peers in my direction. 'It's Stella,' I call.

Finally Susan twists her whole body around, but she doesn't move off her spot. I smile as I walk up to her, her face passive and pale against the bright beam that floods the garden from her kitchen. 'Do you know, Graham looked like a ghost the day he told me you were back,' she says. Fumes of alcohol waft from her breath and a glimmer of a smile hangs off her lips but it isn't reflected in her eyes. 'He's been down on that beach for over forty minutes now. In this weather, too.'

She turns back to the cove which is a sheer drop down from the end of their garden and I follow her gaze, spotting two figures, one with a flashlight that shines out towards the water. I take her word it's Graham as there is no way of knowing from where we stand.

Susan turns to me again and holds out her arms and I fall into her stiff embrace. 'We didn't get a chance to talk the other day before Annie stole you away. I imagine she was telling you to leave the island.' Susan pulls away and turns back to the two figures below. 'Good on you for coming back.'

'I'm not sure anyone else will see it that way.'

'Probably not. She has your best interests at heart, but she still thinks she owns this place and everyone on it,' Susan murmurs before saying, 'You'd have thought he'd realise I can see him from our house, wouldn't you?'

'Why are you watching him?' I peer over the edge.

She glances at me like I've asked a stupid question, but doesn't answer. 'Do you think he's guilty, Stella?'

'Who, Graham?'

'No!' she laughs. 'I know *he* is. I mean your brother. Danny.' She pulls out a packet of mints from her pocket and squeezes one to the top before offering it to me.

I take it, holding it in my hand. 'No, I don't think he is.'

'Everyone on the island does,' she says. 'And by association, they'll think you are too. It's a risky move coming back again.'

'I know.'

'Why are you? Back, I mean.'

'Because I want to know what happened.'

Susan nods. 'There's nothing wrong with putting people on edge,' she says. 'Just look at him.' She gestures her arm towards her husband. 'People get too comfortable, but that's when they make mistakes.'

I squint at her, trying to fathom what she's actually talking about. It seems like there are multiple strands twisting in her head.

'Some people seem very excited that Danny confessed to killing that girl,' Susan tells me. 'There's a lot of gossip about him. Stories that aren't actually true.'

'Like what?' I ask, but she brushes away my question with a swipe of her hand.

'The fact is, he was a good boy. Painfully introverted, but ...' Susan pauses. 'He wasn't bad.' She looks up at me sharply. 'You know, my daughter later told me he never actually grabbed her in the cave. Do you remember that happening? Maybe you were too young.'

'No, I remember.'

Susan watches me with wide eyes. 'They set him up. Or someone set Tess up to do it. I was so cross with her. I never brought her up to be like that, but that summer she was – she was different. She was sucked in by someone who pretended to be her friend.' Susan turns back to the beach, and I realise she must be talking about Iona. 'I didn't realise why at the time, but it was all to do with him.' She flicks a hand in Graham's direction.

'Graham ...?'

'And now she's moved to London and I barely see her or my grandchildren.'

'I'm sorry,' I say as a torchlight from the beach arcs in the sky. 'What's he doing down there?' I ask.

'He's with that little tramp again.'

'Oh.' I step nearer. 'Oh,' I say again, at a loss for any other words.

'Emma Grey,' Susan says as she turns to me, staring pointedly. 'You remember her?'

I nod. 'Yes, of course, but—' My mind flashes back to the two of them together at the end of her road. Is that what he was worried about when he saw me? Did he think I'd tell Susan?

'But she's your age,' Susan says. 'Is that what you were going to say?' She laughs. 'I know. He's always preferred them younger.'

A lot younger, I think. The age gap must be touching thirty years.

'So, what do you think I should do, Stella?' she says, with feigned recklessness. 'What's your advice? Your mum told me to leave him,' she goes on before I can answer.

'My mum? But—'

'Yes. That was many years ago. And you'd have thought I'd have learnt my lesson, wouldn't you?' she interrupts. 'Your mum said if I wasn't going to leave him I should give him an ultimatum. So I told him that if he didn't leave *her* then we were all leaving the island. Starting again.'

'Not Emma—'

'God, no, not Emma,' she says. 'She was only a child back then. The joke is, we only moved to this place because he'd done it before. I thought it would be safe living on an island, but he still manages to find them.'

'You never left, though,' I say. 'I take it that relationship ended.'

Susan doesn't respond. Instead she carries on intently watching the couple below.

'He'll be coming home now,' she says finally and I look down to see the figures pull apart, both of them now with flashlights that bow in front of them as they walk off in different directions: Graham heading for the steep path that winds up towards his house and Emma for the steps leading to the cliff and Jill's bench. 'As if nothing's happened,' Susan adds.

'Why stay with him?'

Susan shrugs. 'You get to a stage in life where the alternative isn't an option,' she says sadly, as rain splashes on to her forehead. 'Be careful, won't you, Stella? Coming back here. Looking for answers. *I* don't care what you find, but some will hate it.' She looks down at Graham. Her gaze penetrates him for a moment too long before she disappears into her house.

Chapter Twenty-Nine

I slip away before Graham arrives and am about to turn left in the direction of the lakes when a shriek from the clifftop stops me. Emma is climbing the far steps, but between her and me stands another figure, precariously close to the edge. As Emma's torchlight flashes towards us it's Meg who is caught in its beam.

'Get back,' Emma shouts at her daughter as I simultaneously call out her name. Meg's head snaps to me and then to her mother who is slowly approaching her. She takes a step away, ignoring me as she storms towards her mum.

'What are you doing?' Meg is shouting.

Emma reaches the clifftop. 'I'm not doing anything.'

'Yes, you are, I saw you down there with him. I'm not stupid,' Meg screams, slamming her palms against her mum's chest. Emma stumbles backwards with shock as I race forwards.

'Meg.' I catch her arm, spinning her around. Her skin is streaked with tracks of tears amid the dampness of the rain.

'She's seeing a married man!' she cries. 'Graham Carlton of all people! You make me sick,' Meg sobs, twisting back to Emma who is lingering behind, seemingly unsure what to do. 'Look at her,' she says. 'She can't even deny it.'

'I was finishing it.' Emma stumbles over her words.

'You're lying!' Meg screeches, sobs catching in her throat. 'I've been watching you both.'

'I don't – I'm going to finish it,' Emma says weakly. She reaches for her daughter who leaps back.

I hold out my hand to steady her. 'Meg, I know you're upset, but don't you think you should both go home,' I suggest. 'Talk about this together. I'm sure your mum—'

'My mum knows exactly what she's got herself into but she can't stay away,' Meg cries. 'For the last six months she's been slinking around the island, pretending nothing's happening between them. She tried denying it, but I know her. It's not hard to see she's dolling herself up for someone, giggling like a stupid schoolgirl whenever she sees him lingering around the village in that revolting hat of his.'

'Meg, it's normal to feel like this—' I begin.

'You asked after him when he came into the café,' she goes on, blindly ignoring another protest from her mum to stop talking. 'He fled pretty quickly when he saw you, didn't he? He recognised you—'

'Meg, stop!' her mum begs.

'Why?' Meg laughs. 'Why shouldn't I tell her?'

'We're going home,' Emma says, her voice shaking and not in the least authoritative as she fumbles for her daughter's arm.

'My mum isn't the first, Stella,' Meg sneers as Emma attempts to tug her away. 'She found out the other night he was seeing the girl who was buried in your garden.'

'Iona?'

'But you already knew that,' she says, yanking away from her mum's grip again.

'No.' I shake my head. 'I didn't.'

'Yes, you did. You saw them together. That's what he told my mum last night.'

I shake my head again, desperately trying to piece together what she means.

Meg hesitates. 'He said you must have told the police because they've been crawling all over him. That's why he confessed to her.' She flicks a hand in Emma's direction. 'But the stupid cow is still seeing him.' Her voice reaches a crescendo.

'I'm going to finish it,' Emma pleads but her words fade into the wind and Meg, having heard enough, suddenly races off down the path towards the village, swiftly followed by Emma.

The rain starts up again, pounding against my hood as I gape at them, watching them disappear out of sight.

Graham was having an affair with Iona? I've always been convinced it was my dad, because of the cap. That damned cap. It was the only thing I can picture in the image I've tried to shut out of my head. But what if all these years I've had it wrong?

It takes a while for Annie to answer the door. When she finally does, I can't help my eyes drifting down her frail body. Even though it's only five thirty, she's wearing a thin pink nightie that skims her knees. Her legs are bruised and patched with dry skin, her arms too fleshy for the bones that hide beneath, and as she opens the door wider I feel guilty for my intrusion. This old lady is possibly the only person on the island who'll welcome me in, but I don't know that I should be putting her out.

I step inside anyway as she orders me to take off my coat and my boots. 'My dear, you're soaking,' she says, hanging my coat on an oak hook that's been shaped to look like antlers.

'Danny made that,' I remember. 'Dad helped him.'

Annie stops to look at it. 'He did,' she says. 'He was always clever with his hands.'

I want to tell her he's still making things, that he's selling them on a website I never ended up looking for. Instead I follow her through to the living room and wait for her to fiddle with a gas fire until a fluorescent orange flame flickers into life. Annie stands in front of it for a moment and my mind drifts back to all the presents she gave us which were always so thoughtful.

Every birthday she bought me something she knew I would love, like the notebook with a lock and key that she handed to me when I was ten. I'd held it up to my face and smelt its leather, running my fingers over the sheets of paper tied in with string. It was as good as the bike Mum and Dad had given me, if not better.

She had done it for Bonnie and Danny too. A palette of eyeshadows for Bonnie on her sixteenth. A set of pencils with Danny's name engraved into the wood the Christmas he'd turned ten. 'For your drawing,' she'd said, and I hadn't known at the time what she meant, but my brother's eyes lit up as he carefully tucked them into his rucksack. Annie must have known my brother liked to draw before even I had a clue.

Annie points to a chair, gesturing for me to sit, but I don't move. 'Graham was having an affair with Iona,' I say. 'I just found out.'

Annie looks at me quizzically and then slowly nods. Of course it wouldn't have got past Annie if the police have been questioning him.

'Bonnie knew he was seeing someone, but Iona never told her who,' I go on. 'My God. *That's* why she befriended Tess,' I say, as realisation dawns on me. 'Susan said as much.'

When Annie doesn't respond, I say, 'He thinks I saw them.'

'Does he?' She raises her eyes.

'I saw someone but I always thought it was my dad.'

'Your dad?' Annie lets out an incredulous laugh. 'Oh, my dear, I think you were mistaken. Like I told you before, your father wouldn't have had an affair. He loved your mother too much for that.'

I sink into the armchair, fighting the urge to cry. I've blamed him all these years, and now the weight of my heart pains me. 'Graham thinks I told the police,' I say. Possibly he was the one who sent me the threat.

Annie nods again, her eyes drifting over me.

'I didn't,' I murmur.

When she doesn't respond, I ask if I can stay with her for the night. 'I've got nowhere else I can go. I promise I'll be gone in the morning.'

'Of course, you must,' she says. 'But you'll have to sleep on the sofa. I have blankets and a spare pillow but I don't have the guest room made up. I haven't had anyone staying over in ... well, as far back as I can remember.'

I breathe out a sigh of relief. 'Thank you, Annie.'

'Though I don't know if you *will* be going back in the morning,' she says. A shadow crosses her face as she glances towards the window. 'A storm's coming.'

I turn to look. Trees silhouetted against the glass sway wildly from side to side. She is right. The island will be completely cut off if the weather gets worse. I have seen it before. I saw it the night we left.

'I'll put the kettle on,' she announces, as if pulling herself together. 'Have you eaten?'

'No, and that'll be lovely.'

Annie hesitates. 'What brought you back, Stella? Tonight of all nights.' The rain is lashing heavily against the pane like stones.

'I went to see Danny,' I tell her. 'The police don't believe he did it.'

'Oh. I see.'

I try unsuccessfully to read the expression on her face before she wanders into the kitchen.

'I don't think he did either, Annie,' I call to her as she fusses in a cupboard, pulling out a tin which she opens and pours into a pan. I lean back in the chair and turn to the bright orange flames flickering like ribbons in the fire. I'm unable to take much comfort from the warmth when the noise against the glass is so harsh. Rain knocks the window in a constant thud.

'Danny is all everyone here is talking about,' Annie says when she comes back in, a tray wobbling between her hands. She sets it down on the coffee table. 'There's soup and a roll. Help yourself.'

'Thank you.' I take a bowl and hold it on my lap. 'I'm beginning to gather that. What are they saying?'

Annie sighs deeply. 'Half the islanders don't even remember him,' she says, dipping her head as she slowly lifts her spoon to her mouth.

'But you do,' I say. 'You must know he wouldn't do something like this.'

Annie takes a sip of her soup and then drops her spoon back into the bowl, frowning. 'Yet he confessed,' she says.

'But he had no reason to kill her.' I'm certain the thought can't sit right with her.

'Yet he's told the police he did it,' she repeats, her eyes drifting up to meet mine, and as she holds my gaze I think she actually does believe him capable. 'There are many people on this island who are glad for the fact,' Annie goes on. 'They have an answer. They know there's no longer any threat, and if they see you back here, they won't be happy, Stella.' Her mouth flattens into a thin line as she hunches forward, her breaths short and quick. 'I understand why you hope Danny isn't guilty, but what do you think you can find here that the police haven't already?'

'I need to talk to people,' I say, turning to my soup. 'This is lovely, thank you.' My cheeks flush as I feel her eyes boring into the top of my head. I realise I'd hoped Annie would unreservedly be on Danny's side. If she's not, she'll want to know exactly who I want to talk to and why.

'I used to worry about your mother,' Annie says, and I glance up. Her eyes are still focused on me but they have misted over. 'She had something inside her you don't often see. Sometimes it can be mistaken for bravery.' She pauses. 'I see it in you, too.'

'What do you mean?'

Annie waves her spoon in the air. 'She thought she knew best but I didn't always agree. I worried about her then and I do for you now. Who are you planning to talk to?'

I don't answer. I don't want to involve Annie, and I also don't want her trying to stop me. I intend to borrow a torch and wait until she has gone to bed before looking for Bob and Ruth. I need to speak to them tonight. Before it's too late and they charge Danny with murder.

'If you are so certain your brother didn't kill Iona then I assume you know something. Or you *think* you do,' she continues. 'Tell me, my dear, what is it?' Her hand flutters as she brings the spoon to her mouth again.

I sigh, shaking my head, as Annie continues to watch me. I know she won't give up. But at the same time I'm scared that if I tell her too much, she might not believe it.

'I think Iona came to Evergreen looking for someone,' I say eventually. 'I want to talk to Bob and Ruth.' My words are lost amid a crack of thunder that fills the room. The sky illuminates with bright white streaks, the lights in the room cutting out instantly.

'Bother,' Annie mumbles. Lit by the dim flickering of the gas fire, I watch her get up and wander out of sight. Soon a torchlight spears its beam across the room. She lays the torch on the sideboard and sets about finding candles and matches which she lights and places on the coffee table.

'Well, you won't be talking to anyone until morning, my dear,' she says and I sense her relief. 'Not in this storm.' She wanders over to the window and holds a candle up to the glass, shielding her eyes as she peers out. 'A tree has gone down,' she says, picking up the telephone that perches on the windowsill. 'Damn it. I'll have to get Graham over when the worst has passed. He can fix the phone lines. Now let me get you some bedding.'

Annie disappears out of the room and I wait while she rummages in a cupboard at the top of the stairs. When she comes down she is carrying two heavy woollen blankets and a plump white pillow which she leaves on the edge of the sofa. She bends over at my side, gently touching my hair.

'I did miss your family when you all left,' she murmurs. 'Your mother was like a daughter to me.'

'I know she was, Annie. She thought the same.'

'I never wanted her to go. Nor you, Stella, you always had a special place in my heart.'

I smile. 'I know,' I say gently.

She takes her hand away and sits back in the armchair opposite. 'Why do you think you need to talk to Bob and Ruth?' she asks. Her eyes don't leave me.

'It's just a hunch,' I end up saying, shrugging. 'No reason in particular.'

I wait for Annie to accept this but the way she continues to watch me, leaning back in her chair, twisting around the gold watch that hangs off her wrist, I can see she's having trouble with it.

I want to tell her not to worry. That I won't go anywhere until morning. That the idea of confronting Bob scares me too, but I don't have any choice. Instead I say none of this as another loud crack of thunder explodes into the room.

At just before nine Annie announces she is going to bed. She places a candle on the table beside the sofa and warns me to blow it out before I fall asleep. I promise her I will, but she wavers in the doorway so I make a pretence of pulling the blankets over me and stretching out. I sense she is about to leave the room when her eye catches sight of the torch and she wanders over and picks it up. My heart plummets as she takes it with her. 'Sleep tight,' she says, pausing again, and I can see how concerned she is that I might still try and go out in this weather so I sink deeper under the blankets.

Her slippers pad slowly up the wooden staircase. Every few minutes the sky lights up, thunder growling overhead, and each time the candle beside me flickers, threatening to send me into darkness.

I close my eyes. I really don't like the thought of going out in the storm but I have no choice. There are only two people who can give me answers and I need them before the morning. Before Danny's time is up.

The floorboards creak overhead and I wait for them to subside so I can search the house for another torch, but

Annie's footsteps pace interminably up and down the landing, disappearing into rooms, coming back out again, and at some point I drift off to sleep.

When another large crack of thunder erupts into the room I jolt upright. The candle is now nothing more than a short stub. Wrapping a blanket around myself, I creep into the hallway, listening, but there's no sound from upstairs, and once I've pulled myself together, I begin rooting through side-table drawers and kitchen cupboards, looking for another torch. When we lived on the island we had at least half a dozen. Everyone needs them as soon as darkness approaches and I know Annie must have more.

Back in the hallway I turn to a locked door, the key hanging from its lock, and as I open it I'm unable to recall if I've ever been inside the small box room that lies beyond. A solid wooden desk sits in its centre; around the walls bookshelves are stacked high, clutter spilling from every surface.

Before I go in I glance up the stairs, the candle in my hand threatening to burn out any minute. Placing the light on the desk, I check the drawers and scan the room, eventually finding a box on the bottom shelf of a bookcase with two torches in it.

Switching on the larger one, I'm relieved as it floods the room with bright light and am about to turn it off when I see a tray beside the box filled with photos.

The top one catches my attention. In it, a much younger Annie is looking at the camera, holding a baby. I pick up a handful of pictures, flicking to the next, one of my mum holding the same child, and as I look closer I see it is Bonnie. Their names have been scrawled on the back, dated 30 March 1976. Bonnie was less than two months old.

All the rest in my hand are of my family. More of my mum and Bonnie, a few of Danny and me as young children. I lay them to one side, about to pick up more, when a sound stops me.

Grabbing the torch, I creep to the hallway, quietly closing the door behind me, as I wait for a moment, listening again before pulling my coat off the hook. It's not until I'm at the front door that I notice the white envelope lying on the floor. My name is slashed across its front in black capitals. I rip into it, pulling out a piece of paper.

I TOLD YOU TO LEAVE. I WON'T TELL YOU AGAIN.

I open the front door, swinging the torch frantically from side to side, but there's no sign of anyone. I could well have missed the note when I headed straight for the box room, it could have been posted at any time during the evening but, more importantly, it means that whoever sent it not only knows I'm back, but they know where to find me.

Someone is trying to stop me finding out the truth, and it's with a sense of unease that I step out into the howling storm, leaving Annie alone upstairs.

Evergreen Island

7 September 1993

Maria's mind was a tumbling mess. So determined had she been to confront Bob about Jill that she hadn't stopped to think about the repercussions.

Her conversation with Iona continued to spin round and round in her head, and if she hadn't faced up to Bob she would have told him Iona was a threat.

But Stella's revelation had overpowered her thoughts and she'd acted on instinct. And now she was almost certain she hadn't done the right thing and was left with the unsettling feeling that she would have to do something about Iona herself.

Maria paused at her kitchen window, spotting David through the trees at the bottom of the garden. She drew in a breath and considered telling him what she knew, asking what they should do.

Confiding in him would of course have been the right decision. But as he lingered at the bottom of the treehouse, leaning his head back as he spoke to whoever was up there, Maria found herself grabbing her keys and scurrying out around the back of the house before he spotted her. There was someone else's advice she'd seek instead.

David waited for all three of his children to retire to their rooms that night and only when their doors were safely closed behind them did he ask Maria to sit down on a comfy chair in the living room.

'You look exhausted,' he said. She did – and normally he'd be worrying about her, but right now it wasn't concern he felt. 'What have you been up to today?' he asked, though he knew damn well what she'd been doing. He'd seen her fleeing out of the house and had followed her to the edge of the woods, where he watched her run to Annie.

His wife glanced up at him, her eyes wide with fear. Once upon a time he would have sat beside her, wrapping his arms around her, but he carried on standing by the fireplace. His arms were linked tightly across his chest, his feet planted apart, and he knew she would notice all this. He wanted her to.

When Maria didn't answer David said, 'I've been with Iona.' He knew this would get her attention.

Her mouth snapped open. 'What were you—'

'She's barely more than a child, Maria,' he interrupted. 'You should never have gone running to Annie.'

'I didn't, I—' Maria broke off. She must have realised he knew she was lying.

'I am your husband. You should have come to *me* first. We should have spoken about it.'

'I tried, David,' she said. 'You know I did. Only you never listened.'

'You didn't try.'

'I did. Many times over the summer I told you something wasn't right, that we knew nothing about Iona, and you brushed me away like you always do. Making me think my concerns are nothing to worry about, only this time they were.'

David sighed, looking away. This time she had been right to worry. He crouched in front of her. 'But what do you think is going to happen now, Maria? You've run to Annie and she's already spoken to me. She'll tell Bob, too.'

'He doesn't know.' Maria shook her head, tears glistening in her eyes, and he wanted to touch her but he couldn't. Fear bled through him. Everything was about to come crashing down.

'If I could go back and redo it,' he cried, pushing himself back to his feet and holding his head in his hands.

'No.' Maria shot out of her chair. 'Don't say that. Don't you ever talk like that, David.'

'We should never—' He broke off. He had never truly admitted how, for their entire lives on the island, he'd felt like he was running on a thin rope. That any moment they could all slip and everything they'd built would collapse around them.

He had never told his wife that every day he prayed to God for forgiveness and begged him not to take it all away from them because they didn't deserve that. Surely.

In many ways David admired his wife's strength, because despite her worries he doubted she was crumbling inside like he was.

'There's only one thing we can do,' he said. 'Make sure Iona gets off this island. She needs to leave before Bob gets to her. She's down by the quay. At least she was when I left her.'

What David omitted to tell Maria was the depth of the conversation he'd had with Iona. Perhaps he should have been honest and revealed his admission, but he didn't want her turning everything on him right now.

He scraped a hand through his hair, drawing her eyes to the top of his head.

'Where's your cap?' Maria asked.

'What?' he said distractedly. 'I left it behind. Graham picked it up. Maria, have you been listening to a word I've just said?'

Maria nodded. 'You want me to talk to her?'

'Yes,' he cried. 'Now. Sort this out, Maria.'

PRESENT

Chapter Thirty

I leave Annie's house as the sky illuminates with another flash of lightning. Rain drives in slants, slapping my face as I avoid the woods, racing along the sodden path, my heart thumping, my mind spinning with thoughts of what I'm doing.

Annie had said I was like Mum, her actions often confused with bravery. I don't recall seeing that side of her, but I see it in myself now.

Am I being brave or completely stupid? The reality is I've lately been so driven by a need for the truth that I've become blind to its fall-out.

My feet slap against the ground, mud splattering up my legs, clothes sticking like glue to my skin.

There's no point contemplating alternatives because there no longer are any. I won't stop until I find out if my brother killed Iona or whether someone else is happy to let him think he did.

I won't stop regardless of what else I find.

A dim light flickers behind Bob and Ruth's thin curtain. I knock on the door and wait only moments before Ruth opens it. Like Annie she is dressed for bed, with a long purple velvet dressing gown tied around the waist. Her face pales when I remove my hood, but she stands aside without speaking.

When I step in she closes the door, swooping past me to the kitchen where she stops short at the table, sweeping a hand across it, gathering photos which she piles in one hand.

'Jill?' I ask.

Ruth nods.

'Is Bob here?' I look around.

'He's out back. A tree came down. It shattered a window.'

'Ruth, I need to speak to you both.'

She nods again, her eyes dropping to the photos clutched tightly in her hand. 'She didn't like it on the clifftop, did she? Jill. She never liked it there. I knew that, but he insisted it was where we put the bench. "Everyone will see it here," he said. But she never liked it.'

'Jill liked the whole island,' I say. Water slides off the end of my coat, making tiny puddles at my feet. I take it off and lay it in a heap on the doormat. She sinks on to a chair and I pull out one opposite.

'But it wasn't her favourite place,' Ruth insists. 'Where was that?' Her glassy eyes look right through me.

'The lakes,' I say. 'Jill liked the lakes.'

Ruth fights back tears, holding a hand over her mouth. 'We drifted apart. When she was little we did everything together, but at some point—' She breaks off. 'I never stood up to him. Jill knew that. I saw in her eyes she'd lost faith in me and still I did nothing.'

'Jill knew you loved her,' I say. Ruth's pain is obvious and, regardless of what she's done, my heart still tears for her.

'My mother always told me to make my husband my priority and for years Bob was all I had. I never expected Jill would one day come along. When she did I still carried on putting him first. Even when I knew he was wrong.

'You know, despite everything, I admired your mother for that,' Ruth goes on. 'Your mother always did what was right by her children.'

My breath catches and I want to ask what she means, but Ruth doesn't give me a chance. 'I shouldn't have always put him first,' she murmurs, dropping the hand that clutches the photos to her lap as the other reaches up to clasp her dressing gown closer together.

'Ruth ...' My heart is reverberating in my ears. 'I know the truth about Jill. I know you're not her birth mother.'

Her hand slips from her gown, her fingers trailing down until they hang midway to her lap. She looks as if she has stopped breathing. Only a slight rise in her chest gives her away.

I wait for her to question this but she looks like she's been expecting it for a long time. 'I had every right to be a mother,' she says, her words barely audible. 'It was all I ever wanted. I looked at people like *her* and I thought, how could she have been given two babies and I can't even have one? It wasn't fair.' Her eyes dart up to find mine, challenging me to contradict her. 'Annie told you,' she adds, quietly. 'I didn't think she ever would.'

'No.' I cock my head. 'I didn't realise Annie knew.'

'Then ...?'

'I met Iona's mother. Iona came to the island looking for Jill, didn't she?'

Ruth gives a short laugh and shakes her head. Ignoring my question, she says, 'She was never a mother. She didn't want either of her children. She wasn't interested in whether they had enough food or that the stench of their nappies filled the room because they hadn't been changed all day. Her daughter was seven and was still wearing one,' she continues, her eyes widening, glaring. As the realisation dawns on both of us that she must be talking about Iona, Ruth looks away.

'She was too high or drunk to care. Being a mother is a gift and she didn't deserve it.' Ruth sticks her chin out defiantly.

'What happened?' I ask, grateful that she clearly wants to talk and eager she does so before Bob walks in the house.

'Bob blamed himself for the fact I never got pregnant, though we never actually knew if it was him or me. Then one day he came home and gave me a solution. A baby girl who needed a good home and good parents. And a chance to live on a perfect island. What was I supposed to do?' she asks, splaying her palms upright, like she thinks anyone would have done the same.

'Adopt?'

'And what's the difference?' She shakes her head. 'We'd tried that anyway. I'd already done everything by the book but someone was still looking down on me, deciding I shouldn't be a mum.'

Or perhaps that Bob shouldn't be a father, I think.

She carries on, proving me right. 'Bob came home drunk for one of the adoption visits, saying he couldn't get away from work, though it was obvious he'd forgotten. I saw my last chance fly out the door with the social workers as they left. But it wasn't my fault. The system failed me, and it would have failed Jill too, and I *knew* I could give her a wonderful life. And she had one. She didn't spend precious years worrying about where her next meal was coming from or sleeping on a damp mattress.'

'But it still doesn't make it right,' I say.

'I loved her,' Ruth goes on breathlessly. 'I loved her so much.'

'I know you did.'

'But I failed her too in the end, didn't I? I didn't know she was sick.'

Despite myself, I reach for Ruth's hand.

'Jill missed you a lot when you left, she – she never stopped hoping you'd come back,' Ruth says, looking to the corner of the room. 'She never knew you wrote. Bob kept your letters from her, so she never knew how to find you.'

'Why would he do that?' I gasp.

'I'm sorry.' She pulls her hand away. 'I didn't want him to, but after everything that happened—'

'Do you mean with Iona? Ruth, what happened to her?' I press forward, leaning across the table.

Ruth draws in a deep breath and releases it slowly. 'I wasn't there. I don't know.'

'I think you do.'

'Only what I've been told.' She looks at me, tears sliding down her cheeks. Running a hand up and down her dressing gown, she scratches at her skin through the thick fabric.

A door slams at the back of the house. Only my eyes move as they flick to the side, expecting Bob to have appeared in the room.

Another slam. A heavy thud.

'You should go,' Ruth whispers, her words so quiet I'm not sure I heard them. 'Go,' she says again, but I don't budge, and suddenly Bob is standing in the doorway, a heavy dark coat slicked damp with rain, black hair sculpted off his face, eyes boring through me.

Fight or flight.

I answered flight in my counselling training. I always knew I wasn't brave. Not when it came to it. But tonight I freeze.

Evergreen Island

7 September 1993

Iona was sitting on the bench by the quay as David said she would be. She looked up when Maria emerged from between the trees and Maria hesitated for a moment before walking over and sitting beside her.

'We're not who you're looking for.' Maria studied the girl. Iona didn't look as confident as she had earlier and Maria wondered what conversation David might have already had with her. 'I think you're here looking for a sister, and while you look alike, it's not Bonnie.'

'That would suit you, wouldn't it?' Iona said, but it was spoken with resignation rather than malice.

'Why do you think your sister is here, Iona?' She needed to understand what the girl knew.

Iona hugged her knees to her chest. 'I always remembered I'd once had a baby sister, but my mum used to tell me I was wrong. She said I was making it up. I knew I wasn't, though. I remembered her being in the room. I remembered her cry. Her smell. You don't make things like that up, do you?'

Maria gave a small shake of her head.

'She was there one day and not the next. I never gave up on the idea of her, finding out what happened. Part of me thought my mum might have done something to her.' She shuddered. 'Then three years ago I decided to look for her. I told Mum and she completely flipped. She got really angry and wasn't making any sense, but she was so out of it, she suddenly blurted the truth.' Iona gave a short laugh. 'She admitted she'd sold her baby. How sick is that? I couldn't look at her after that. There was no way I could speak to her again, and thank God she realised that and had enough intelligence to leave me alone.'

'What did you do?'

'I saw this TV programme about adoption. I'd started seeing a guy who worked at the hospital and he was a useless idiot but he helped me look up all sorts of records. There was one care worker who used to visit us all the time and I recognised her name when we found it. My mum used to mutter, "Oh look, Joyful is here"' – Maria flinched at her mother's name – 'but I always looked forward to her coming because she was kind. She brought me treats.

'Then I found her obituary in the paper,' Iona went on. 'It said she'd had a daughter.' She turned and looked at Maria. 'I kind of thought that lead had come to a dead end but I looked up your name anyway and found a picture of you in a newspaper. You were protesting about some developments on the island.'

Maria remembered the article. Stella had proudly stuck the clipping in her scrapbook.

'Your name was in the headline clear as day, and right next to it was another one I recognised. At first I couldn't work out why I'd heard of Annie Webb, but then I remembered seeing her in the records as a midwife. Maybe I shouldn't have read anything into you and Annie both living on this remote island together, but it seemed strange. I wanted to come and see it for myself. So I came over for a day trip. And then another. And I watched you and your precious family and—' Iona suddenly stopped.

'Go on,' Maria urged in a whisper.

'You all looked so perfect from the outside. Or you did at first. But Bonnie – she looked nothing like the other two, I could see that straight away. And the more I watched her the more I realised she was an outcast. I knew she must be the sister that had been taken from me and I hated that she had all this and I'd been left with nothing.' She spat out the last word.

'Only she isn't the sister that was taken from you,' Maria said.

'But when I came over at the start of the summer she latched on to me, telling me all these things like she never felt she belonged here and didn't feel like part of the family ...' Iona drifted off as Maria caught her breath. She couldn't bear to hear Bonnie actually felt that way. All the things that had always worried her might be true.

'I promise you Bonnie is not the girl you're looking for,' Maria said.

'I know,' Iona replied and Maria was taken aback.

She opened her mouth to ask, *how do you know?* but the words caught in her throat.

The ensuing silence was unbearable until Iona said, 'David told me she couldn't be. He said Bonnie's mother was only fifteen.'

Maria's heart leaped into her mouth. She felt her skin turn cold, inch by inch, until her whole body was frozen.

David told her that? He had admitted what they'd done?

'I know my mum was older than thirteen when she had me, so ...' Iona shrugged. 'Why did *you* do it?' she asked.

Maria couldn't speak. She wanted to. She wanted to scream that her husband had betrayed them in the worst possible way. He had failed their family. For this girl. This stranger.

Slowly the blood drained from her face.

'Please tell me why you did it,' Iona went on. 'I just need to understand, and then ...' She waved a hand towards the water.

And then you'll go? Maria thought. *And then I'll get rid of you forever?*

'I'd lost two babies,' Maria said in a tight whisper. 'I was worried I wasn't ever going to have one of my own.' Her body was rigid with fury. That, she realised, had overtaken fear and now all she could think was that she had to get this girl off the island, but not for Iona's safety, which David seemed so concerned about – for her family's.

'So you thought you'd take someone else's?' Iona asked.

'It wasn't like that.' Maria shook her head vigorously. 'I met her once. I had to. I needed to have some kind of—' Maria bit her lip. 'I wanted to reassure myself we were doing the right thing.'

'You wanted to clear your conscience.'

'No,' Maria said adamantly, twisting round to face Iona. 'This young girl's parents refused to have anything to do with her after she got pregnant. She'd lost everything and she was desperate. She was living in a bedsit and she thought ...' Maria paused. 'She believed the only way through it was to start again. On her own.

'I know what we did might not have been legal, but Bonnie would have been put into foster care and I saw what some of those places were like when I went with my mum. I also knew our money would do much more for that girl than any other so-called support. So actually – actually, my conscience was clear. Bonnie's birth mother straightened herself out with what we gave her.'

'Unlike mine,' Iona said solemnly. 'So, who *is* my sister then?'

'I don't know,' Maria said faintly. 'I don't know anything about your sister.' This was of course a lie, but Maria wouldn't tell her the truth.

Iona let out a sigh and turned away. 'So she might never have been brought to this island? She could be anywhere.'

'She could be, yes.'

A part of Maria's heart fractured at the thought that the sister Iona was looking for was within grasping distance. But she needed Iona to leave. If Bob had been told who Iona was searching for, she wasn't safe.

'I'm so sorry about what you've been through, but there's nothing on this island for you,' Maria said. 'I think it's best you don't stay any longer.'

'So that I don't tell anyone?' Iona turned to her. 'Is that what you're afraid of?'

'We can make sure you're alright,' Maria went on.

'You mean pay me off?'

'We can help.'

Iona laughed. 'You think I'm here for money?'

'No, I can't give you what you're here for. But I do think money could give you a new start. Don't you?'

'So I just go now, do I?' Iona smirked as if the idea were ludicrous.

'First thing in the morning,' Maria said. 'I think you should say goodbye to Bonnie. Tell her you've got a sick aunt who needs you urgently. David will take you to the mainland at eight.' Maria leant over and clasped her hands around Iona's. 'We'll get your money for you then, but I'm begging you not to say anything to her. I promise we can help you.'

Maria's heart thumped an unsteady beat as she waited for Iona to refuse.

'Fine. I'll be there.'

Maria's eyes widened as she nodded. 'Great. Okay. Good,' she said as she let go of Iona's hands and stood, all the while tearing herself into little pieces. It wasn't right to deny Iona her sister, but what else could she do?

Maria passed through the white picket fence, kicking it shut behind her as she looked up to see David waiting for her at the kitchen window. All those little broken pieces began to mould together into an iron clump in her chest. His own guilt had led him to admit to the girl what they'd done, and she knew in that moment she would never be able to forgive him for that.

PRESENT

Chapter Thirty-One

'What the hell are you doing here again?' Bob growls, peeling off two thick black gloves from his hands and tossing them to the side. 'I told you—'

'She was just leaving,' Ruth interrupts, quickly standing and trying to bustle me up too.

Bob steps forward. His hand blocks me from moving as he stretches it across me, leaning on the back of my chair. 'I asked what you're doing here,' he says, eyes roaming my face, an action that makes him look nervous though the rest of him gives no such impression.

'I just wanted to speak to you both,' I tell him.

He raises his eyebrows. 'Go ahead.'

Ruth patters behind him, tapping from one foot to the other, but when Bob turns to look at her she immediately stills. 'What have you been telling her?' he demands.

She shakes her head, her lips part. 'She knew,' Ruth says quietly. 'She already knew about Jill.'

Bob raises his hand and slams it back on the chair, glaring at Ruth.

'She's telling the truth,' I say. 'I knew about Jill before I came back today.'

'Go upstairs,' he tells his wife.

Ruth hesitates. She glances at me, then back at Bob, but it only takes a moment before she disappears and her footsteps race up the stairs.

Confident she's gone, Bob turns back to me, glowering, and strides around the table to sit down opposite me. His movements are slow and purposeful as if he's not fazed by me one bit. 'So what are you doing here?' he asks me again.

'I want to know the truth,' I tell him.

'And what business do you think it is of yours?'

'My brother is innocent,' I say. When Bob doesn't react I go on, 'I don't think he killed Iona but I believe someone's happy for him to take the blame.'

Bob dips his head ever so slightly to one side.

'Iona came to the island looking for her sister. She was here for Jill.' I try keeping my words level, though each sentence comes out in sharp puffs.

'And I take it you've gone to the police with your so-called information?'

I open my mouth, pause, clamp it shut again.

Bob laughs, his head lolling back. 'No, I didn't think so. Why is that?' When I don't answer he goes on, 'I killed Iona. Is that what you think?'

'You had reason to,' I say. My hands tremble behind me and I tell myself he won't harm me while Ruth's upstairs, though she's been covering up for him for years.

My eyes flick to the front door, an action that seems to amuse him, but I'm certain I could outrun him if I need to.

'You think I'm the only one with a motive?' he asks. 'I imagine you've already worked out someone else had one too, only you don't like the thought of that.'

'I don't know what you mean.' The words tumble out of my mouth.

Bob laughs again. 'It was your parents who were freaked by her arrival, not me. Though I think you already know that.'

I bite my lip, willing my heart to stop hammering.

Bob presses his fists to his mouth and then splays his hands flat against the table as he considers his best option. 'You see, whatever I might have done, I only agreed because your parents had set a precedent. I assume you know Bonnie isn't actually your real sister?'

The air around me stills.

'Iona knew that but she didn't have a clue about Jill,' he goes on as if he hasn't just told me the one thing that has split my world in two.

My ears buzz and I shake my head, trying to stop the noise so I can focus on what he's telling me, but the room is beginning to spin and I feel like I might throw up.

'It was your parents whose exposure was being threatened, not mine,' he is saying, 'so I had no reason to kill her, did I?'

'Of course you did.' My words sound foreign, hazy, like they don't belong to me.

'Your parents were determined that girl was going to ruin their lives. So, you think you can come here and get your brother off the hook because he's innocent? Well, he probably is,' Bob leers, leaning back in his chair like he's played his trump card. 'But I'm not your killer.'

His eyes bore into me as he leans forward until his face is only inches from mine. I smell sweat, and stale onion on his breath, and automatically pull back, trying to find my footing as I edge myself out of the chair.

'I told you before you shouldn't be here, digging around. You were never going to like what you found.'

'I know you sent me the threats,' I say.

'Threats?' He screws his face up.

'The notes you've been leaving me. I've taken the first one to the police. They'll know you've got something to hide, so there's no point trying to put this on my parents.'

Bob laughs. 'I can honestly say I have no idea what you're talking about.'

'You want my brother to go to prison so the police don't come looking for you,' I say.

Bob prods his thick fingers against his chest. '*I* didn't kill her. *I* didn't run away,' he sneers, his eyes roaming over my face as he presses closer again. I inch my way around him, desperate for him to get out of my face. Whatever I'd come here for, I no longer want to hear. Whatever Bob tells me, I need to go to the police with what I know.

'Who made the decision to up and leave in the middle of a storm?' he says.

I flinch as a drop of his spit lands on my lip, and I push back further until I'm almost in the doorway to the hall. 'I don't believe you. My dad could never—'

'No,' Bob laughs. 'No. I don't actually think your dad could.'

My hand grips the door frame and I use it to steady myself. *I don't want to hear what you're telling me, Bob.* The words scream inside my head but they don't come out.

'Not the answers you came here for?' he is saying. 'What a shame. You were so keen to find out what happened.'

'You can make anything up because my parents can't defend themselves.' I stumble backwards, feeling for the front door behind me. I want to hold my hands over my ears, sing loudly, do anything to stop his lies.

'Thing about this place is that secrets can stay hidden for a very long time.'

I reach down for my coat and when I straighten up he is right beside me. I'm surprised at his sudden agility. He moves quickly for such a big man.

'You really want the truth?' Bob says.

No. I really don't think I do any more. I turn the door knob, opening the door as a rush of cold air slaps me, and I stumble outside.

'Your mother killed Iona,' he says as I start scrambling up the driveway. 'And I'm the one who's been keeping her secret all these years.

'You can run but you can't go far,' he calls after me. 'You know there's no way off this island tonight.'

I reach the top of the path, falling against a tree. A rise of nausea swells inside me, making me retch over my shoes and my already sodden jeans. Rainwater smears my vomit into streaks and stings my eyes, but none of these things matter any more. None of it matters.

Evergreen Island

8 September 1993

David punched his fist into the kitchen counter. Iona hadn't turned up for the eight o'clock ferry that morning. He supposed there should be a part of him that shouldn't be surprised, but Maria had been convinced she would show. He'd even heard Iona regurgitating the lie about her sick aunt to Bonnie. 'Have you seen her?' he demanded.

Maria shook her head. 'What about Bonnie? She was supposed to say goodbye.'

'No.' Bonnie was still upstairs in bed. He'd looked in on her only moments ago. 'What if something's already happened to Iona?' he hissed. Maria had barely spoken to him all night, barely looked at him. He knew he'd done wrong. He shouldn't have admitted the truth to the young girl, but she'd opened up her heart and he couldn't bear to see her pain. Not when he felt partly responsible.

Besides, Iona already knew what they had done seventeen years ago. He'd seen it in her eyes. She might have come for the wrong child, but Iona was clever, she'd worked it out. David shook his head as he stared at his wife. She looked like a stranger to him that morning.

He sighed deeply. The truth was he could tell himself it was Iona who brought the confession out of him, but deep down he'd been waiting to unbridle his guilt since the moment they'd made that terrible decision all those years ago. He'd lived with the burden for years, and many times he'd considered whether there'd be relief when he finally was honest. He'd convinced himself there would be. That maybe then he'd feel like he'd paid for what they'd done and the heavy weight of culpability would be lifted. Iona had pressed a button inside him and he'd wanted to be liberated.

Only he didn't feel relieved. It hadn't actually surfaced.

'Is she all you're worried about?' Maria was crying, having turned to glare at him. 'What about us?' She slapped a hand hard against her chest.

'You know she's not all I'm worried about,' he replied, as calmly as he could. 'But we do have to find her.'

'You mean *I* have to find her,' his wife snapped, picking up her house keys, tossing them in her bag.

By midday Maria had found no sign of her.

Every time she returned to the house she would check in on all the children, who thankfully seemed blissfully unaware their family was hanging by a precariously thin thread. Bonnie was in her room, refusing to come out. Danny was in the treehouse and Stella was reading at the bottom of the garden.

Each time she would ask them if they were okay, her voice high-pitched, her feet tapping the ground, desperate to get back to her search. She knew she looked frantic but the children were luckily absorbed in themselves. How she had wanted to scoop them into her arms, hold them together. Get off the island themselves. Run.

She'd lost count of the number of times she'd scoured it for signs of Iona, but each time she'd returned home she would linger again, watching one of them, her pulse ticking like a bomb. What would she have to do to keep them safe?

Anything, she'd told herself, as she set out again. Anything.

She didn't see how else the girl could have got off the island, but by evening, when there was still no sign of Iona, she began to think she must have. Yet Maria went out once more.

As she left the house she noticed Bonnie watching from her bedroom window, her hands splayed against the glass. Maria turned her back on her eldest and carried on towards the woods. Stella was fast asleep in bed. Danny had gone out an hour ago. Usually she would ask where her son was going, but that night she hadn't.

The woods were dark but she carried a torch, arcing it wide as she scurried between the trees. When she came out on the path she scanned the lakes and then took the route that circled the island, leading past the clifftop and Pirate's Cove, all the time flashing her light on empty beaches. She briefly hesitated outside the pub but didn't linger, and wasn't far from home when a scream filled the air. It wasn't a piercing one, but it was enough for her to stop and turn to the right.

When she heard another, she flashed the torch in its direction and stepped off the path. As soon as she saw the two figures in the small clearing by the edge of the cliff, she knew who they were.

Danny had heard his mum's voice, crying out, demanding what was going on, but he couldn't let go of Iona's arm. In her other she had his drawing book, stretched out of his reach, and as much as he'd yelled at Iona to give it back, she wouldn't. She just laughed at him instead.

'Danny, what are you doing?' his mum cried. She was right behind him now and he knew she'd make him let go of Iona, but if he did he might never get his drawing book back.

But then his mum seemed more interested in her instead. 'Iona, you were supposed to have left,' she said.

'Silly me,' Iona replied, her teeth gritted as she turned to look at Maria. 'I must have missed the ferry.' Her eyes were as black as coal yet they still sparkled fiercely bright. Maybe Danny's mum would finally see in her what he had for weeks – that Iona wasn't actually that nice.

'You never had any intention of going?' his mum was saying. She sounded pretty annoyed about it, but then if her aunt was sick she should have gone.

'I was never here for the money,' Iona snapped.

Danny didn't have a clue what they were talking about, but in the moment they both seemed to have forgotten he was standing there.

'So what are you going to do now?' His mum's voice was shrill and he could tell by the way she panted that she was scared of the answer.

Iona laughed. 'Oh well, let me see.' Danny watched the arm that was clutching his book relax. If he caught her off guard ... 'I could start by telling Danny here what you did. Would you be interested, *Dan*?' she said, cocking her head to one side.

His mum took a step closer. 'Danny, get back to the house,' she hissed.

He didn't move as he kept his eyes on his book. Of course he was interested in what his mum had done, but he was more focused on the fact that if he just reached out he could probably grab the book while Iona wasn't paying attention.

'Danny,' his mum said in her firm voice. 'Let's go back to the house.' Finally she must have clocked his drawing pad in Iona's hand because she said, 'Give it to him. Please. He doesn't deserve to be brought into this. Then you and I can talk.'

Now he was annoyed because Iona stretched the book further out of his reach. 'He watches everything, everyone, you know that?' she was saying, flapping it in her hand. 'It's weird.'

'Give me back my book.' His cry was louder now, more desperate.

'And Bonnie's got issues, I assume you realise?' She wasn't listening to him. 'I really don't think we'd have been friends in a different life. I'm not surprised she doesn't have any others.'

'Don't say that,' his mum roared. 'Don't say that about my daughter.'

'Only she's not your daughter, is she?' Iona yelled as Danny finally saw his chance: Iona's arm had dropped again. 'She knows you don't like her as much as the others. Everyone can see you don't have as much time for her, but then I don't blame you. I wouldn't have much time for her either—'

'Stop!' Maria shouted just as Iona was screaming, 'She has what *I* should have had,' and Danny yelled, 'Give me back my book.'

He lunged at it with such force that Iona lost her footing, stumbling backwards. He didn't notice in the dark how close she was to the edge as he reached out again, knocking into her, and then suddenly, she wasn't there.

Maria didn't move. It felt like an eternity that she stood rooted to the spot but in reality it was probably no more than three seconds. 'Oh my God. Oh God,' she finally muttered, running forward, peering over the edge of the cliff as she flashed her light on the beach below.

Beside her Danny was whimpering loudly. 'Is she dead?'

'No, shush,' Maria replied, pulling back to look at her son. His eyes danced with fear as he hopped from one foot to the other. 'No, of course she isn't dead.'

God, how Maria hoped she wasn't. She wasn't moving. Maria looked back over her shoulder, but from here she could no longer see the girl. As Danny continued to bounce nervously in front of her she knew she couldn't check while he was with her.

'Tell you what, let's get you home and then I'll come back to make sure she's alright. And I'll get your book,' Maria added as she led him away, all the time glancing behind her as if she expected Iona to suddenly appear.

Danny was surprisingly obliging. She deposited him at the kitchen door and told him to go to bed and that she wouldn't be long. She hated leaving him so traumatised but she had no choice.

As soon as Maria got back to the small slip of beach she saw Iona's body lying on the sand. Only she quickly noticed there was someone crouching beside her. Maria's heart must have stopped for she could no longer feel its beat.

She slowly stepped forward until the person looked up, their face ghostly white against the moonlight.

'Annie?' Maria breathed out.

'She's dead,' Annie whispered. 'Do you know what happened?'

'Oh, Annie.' Maria collapsed next to her. How was she going to explain what she was doing running along the beach so late at night? She couldn't think of any good reason why she'd be there.

She couldn't pretend she knew nothing about it. Not to Annie who'd always been so fiercely loyal to her. And thank God it was her on the beach. There was nothing her dear friend wouldn't do for her.

But she couldn't tell her the truth.

'We had an argument at the top of the cliff,' she blurted. 'It was an accident, but I—'

'*You* did?' Annie said, her eyes wide.

It looked like she didn't believe her, but Maria was sticking to that story. 'I didn't mean to,' she insisted.

'No, no, my dear. Of course you didn't.'

'Only she was saying such awful things—' Maria really should stop but the need to absolve her son was overwhelming. 'What's going to happen?' she whispered, knowing she needed Annie to take care of it.

Often David would ask her what Annie had been doing on the beach at that moment, how long she'd been there. Maria couldn't tell him because she never did ask.

David had never liked the way Annie had looked after them since the day they'd arrived on Evergreen, and there was a time when that had been the one thing they'd openly argued over. Maria would see the glint of mistrust in his eyes when he questioned her about that dreadful night, but she no longer cared what he thought of Annie. By then they both knew that trusting her was all they had left.

PRESENT

Chapter Thirty-Two

I fumble Annie's key into her lock, throwing the door open, crying out with shock when I see her standing in the hallway. She looks ghostly in her nightie, a candle flickering on a plate in one hand. Her eyes drift down my body and I see her intake of breath but she doesn't comment as she carefully puts the candle to one side and reaches for my coat, gently peeling it off me.

'I was worried about you,' she says, shaking it on to the doormat before hanging it on an antler. 'I came downstairs and found you gone. Where have you been?'

Annie slowly bends on to her knees and begins lifting up one of my legs so she can take off a boot. One by one I allow her to do this, before she carefully lines them up by the door. It's an effort for her to push herself up again.

'I'm running you a hot bath.' She turns, gripping on to the banister as she climbs the stairs, then disappears around a corner at the top.

Still I stand rooted to the doormat, silent, streaked in sick and soaked through to my skin. She appears again with a thick grey towel in one hand. 'Remove your clothes,' she demands and I glance down, finally taking hold of my top and lifting it over my head.

When I am undressed to my underwear Annie wraps my shivering body in the towel and leads me up the stairs. When we get to the top I stop on the landing. 'He said my mum killed Iona.'

Annie draws a deep breath, biting down on her lip, before finally releasing it and manoeuvring me towards the bathroom.

Once inside she lets go, leaning over to swirl her hand in the water and turning off the taps. I feel like a child as she gently removes the towel and hangs it on a rail, nodding towards my knickers and bra. Silently I remove them and climb into the bath, sinking under the heat of the water, grateful for the bubbles that cover me.

'Annie, tell me what happened. I need to know.'

'We can talk downstairs when you've warmed up,' she says.

'No.' I shake my head. 'I need to know now. It wasn't Mum, was it?'

Annie frowns and says softly, 'Yes. I'm afraid it was.'

'No!' I let out a painful wail as I close my eyes, sinking deeper into the water. When I open them I see the same pain etched into the lines of her face.

'You knew. All this time you knew what she'd done. Was it you who told them to leave the island?'

'No. Your parents made their own decision about that.'

'How could you? I mean, you've lied for her, for so many years. Why did you do that?'

'I loved your mother,' she says simply. 'I loved you all. What she did might have been wrong, but ...' Annie pauses, pulling out a wicker stool from beside the basin and lowering herself awkwardly on to it. 'I don't believe she intended it to happen. It was an accident. Your mother was scared.'

'So she should have been,' I say, gulping back a sob. 'After what she did.'

Annie's eyes bore into mine but she is expressionless. I can't read her.

'You know about Bonnie?'

'I know,' Annie says.

'Who else does?' I cry.

'No one. No one else at all.'

'Apart from Bob and Ruth.'

'Yes, apart from them.'

'God! I don't believe what they all did. Did you help Mum and Dad come over here? Dad said they knew you before. Was it you who did that?'

'Yes,' she says calmly.

'Why?' I gasp, incredulous. 'I mean, why would you?'

'I knew your gran for a very long time. She was a good, old friend of mine. She did something once for me that I will never forget. She saved my life. She saved me from someone who would have hurt me. So when she asked me for help, I would have done anything.'

'It was my gran's idea?' I cry.

'She saw how those families lived in squalor. Ways you couldn't imagine. Wallpaper peeling off damp walls, holes in the bare floorboards. She used to tell me it was like they were in the midst of a war zone, some of them six children sleeping in the same dirty room they ate and washed in. One day she arrived to find one of her mothers holding her baby as she tried to stop a bulldozer knocking her home down.

'The poverty was sickening but at least most of the mothers cared for their kids. Imagine adding in those who were high on drugs, or only kids themselves. Your gran got to know every one of them, including those she knew couldn't look after their babies.'

'But even so, getting them to sell their children—'

'She hoped the money would help them out,' Annie says, seeming exasperated that I still can't accept this. 'And for Bonnie's mother it did. But like I said, I owed your gran everything, and I grew to love your mother like she was my own.'

'Why did you help Bob and Ruth—' I start as Annie pushes herself off the stool.

'Have your bath and warm up.' She flicks a hand towards the water. 'I'll make us a drink and we can talk downstairs.'

A loud thud makes us both jump. I shoot upright as Annie reaches a hand to steady herself.

'That wasn't thunder,' I say. It dawns on me only now that the storm has stopped, though rain still hammers against the small pane in the bathroom.

'I'll check it out.'

'Annie, be careful,' I say as she goes to the door. 'Bob – I don't trust him. I think he's been sending me threats and tonight he told me I can't get off the island.'

She hesitates in the doorway. 'You can't,' she says plainly.

'I have to. Bob doesn't want me going to the police, but I can't let Danny go to prison for something he didn't do. They'll charge him with murder by morning if I don't tell them the truth.'

'But your family – your mother – this all comes out and – it *can't* come out, Stella.'

'You can't expect me not to say anything?' I gape at her. She's known Danny's confessed for days. 'You'd let him go to prison for something he didn't do?'

'Oh, my dear ...' Annie's eyes water.

'Annie, I know what you've done for my mum, but Danny – you know you can't do that to him.'

'Only ...' She hesitates, one hand holding on to the open door.

'What is it?'

'The night it happened – I only have your mother's word for it.'

'I'm not following.'

'She told me she was the one who pushed Iona, yet—'

'What are you suggesting, Annie?'

'Deep down?' she says gravely. 'I always thought she might be covering for him. He was arguing with Iona on that clifftop right before it happened.'

'No,' I say defiantly.

'And if that's the case—'

'It's not,' I cut her off angrily, 'and even if it were, Mum didn't want anyone to know and she would never want her son to be blamed for murder. You just told me Mum did it, you can't start twisting it around now. This is getting too much,' I cry. 'I don't know what to believe any more.

'I have to talk to the police,' I add more quietly when she doesn't answer. 'I have to.'

Annie pulls in a tight breath. 'I'll make us that drink,' she says before closing the door behind her. 'Try not to worry,' she calls. I swear I hear her locking the door.

Chapter Thirty-Three

Exhausted, I let the hot water burn into my cold, aching muscles, but I can't relax, and after a while I pull myself out, grabbing the towel from the rail and wrapping it around me before trying the handle.

It doesn't open. I pull at it again, futilely twisting it, calling Annie's name, and after a while I hear her approaching, finally unlocking it with an apology that she hadn't realised.

I stare at her in disbelief as I follow her downstairs to where she's laid out a pair of old jogging bottoms and a fleece, both of which are far too small for me but I put on anyway. 'Are you sure you didn't mean to lock the bathroom door?' I ask, following her into the kitchen where she's fiddling with a lighter, her shaking hand attempting to light another candle.

'I thought we deserved something stronger,' she says, ignoring me. 'I've poured us both a sherry.' She finally lights the wick and tosses the lighter into a drawer, shutting it quickly, pressing her hand against it for a moment too long.

'Did you find out what the noise was?' I ask as she gestures to two glasses. I take a small sip of the sweet drink, grimacing but thanking her anyway.

Annie shakes her head. 'Must have been something outside.'

She seems nervous, evading my questions. There is more she's not telling me, but with nowhere either of us can go, I resolve that at some point during the night I'll find out what it is.

Annie brushes past me, back to the living room. 'You know, I never knew how your mum could have pushed her with such force,' she says. 'Her being such a slight woman. The way Iona hit that rock ...'

I feel myself stiffen. I don't like her insinuation and there's something about what she's just said that doesn't sit right, though I can't put my finger on it. 'Annie, I realise you don't want me speaking to the police,' I say, 'but you can't suddenly be happy to put the blame on Danny.'

'I just wish I could tell you exactly what happened,' she sighs.

'And that's just it. You can't. But you told me upstairs you always believed it was my mum. Now Danny thinks he did it and—' I break off, waving my arm in the air as tears fill my eyes.

There are two possibilities, neither of which bear thinking about, and I'm left suspended between them with no idea what I'd prefer the truth to be.

I take another sip of sherry and sink on to the sofa, closing my eyes as I picture myself opposite me in my counselling room.

What would you prefer? I ask. *That your mum was a killer, or your brother?*

It's a trick question. There's no good outcome. It's like the story of the mother we discussed in training who had two sons and one murdered the other.

What did she do again? I ask.

In the end she stood by the son who'd killed the other because he was all she had left.

'True story,' I say aloud.

'Sorry?' Annie asks. 'Stella, are you okay?'

My eyes snap open. 'I know you're worried about what might happen to you, Annie, but regardless, we need to go to the police.'

'Oh, my dear, I'm too old to be worrying about myself any more.'

I lean forward, even though it feels like an effort to do so. 'I need to get off the island, Annie.' The thought of being trapped here is suffocating. I can almost see an imaginary clock sucking the time away, just like the air around me. I flap the neck of the fleece I'm wearing, wondering if Annie feels as hot as I do.

'I don't see any way you could possibly do that. Who knows you're here?' She takes a slow sip of her drink, peering steadily over the rim of her glass.

'No one. I didn't even tell Bonnie.'

I take another sip myself, resting my head back as the room sways softly out of focus.

'Oh, God. Bonnie,' I groan. I had almost forgotten my sister. Everything she's feared will slot together and make her realise she was right to feel the way she always did – that she has never belonged.

Bonnie must have been taken from her real mother at such a young age. I know the impact that can have; I have clients with adopted children who have attachment disorder. Triggers are set in place before we can even imagine.

Bonnie was obsessed that Mum was always trying to fix her with those sessions – maybe Mum was trying to prevent something from happening even if she didn't know what.

'Stella?' Annie's voice stirs me but it's an effort to lift my head. 'You obviously need to rest.' She pulls a blanket over my legs, rubbing a hand against my shin. 'Lie down.'

'No.' I force myself upright. 'I have to find a way to get back.'

She takes a deep breath and releases it in a sigh. 'I have something I need to show you.' Her slippers patter across the hallway floor.

My head is beginning to throb. I press a hand against my hot skin. My mouth feels dry. I need a drink. When I stand it takes a moment for me to right myself as the room swishes in circles.

At the sink I lean my head under the tap, gulping down water, then, pulling out drawers, I search for paracetamol, my fingers trailing over elastic bands and old postcards when they suddenly stop, resting on a white piece of card.

On it are three words of an incomplete sentence. In block capitals they say I TOLD YOU –

Half dazed, I pick it up, staring at the writing, looking over my shoulder before clutching it tightly and making my way to the hallway.

Annie has disappeared into the back room. The door is wide open, its key dangling from the lock. I hover in the doorway, lifting the card. My heart is beating far too rapidly. '*You* sent me the notes.'

She turns around. Out of her hands spill a fan of photographs, their box lying open on the table next to her.

She doesn't speak.

'It was you,' I say. 'You sent me threats. Why would you do that?'

'I didn't want you here,' she says eventually.

'So you tried to scare me?'

'You were threatening us all—'

'I thought you were on my side,' I cry.

'I *am* on your side.'

'No.' I shake my head. 'No. If you were you wouldn't send me anonymous notes telling me to stop digging, that I wouldn't like what I'd find.'

Something at the bottom of the box catches my attention. My hand reaches out for it but she pulls it out of my way.

'What was that?' I say.

'What was what?'

'In that box. It's Danny's drawing book. What are you doing with it?'

My head is spinning and I grip on to the desk to stop myself swaying. 'There are no rocks,' I say suddenly.

'What?' Annie frowns.

I shake my head, pieces of a puzzle flitting around it, trying hard to make them fit together. 'Earlier you said *the way Iona hit that rock*. There are no rocks on that part of the beach. She couldn't have hit one.'

The overheard snatches of conversation in the police station dance in front of me. What had been said? The injuries from the fall could have killed her but they weren't sure. It was made to *look like* she hit a rock.

If Annie answers I don't hear. My head is whirring, thoughts wrapping themselves around each other. 'I don't feel right,' I say, stumbling forward. 'Annie? I don't feel well.'

I wait for her to help but she steps further away.

'What did you do?' My words are little more than a whispered slur. Even I hear the way they snake out of my mouth, twisting in the air. I no longer know if I'm asking her what she did to Iona or to me.

Annie's eyes have darkened. Or maybe it's the effect of the flickering light. Either way I try hard to focus, to gauge her reactions, because I know well enough it's the little things that give people away.

Her fingers grip her desk. She takes a deep breath that she isn't able to let go. Her eyes try to focus on me but she blinks frequently as if searching for the answer she should give.

Her hands shake now as she looks away. 'I never wanted it to get to this, Stella, but you wouldn't stop.' She says it like this is my fault.

I hold my hand over my mouth as nausea soars through me again.

'You just kept going,' she says, as if tired by the thought of it. 'Like your mum always used to. When she got hold of something she wouldn't let it go. She got herself into a state about Iona, panicking everyone. You know, I could have done something about it if she hadn't gone and admitted to the girl what we'd all done.'

'Annie, I really don't feel right.' I slide on to a green leather chair that sits beside the desk. She either doesn't notice or doesn't care as she ignores the fact I've slumped forward.

'Iona would have had us all sent to prison, but I could have prevented it if your mother hadn't said anything. I had no choice in the end. She fell off the cliff, it could have been Maria, it could have been your brother, I've no idea who did it. The fact is by the time I got to Iona, she was screaming bloody murder. I had to clean up the mess your mother made.'

As hazy as the room is, these words hit me.

'That's all I'm ever doing, cleaning up your family's messes,' she says, and this time her words fizzle out and darkness hits me.

Evergreen Island

8 September 1993

Maria waited for Annie to speak for what felt like an eternity. 'Who else knows she's still on the island?' Annie asked finally.

'No one.'

Annie raised her eyes.

'Only David. He knew she didn't get on the ferry.'

'Then we get rid of the body.'

'What – we can't – what are we supposed to do with her?' Maria glanced out to sea where the waves were beginning to whip up. She could feel the air still. It was always this way before a storm and the thought unsettled her even more.

'Go home,' Annie told her, 'before your family comes looking for you. Leave it with me.'

'Not Bob ...' Maria gasped. She didn't want him getting involved.

'Leave it with me,' Annie said again, firmly.

Maria ran back, her head spinning with what she'd just agreed to. There was no way they could get away with this, surely? But what would happen to them otherwise? An investigation could find her guilty, or worse, Danny. Involving the police would open up all their other secrets and she still wasn't prepared to do that.

Inside, she crept up to Danny's bedroom and gently opened his door. He pulled himself upright, his eyes filled with panic.

'She's fine,' Maria breathed, her voice rising patchily. 'There's nothing for you to worry about.'

'Are you sure?'

'Yes. I'm sure.' She tried to smile, watching her son's shoulders drop though he still looked at her uneasily.

'Did you get my book?' he asked.

She shook her head. She hadn't even thought of the damn book. 'I'll look tomorrow.'

Maria crept out of his room, closing the door behind her, her eyes filled with tears as she leant against it.

Now she had to tell David. And then they would have to leave. There was no way she could stay on this island after what had just happened.

Maria wished David would hold her close, but he was clenching her shaking body at arm's length. She'd told him it was an accident, that Iona and Danny were arguing and she'd tried to get Danny's book when Iona slipped backwards over the edge of the cliff.

She sensed he didn't believe her, but she'd started on this story now, and even though it wasn't too late to admit what had really happened, she never did. Maria would rather he always thought of her as capable of manslaughter than their son. She couldn't bear to see that in David's eyes every time he looked at Danny.

Instead she begged that Danny must never know Iona was dead. That he had to believe she was alright.

No one else would see it as an accident – at least they agreed on that. Because as soon as the police were called, they'd turn up all kinds of interesting information including what Iona was doing on the island in the first place.

Then the secret that they'd been hiding on Evergreen for seventeen years would be out.

Maria couldn't stop sobbing, gulping lungfuls of air she couldn't swallow. 'We need to leave,' she told David. 'As soon as possible.' She would have dragged the children out of their beds and fled that night.

But they agreed that would be unwise. They would go the following night. Tell everyone David had found another job because the ferry was losing them money. She would lie to Susan about the extent of their financial troubles and come hell or high water they would be off the island within twenty-four hours.

David agreed, but he remained nervous about not telling the police. Maria carried on begging him not to, that Danny couldn't possibly know Iona was dead.

That was when she saw the light dawn on him, and she wondered if he'd guessed she was covering for their son. Only he didn't ask. Maybe he would rather think she was the one capable, too.

That night they made hurried plans for the next few days, both of them talking as an invisible wall grew between them. At some point David had cried out, 'We should never have done what we did.'

Maria's heart had stopped beating in that moment, her mouth hanging open. It was a despicable thing to say when they both knew it meant they'd never have had their daughter.

Right then she'd seen their future clearly and she knew for certain at some point it would no longer be together. It broke her heart.

Months later Maria sat alone one night and considered what she finally knew to be the answer to her friend's question. When Susan had asked her if she could ever trust anyone, there was in fact only one person she believed she could hand-on-heart trust with her family's life. And she spent the rest of her days thinking this was Annie.

PRESENT

Chapter Thirty-Four

The rain has stopped. This is the first thing I notice. The second is that it's pitch-black and I'm now lying face down on the back-room floor.

I try moving my head to focus on the golden carriage clock that sits high on a bookcase, but it's heavy and my eyes swim as the clock hands go in and out in wavy lines. I cannot make out the time.

Next I try shuffling my legs to push myself to sit, but it feels as though I've been anaesthetised. Bonnie described once how it felt like she'd had the legs of an elephant when she'd had an epidural. I'd laughed at the time.

Bonnie.

Sickness surges through me and my head drops back on to my hands. An unbelievable wave of sadness hits me at the thought of my sister. I wish I'd told her I was coming. I wish I'd told anyone. I never should have come in the first place.

My eyes flutter closed again, their lids pressing together. It feels much better like this.

There's a dampness between my legs and I inch my hand closer to touch it. Have I wet myself?

My eyelids flicker open again. There are voices the other side of the door. Annie. I hear her talking to someone, telling him – what is she saying? She says they have no choice.

Bob answers – something undecipherable.

'You'll have to,' Annie says.

She's brought him here. He knows I'm lying on the other side of the door. Why's she done that?

I let out a barely audible groan as I roll my head forward, face flat against the floor, hoping to muffle the sound.

Tears of frustration leak from my eyes, pooling around my face.

Bonnie will know I'm missing, so I won't be left for twenty-five years, yet it still might be too late. By the time she starts looking I could be long gone.

It hurts to lift my head to look at the carriage clock again. Still its gold numerals flicker out of focus. The sweet taste of sherry lingers on my tongue. My mouth is so dry. Annie must have drugged me. I'm not sure if the pain at the side of my head means she also hit me or I fell out of the chair.

My arm is a lead weight, but I reach it slowly to a small, sticky patch of blood on my temple.

The voices are still outside the room but they are more muffled. I need to get out before they come back for me, though the door must be locked, and with them on the other side of it, the only choice I have is a small window behind the desk.

I close my eyes one last time, pulling in all the strength I have, taking long, deep breaths before I force myself on to my palms.

Finally the hands of the clock come into focus. It is nearly midnight. Only hours before they'll charge Danny or let him go.

Fight or flight? I'll do either.

I ease myself on to my knees, grabbing the edge of the desk as my eyes blur and bile fills my mouth, and, despite the closeness of the window, it still feels out of my reach.

There is a slam outside the door as Bob asks, 'Are you ready?'

I try to push myself to my feet, but the room spins around me like a waltzer. My elbow gives way, I drop down again, my head thudding against the floor once more.

'Where is she?' Bob's voice booms into the room and my eyelids twitch.

Annie's distant response comes quickly. 'I left her on the floor.'

He steps inside and sees my feet. I close my eyes again to his panting breath; one hand curls around my ankle as he finds his way in the dark. 'She's out cold.'

I'm grateful my head is turned away from him. Flight is no longer an option so I have no choice but to fight, though I don't see how when I can barely move.

Bob's wrapping both his hands under my legs, dragging me out from beside the desk.

'Is she breathing?' Annie asks from behind him. Her voice is close now.

Bob grunts. Thick fingers wrap around my wrist, squeezing too tight. 'Yes, but her pulse is slow.' His fingers release and I hear him shuffling to his feet. 'What do you want me to do?'

'I don't know,' Annie says quietly. 'I don't know, I guess – I can't . . .' Her words hang in the air before she scoops them up and says, 'She knows too much.'

He sighs, resigned. 'If you want me to bury her I'll need tools.'

'We can't do that. Not with the police still crawling all over the island.'

'What choice do we have?' he says gruffly and then adds, 'I can't believe I'm doing this again. First for her mother, now . . .'

'Now for me? Is that what you were about to say? After everything I've done for you, Bob.'

There is a moment's silence before he answers. 'Yes. I know.'

'We've always been in this together,' Annie goes on. 'You and me. I'm your godmother ...' This hangs in the air before sinking in to me. How had I never known how close they were? How much one might do for the other?

'I know,' he says again, resigned. 'I know. Anyway, it'll be fine. The police won't be looking for another body.'

'But they will when they know Stella is missing. She has people who'll notice.'

'I'll make sure she won't be found.'

'Like Iona was,' Annie whispers.

'This time—'

'This time don't bury her right outside *my* garden.'

'You know why I did that,' he says, like a scolded child.

My throat tightens as the words register. Not only did Bob bury Iona; he chose the exact spot on purpose, so that if anyone found her, fingers would point at my family.

'You did it for revenge,' Annie says. 'But look where it's got us.'

'I did it because Maria accused me of hurting my daughter,' he growls and my body tenses so hard I fear any moment I will cry out with the pressure.

I sense Bob getting to his feet as he says, 'I'll get my things.'

'Okay,' Annie says finally. That one word cracks in half, a give-away that she wishes it hadn't come to this. Bob leaves the room before Annie adds, so quietly I can barely hear, 'Oh, what have I done, Stella?'

*

I need to get to the window before they come back. I push myself up again, on to my knees, a slow movement that makes my head splinter with pain. The room whips around me and I hang my head forward. Objects come in and out of focus. I know if I stand I'll likely be sick.

Outside the door Annie's footsteps pad back and forth and then finally stop. I freeze too. Slowly the key turns in the door and I slide down again, back on to the floor. Light trickles in with a cold blast of air.

I hear her pause, an intake of breath as she creeps closer to me, bending down. Finally she rests a hand gently against my head, her fingers sliding into my hair, stroking it softly. It's such a caring gesture that I can't help but open my eyes, and when I do she's staring right at me.

She gasps, pulling back. There are tears in her eyes and I wonder if I could talk her round from whatever she plans to do. This is, after all, what I am good at. My job is to talk to people, to reason, find solutions when it feels like there aren't any.

But even I know there aren't and so it's only a brief thought. I have seen all too clearly that Annie's prepared to do whatever she has to to remove the threat, and that is all I am to her now.

Annie is off guard because she didn't expect me to open my eyes and stare into hers. This is my chance. I could hurl myself into her, knock her off balance.

I go to push myself up again but I am too weak, too slow, and with one hand she grabs for the carriage clock as the front door slams open and someone behind us yells.

It only takes a second for her to pause, glance towards the hallway, and in that time I manage to push up further, leaning unsteadily on one hand as I use the other to grab the clock from her grip.

Her eyes are bright with fear as she turns back to me and I open my mouth to tell her we can sort this out because deep down it's what I still want, but already my hand is drawing back and instinct is taking over as it crashes down.

Annie yelps, sinking back against the bookcase. Only a tiny trickle of blood seeps out of a small cut at the side of her head.

Oh God, what have I done?

My arm is weak and what I'd thought of as a crash must have only just scraped her skin, and now there are noises in the hallway. I missed my chance.

'Hello?' someone calls.

I can't see through to the hall, unlike Annie who turns to look. I open my mouth but no words come out.

'Annie? Oh my God. Stella, what happened? Are you hurt?'

A figure is in the room, crouching in front of us. Only now do I see it's Meg.

'Need help,' I manage.

'Yes. Yes. I'll get help,' she says but she doesn't move as her frightened eyes glance from me to Annie.

'Who did this to you?' she says, grabbing my hand and squeezing it as there's another sound from the hallway. Annie's gaze trails over Meg and then towards the noise.

I know it is Bob. I see it in the way Annie draws in a long breath, her eyelids fluttering half closed with what looks like relief.

No. Please don't, Bob. Not Meg, who is innocent in all this. Who is only fifteen and has turned up at Annie's house for a reason I can't explain but somehow I think she came looking for me. Not Meg, who is continuing to study me with concern, waiting for me to tell her who put me in this state.

It was her, I plead with my eyes, *the old lady lying next to me. But we're all in danger now.*

I squeeze Meg's hand back. I don't want her to see him standing in the hallway but at the same time I should prepare her for what's coming.

But then Annie does the one thing I least expect. She gives a small shake of her head. Only a flicker, but enough to tell him, *don't come any further.*

I hold my breath until it burns my lungs. Until there is a creak of a floorboard and then nothing more and finally Annie looks away.

'Okay, I'm getting help,' Meg says.

I have no idea why Annie's done what she just did.

'Don't go,' I say as Meg reaches into a deep pocket and pulls out a walkie-talkie.

'Stupid thing,' she mutters, 'my mum makes me take it everywhere because there's no phone reception.'

As it crackles and Meg pulls away her hand, getting to her feet, talking to Emma in short, sharp bursts of urgent conversation, I want to laugh out loud with relief. But I don't. Instead my eyelids droop and I drift into some semi-state of consciousness, aware much later of a pillow plumped under my head, a blanket wrapped over my body, hands held lightly against my forehead as we're told help is on the way.

Every time I open my eyes Annie is still beside me. She hasn't moved or spoken but her eyes snap around the room, occasionally settling on me. I consider what she will tell the police when they arrive, how she will spin what has happened, but for now she says nothing.

I pass out again and the next time I wake there are more voices murmuring around me.

'Stella, can you hear me? I'm a paramedic. We're going to take you back to the mainland and get you checked out in hospital, can you understand?'

I nod.

'Okay. We're going to lift you on to a stretcher—'

'Annie—' I say.

'Your friend's being taken care of, no need to worry.'

I try to shake my head. 'She did this to me.'

Chapter Thirty-Five

Bright lights drill through my eyelids. My mouth is sore, my head banging. 'Where am I?' I croak at a figure hovering in the corner of the room.

As she approaches she says, 'Poole Hospital. It's good to see you awake, love. How are you feeling?'

'Tired. Sick,' I tell the nurse. 'What day is it?'

'Monday morning.'

I try looking out of the window at the light streaming in between the blinds. Piece by piece the night comes back to me. 'Annie,' I say, 'the woman I was with.'

'She's fine, dear, don't worry about anyone but yourself at the moment.'

'No.' I try shaking my head but it hurts too much. 'She drugged me.'

'Oh.' The nurse looks perplexed. 'Actually, there's a detective waiting to speak to you. I can keep him at bay—'

'No,' I say again, 'I want to talk to him.'

'Well, only if you're up to it.' She hesitates. 'Your memory *will* be patchy and you need to take it easy.'

'I'll be fine.'

'And I'll be keeping an eye on you,' she says sternly, as she leaves the room.

Moments later Detective Harwood appears. 'Ms Harvey.' He smiles grimly as he walks over to the bed. 'It's been a bit of a night for you by all accounts.' He pulls out a plastic chair. He looks worried. There's a thick crease in his forehead where his eyebrows are pinched together. 'Are you okay to talk?'

'Yes. What's happening with Annie?' I ask.

'She's in the hospital.'

'She drugged me. You can't let her go.'

Harwood nods. Still his eyebrows are knitted together. His gaze roams my face, trailing down to a tube I've only just noticed is attached to my arm. 'We're going to need to take a statement from you. Are you up to doing that?'

I sense his impatience but there are too many things I don't have straight in my head. Not least the fact that as soon as I start talking I'll expose my family for what they've done. I need to speak to Bonnie first. 'I'm not sure.'

He nods, squeezing his lips together, and I can see he's weighing how much to push me, which immediately makes me think of Danny. If I don't speak now, will he be charged with murder?

'Oh God,' I groan, closing my eyes.

'Do you need the nurse?'

'No. I just— My brother didn't kill Iona.' When I open my eyes again he is staring at me, his mouth parted. 'I'll make a statement now if I have to.'

Harwood's face relaxes. He tells me he'll need to record the interview and, as he sorts out the equipment, my mind is plagued with visions of my dad being arrested, Bonnie falling apart at the truth, my relationship with my sister irrevocably breaking.

I think of the woman in the story with her two sons. We'd argued it out in training. I'd said she should have told the truth and stood by her murdered son, but now I see that wasn't an option when the other was still alive.

It's not so clear-cut for me. Three of my family's lives are hanging on threads and I'm the one holding the string.

Harwood tells me he is ready and asks me to start at the beginning of the evening.

Instead I dive into the middle and say, 'Annie Webb drugged me.'

'There was a high level of midazolam found in you and traces on one of the glasses. It's used as a sedative,' he adds when I look blank. 'We're aware of this, but it would be really helpful if you can tell me what happened in the lead-up to that.'

'She told me she'd killed Iona,' I say. My heart is pitter-pattering quickly, inside my chest. 'And I found a note in her kitchen drawer. She was the one who sent me the threats. I don't know what happened to the note.'

'We found one partially written in her office,' he tells me.

'I thought of Annie as an aunt,' I say sadly. Tears prick at my eyes. 'I thought I could trust her. Has she admitted it? It wasn't Danny.'

'Ms Harvey, I really need you to start at the beginning of the evening.' He's trying to stay patient.

'But Danny—'

'Your brother's already been released,' Harwood says. 'We didn't have enough evidence to charge him and there were too many inconsistencies in his version of events.'

'Oh!' I hold a hand over my mouth. 'He's free?'

He nods. 'We'll be keeping an eye on him but he's free.' Harwood shuffles to the edge of his chair. 'I know this isn't great timing for you, but we really need you to tell us what happened. Annie Webb isn't talking. She's neither confirmed nor denied anything at the moment.'

'She hasn't admitted she did it?'

'She hasn't said a word. That's why we need you to tell us exactly what you remember. Why she told you she killed Iona.'

'She—' I break off, screwing my eyes up.

Harwood nods encouragement. He thinks I've stopped because my memories are patchy, just like the nurse told me they would be.

In reality they're crystal clear. I remember every part of my conversation with Annie, from her telling me Mum pushed Iona off a cliff to Annie having to clean up the mess Mum made. 'She's not said anything?' I ask.

He shakes his head, pursing his lips, edging closer. He's so eager for the story and I could tell him exactly what he wants to hear. In doing so I could implicate Bob, but then I'd also be pulling my own family's lives apart in an instant.

I think back to the nurse's helpful warning. 'I'm sorry. It's all so patchy. If she told me I don't remember.'

Harwood doesn't move. He's pressed forward so much that he's almost touching the side of the bed. The air between us is heavy and it's a relief when he finally pulls back.

'I'm sorry I couldn't be more useful,' I say as the nurse appears in the doorway.

'Ms Harvey, we're going to need to talk again,' Harwood sighs, reminding me this is by no means over.

'I know,' I murmur. I understand it's far from finished. But there are two conversations I need to have first, before my patchy memory returns, though I don't relish the thought of speaking to Bonnie or Dad.

The nurse bustles Harwood out of the room as my phone rings on the table beside the bed. It's Freya. She must have been trying to get hold of me since I hadn't updated her about my search for Ange, because I have a few missed calls from her.

'Oh my God,' she screeches when I pick up the phone. 'I knew something must have gone wrong when you didn't call me back yesterday, but this—' She breaks off dramatically. 'Are you okay?'

'I'll be fine,' I tell her.

'I heard they're talking to Annie Webb.' Her voice quietens. 'I can't believe it,' she murmurs. 'Did you find Ange yesterday?'

'Yes.'

'And? Did she say any more about the sister?'

'No,' I lie. 'She wouldn't tell me anything.'

'I didn't think she would,' she sighs. 'Oh well, maybe there's nothing else to it ...' Freya drifts off as I catch Meg lingering in the doorway. I hold up a hand in a wave and she smiles back at me.

'I want to thank you, Freya,' I say. 'Without your help I don't know that my brother would be free.'

'Any time,' she says as Meg tentatively steps into the room. I beckon her over.

I tell Freya I need to go, with a promise we'll keep in touch, because there's someone else I need to thank too.

Once I hang up Meg rushes across, almost flinging herself on top of me. 'Oh my God. I've been so worried about you. How are you feeling?'

'Like I've been run over,' I smile. 'I can't thank you enough.'

'I can't even imagine what would have happened if I wasn't there,' she says. 'It doesn't bear thinking about.'

'I know.' It doesn't. 'How come you were?' I ask.

'I wanted to talk to you,' she says. 'It was the third time I'd come by Annie's house. Long story, but Susan Carlton showed up at ours, closely followed by Graham.' Meg screws up her nose. 'It turned into this horrible argument and I just ran out. I went straight to Rachel's. When she said you weren't there, the only other place I thought you might be was Annie's. The first time it must have only been just after ten but I got her out of bed.'

'I must have just missed you,' I say. It was the time I'd slipped out to Bob and Ruth's. It must have been why Annie was waiting for me when I got back.

'Well, she denied you were there but I saw bedding on the sofa. She always invites me in but she couldn't get rid of me quick enough, even though I was outside in the middle of a storm.

'Mum was a complete mess when I got home, quoting Graham that if you hadn't come back he wouldn't have had the police on to him. According to her, if that hadn't happened then Susan wouldn't have found out and turned up on our doorstep, meaning Graham wouldn't have called off their relationship.'

'Seriously?'

'I know. She'd gone totally nuts. But she was mad at you, and I was so certain Annie was lying that I went back. That time she told me you were having a bath!' Meg snorts.

'Funnily enough I was,' I smile weakly. 'But you were right to be worried.'

'Annie looked so pissed off when I turned up, and with Graham so wound up and my mum and ...' Meg trails off. 'I *was* worried, but I was looking for you for myself, too. I just really needed someone to talk to.'

'I don't care why you were there, I'm just glad you were,' I say. 'Thank you.' I reach out and take her hand as the nurse comes back in again.

'I can't believe what happened and that you were drugged and—'

The nurse clears her throat loudly. 'Visiting time's over for now,' she says. 'Stella needs rest if she wants to go home later.'

'I'm pleased I met you, Stella.' Meg leans forward and kisses me on the forehead. 'Promise me you'll come back to Evergreen?'

'You know, I don't think I will,' I say, smiling sadly. 'But I'd love for you to come see me some time.'

Eight hours later I'm wrapping my cold duvet around me in my own bed. I snuggle into my pillow, tears dampening the cotton beneath my cheeks. All around, our young faces beam back at me from behind their glass frames and I fight the urge to rip them all down.

I lied to the detective. Still I'm playing God, trying to keep my family safe. I don't know how Mum did it for all those years. Whether she nearly broke, or if it came easy because the alternative wasn't an option.

I don't have that choice. Sooner or later Annie will talk or Bob will come forward, but if they don't, I'm not like them. I can't bury the truth like they did.

I think of the two people who will suffer the most. Technicalities might excuse my dad from going on trial, but it will break him nonetheless. Yet every so often the question knifes into me: doesn't he deserve to pay?

But it is Bonnie who pains me most. My fragile sister, already broken. She will take the facts in black and white and decide for herself that she was never a part of our family, that she was right to think she never did belong.

Chapter Thirty-Six

I've avoided calls from Bonnie and Dad, messages assembling in my inbox that I couldn't bear to listen to. Instead I sent them both a brief text telling them I was alright but needed to sleep and we'd speak in the morning.

Only now morning has come and my stomach is bubbling with dread. There is no more word from Harwood. I don't know what Annie is telling them, but I do know I must face my family.

I'm in bed, still deliberating the thought, when my mobile rings, Dad's home number flashing. My heart plummets into my already knotted stomach as I pick up.

'Hello, Stella.' Olivia's voice fills the line. 'How are you?'

'I'm doing okay. Thank you.'

'Well, that's good … Your father's been worried sick. Hopefully he can put everything behind him now.'

'Hopefully. Is he there?' I ask, not interested in engaging in any more one-way conversation with his wife.

'Yes.' For a moment Olivia continues to breathe down the line and I wait for her to either tell me he can't talk at the moment or if he does I'm not to mention the island. It surprises me when she does neither.

'Stella, my darling,' Dad says when she passes him the phone. 'I've been so worried.'

'Don't be, Dad, I'm fine now.'

'What happened? What did they do to you?'

'It's a long story,' I tell him. 'It can wait for another day. The important thing is I'm home and Danny's been released. It's good news, isn't it, Dad?'

'Yes,' he says but I hear the word catch.

'Danny didn't do it. The police know this,' I reiterate.

'No,' he says quietly. 'Danny didn't do it.'

'Is everything okay?' I don't know why he doesn't seem happy about it. 'I thought you'd be pleased.'

'I know, my love, only ...' He hesitates before adding, in no more than a whisper, 'I always thought he had ...' I hear the pain in Dad's words as they trail off. 'Your mum was adamant it was her, but I never believed her. I thought she was protecting him.'

'You really thought Danny was capable?' I ask.

'No, no, it wasn't like that. I knew it was an accident, I knew he wouldn't have meant to hurt her. You know Danny,' he cries. 'He never hurt anything.'

'So you and Mum never talked about what actually happened? You never knew for sure?'

'I thought she was trying to shelter him. But clearly I was wrong,' he says, as if pulling himself together. 'So do the police know it was your mother now?'

'It wasn't Mum,' I say. 'It was Annie.'

'Annie?' he roars as I pull the phone away from my ear. 'Annie?'

Olivia fusses in the background, asking him what's wrong, demanding he pass the phone to her, but still clutching it he shouts, 'Leave me alone. Just piss off.'

I reel back. It is the first time I've heard Dad raise his voice, let alone swear.

He clears his throat and when he still doesn't speak I ask him if he's alright.

'Yes,' he says finally. 'I'm alright. But Annie Webb,' he growls. 'She killed Iona? She made us all believe it was Danny?'

'I know this is a lot to take in, but there's more I need to talk to you about. Can you move somewhere you can't be heard?'

'Olivia's in the kitchen.'

'Okay.' I hold a breath, releasing it slowly. He must be able to hear my nerves. 'It's about Bonnie,' I say, squeezing the words past the tightness of my throat. 'I know what you and Mum did.'

Questions are freefalling. I'm ready to stop on the one that seems most appropriate. What the hell were you thinking? What gave you the right to lie to us all our lives? Did you never consider what you'd done was wrong?

In the end I say, 'Annie knew Mum had told Iona what you'd done. I think that was why she was angry enough to let her think it was her fault.'

'Oh no, Stella,' Dad groans. 'Oh dear God, no.' He starts to cry. I picture him curled into a ball, clutching the phone tightly against his ear. It's a pitiful thought, yet for once I feel no sympathy for him.

Isn't it too late to break down now, Dad? Forty years on. It doesn't escape my notice how lucid he is. It's like taking him back to such a significant moment has anchored him in a way nothing has for a long time.

'We should never have done it,' he sobs. 'We should never have done what we did.'

'What?' I cry. 'You can't say that. You can't regret Bonnie.' The tightness inside me squeezes harder until every muscle in my body is clenched. I'd thought I wanted him to show remorse, but now I know it's not what I want to hear. 'You can't tell me you wish you didn't have her?'

'No. I don't know,' he cries. 'It was wrong. It was so wrong, and your mum could never see it.'

'But you must have made the decision together,' I say angrily. 'You can't blame it all on Mum.'

I want him to defend what they did, not regret it. I want to hear him tell me they had no choice because they loved Bonnie and they wanted to give her a better life. I don't want to listen to him snivelling down the phone at me that they should never have taken her.

'Of course we did. Of course we did,' he repeats, more quietly.

'So why did you?' I plead. 'Tell me why you did it, Dad.'

'We were young and desperate for a family. And your mother had lost two babies and we thought— We thought we couldn't have our own. I love Bonnie. You know that.' He pauses. 'But we shouldn't have done it.'

'Does Bonnie know?' he asks.

'Not yet,' I snap. *And I'll be the one to tell her, won't I, Dad? It should have been you but neither of you could do it.*

My fingers tingle from where I'm gripping the phone. Blood races through my veins, heating my skin. I'm angry that I won't get what I now realise I want from him. I wanted what Ruth had given me – a refusal to believe they'd done anything wrong. A conviction I think I'd have seen in Mum.

'It wasn't your mother.' Dad is sobbing into the phone. 'I was the one who told the girl what we'd done.'

'Oh God—' I start as Olivia's voice breaks in.

'I don't know what's going on,' she says, and I realise I've lost him.

'Nothing's going on,' I snap as I hang up the phone.

Only now do I see snatches of my parents' relationship for what it was. I can picture them sitting in front of me as I draw a portrait of their marriage and it's clear they could never have moved past what happened.

They'd done something they never agreed on. That made Dad tear himself apart with guilt to the point he admitted it to Iona, while Mum tried her best to hold us together. They didn't stand a chance of survival in the end.

Ten minutes later my doorbell pierces the silence. I expect it to be Bonnie and pull on a jumper before opening the door, but it's Detective Harwood.

'I'm sorry, I got you out of bed,' he says, eyes drawn to my pyjama bottoms before quickly returning to my face, a pinkness appearing on his own. 'I wanted to bring something by and I – how are you feeling?' he asks, as if registering he should have phoned first.

The truth is, physically, I feel much better today but I'm not ready to be hauled in for more questioning. 'Like I just want to sleep,' I tell him. 'And sick,' I add for good measure.

Harwood's front teeth clamp down on his bottom lip. 'I was hoping we'd be able to finish our conversation, Ms Harvey. Annie Webb has started talking.'

He must know this would stir me and I'm unable to hide the fact as my fingers drum against the door frame, my foot scuffing anxiously on the mat.

'I rather hoped some more of your conversation had come back to you,' he goes on.

I give a small shake of my head and, when I don't say anything, he pulls in a tight breath before handing me a carrier bag. 'What's this?' I ask.

'Your brother asked me to give it to you. We found it in Ms Webb's house. He says he doesn't want it.'

I look inside the bag, pulling out Danny's drawing pad. 'Oh!' My fingers trail across its cover. 'He wanted me to have it?' I glance up for confirmation. 'Thank you. Thank you so much.' He has no idea how much this means to me.

'Ms Harvey,' Harwood says, taking a step back as if what he's about to say is just an aside when actually it's anything but, 'Annie Webb is saying it was an accident, that she never intended to hurt Iona Byrnes.' He pauses, waiting for this to register. 'I really need you to recall if anything to the contrary was suggested in your conversation the night before last.' It's clear he believes it was.

But Annie is saying it was an accident. That means she's suggesting there was nothing pre-emptive about what happened. Nothing linking her to Iona, nothing that would help Harwood drag up the past. It means not only is she protecting Bob, she's protecting my parents too. And after she'd so carefully manipulated it to look like Mum's fault.

It's possible Annie has weighed up her options and considered a charge of manslaughter is better than admitting the truth.

'Ms Harvey?' Harwood's head hangs to one side. I blink and look up at him.

I need to tell him the truth. I have to. But I still need to speak to my sister first.

'I'm really sorry, I still don't ...' I wave a hand in the air. 'I'm hoping after some more rest ...'

He shakes his head and sighs. 'We need to finish that statement,' he says, raising his eyes before finally turning away. 'I'd be grateful if you could come into the station later.'

I slam the door shut behind him, clutching Danny's book to my chest. I can't do this for much longer, I think, tearing myself away and going back to bed.

Laying the book across my lap, I stare at its cover. It reminds me of the feeling I'd have when I opened my advent calendar. The anticipation of what would be inside. Finally I open the first page. An envelope has been wedged into the spine. Tugging it free, I reach inside and pull out a letter.

Dear Stella

I want you to have this book. Do with it what you like – burn it if you want – but there might be a part of you that wants to look. You were always begging me to when we were kids!

There was a time I wanted it back more than anything, but the cost of that became too great. I haven't even been able to look inside because I know I'll see memories of a summer I've spent my life trying to forget.

When Mum came into my bedroom and told me Iona was alright, I knew she was hiding something. I saw it behind her eyes – you always told me I was good at reading people. The next day they told us we were leaving but I never believed Iona could be dead. My fifteen-year-old brain thought she'd threatened us and Mum panicked.

Mum gave up everything to keep me safe and it was too much of a burden for me. After seven years I couldn't do it any more and had to get away, start afresh. I hated seeing you beg Mum to take us back when I knew she never would and I blamed myself for everything, including Dad leaving.

But before that summer we were happy, weren't we, Stella? We did have a great life on Evergreen, and what's happened will never change that.

I'm also happy in Scotland now, it's where I want to be, but if I let myself acknowledge it there's one thing missing, and that's you. I miss you, Stella. I miss the feeling of knowing you were by my side in the treehouse.

I'd like it if we could write to each other and maybe, one day, you might come up and visit.

Danny

Tears stream down my cheeks as I press my brother's note against my chest. No matter the distance between us, we will be forever tied together. 'Yes, Danny,' I say, 'I would like that very much too.'

Chapter Thirty-Seven

'It's good to see you,' I smile when Bonnie turns up. 'I've missed you.'

'Yes, well, if you go gallivanting all over the country like some crazed Miss Marple, what do you expect?' She breezes in before looking at me carefully. 'You could have been killed. You know that, don't you?'

'I do, actually. But it *is* good to see you, Bon.'

'I worry about you,' she murmurs as she takes off her coat and lingers with it in her hand before I sling it over a chair. An overwhelming scent of perfume hangs in the air. 'Why are you looking at me so oddly?'

I shake my head and glance away. 'I didn't know I was.'

'You were. You were staring at me. Have I got something on my face?' She reaches a hand and swipes at her chin.

'No. I wasn't looking at you in any way,' I say as she walks off to the kitchen. I take a breath as I watch her go.

It's weird seeing her again, a face I've known my entire life, only now I know we're not related. The similarities I'd once told myself were there must have all been in my head.

'Thank God you have no need to carry on your little search now, though.' She stops in the doorway and turns back. 'I assume you don't, anyway?'

I shake my head. 'Coffee?'

'Yes.' She moves out of my way and stands by the small breakfast bar, her fingers scratching its surface.

'I'm not offering you anything stronger,' I say as I fill the kettle.

Bonnie doesn't reply and I don't look at her as I hear the scrape of a stool against the tiles. 'So Annie is our killer,' she says flippantly. When I turn I can tell by the way she leans forward, her eyes wide, that Bonnie is shocked. 'Why did she do it?'

'She's saying it was an accident,' I reply carefully, 'but it meant Mum left the island thinking it was Danny.'

Bonnie nods slowly. 'But then she drugged you. Was she going to kill you too?'

'I don't know,' I tell her, though I'm certain she was. 'I guess she was scared.' I avoid telling Bonnie that I'd overheard Annie's plan to get rid of me. Or that only moments before Meg arrived she'd been about to hit me over the head with her carriage clock.

Bonnie's fingers have stopped scratching but they trace circles on the surface between us. 'You know, Luke wants to book us a holiday. To Jamaica,' she says suddenly. 'Why do I want to go to Jamaica?'

'Why don't you?' I laugh. 'It'll be amazing.' I know she has changed the subject through fear. As much as Bonnie has plenty of questions, she isn't sure she wants to ask them.

'It'll be hot,' she goes on.

'That's a good thing.'

'Yes. I suppose.' I see the flicker of a smile on the edge of her lips before it passes. 'You are looking at me weirdly. Will you just tell me why, because you're beginning to freak me out.'

'I'm sorry.' I hold up my hands. 'It's just so much has happened. I'm relieved to be back. And safe.'

Bonnie seems to accept this but says, 'So I'm assuming you did go back and see Iona's mother on Sunday? When you told me you were coming home.'

'I did.'

'Right.' Her shoulders rise and fall quickly as she battles her need to know and her resistance to hearing it.

'Iona is definitely not your sister,' I tell her.

She looks up.

'I promise. She isn't.'

'How do you know?' she asks, her breath slowly releasing.

I open my mouth to tell her it's Jill, but for now something stops me. Instead I reel out another lie. 'She showed me a photo of the baby. It looks nothing like you. She had ginger hair.'

Bonnie looks away as tears swim to the corners of her eyes. 'Oh God,' she says finally. 'Oh my God.' She lets out another deep breath and laughs as I slide on to a stool opposite her. 'I was so sure Mum was lying. But she's really not?' She turns back, her eyes imploring me. 'You're telling me the truth.'

'I am, Bon,' I say, reaching for her hand. 'But—' I start as she carries on speaking over me. I can't let her revel in relief when I still need to tell her what she's most dreaded hearing.

She is talking about Mum, bringing up the Stay and Play sessions again. 'Maybe it was my jealousy of Danny,' she says, reassuring herself there was nothing more to it. 'Maybe that's why they took me. I mean, I hated him as soon as he was born.'

'That's really why you didn't get on with him?'

'Yes. I think it was really,' she says.

'So what about me?'

'Oh, you were different. I couldn't shake you off. I tried, but you just hung around me, and in the end I suppose I grew to love you.' Her voice has the carefree tone of someone who's received good news.

'You know, I read this article about being the oldest sibling the other day,' she starts, and when she turns back to me the edges of her mouth twitch up.

'Oh yeah?' I smile.

'It said one of the most positive experiences of being the oldest sibling is nurturing the younger ones. Apparently my doing that has expanded my ability to be sensitive to other people's needs. Think I got that spot on, didn't I?' she asks, her eyes sparkling.

I squeeze her hand a little tighter. I could leave her blissfully unaware for longer but what good will that do? Our family has lived a lie for over forty years and Bonnie deserves the truth.

'I don't know what I'd have done without you all these years,' she is saying. 'You know that, don't you? I don't tell you as much as I should, but ...'

'I know,' I say, when she doesn't finish.

She tilts her head to one side and I can see she's scrutinising me again. I realise I must be staring. 'What is it?' she says finally. 'What aren't you telling me?' She pulls her hand away, clutching hers together in her lap.

I close my eyes and when I open them she's watching me, waiting, and I know what I need to say goes something like this: *Bonnie, you were right. You weren't Iona's sister but our parents still did something awful. They bought you when you were a baby, from your mother who lived in the slums. They brought you up like you were their own and you were, you were as much a part of the family as Danny and I have ever been.*

Then I picture her face falling in slow motion.

Blood is thicker than water. I can almost hear her words ringing through my ears.

I will lose her. I know that without doubt. If there are no blood ties between us I will lose my sister forever.

And I can't. I can't do that. I won't survive it.

Her eyes trail down my cheeks and I wipe them with my palms.

She leans forward, her face set, and I can see how angry she is. 'Will you just tell me,' she says, her eyes flaring wide as her fist slams down on the counter.

'I know you've been drinking again,' I blurt. 'I don't want to go through this again.' It's a risky move and there are only little things that make me think she has been, like the strong scent of perfume to mask the smell of alcohol and the fact she didn't answer when I told her there was nothing stronger to drink.

Bonnie flinches as she sits back, arms crossed in front of her chest, and I know I'm right.

'That's it?' she snaps.

'Yes. That's it.'

Can I live with a lie? Do I have the strength Mum did?

'That's it,' I say again, 'and I'm sorry, but you need to hear this. If you're not careful you'll lose Luke and the boys and—'

'Okay.' She is holding her hands up. 'Okay,' she adds a little more gently. My heart continues to pound, echoing through my ears. 'I know all that. I know. I just – I'll get help. Again,' she says. 'With everything that's been going on—'

'It's no excuse,' I say firmly, and I feel harsh doing so but it's what I would have said if this is what I'd been building up to.

I sit back too, my arms aching to pull her in and hold her against me. Bonnie bites her lips and eventually looks away, and I hope that if her drinking is the hardest thing we have to deal with, we'll be alright.

Yes, I decide, I can live with a lie, because the alternative is unbearable. I'll spend the rest of my life having to trust Bob and Annie, just like my mum did, but I will do it because I won't lose my sister. I have lost too much already.

And I'll live with it hanging over me forever, because that's the trouble with secrets. They never go away.

ACKNOWLEDGEMENTS

This book has been inspired by own my childhood memories, which may sound odd given that I didn't live on an island and there were thankfully no dead bodies in our garden. . . But through Stella I was able to relive my own past, and the many happy times I had. For this I have my mum to thank. She taught me that a happy child doesn't need money – they need love, support and security. So, for my mum – Jo Welch – thank you for giving me all of this in abundance.

Writing is definitely a team effort and I feel incredibly lucky to be surrounded by the best, starting with my fantastic agent, Nelle Andrew. You are a star and I am so grateful to have you on my side. I could not have done any of this without you.

Emily Griffin, I could not ask for a better editor to work with and I'm so thrilled I get the chance to write more books with you. The entire team at Century and Arrow have made what is already an exciting journey even better. I am grateful to each and every one of you, and I would like to pay particular thanks to: Natalia Cacciatore, Rachel Kennedy, Claire Simmonds, Amber Bennett-Ford, Jess Ballance, Linda Hodgson and Emma Grey Gelder.

Chris Bradford, for all the times I've picked your brains and called you with odd questions – thank you. I am still in awe of your knowledge and hope you won't mind me continuing to bother you with plenty more queries as I write.

Similarly, Phillipa Shawyer, thank you for your medical input – especially when I rap on your window in a dark car park to ask you about drugs!

Writing can be a lonely business but, Melissa Carr, our coffee-shop sessions are always great fun – though possibly I don't get as much done when there are too many other things to talk about!

And, Lou Gill, I promised I'd get you in here. Thank you for all the wonderful inspiration you have given me with your weird stories that often end with: 'hasn't everyone done that?' (The answer is no – they haven't!)

For my friends, Lisa and Susie, who seem proud to call themselves stalkers – what lovely ones you are! And to all the other gorgeous senoritas: Lara, Cris, Olga, Lou, Alia and Jen. Here's looking forward to a pool shot with this book!

To my friends, Debs, Lucy and Donna, who read early copies and continue to be amazingly supportive – thank you for being almost as excited as I am.

To my wonderful family who enable me to do what I love, and to my husband, John, without whom I'd probably never have started writing. You never stop believing in me. Thank you for checking in daily on rankings and reviews, for your constant support, encouragement and love, and for all the laughs along the way. You're amazing.

And finally, to my two gorgeous children, Bethany and Joseph. Being your mum is the most precious gift. I hope I have shown you that, if you never give up, you can achieve your dreams. I love you most. No returns.

**Read and loved *Come Back For Me*?
Tell Heidi what you thought.**

f @HeidiPerksAuthor
y @HeidiPerksBooks

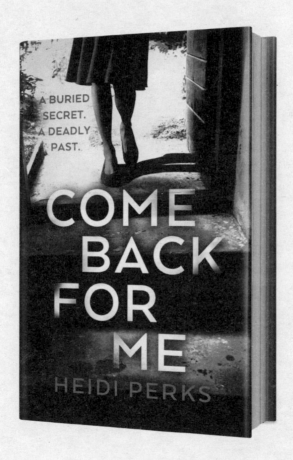

We all have something to hide . . .

#COMEBACKFORME